Out of Bounds

The White Series
Book 1

Sallyanne Johnson

Out of Bounds
Copyright © 2021 by Sallyanne Johnson
The moral right of the author has been asserted.
All rights reserved.

Without limiting the rights under copyright reserved above, no part of this book may be reproduced or transmitted in any form or by any means (electronic or mechanical, including photocopying, scanning, recording, or otherwise) without the written permission of the copyright owner and the publisher of the book.

All characters and events depicted in this book are entirely fictitious. Any similarity to actual events or persons, living or dead, is purely coincidental.

Designations used by companies to distinguish their products are often claimed as trademarks. All brand names and product names used in this book and on its cover are trade names, service marks, trademarks, and registered trademarks of their respective owners. The publishers and the book are not associated with any product or vendor mentioned in this book. None of the companies referenced within the book have endorsed the book.

Published by Sallyanne Johnson
29 October 2021

Editors: Jackie Bates & Magnolia Author Services
Proofreader: Book Nook Nuts
Cover Designer: Angie Oltman
Formatter: Sallyanne Johnson

PRAISE FOR SALLYANNE JOHNSON

"It has been some time since a story has tore at me from all directions like this one did. But heck, was it absolutely worth it! Johnson's books have been amazing and so breathtakingly beautifully written. She pulls at you with her words and has you experiencing all the emotions. This author knows how to get you in the gut and heart." – Amazon Reviewer on *Dark Soul* and *The Black Series*.

"This was a passionate and consuming love story that truly gave me goosebumps. The chemistry took my breath away…" – Amazon Reviewer on *Dark Heart*.

"Amazing story, incredible romance, intriguing characters, *Dark Desires* has it all." – Amazon Reviewer on *Dark Desires*.

ACKNOWLEDGEMENTS

As always I couldn't have written this book without the ongoing help and support of a few lovely people.

My fabulous editor, Jackie who's advice and guidance is always spot on. All the improvements in my writing are down to this wonderful lady.

My team of beta readers; Zoe, Ashley and Dani who's suggestions made the story the best it can be. Zoe, my friend and superstar PA who keeps me on track and who I could not do this without. All the bookstagrammers, bloggers, fellow authors; everyone who helps promote my work and spreads the word about my books, thank you!

Finally, I'm incredibly lucky to have a met a small group of people through my writing, some of whom I've already mentioned. They're always on hand to offer support, troubleshoot and pick me up when I've had a bad day. Without them this process would be a whole lot more difficult. You know who you are ladies. I'm so grateful to have met you.

CONTENTS

Praise for Sallyanne Johnson
Acknowledgements
Playlist
Prologue
Chapter 1
Chapter 2
Chapter 3
Chapter 4
Chapter 5
Chapter 6
Chapter 7
Chapter 8
Chapter 9
Chapter 10
Chapter 11
Chapter 12
Chapter 13
Chapter 14
Chapter 15
Chapter 16
Chapter 17
Chapter 18
Chapter 19
Chapter 20
Chapter 21
Chapter 22
Chapter 23
Chapter 24
Chapter 25
Chapter 26
Chapter 27
Chapter 28

Chapter 29
Chapter 30
Chapter 31
Chapter 32
Chapter 33
Chapter 34
Chapter 35
Chapter 36
Chapter 37
Chapter 38
Chapter 39
Chapter 40
Chapter 41
Chapter 42
Chapter 43
Chapter 44
Chapter 45
Chapter 46
Chapter 47
Chapter 48
Also by Sallyanne Johnson
About Sallyanne
Author's Note

PLAYLIST

"River" by Bishop Briggs

"Miss Independent" by Kelly Clarkson

"Paradise" by MEDUZA, feat. Dermot Kennedy

"Stop This Flame" by Celeste

"Addicted To You" by Avicii

"Without You" by David Guetta, feat. Usher

"Partition" by Beyonce

"Friday I'm in Love" by The Cure

"Levitating" by Dua Lipa

"This is Real" by Jax Jones, feat. Ella Henderson

"Wish You Were Here" by Incubus

"Head & Heart" by Joel Corry, feat. MNEK

THE WHITE SERIES

Out of Bounds
Out of Love

Prologue

Ella

Eight years earlier...

Bright strip lights sting my eyes and hurt my aching brain. A clinical disinfectant stench fills my nostrils and makes my stomach roll with nausea. Other than me and Kate, there's only one other sombre looking woman in the silent waiting room. She looks as though she'd rather be anywhere else. Just like me. Just like every woman who ends up here.

The door to the doctor's room opens and a woman walks out, wiping her eyes and stuffing a leaflet into her handbag. I recognise the glossy front page. It was the same one they gave to me on my first visit. It listed my options. Truth is, there are no options. Not for me.

I'm up next.

My mouth fills with saliva. I dig a hand into the pocket of my black puffa jacket and pull out a packet of Polo mints. They're the only thing that take the edge off. The constant gut churning feeling I get in the mornings or whenever I smell coffee has definitely got worse these last few days. I suppose that's to be expected.

I offer Kate a mint and she looks up from her phone, scrunching up her nose. "No, ta." She gives me a sympathetic smile and asks the same question she's asked nearly every ten minutes since we arrived. "Are you okay?"

I push the packet of mints back into my pocket and force a smile, giving the same reply I always do. "I'm fine."

She heaves a sigh but remains silent. She doesn't need to say anything. We've been friends since we were eight. I'm closer to Kate than I am my own sister.

"Thank you for coming with me," I say, even though I've already told her this loads today. If it wasn't for her, I'd be going through this alone. "What have you said to Gav?"

"That we're shopping this afternoon. And of course I've come. You can't go through something like this by yourself. They said you'd be a bit out of it when you come round, didn't they? I need to make sure you get home all right." She gives me a weak smile. "Anyway, you've helped me out of enough pickles in the past, and I'm sure there'll be many more times to come where you'll save my arse."

She's trying to make me feel better. She's never fucked up this royally and I doubt she ever will. Getting knocked up a couple of months before your eighteenth birthday will take some beating. No one knows; only me, her and the bastard who got me into this fucking mess. Embarrassment, shame and guilt hang around my neck like a noose – I'll take this shit to my grave. Everyone has their cross to bear, I guess this is mine. Amy's far too young to know, and Mum doesn't deserve me bringing this worry to her door. All her life she's worked her fingers to the bone, making sure me and Amy have everything we need. Now she's working all hours in the shop she relies on me more than ever; to make sure Amy has her tea when she comes home from school and ensure she's done her homework for the next day. I'm the eldest. I'm meant to be the responsible one who gets good grades and gets into a good college and who wants to go to university. This stupid mistake will sabotage my future and crush Mum. She's got her own shit going on at the moment. *That's* where I should be right now. At the hospital, supporting her while she gets her test results. Instead, I'm sat on a hard plastic chair, having made possibly the biggest decision of my life, and waiting for what feels like eternity. But I don't have a choice. The clock's ticking. I can't put this off another week.

My mobile beeps in my pocket telling me I've got a text. I pull it out and pray it's Mum telling me she's got the all-clear, but it's not.

Is it dead yet?

Tears prick at the corner of my eyes as the cruel words slice through me. Harsh and cold. I blink them down, refusing to cry. I've shed too many tears over that bastard.

"Logan?" Kate asks. Her gaze hardens as I look at her. She already knows the answer.

I shove the phone back into my jacket, anger blazing inside me, extinguishing the hollowness I feel about what I'm about to do. I'm incensed; maddened by the situation but most of all furious with myself, for not listening to that little voice in the back of my head telling me it was too good to be true. *He* was too good to be true; that Logan Marshall, the most handsome, popular guy in college wanted little old me. I didn't believe it at first but over the weeks he wore me down, seducing me with his silver tongue and snazzy sports car. His family were loaded thanks to his dad's job on the trade floor and I fell hard. He told me he wanted to be my first and he'd wait until I was ready. But he didn't. I foolishly ignored the red flags popping up in my brain telling me to break it off, because he was Logan Marshall. No girl dumped Logan, he was a *catch*. All the girls wanted to shag him and the boys wanted to be his mate. After two weeks of pressure, emotional blackmail and being told "if you loved me, you'd let me," I caved. He said he was allergic to condoms, he promised he'd pull out. Then he was gone. Ghosted me. Stopped returning my calls. Text me to admit he'd only slept with me because of a bet he'd made with his mates. Told me I was the easiest hundred quid he'd ever made.

The door to the doctor's room opens and a well-spoken voice calls, "Ella Anderson."

Kate squeezes my hand as we stand together. "Are you sure about this?"

I let out a deep breath to try and calm my nerves. I nod and grip her hand tight. "Positive. Let's go."

Gabe

Sixteen years earlier ...

The early July sun shines through the windows of the black Mercedes, warming the leather seats. Another term of boarding school done. I'd like to think I'll be spending the next six weeks doing whatever I fancy but I know that isn't an option. Dad's forewarned me he's got plans to "educate me in the family business". He's a self-made millionaire and one day the baton will be passed to me. In another ten years he'll be retiring, which means my life's already mapped out for me; school, sixth form, Oxford then the business. It's not even been discussed. In his eyes it's a given. I'm the son with the "most potential." Jake's left to join the army and Spencer...

I glance over at my younger brother, who sits beside me engrossed in his phone. I make the mistake of looking at the screen and see a photo of a pair of tits belonging to some girl he's managed to persuade to send him a nude selfie. I roll my eyes and look out of the window.

He's only thirteen and already thinking with his cock. *Fucking great.*

I look back out of the window and watch the trees and hedgerows of the familiar Surrey countryside whizzing past. We're nearly home. But something doesn't feel right.

"How come Mum didn't come to collect us from the station?" I ask Grayson, Dad's driver who sits behind the wheel.

A tension appears in his shoulders, and he forces a laugh. "You telling me you're not pleased to see me?"

"Of course, it's just that Mum usually comes to pick us up."

He shoots me a hesitant look through the rear view mirror. "Your mum's not been feeling too well recently. But she's better now, I think. Your dad was going to come, but he had to take an urgent business call."

"Dad's back?"

"Yeah. He wanted to welcome you home."

Now I know for certain something's up. Dad spends eighty per cent of his waking life in London. I'm not knocking him, without his sacrifices we wouldn't be living in a three-million pound mansion in the Surrey countryside, and Spencer and I wouldn't be enrolled at one of England's most prestigious schools.

I look at my little brother to see if he's picked up on the fact that something's amiss too, but he's still absorbed in his tit pic.

Before long, we're home. The car crunches along the gravel driveway, coming to a stop at the bottom of the stone steps that lead up to the black double front doors.

Nessa, our housekeeper, stands at the top of the steps waiting with a big, ready smile on her face. I'm filled with a warm feeling of familiarity at the sight of her. I've never not known her to be around. She practically helped raise us when we were younger, when Dad was in the city and looking after three young boys became too much for Mum. Nessa *is* home. I'm relieved and comforted that some things never change.

Her blue eyes sparkle as she looks proudly at us as we head up the steps. She shakes her head in disbelief, sending her greying dark brown bob swinging from side to side. "I can't believe how much you two have grown. Such handsome boys."

"Good to see you, Ness." I give her a kiss on the cheek and Spencer ducks out of the way as she ruffles his hair.

I step into the house and scan the hallway, noting nothing's changed. The cream porcelain floor is so highly polished you can almost see your face in it. The usual ostentatious floral arrangement of white calla lilies sits in a cut glass vase on top of the antique oak sideboard. Mum insists on them because "they look good," even though she's allergic.

"Where are Mum and Dad?"

Nessa fiddles with the string of her pale green gingham apron and looks out of the front door, watching Grayson haul our luggage from the boot of the car. "Your dad's on a work call in his office and your mum went for a lie down because she's got one of her bad heads."

I glance up the carved oak central staircase. "I'll go and surprise her, then."

Nessa forces a thin smile which doesn't reach her eyes and focusses her attention on Spencer. "I've baked some of those chocolate chip cookies you like. Shall we go into the kitchen and you can have one?"

Spencer looks up from his phone with a start; the prospect of food the only thing to interrupt his ogling of naked girls. "Yeah, cool, Ness."

***

I reach the top of the stairs and hear Dad's voice coming from his office down the landing. I gently knock on the bedroom door. If Mum's still sleeping I don't want to wake her, but I haven't seen her since we went to Monaco for May Bank Holiday. I might be fifteen, but she's still my mum.

She doesn't reply so I quietly push open the door and head into the bedroom. She's in the middle of the queen size bed on top of the cream sheets, wearing a white and red patterned silk dressing gown. She's asleep. I don't want to wake her, but I *do* want to wake her. I want to tell her everything I've done at school over the summer term. I move closer.

That's when I see it.

The moment everything changes.

The second my life turns upside down.

A large pool of deep red blood covers the sheets and soaks the sleeves of her dressing gown. The material isn't patterned red and white; it's blood. The glint of a razor blade on the cream carpet catches my eye. A loud ringing noise fills my ears and dark spots float on the edge of my vision. I'm frozen, paralysed with shock as reality hits me like a steam train.

I'm going to pass out.

I can't.

I need to do something.

I need to get help.

She may not be dead.

The thought that there's a chance I can save her sobers me up like a shot.

"Mum!" I cry out, in a voice I've never heard before. Adrenaline kicks in as I rush over to the bed and drop to my knees grabbing her arms. Two long slashes on her wrists continue to seep blood. She's ice cold to the touch. Her pallor's white and waxy. It's too late. *I'm* too late.

I hear the door open and Dad's voice as he shouts. "Fucking hell!"

He shoves me out of the way, pushing me back on my arse as he frantically talks to Mum and tries to get her to come round.

"It's too late," I stutter through shaky breaths, staring down at my trembling hands that are covered in her blood.

He staggers backwards, staring aghast at the horror in front of our eyes. Then, in a second his eyes narrow in menace and his jaw tightens. "Fucking bitch."

My heads snaps up in shock. He can't have said what I think he's said. I scrabble to get to my feet. "What?"

Dad grabs me by the collar of my navy school blazer and glares at me. "You listen up, Gabe. Now's the moment you grow the fuck up. You're never going to forget this fucking moment for the rest of your life, which is exactly what she wanted. Manipulative bitch."

Tears burn in my eyes. To hear him calling her these horrid names when she's lying dead next to us, makes my head spin. "Why has she done this, why has she left us?"

His grey eyes blaze with anger at my emotional response. He roughly grabs my face with his sticky, blood-soaked hand and forces me to look at him. "No fucking crying. You need to man the fuck up, right now. Your mum did this because she couldn't cope."

"With what?"

He looks at her for a moment, like he's deciding something.

"With the fact I found out she's been having affairs with different men over the years."

My stomach twists with nausea. I think I'm going to throw up. I shake my head in disbelief. Mum. Unfaithful? No.

Dad tightens his grip on my face so it hurts. "It's true. She couldn't cope with the guilt and what it would do to the family. How it would ruin our reputation."

Something doesn't add up. "So, she did this? She saw this as her only way out?"

"The last few months have been hard. She's been feeling down and taking anti-depressants." He fixes me with a firm look. "Women are trouble. The more money you've got, the more they want to fuck you. They're good for one thing and one thing only. Take my advice kid, don't get yourself tied down to one." He grins. "And you need to watch out, because they'll be making a beeline for you in a few years' time. Now, go and clean yourself up. I'll call an ambulance. Keep Spencer the hell out of here. Don't tell him what I've just told you. That'll just be our secret. Get Nessa, she can clean this fucking mess up."

Dad's reeling off orders and I don't know what to do. I can't even bring myself to look at the bed. My hearts shattered and my fucking head's set to explode.

Fuck.

I need to do what he's said.

I can't let him down.

Man the fuck up.

I sniff back tears and dig deep. "Okay, Dad. I'll help sort it."

He smirks and pats my cheek. "That's my boy. You know it makes sense."

Chapter 1

Ella

Present day

I'm always late. Running behind, tardy, whatever you like to call it. Kate jokes that I'll be late for my own funeral. Ironically, I was *nearly* late for Mum's. The hearse broke down, we had to wait for another... you get the picture.

"For fuck's sake, Ella, are you going to be much longer?" Kate yells up the stairs.

"Coming." I swipe the bronzer brush over my nose and cheekbones. That will have to do. If I don't emerge from my bedroom soon, Kate will come and drag me out herself. She's bossy like that.

"Good, because the Uber's four minutes and thirty-six seconds away."

The irritation in her voice is crystal clear. She's never understood my inability to be on time. That's just one of the many ways we're so different. Kate's wristwatch is always set ten minutes early.

I chuck the brush down on top of the glass dressing table and run my fingers through my hair, checking my reflection in the mirrored wardrobe door. I smooth a hand over the scarlet material of my dress. It's a halter neck and clings to my figure, resting just below the knee. I think I look okay, considering I bought the dress two years ago in a sale, and retrieved it from the back of my wardrobe less than an hour ago.

"Are you coming or what?" Kate hollers.

Bossy sod.

Honestly, it's a good job I've known her forever, otherwise, I'd tell her to piss off.

She's standing at the mirror in the hall, applying a coat of red lipstick when I finally get downstairs.

"Nice dress." She grins in approval eyeing my outfit. "That colour red looks hot on you. You're definitely going to get noticed wearing that."

I tug the dress down, feeling immediately self-conscious. "Hmmm... I want to look nice, I don't want to be noticed. I've been there, done that."

Kate gives me a look because she knows exactly what I'm referring to. She didn't approve of my choices a few years ago, but the reality was that I didn't have a choice. Now, thankfully, because of her, I do.

I admire her simple black dress that fits her tall, slender figure perfectly. Why couldn't I own something black? Black blends in. Red stands out. I thought I looked okay. Now I'm not so sure. "It's the only dress I could find in my wardrobe that isn't yonks old. Do you think I should change?"

"Absolutely not." Kate shoves her lipstick in her black clutch bag. "You look perfect. Remember where we're going. It's a classy joint. The place will be teeming with VIPs, celebs, footballers. Everyone will be dressed up."

Her words don't reassure me in the slightest. My stomach cramps with nerves at the thought. I haven't really been "out out" since Mum died and I've never been anywhere *that* exclusive. All those super rich arseholes, floating about the place looking down their noses at you. No thanks.

I wrinkle my nose at the thought. "Kate, I'm not so sure about tonight..."

"No." She points a finger at me, cutting me off. "You're coming out with me. You're going to let your hair down and you're going to have a bloody good time. Besides, it's the perfect opportunity to celebrate the new job."

My stomach tightens even more. I'd put that out of my mind. After temping for the last six years I've landed an Executive Support job at one of the city's most successful property development companies. It's a proper grown-up job with a pay packet to match. No more scrimping and saving, which has become a way of life over the past few years.

Kate runs a hand through her light blonde poker straight hair, does a double-take at my feet and frowns. "Where are your shoes?"

I glance down at my red varnished toenails. "Oh shit, yeah."

She rolls her eyes impatiently and looks at her watch. I can almost hear her last thread of patience straining to snap. "Oh, for God's sake, El. Hurry up. The cab's nearly here."

"I can't help it." I start up the stairs. "It's your fault for rushing me. You'd think after twenty years you'd know I'm not particularly organised. The first I heard that we were going out tonight, was when you got back home from work an hour and a half ago."

"Yeah well, Harry didn't tell me about the tickets till this afternoon."

Harry. Kate's done nothing but harp on about the "sexy account manager" since he transferred to her department at the bank, three months ago. When she sets her sights on someone, she usually succeeds in getting him, so for her to learn he'd hooked up with someone else a few weeks ago was a bitter blow. But things seemed to have changed – I can never keep up.

I pause half-way up the stairs and turn to her. "So, what's the deal with you and him now then?"

"Nothing." She shrugs and rummages through her clutch bag avoiding my gaze. "We're just friends."

"Oh, come on. Cut the crap. Something's going on." I pause as an unwelcome thought hits me. "He's not still seeing someone is he?"

"No!" Kate replies firmly, meeting my eyes. "Do you really think I'd go out with a guy knowing they were in a relationship? After all the shit I went through with Gav."

She's right. Kate was a wreck when she and Gav broke up. They were one of those couples who you thought would be together forever. When she discovered he'd been having an affair with a woman from work her world collapsed overnight. She moved out of their flat and in with me and has been here ever since. We helped each other to heal; her getting over Gav, and me losing Mum. It's been just over twelve months and she hasn't really dated properly since, but Harry's got her whipped up into a right frenzy.

"Okay, maybe not," I admit.

"He's not seeing her anymore. They went out on two dates, didn't even shag."

"And now he's got his eye on you."

Her cheeks flush giving her away. She fiddles with the metal zip on her bag. "Possibly."

"I don't think there's any doubt. He's given you two tickets to the opening night of an ultra-exclusive, hip and trendy club in Mayfair. If nothing else, he's going all out to impress you. I'm guessing he'll be there?"

She pulls her mobile from her bag and avoids my gaze. "He mentioned he might pop by."

I know she's playing it down. There's no "popping by" to opening nights at these types of places. You've either got tickets, or you're not allowed in.

"What a surprise."

Kate gives me a stern look. Her patience is nearly frayed, I can tell. "Listen, can we chat in the cab that's going to be arriving in exactly two minutes? Go and put some bloody shoes on!"

"Okay, okay, I'm going. I'd hate for you to be late for Harry," I call over my shoulder, heading upstairs.

I retrieve a pair of black, strappy heels from the bottom of my wardrobe which haven't seen the light of day for a while, and my small black clutch. I head back downstairs, checking the contents to make sure I've got everything. If I forget anything and we have to come back, she'll kill me. She's always been slightly uptight but tonight she's in overdrive.

Cold air blasts through the hall, making me shiver. Kate's standing at the front door talking to someone. She glances over her shoulder as I reach the bottom of the stairs.

"Oh, here she is." She steps aside to reveal Margot, my mum's oldest friend. She took over the running of Mum's business, The Enchanted Florist, in the high street after she died. A place

I haven't stepped foot in for a long time. In fact, I haven't seen Margot since the funeral. Why's she here?

Margot pushes her tortoiseshell framed glasses onto the bridge of her nose and gives me a nervous smile. "Hello Ella. Kate said you're on your way out. I'm sorry to drop round on a Saturday night, but well, I think you need to know about this." She retrieves a crumpled letter from the pocket of her dark green padded gilet and hands it to me. "It came in this morning's post, but I've only just got round to opening it."

"Thanks," I say, looking at the white envelope.

Margot nervously nibbles her bottom lip. This feels ominous.

Kate hovers beside me, sensing somethings up too. I pull out the letter, open it up and begin to read, but barely reach the second line.

"He's selling." Margot blurts, unable to wait any longer to share the burden.

I frown in confusion. "What? Who is," I ask scanning the rest of the letter.

"The landlord. He's selling the shop. And it's not just us who's had a letter. The newsagents next door has and the launderette next to that. It looks like he's selling all of the shops he owns."

I look at her in disbelief. "But that's practically the whole high street."

Margot nods gravely. "All the old shops that have been there years. From the roundabout up to the old textile warehouse."

The unwelcome thought sinks in. "But he can't just do this, can he? I mean those shops ... Mum's shop's been there forever. They're part of the community."

Margot gives me a weak smile. "Looks like he can. Bob from the grocers says he's going to launch a petition. We can't go down without a fight. I mean if anything happened to the shop I'd be okay financially, but that's not the point, is it. And that's not the case for everyone. It's their livelihoods, they've got kids to feed and bills to pay."

My heart twists with sadness. I know that feeling all too well. Not knowing how you're going to afford to pay the next bill.

"But what happens if the petition doesn't work?" I ask, already knowing the answer.

"Then we haven't got a choice, love. We'll have to close, for good."

I grip the letter tight, staring at the page willing the words to magically rearrange themselves into another far more positive message. One that's not quite so heart breaking. Close Mum's shop. The business she ran for twenty years before she died. The place she spent countless evenings and weekends working all hours. It was such an important part of her life and ours. The idea of it no longer being there is inconceivable.

Kate puts an arm around me. "I'm sorry, El."

"But why? Why is the landlord selling?"

Margot shakes her head, looking as clueless as I feel. "I don't know love. He must need the money. Maybe he's had an offer from a developer or something."

The sound of a car engine rumbling outside and the beep of a horn signals the Uber's arrived.

Margot glances over her shoulder down the front path. "Oh, your taxi's here. I'd best be off."

I give her the letter back. "Erm, yeah thanks for coming round and telling me. I appreciate it. I'll help you however I can. The shop's part of Mum's legacy. I owe it to her to try my hardest to stop this."

She gives me the once over and becomes glassy-eyed. "Thank you. Your mum would have been proud of you. I'll let you know when I hear any news."

"Are you all right?" Kate asks after she's gone.

"I'm not sure. I mean, it's come out of the blue."

She gives me a squeeze. "Tell you what. Why don't we sack off going to the club. We can stay in, open a bottle of wine and watch *Sex & The City* re-runs."

"What about Harry?"

"He'll survive. This is more important."

I look down the front path at the taxi waiting for us. Kate's done more than her fair share of looking after me this past year. She's got her heart set on tonight. The least I can do is go. "You're joking. Now you've made me get all bloody dolled up, I'm not going to let it go to waste. We're going."

Chapter 2

Ella

Thirty minutes later we arrive at the club and climb out of the Uber. A couple of stone steps lead up to a set of black double doors, where a very large bouncer dressed in black stands beneath a glass canopy, seeing to the queue of guests. Two topiary trees adorned with white fairy lights sit in planters either side of the door.

My mobile beeps inside my bag and I pull it out as we join the back of the queue. It's a text from Amy.

Hi sis, any chance you could transfer 50 quid into my account? Out tonight and I'm out of cash.x

My heart sinks. She's more of a financial drain now that she's at uni than she ever was at home. And she's only been there a few weeks. It seems not much studying gets done, but a whole lot of partying takes place.

Kate reads my expression and sighs. "Don't tell me. She's asking for money again."

"She says she's out."

"She's always out, El. It's about time she stopped sponging off you and got herself a part-time job."

The mention of my sister to Kate is like red rag to a bull. They've never gotten on. In the six months they lived together I was forced to act as referee on more than one occasion.

The queue moves forward. We're in next.

"Yeah, I know. I think she's got one lined up at GAP this week," I say, stuffing my phone back into my bag. Amy will have to wait.

Kate frowns in annoyance at my defence of my sister but remains silent. It's a sore subject.

The couple in front of us disappear through the doors of the club and it's our turn to be let in.

"Good evening ladies, welcome to Whites. Can I have your tickets please?" asks the bouncer with a curl of his lip. He's as broad as the door, with raven black shoulder-length dreadlocks and deep brown eyes that say he doesn't stand any messing.

Kate smiles sweetly and passes him the tickets. "Of course."

He checks them, nods in approval and steps aside to let us through.

The entrance hall is vast, with dove grey panelled walls, an oak floor and magnificent crystal chandeliers. If this is just the entrance, I can't wait to see what the rest of the club looks like. A group of young men and women are lounging on the white leather sofas, knocking back champagne and laughing. Designer clothes, perfect hair and make-up. Just by looking at them I can tell they've all got one thing in common. Money.

I roll my eyes, knowing I'd better get used to it. This place is going to be teeming with these types; rich, self-entitled, never had to work a day in their lives, living off Daddy's money …

"Oh my God," Kate hisses as we pass the group. "That's Trixie Delivive. One of the L'Oreal cover models."

I glance back at them, but I'm not sure who exactly she's referring to. All the women look the same; thin, high cheekbones, long blonde hair. Any one of them could be a model.

"I suppose it's no surprise she's here. Last I read, Spencer White's shagging her." Kate catches my confused expression. "Tell me you know who Spencer White is?"

Everyone knows who Spencer White is. The infamous super-rich star of the reality TV series *Young, Rich & Reckless,* who's made headlines for his womanising and partying since joining the show a year ago. You'd have to be living in a cave not to have heard of him.

"Of course I have," I scoff. "I just don't get why him shagging Trixie-whatever-her-name-is, has any bearing on her being here."

Kate looks at me like I've just landed from out of space. "Because this is Spencer's club."

Whites. Of course it is. What better way to take advantage of his party boy reputation than to open a club.

Kate's phone beeps and she retrieves it from her bag. Her face lights up. "Harry's here. He says he's found some seats over by the bar with the largest dance floor."

I raise my eyebrows. "How many bars has this place got?"

She grins. "Loads, so I've heard. Come on, less standing around out here. Let's get drunk."

A wall of dance music hits us as we head through another set of double doors into the main club. The thud of the bass beat reverberates through my chest as I follow Kate, squeezing through the crowds of revellers and taking in the impressive surroundings. It's all shiny floors, white sofas and glass tables with backlit walls. This part looks super sleek and modern in contrast to the traditional entrance at the front of the building. The club goes back and back and just when I don't think it can get any bigger, the place opens out into a huge dance floor with a vaulted ceiling. There's a bar to the left and the large dance floor in the middle is heaving. White leather booths are tiered around the room on different levels, looking down over the dance floor. It's like no other club I've ever been to before and I'm not sure where to look first.

Kate grabs my arm and gestures towards the other side of the dance floor mouthing something to me, but I can't make it out over the music. I follow her lead around the tangle of dancing bodies and up some steps to one of the seating areas, where it's thankfully a little quieter.

A tall, stocky guy with a mop of corn blond hair and a rugby player physique gets up from one of the sofas as we arrive, joined by his slightly shorter, dark-haired friend.

"Great. You found us." The blond guy, who I take to be Harry, flashes a smile and gives Kate a kiss on the cheek. She blushes furiously but quickly recovers.

"Yeah, this place is great, isn't it. Thanks for the tickets."

There's an awkward silence for a few minutes as they look at each other all googly-eyed. The other guy glances around the club and sips his pint, looking completely disinterested.

Well, this is great.

I clear my throat to remind my friend I'm actually here. Kate snaps out of it and gives me an apologetic look.

"Oh, sorry. Ella this is Harry. Harry this is my friend, Ella."

"Hi," I say.

Harry gives me a charming smile. "Hi. This is my mate, Sam."

"Yeah, nice to meet you, El," Sam says with his eyes on my breasts.

Creep.

"So, what can we get you lovely ladies to drink," Harry asks rubbing his hands together.

"Ooohh, how lovely." Kate giggles, flicking her hair over her shoulder and locking into full-on flirtation mode. "Pornstar Martini for me, please."

I shoot Sam an icy glare, but he doesn't get the message and carries on staring at my chest. "I'll have the same," I reply stiffly.

Harry and Sam disappear off to the bar and we sink down onto one of the plush white leather sofas.

I need to get something straight. I fix my friend a firm look. "I know what you're doing."

Kate crosses her legs and stares out at the dance floor. "What?"

"Don't what me," I warn her. "You're trying to set me up."

"I'm not."

"Yes, you are. You've been trying to set me up with that guy from your work for months, and because I haven't agreed to go on a blind date with him, you're now trying to set me up with Harry's friend."

I know all her stunts, we've been friends too long. Kate sighs defeatedly and I know I've hit the nail on the head. Now it's her turn to give me a firm look.

"I'm not really. Harry just mentioned he might be bringing a friend along. Come on, El. Would it really be so bad if you spoke to a guy, dare I say, even flirted a bit? It's been nearly two years since you had anything close to a relationship."

Ryan. We dated for six months.

I shrug. "So?"

"So, it's not natural. You're twenty-six, for fuck's sake." Her gaze softens. "I know how hard it's been for you these past few years, looking after your mum and Amy, and I know you haven't had the best experiences with men, but now it's time for you to put yourself first for a change, instead of looking after everyone else."

She's right. For almost the last eight years I've spent nearly all of my spare time looking after Mum and Amy. They've been my focus and I've been fine with it.

"I don't need a guy to make my life complete."

Kate sighs because this isn't the first time we've had this discussion and it won't be the last. "I know you don't, and I get why you're wary..." She trails off, not wanting to finish the sentence.

Men betray you, let you down, then leave. Just like Dad did when he walked out leaving Mum a single parent to a seven-year-old and a one-year-old. Just like Ryan when he dumped me after finding out what I did to earn a bit of extra cash. Just like Logan...

Fuck, I need a drink.

I shift uncomfortably in my seat. "Maybe. But you can forget about anything happening with Sam."

"Why? You've only just met him."

"Yes, I know, and he stared at my tits the entire time."

A wry smiles stretches across her face. "I told you, you look hot in that dress, but if that's the case I take your point."

Before I can squash any further ideas she might have about setting me up with anyone else, Kate's eyes widen as she spots something behind me. "Oh my God," she gasps, grabbing my arm. "There's Spencer White."

I follow her gaze. Overlooking the club is another seating area. Tucked out of the way at the top of the stairs, sectioned off from the rest of us mere mortals by a red rope barrier, is the VIP area. A tall, well built, muscular guy stands behind the barrier with his hands clasped in front of him. He surveys the club below, watching, waiting. His buzz cut, physique and sharp black suit tell me he's security. Behind him are low-backed, white leather seats filled with a few men in suits who look like businessmen. Spencer stands looking down at the dance floor, chatting to a blonde and swigging from a bottle of Cristal. He looks the same as when I last saw him on TV; clean shaven with haphazardly styled, mousey brown hair which skims the bottom of his ears. He's wearing a black t-shirt and jeans like he couldn't be bothered to make a special effort for tonight.

"Do you think if I go and ask, he'll have a selfie with me?" Kate says.

Two women walk hand-in-hand up the stairs to the VIP area. Both have stunning figures and are wearing short, tight sequinned dresses, but one's blonde and one's brunette. They swoosh their long hair over their shoulders as they reach the barrier and giggle flirtatiously at the security guy.

He gives them the once over, unhooks the rope and steps aside to let them through.

"I'd say Spencer's got his hands full at the moment."

Kate sighs wistfully. "Lucky cows."

The women sashay across the floor and brazenly drape themselves all over him. Spencer's eyes light up. He grins like a Cheshire cat, sandwiching himself between the girls and slinging his arms around them. The woman he was talking to looks fit to burst with rage and storms off. He's clearly not a one-woman man.

A guy gets up from the seating area and heads over to the stairs. He's not one of the businessmen. He's wearing dark blue jeans and an ink blue, long sleeved, button up jumper. Smart but casual. The brunette's eyes light up as she claps eyes on him and darts in front of his path, forcing him to stop. She runs her hands across his chest and tosses her hair back, batting her eyelashes and laughing flirtatiously.

The guy smiles politely, says something, then gently removes her hands from his chest, and heads over to the security guy at the top of the stairs. The brunette looks miffed and retreats back to Spencer. Her moves haven't worked on him.

"Who is *that*?" Kate says.

"Dunno," I mumble distractedly as I watch him more closely. Now I get why the brunette was so excited to see him.

The security bloke's built but this guy's nearly matching him on height and size. But he's not security. He stands with his arms folded, casting a scrutinising gaze around the club and giving off an air of something else entirely, but I can't put my finger on it. His strong jaw is adorned with scruff and his dark brown hair is longer on top and slightly dishevelled, like he's in the habit of running his fingers through it. The thin knit jumper clings to every undulation of his taut, muscular body and I can't stop myself from admiring him.

Fucking hell, he's hot.

Most women's dream.

I briefly close my eyes and press my thighs together to stem the fluttery ache between my legs.

What's happening to me?

I haven't reacted to anyone like this in a while. Okay, ever. But he's like no one I've laid eyes on before. Apart from the fact he's knicker-scorchingly attractive, there's something about him...

Who are you?

I open my eyes. He's staring directly at me. My heart double times. His direct gaze cuts through me causing a hot flush to creep up my body. I shift uncomfortably beneath his penetrating stare because he's doing more than just looking at me. I feel exposed, cracked open; like he's seeing into my soul and my deepest, darkest secrets.

Then I see it. The thing I couldn't put my finger on. The quality he possesses that makes him different to all the rest; power. He oozes it. From every pore. But as he carries on looking at me, something shifts. The iciness thaws, the steely exterior dissolves and I see sadness. My heart twists. I *feel* it. A dark, biting melancholy buried deep inside him calling to me. I can't pull myself away. He must feel it too, because his eyes don't leave my face. The beat of the dance music, the revellers having a good time, all fall away to nothing. It feels like we're the only people in the entire place. A silent, magnetic connection closes the distance between us. His eyes rake over my body, scorching my flesh like he's touching me with his big, strong hands and I yearn to feel him. I need his perfect lips on mine. I need *him*. All over me.

"Oooh, here are our drinks," Kate gushes.

I'm pulled back to reality with a bump at the sight of Sam standing in front of me holding two drinks and interrupting my view of mystery man. "One Pornstar Martini, for the lovely Ella." He hands me my drink with a smirk and sits down beside me, a little too close for comfort.

If he thinks flattery is going to get him anywhere, he's got another thing coming.

I force a polite smile and wriggle away so his thigh isn't pressed up against mine. "Erm, thanks."

Harry sidles onto the other end of the seat and slings an arm around Kate's shoulders. She giggles and relaxes against him and they become absorbed in one another again.

I look up at the VIP area. My mystery man is looking down at his phone. Probably texting his extremely attractive wife or fiancée. Huh.

Sam takes the opportunity to sidle up closer to me. His eyes land on my breasts once more.

Fucking great.

I grab the Prosecco shot and down it in one. Tonight's going to be a long night.

Chapter 3

Gabe

My hands clench round my mobile in frustration as I re-read the text. "Fucking great!"
Another company has their eyes on the prize. U need to act quick.

Jake glances at me before returning his gaze to the club. "Trouble?"

I slide my phone into the back pocket of my jeans. Just what I need – competition. Whoever seals the deal on the land is set to make billions in a couple of years. And that's got to be me. It *will* be me. I don't give a fuck about the competition, they're just a fly in the ointment of success. I'll trample over whoever to get what I want, like I always do. You either win or you lose in this game. And I *never* lose.

I drag a hand across my face, contemplating our next move. "We've got competition. We need to act fast otherwise we're going to be left with our arse in our hands."

Jake lifts an eyebrow, looking as thrilled about the news as I feel. "Fuck. Who says? K?"

K. My man on the inside – the guy I pay a whole lot of cash to keep me ahead of the game.

I don't need to reply. Jake's blood. We're cut from similar cloth.

He sighs, taking in the news. "You need me to ... intervene?"

"Not yet. I need everyone with their jaws still intact so we can talk it out and reach an agreement. And when I say we, I mean you."

A flicker of a smile crosses his face and he cracks his knuckles. Despite leaving the SAS eight years ago, the fight's still ingrained in his character. I don't think it will ever leave. He's the brawn, with a never-ending list of useful contacts, ranging from bent coppers, gang leaders and council officials partial to the odd backhander. I head the business; make the deals, ensure its sparkling reputation remains intact because image is everything. We make a good team. We've got each other's back, unlike our other flesh and blood …

"And if they don't want to talk?"

"Then you know the score."

A piercing shriek of female laughter comes from behind me. I don't need to look to know Spencer's the root cause.

Jake casts a disparaging glance over his shoulder. "Looks like the girls I arranged for our guests have been distracted by Spencer."

My jaw twitches with irritation. Good job I've already closed the deal. I've got what I want. If I'd had a choice, I wouldn't have brought them here, but they seem to actually like all this shit and fakery. But needs must.

"He fucks anything that moves," I mutter in disgust.

Jake chuckles. "Don't worry. Our guests haven't even noticed. The two lines of blow they sank in the toilets has made sure of that."

I fix him with a fierce stare. "Are you fucking serious?"

"Calm down. It was in the VIP toilets. There was no one else around. I cleaned up all the evidence." He shrugs. "Anyway, that's what they wanted, and it's my job to keep the guests happy so you can close the deal. Have you?"

What kind of question is that? "Of course."

"So, I've done my job." He gives me a long, assessing look. "You need to chill the fuck out. Have a drink, get laid, whatever, but calm the fuck down, little bro." He smirks. "Not that you usually need my help with these things, but do you want me to sort you out some skirt?"

Within seconds I find her. She's still sitting in the same spot with her blonde friend. Now two guys have joined them, and the dark haired one is chatting to her.

Boyfriend?

I narrow my eyes in contempt and study her body language closely. Her slender legs and arms are folded in a typical defensive posture. Her lips are twisted, but she's not smiling. She looks bored as fuck as she stares at the guy who's jabbering on, oblivious that she's zoned out. There's no spark in her eyes. Not like when she looked at me. My cock jerks at the memory.

Fuck.

He's hitting on her and failing to impress if the look on her face is anything to go by. She's got an edge. I like it.

"I said… do you want me to fix you up with a girl?" Jake presses.

I shake my head, unable to tear my eyes away from the dark-haired beauty in the smoking red dress. Just like the first time I saw her. Her hair tumbles over her breasts, giving her an untamed, wild vibe. I've dated models, the aristocracy, heiresses but she's a natural beauty. And it makes her all the more appealing.

She flicks her hair, sending soft curls cascading over her shoulder and my mind wanders.

How soft would her hair feel in my fist as I came in her mouth?

Shit.

Jake's right. I need to get laid. It's been a few days.

But not her. A woman like that deserves more than a one-night stand with yours truly. Because that's all I've got to offer. She needs someone who'll treat her right and won't just use her for sex, then drop her once he's done.

I force my gaze away from her and scan the glitterati that have dragged their super rich arses to tonight's opening. Actresses, z-listers, and models fill the place, all here for the publicity and paparazzi who'll be waiting when they stagger out at two in the morning, because there's no such thing as bad publicity in their world.

They wouldn't know hard work if it smacked them round the face.

I don't even realise that I'm staring at her again. It's like there's a weird pull that keeps drawing me back to her. And this time she's looking at me. Her eyes widen as our gaze locks. She absentmindedly winds a lock of her hair round her finger, bored out of her mind, while the guy beside her continues to chat away.

Her eyes tell me everything. She couldn't give a fuck about him. She wants me.

Chapter 4

Ella

"Another drink?" The words pull me back to the moment. Sam lifts his half-drunk pint of lager to his lips and drains it, then raises his eyebrows, waiting for me to reply.

I blush. I've been staring up at my mystery man. Again.

What the fuck is the matter with me?

Sam slurps his pint and leers at my breasts.

Oh yeah, that's what's the matter. Not to mention the fact I've spent the past ten minutes being spoken at. I know everything there is to know about Liverpool's chances of winning the Premiership this season.

"Well, do you want another or not?"

I frown and stare at the half-drunk cocktail in my hand, suspicious of his motives. "I haven't finished this one yet."

If he's planning on getting me drunk, he's going to get a shock.

"Come on, El. Harry and I are going to get more drinks. Why don't you have another to celebrate?" Kate enthuses, getting to her feet.

"What are we celebrating?" Sam pipes up.

If you'd have let me get a word in edge ways you might know.

"I'm starting a new job on Monday."

Harry loops an arm around Kate's waist. "Great. Whereabouts?"

"White House Developments. They're a property company based in Canary Wharf."

"Nice," Sam nods thoughtfully "I've seen signs on buildings with their name on all over the city. Aren't they a pretty big deal?"

"Yeah, pretty big," I agree.

They're one of the wealthiest property companies in London, or so Google informed me when I did a bit of last-minute research for my interview last week. Maxwell White founded the company thirty years ago and it's gone from strength to strength. They're responsible for a lot of redevelopments in the capital. Turns out I needn't have bothered doing the research. My temping experience over the last six years spoke for itself and Maxwell's PA, who interviewed me, didn't throw any curve balls my way.

"We'll get you another drink to celebrate. You can't nurse that one all night. Anyway, Harry thinks he's just seen Dante Pearce over by the bar," Kate says decisively, craning her neck to see if she can catch a glimpse.

I frown. "Who's he?"

"Chelsea Midfielder. You know, the hot one with the little dreads."

"Have you?" Sam shoots out of his seat, spilling lager all down his white shirt and narrowly missing my feet. He doesn't notice.

I silently will Kate and Harry to take him with them, but sadly they don't. They disappear off towards the bar hand-in hand. I'm thrilled Kate seems to have finally snared her man but I'm less than delighted by the prospect of being stuck with Sam.

"So, it's just you and me then," he tells me, sitting down beside me and resting an arm across the back of the seat.

I shift away from him in the hope that he'll get the message. He doesn't. Instead, he puts his sweaty palm on my thigh and gives me a smarmy grin.

"We can get to know one another a bit better."

Is he serious?

I push his hand off my leg in disgust. I've experienced enough drunken, handsy men over the years to know how to deal with them.

"Cool it, hotshot. I'm not looking to start anything right now."

He doesn't get the message and sees my rebuke as a challenge. His hand lands on my knee. "Oh, come on," he mutters pushing it up my thigh and with it, his luck. "Don't be a prick tease."

I see red and jump to my feet. "Fuck off, you creep!" I shout, chucking the remainder of my cocktail all over his shirt.

Sam leaps up and peers down at the large orange stain seeping through the white cotton and glares at me. "What the fuck did you do that for, you silly cow?"

The next five seconds happen in a blur. He lunges at me and I dart backwards to get out of his way but stumble. I feel a sharp pain, my ankle gives way and I fall flat on my arse, just as my mystery man and the security guy crowd in.

Mystery guy grabs Sam around the throat and squeezes. "Apologise to the lady."

Sam's face turns puce. His eyes bulge out of his head and I'm pretty sure he's going to pass out any second.

"Are you fucking serious?"

He's barely finished choking out the words when the guy squeezes harder.

Other guests start to crowd round watching the scene unfold. I'm still on the floor watching transfixed.

So raw, so powerful…

Fuck. This is turning me on.

"I didn't do anything," Sam splutters in defence.

The frown line on the mystery man's forehead deepens at the blatant lie. "You touched her and she didn't want you to. Apologise."

"For fuck's sake, I'm sorry. Okay, I'm sorry," Sam gasps.

"See, that wasn't so hard, was it?" my mystery guy growls, removing his hand from around Sam's throat. The security man grabs him by the shoulder and shoves him towards the exit.

Mystery guy straightens his jumper and glances round at the other guests.

"Show's over."

He lowers himself onto his haunches beside me. The frown line dissolves and his gaze softens. Piercing eyes hold mine, making my stomach tighten with lust. From a distance he's hot, up close he's breathtaking.

"Are you okay?"

His deep, husky voice pulls me back to the unfortunate reality; I'm ungraciously sprawled out on the floor at his feet, thankfully not flashing my knickers.

"Erm ... my ankle hurts a bit."

"Do you think you can stand?"

"I'm not sure." I go to move but he puts out a hand to stop me.

"It's okay. Stay there. Don't try to walk on it. If it's broken, it'll just make it worse."

Broken? Fucking hell, I hope not. That's not going to make a good impression on my first day at my new job, is it?

"I'll help you up."

I offer him my hand but he doesn't take it. One minute I'm on my backside sat on the hard floor, and the next he's scooping me up into his arms as though I'm light as a feather.

He hasn't asked my permission. He's just done it. This should feel wrong and weird, but it doesn't.

I relax against his warm, firm chest and press my lips together to stem the sigh threatening to escape me. He smells delicious. All fresh and clean and there's the scent of sandalwood in there too; no doubt some expensive aftershave. No one I've dated has ever stood up for me like he just did, or whisked me off my feet. For the first time in my life I feel protected by a guy. I fight the ridiculously strong urge to rest my head against the curve of his neck as he carries me over to the seating area, because if I give in, he'll think I'm a weirdo. He carefully lowers me down, sliding his arms from underneath me and making me immediately feel bereft at the loss of contact.

"Which ankle is it?"

I lean back on my hands. "My right."

He pushes up his sleeves. Designs in black ink decorate his muscular forearms from the wrist up and disappear beneath the material of his jumper.

My stomach backflips. I swipe my tongue across my dry bottom lip and think back to the sight of his hand around Sam's throat. The look of menace in his eyes as he squeezed his fingers round his neck, cutting off his oxygen supply. Outwardly he's Mr Put-Together, but he's got a dangerous streak. And I don't care, because all I can think about is where his tattoos stop. Maybe, they don't. Maybe they carry on across his chest and back and down to his well defined waist. I don't even realise I'm staring until he clears his throat and my eyes dart to his.

His eyes glint in amusement at the fact he's caught me checking him out. Not for the first time tonight.

Shit.

"May I?" he asks, gesturing towards my foot.

I blush furiously, hating myself. "Um, sure."

He curls a hand around my ankle with the gentlest of touches and slowly moves my foot from side to side.

"Does that hurt?"

I shake my head.

It feels heavenly.

I think he's going to carry on doing what he's doing but he doesn't. He slips my shoe off and gently presses the palm of his hand against the base of my foot, curling his fingers around my toes. My foot looks tiny in his large hands and the sight of his long fingers wrapped around my ankle makes my pulse speed up. I watch mesmerised, as he carefully manipulates my foot with the lightest of touches like I'm fragile glass and he's scared he'll break me. He brushes his thumb over my ankle bone in small, slow circles. I swallow hard. My imagination's running wild.

How soft would his palm feel running up my thigh?

What would his fingers feel like inside me?

I open my eyes and notice a signet ring on his index finger. There's a dark stone in the centre but I can't make out the detail. He's not wearing any other rings. My stupid heart skips at the meaning. I'm relieved when he speaks and distracts my mind from wandering down a dangerous path I've forbidden

ing out my phone. "Amy calling" flashes in the display.

For fuck's sake, Ames, impeccable timing.

I cancel the call and slide the phone back into my bag.

"My younger sister," I explain, because I don't want him to think it's a guy. "She's asking to borrow money from me, again."

His lips twitch into a knowing smile and he picks up my shoe. "Don't tell me. The bank of mum and dad ran out."

"No, well… there isn't one. I mean, well … we don't have a dad and our mum, well … she died."

His faint smile vanishes. "I'm so sorry."

I'm used to the awkwardness and apologies by now. "It's okay."

He carefully slips my shoe back on. "What's your name?"

Another question about me. I seriously need to even this up a little. So far, I know barely anything about him. "Ella. What's yours?"

His gaze washes over me before returning to my face as though he's thinking about it. Like to tell me would be sharing a part of him, and that's not something he does easily. "My friends call me G."

The next words fall from my mouth before I can stop them. "So, we're already friends?"

"We could be a lot more than that."

His perfect lips widen into a smile and my chest tightens. He's flirting with me. But is he playing with me? I've had enough lines thrown at me by guys over the years. I know how to handle them – usually.

"That's a line, if ever I've heard one."

A deep, throaty chuckle sounds from the back of his throat and sends goosebumps prickling across my arms.

His eyes glint at my challenge and it takes all I've got not to look away. "I've no time for lines. I say what I mean. And mean what I say."

The commitment in his statement makes my stomach somersault with nerves. I ignore the pounding of my heart in my ears and keep my eyes on his, hoping I sound braver than I feel because when he looks at me, I forget who I am.

"I'm glad to hear it. Although that *definitely* sounded like a line."

He inches his brows upwards. "You want me to be more direct?"

My mouth dries. That sounds like a challenge; like he's telling me to think carefully about what I'm about to say. My brain's telling me to run in the opposite direction, but I can't move. I'm riveted to the spot. I need more; I want all he's got to throw at me.

"Yes."

I expect him to say something but he doesn't. He stands and offers me his hand instead. "Shall we?"

I take it without hesitation. The feel of my hand in his causes a shiver to travel up my spine. Heat prickles up the length of my arm as I look at our hands together and shift round on the seat, waiting for him to help me up. But yet again he doesn't do what I expect him to. He doesn't move a muscle. For a few seconds he stands motionless staring at my hand in his, then, just before it starts to get weird, he closes his fingers around mine and helps me up. Even in my stupid high heels I only reach his collarbone. It's only when I lift my eyes to his that I realise how close we are. Within touching distance. Far too close for strangers. So close, he could bend down and kiss me right now. His eyes drop to my mouth like he's thinking the same thing. I stare at his lips, wondering what they would feel like on mine. What would he taste like?

Kiss me!

Just when I think my heart's going to burst out of my chest in anticipation, he drags his gaze to look behind me. I follow his stare to find him looking at the VIP area.

"There's a sadness inside you." His voice rasps in my ear making my whole body tingle with awareness. His warm breath hits my cheek and sends shockwaves of pleasure shooting through to my core. "I saw it straight away. A beautiful sadness in your eyes."

"I saw the same in you."

I steel myself to look at him, but I needn't have bothered. It doesn't work. No amount of preparing myself is going to work when it comes to looking at this man. Steely blues pin me to the spot. I've received similar looks from men knocking back their drinks while they wait for me to get on with it, but nothing as intense as the way G's looking at me. He shifts a millimetre closer, like he's not quite close enough.

He arches an eyebrow. "You don't know me."

I run my tongue across my dry bottom lip and watch his eyes slide to the movement. "You don't know me either."

"I know you want me."

Arrogant dick.

"No, I don't," I lie.

His gorgeous mouth widens into a smile. He reaches up and touches a lock of my hair, smoothing it between his finger and thumb. I can't breathe.

"Yes, you do."

Of course he knows. I've not been exactly discreet about it, and he's got a cocky self-awareness which tells me he knows all too well the effect he has on women. He must get it all the time – like the brunette from the VIP area. An uneasy feeling takes root in my stomach as I mentally join the dots. He's hot, connected to the super-rich clique in this place and loaded, if his expensive knit jumper and glossy black Tag Heuer watch are anything to go by. I'm not young and naïve anymore. Designer tags and money don't impress me, they have the opposite effect. And I'm not going to throw myself at him like the groupie from the VIP area either. And it's about time he knows it.

"And you want me," I say firmly.

He looks deep into my eyes and ghosts a fingertip along my jawline with the lightest of touches, leaving a trail of fire in his wake. I shiver. The butterflies in my stomach are back with a vengeance and when he finally speaks I'm gone.

"Very much. I want to do all manner of sinful things" – his eyes slide down my front – "to your beautiful body" – then up over my waist, my breasts and back to my face – "to that beautiful mouth, Princess."

If anyone else said this to me they'd get a slap.

But he's not anything like the other creeps I've encountered. He's not like anyone I've ever met. And I want him to do everything he's just said, and for me to return the favour.

This isn't normal. I'm fantasising about doing naughty things with a total stranger.

"Would you like me to?" He puts his hands on my shoulders, his warm palms heating my flesh. "Would you?"

"Yes," I breathe.

He slowly caresses the tops of my shoulders with his thumbs, his eyes burning into mine. "Tell me." His measured tone laps across my skin. "Tell me what you want me to do to you."

He's a stranger. And that's a personal question.

My cheeks flush at the fact I don't need to think twice about my answer.

Ryan didn't get my tastes in the bedroom; my need for him to be dominant, but this guy would. Everything about him is calm and controlled.

He leans in a fraction closer, like he knows this will seal the deal. "What's your forbidden fruit, Ella?"

Fuck.

"To be controlled –" I draw a shaky breath in, unable to believe I'm about to confess this to a guy I've only just met "– in bed."

The rise of his chest at my answer, tells me I've found a chink in his masterful façade. His eyes glitter with desire.

I seize the chance and meet his gaze challengingly. "What's yours?"

He looks at my mouth, lost in thought for a few moments. "You."

I'm floored. My mind turns over what he's said.

He gives me a regretful look. The shutters have come down extinguishing the heat from moments earlier.

"You don't want to get involved with someone like me."

Disappointment drops like a rock in my stomach. I can't believe it. He's set me up, hasn't he. Got me to admit – what I admitted, and then backed right off.

"Erm… what's going on? Where's Sam gone?"

Kate's voice shatters the moment in two.

I take a step back from G, and wrap my arms around myself, focussing on the question.

"He's been thrown out."

Harry looks worried. "Fucking hell, why?"

"He tried it on and wouldn't take no for an answer."

Kate puts an arm around me. "Jesus! I know you said he was a bit of a lech but … are you okay?"

I give her a reassuring smile. Sam's a distant memory after what's happened to me in the last five minutes.

"I'm fine."

Harry dashes a hand through his hair and looks awkward. "Shit. I'm sorry about Sam. What a fucking twat."

Kate eyes G quizzically. He's looking at the floor with his hands in his pockets. I hope it's the weight of his prickish behaviour weighing him down, but I doubt it. Twats like him don't have a fucking conscience. Even so, I think I need to at least mention who he is, before Kate keels over with curiosity.

"G intervened and got Sam thrown out."

Kate's eyes dart between me and G, sensing something's up. "Okay, well we're going to move onto another club. Every bar's three deep in this place."

"Yeah, the drinks prices are fucking ridiculous as well," Harry interjects, shaking his head in annoyance.

"I'm going to order an Uber." Kate pulls her phone out of her bag and glances at G. She's got so many questions. I know it. "Are you coming El?"

This couldn't be any more awkward.

I fleetingly glance at him. A wall's come up behind those beautiful eyes.

He slowly nods his head like he's convincing himself, even as he says the words, "Goodnight, Ella."

My stomach drops. His response solidifies my fears. He's been playing me all along. Reeling me in with his bloody lines, making me think he likes me. It's all one big game to him. It always is. Well off, well educated, self-important pricks who are used to everything and everyone falling at their designer leather shoes. But instead of looking smug about it, he looks dejected.

It's all part of the act, you silly cow.

I force my expression to remain neutral. There's no way I'm giving him a reaction. I've already given away too much. Not that he waits to see. He turns round abruptly, like he doesn't want to hear my response and disappears into the crowd. And I watch until he's out of sight.

Fuck him.

Chapter 6

Gabe

The silhouettes of the London Eye and The Shard carve into the midnight blue sky. Lights from the traffic on Tower Bridge in the distance confirm the city is still wide awake, just like me.

Most of it belongs to me. Every mile or so you'll be sure to stumble across a building I own or have got my sights on. Over the last thirty years the family name has become interwoven into the fabric of the city and I'm not about to take my foot off the pedal now I'm at the helm. It's not just a business. The company and the family name go hand-in-hand. The reputation of one affects the other; the family image impacts on business and how we're viewed by our competitors and potential clients. I was primed to take on the role from the word go. Straight out of uni and wet behind the ears, I'd had a lot to learn. I was clueless to the shady dealings, corruption and dog-eat-dog game I was entering. Now, I'm the Ringmaster, and everyone plays by my rules, or they suffer the consequences. We're taken seriously. Deathly. The family's name and reputation sit on my broad shoulders and I'm fucked if I'm going to let the side down.

I raise the tumbler to my lips and welcome the burn as the eighteen-year-old single malt slides down my throat, coating my lips. It's sweet and heady.

And just like that she's back in my head.

What the fuck's the matter with me tonight?

I grit my teeth, pissed off with myself, and swig back the remainder of the Scotch. I know better. This stuff should be savoured, but I'll try anything to get rid of the sight of her each time I close my eyes. I blow out a long breath, raking my fingers through my hair, still damp from the shower, mentally revisiting what happened tonight for what feels like the hundredth time. I'm the guy in charge, the one everyone looks to. So why do I feel so fucking clueless?

Instead of having all the answers, tonight's left me with a host of questions. Like why the sight of that guy feeling her up ignited a white-hot fury inside me that I hadn't felt in a long time. Why I picked her up and flirted with her. Why the look of contempt in her eyes when I told her to stay away from me is burned into my brain, and why I walked out of the club leaving Jake to deal with our guests. I had to. I needed to get the lingering scent of her floral perfume from under my nose and the feel of her baby soft skin out of my thoughts. If I hadn't left when I did, I'd have brought her back here and fucked her. And above everything else, I have no clue why I hate myself so much for leaving her.

I glance down at the empty glass in my hand, wishing it was full. Dad's words ring in my ears from all those years ago, *"Women are trouble. The more money you've got, the more they want to fuck you. They're good for one thing and one thing only..."* I'm not sure my fifteen-year-old self got it at the time but I sure as hell do now. Women are a distraction. They always complicate matters. If I'm thinking about a woman, I'm not focussing on the business. Women are a means to an end. Nothing more than a stress relief and I don't usually have to work hard to get my next dose.

The sound of the lift doors opening, followed by heels clicking across the marble floor of the hallway, tell me my stress relief has arrived.

"It's late." Laura sounds pissed off.

"You didn't have to come," I point out, taking my time to turn round.

The flimsy black material of her dress clings to her slim frame. I catch a glimpse of lace emerging from her cleavage. She might be pissed off, but she's still made an effort.

"You could have told me to fuck off," I tell her, purely for effect. We both know she'll never do that. As long as I keep asking, she'll keep turning up. My looks and money make her wet.

Do I like it? No, but it gets me what I want.

She flicks her blonde hair over her shoulder and gives me her best defiant stare, even though we both know it's an act.

"I thought you'd be at the opening of the club?"

"I was," I say, putting my empty tumbler down on the glass side table.

Her lips twist into a coy smile. A dangerous look I recognise all too well flashes in her eyes. Hope. Her next question confirms my fear.

"And you came home to spend some time with yours truly?"

Not exactly.

I notice her cheeks flush as I approach her.

"Well? Did you?" she pushes.

She's getting the wrong end of the stick and asking too many stupid questions.

"Bend over."

Her brown eyes widen at my directness and her glossed lips part. Her hair frames a heart shaped face and killer cheekbones. Model perfect. But she's not the reason why my cock's been throbbing all night.

She lifts a perfectly groomed eyebrow. "No kiss?"

Her citrussy perfume sticks in my throat and makes me want to gag. Why has it never affected me before? I clench my jaw in irritation. My non-existent patience is wearing thin.

I purposefully step forward, forcing her back against the grey velvet sofa. With one push, she falls backwards onto the pile of cushions. Even though she gives a little-girl-lost cry of surprise, she parts her legs ready for me.

I kneel between her thighs, flip her over onto her front, push her dress up and thong down. I don't want to look at her. She's a mere vehicle for my release.

I roll on a condom, grip her hips and pound into her. She lets out a stifled cry at the intensity and I think I hear her nails claw into the sofa but can't be sure because my eyes close and I lose myself. Doeful hazel eyes and perfect plump lips flash into my mind and I'm thrusting, hard. I do my best to ignore the muffled groans from the woman at the end of my cock, trying not to focus on the way her skin isn't as soft and her non-existent curves don't feel nearly as good as Ella's.

Fuck.

The name conjures her in my mind like a spell and my cock strains. Then it's her I'm fucking, that I'm losing myself in and not for the first time tonight. I'm fucking one woman while imagining another. This is a whole new level of shitty behaviour for me, something else I've not done before tonight. Something else I didn't know I was capable of. Another unwelcome surprise. All because of the sassy, dark haired beauty with the curves wrapped in red, who admitted she likes to be controlled.

I groan at the thought of her beneath me and pound home, searching for my release. My mind blanks and I welcome it. Erasing the night that's got me acting totally out of character. The haunted look in Ella's eyes as her gaze met mine across the club. How nobody else seemed to exist for those few seconds; straight out of some romantic bullshit novel. Not like the real world; where love equals pain and suffering, and women aren't worth the fucking hassle.

I come with a growl, emptying myself with a roll of my hips, feeling the tension slip from my body and taking with it all thoughts of tonight – job done. I pull out, tie off the condom, stand and pull up my sweatpants.

Laura twists round and pushes her dishevelled hair out of her face with a hand. "What about me?"

I'm not in the mood. I'm being a selfish bastard. If she's under the illusion that this is about anything other than fucking, she's about to get a shock. "You know your way out."

I turn and head towards the bathroom, delivering the final blow. "And I want you gone by the time I come back."

Chapter 7

Ella

"Ella, you're going to be late, if we don't set off in five."

Kate sticks her head around the bedroom door and breaks out into a smile at my appearance.

"Someone looks the part." She pushes the door open wider and steps inside. "Very professional."

I self-consciously smooth the material of my new black pencil skirt over my stomach. "Do I look okay?"

"Very nice. I might be borrowing those beauties." She eyes up my new black suede heels, impressed. "You'll knock 'em dead, looking like that."

Hopefully. I want to make a good first impression so I've spent time getting ready to make sure I look the part this morning. I've managed to style my wayward hair into some semblance of smooth waves and applied minimal make up.

"I decided it was time for something new. I'd worn the same old things for years so treated myself to a few new outfits. This job's a big deal."

"Your mum would have been really proud of you. She always thought you could do better than those temping jobs."

Tears prick at my eyes at Kate's kind words and she rushes over and gives me a hug. "Come here. Sorry, El. I didn't mean to upset you."

"It's okay. I'm fine." My default reply to everything, even when I'm far from it. Even when my world's crashing down around me; when mum got diagnosed, when Ryan made me feel like a cheap tart, when I got the abortion.

"No, it's not. I'm sorry I shouldn't have said that," Kate assures me.

I smile weakly. I'm not sure what I've done to deserve a friend like her. She's always had my back but I'm really not sure what I'd have done this past year if it hadn't been for her. She's been by my side every step of the way; helping me sort out all the legal and financial stuff after Mum died. Some days I just wanted to stay in bed and cry, and she was there, checking in on me and bringing me up cups of tea and custard creams.

"And I've been thinking about the shop. We can have a look at things tonight if you like. See what we can find out about what's going on, if anything."

Mum's shop. Something else I'm far from "fine" about.

"Thanks, I owe it to her to at least try and do something. Sounds like a plan." I straighten my blush pink blouse and cast her a sideways glance. "You're not seeing Harry tonight then?"

She fiddles with the button on her black blazer, trying to act nonchalant and failing. She couldn't if she tried, especially not about him. "No, not tonight, he's at football training."

My lips curl into a smile. I can't help myself. "Oh right. It's just I thought he might have worn you out."

Her cheeks turn berry red. I can't believe she thinks I won't mention it. "Ella!"

"Don't 'Ella' me. You've spent the last day in bed together. The walls aren't that thick you know. I'll make you a deal; if you and lover boy keep it down and let me have a decent night's sleep next time he stays over, I'll let you borrow my shoes."

She grins like a Cheshire cat. "Okay, okay. I promise. He's just got a very high… sex drive, that's all."

I reach inside my wardrobe and grab my black trench coat off the hanger. "Spare me the details. And I gathered."

"You're just jealous," she teases.

Am I?

Maybe she's got a point.

A week ago, I wouldn't have felt like this. I haven't slept with anyone since Ryan. Lack of sex hasn't bothered me. I'd got used to it and it's nothing my vibrator hasn't sorted out, but since Saturday, since I met *him*, the sound of my best mate and her new boyfriend through the bedroom wall have left me feeling like I'm missing out.

I wrinkle my nose and pull on my jacket. "Not jealous, but, I dunno…"

She tilts her head to the side and gives me a knowing look. "This is because of him, isn't it?"

"Who?"

"The mysterious hot G who swooped to your rescue on Saturday night and who you've been thinking about ever since."

Damn it Kate!

I pull my hair out the collar of my jacket and tell the biggest lie, ever. "I haven't been thinking about him ever since."

Or how his fingers caressed me with the gentlest of touches.

Or imagining what his lips would feel like on mine.

Stop it. He's bad news.

"He was a prick."

Kate's eyebrows draw together. She doesn't believe me. But she wasn't the one he reeled in, then made a total dickhead out of. "You don't *know* that."

"He was in the VIP area, he said he was friends with Spencer. He was a well-off, cocky prick," I mutter staring at my reflection in the mirror and fastening my jacket. I've had enough of those types to last me forever.

"Yeah, but I think we can both agree that he was a good-looking prick."

"Good looks and loaded, the perfect combination for some women." *Some* women. Not me. Once bitten. Twice shy. I try to fight to keep the bitterness from my voice, but it remains, as clear as a bell. "He must get women throwing themselves at him all the time. In fact we witnessed it with our own eyes. Probably boosts his already massive ego."

"Maybe he does, all I know is that when me and Harry came back, things seemed pretty intense between the two of you." Kate cocks her head in thought. "He looked like he was about to kiss your face off."

The thought of his mouth on mine makes me go all hot. I hate the effect the mere memory of him is having on me, forty-eight hours after I last saw him.

"Not a chance. I'd rather I poke my eyes out than fall victim to another guy like him. Besides, it was obviously one big joke to him; reeling me in, getting me to … tell him things … then pulling the shutters down and backing away. He probably had a right old laugh at my expense. Wanker."

"Maybe he wanted to take things further but couldn't," Kate muses, clearly not ready to let this go. "Maybe he's married."

Apart from the signet ring I spied, he'd been ringless. I frown. "Or maybe he's just a rich dickhead. Can we forget about him please? He's a stranger. It's done. And more to the point, I'm never going to see him again."

Kate raises her hands, sensing she's touched a nerve. "Okay, okay. It was just amazing to see you'd actually had a conversation with a member of the opposite sex. Why don't you let me set you up with Tom? *He's* not a self-entitled prick."

I sigh. Tom from Mortgages. "I'm not that desperate. Yet."

"He's really quite nice actually. Cute too."

Now I feel bad. "I didn't mean it like that, it's just, well, the idea doesn't exactly fill me with sexual anticipation."

"I'll get a photo of him."

"No, don't do that."

"Why not, I've already shown him one of you, and he thinks you're very nice."

I could kill her sometimes. "You've done what?"

"Oh, calm down, El. It's just a bit of fun."

A date with a guy. All that awkwardness and inevitable long silences.

"I dunno. Let me get through today and I'll think about it."

Kate looks at her watch and raises her eyebrows. "Speaking of which. You need to get a wriggle on, otherwise you're going to be late."

***

The heavens open. The temperamental September weather plays a wild card. At two minutes to nine I bustle through the sliding doors of White House Developments, flustered and soaking wet.

My feet squelch in my heels as I hurry across the black shiny floor of the cavernous foyer towards the reception desk. In a perfect world, I'd fix myself up in the loos first, but there's no time. I *cannot* be late on my first day.

The receptionist takes in my bedraggled state and gives me a polite smile. Her perfectly straight blonde hair and smart grey suit jacket only make me feel even more self-conscious.

"Good morning, madam, how may I help you?"

I run my fingers through my damp hair in a bid to detangle my curls. So much for smooth waves. It's going to look like a frizz ball once it's dried out. Great.

"Hello. I'm Ella Anderson. I'm starting a new job here today."

She nods briskly like she's expecting me. "Of course. You'll be working alongside Judy Morris, Mr White's PA. She mentioned you were joining us today. Welcome to the team." The receptionist slides a form across the glass desk and a visitor's badge in a plastic cover. "Would you mind filling this out, just for HR purposes. Wear the visitor's badge for now. Judy will see you get set up with your ID badge later."

I pick up a pen, fill out the form and attach the badge to my jacket. The receptionist calls Judy to let her know I've arrived and my eyes begin to wander around the foyer. It appears no less impressive than when I came for my interview. From outside, the one hundred-storey building holds its own amongst its banking counterparts on the wharf. Inside it's all sleek black, shiny surfaces. Two huge glass lifts occupy the far side of the foyer.

My phone rings in my handbag and I pull it out. "Amy calling" flashes in the display. Nine o' clock on a Monday morning. I'm surprised my little sister is awake.

"Hi, Amy, are you okay?"

She yawns down the phone. "What? Yeah."

I glance at the receptionist who's thankfully still on the phone. "Then you'd better be quick because I'm at work. Speaking of which, have you heard any more about those jobs you applied for?"

"Erm…" There's silence as she thinks. I can feel my stress level rising even though she's not even in the same post code. She hasn't applied for that many jobs. It can't be that difficult to remember. "No, just the one at GAP. I've got an interview Wednesday."

One's better than nothing I suppose. At least she's trying. "Okay, good. What do you want?"

"Can you lend me twenty quid? I need to buy a birthday present for Becky."

Here we go. "Who's Becky?"

"My friend. I've told you about her." She hasn't. The only conversations Amy and I have since she started uni, involve me badgering her to get a job, and her asking for money. "Please, El. I can pay you back when I get the job at GAP."

I haven't got time to argue with her right now. "Okay, okay. I'll transfer it over to you later."

"Cheers, sis. Catch you later." And with that, she hangs up.

"Excuse me, Miss Anderson."

I turn to see the receptionist looking at me expectantly. I blush and stuff my phone back into my bag. "Can you take the lift to floor ninety-eight. Judy will meet you there."

I thank the receptionist and head over to the closest lift, step inside, press the buttons for the ninety-eighth floor and watch the lift doors close. This is the first time I've ventured any further than the ground floor. My interview was held in one of the posh meeting rooms off reception.

I grip my handbag tight as the foyer disappears beneath my feet. I'm pretty sure the last time I travelled at this altitude was the one and only time I've been in an aeroplane. Mum scrimped all year to take me and Amy away for a week to Majorca. I wasn't sure I liked heights then and I'm still not convinced.

Eventually the lift stops and the doors slide open. Judy Morris, Mr White's PA, stands on the landing waiting. Her forest green knee-length skirt and matching jacket fit her buxom frame perfectly. I only reach just over five foot but even in sensible navy heels Judy is a few inches shorter than me. Her greying hair is swept up into a bun and her cream blouse gives her a school headteacher vibe. Kind blue eyes look at me curiously. She takes me in and gives me a hesitant smile.

"Oh, hello, Ella. Erm... would you like to have a moment to freshen up?"

Nerves I'd managed to squash reappear with a vengeance. *Shit. Do I look that bad?*

"I forgot my umbrella and it started to rain," I explain, stepping out of the lift.

Judy laughs softly. "Not to worry, we've all been there. The ladies' is on the left. Once you're ready, I'll get you settled in and show you round. We're just over here." She nods her head towards a corner of the floor. Through a wall of glass, I see a couple of desks and another door.

"Thank you." I smile, grateful for the help, and scurry off into the toilets.

The ladies' is bright and all white, giving it a sterile feel. I inspect my reflection in the mirror over the sink, in horror. The stark lighting's not softening the blow one bit.

Black smudges sit under my eyes from where my mascara's run and my hair looks like I've been in a wind tunnel. I look like Alice Cooper and Brian May's love child.

Thank God for Judy.

I manage to rub off the mascara smudges with my fingers, fix my make-up, give my shoes a blast under the supersonic hand dryer and run a comb through my hair to detangle and tame my unruly curls. Five minutes later, I feel and look far more professional.

The gleaming black floor of the landing stretches on and on across the open plan office as I head out of the toilets. Glass partitions separate the different working areas which are filled with white desks and state of the art laptops. Everyone has their head down and is busy at work.

"Ella." Judy's hovering over by the door to the office she pointed out to me earlier. "We're through here."

I follow her through the door into a smaller working space. A closed grey door is on the far side. On one side of the room is a desk covered with files. On the other sits a sparsely furnished desk which I take to be mine, but I don't pay too much attention. I'm immediately drawn to the view behind it. Floor to ceiling windows look out over Canary Wharf and the bustling city beyond. Even on a bleak, rainy day like today the view's spectacular.

"Wow," I breathe. "The view's pretty wonderful from up here."

"It is," Judy agrees. "I hate to admit it, but after thirty years I've almost become a little blasé about it."

My eyes swing to her. Thirty years. That's a lifetime. It must be an okay place to work if she's been here that long. "That's a really long time."

She smiles fondly and walks round to her desk. "Yes. I've been here from the very beginning. When Maxwell was just starting it up. Of course, it was a very different world then."

Maxwell White. CEO. The big boss. I look at the closed office door and picture the older, grey haired, suited man, sitting behind his desk on the other side. The research I did in preparation for my interview said the company is worth billions. He's minted.

"He's in meetings at the moment, but I'll introduce you later," Judy tells me, following my curious gaze.

"I'm guessing it's an okay place to work then, being as you've been here that long?"

Judy titters like it's a given, and I feel the knot of first-day nerves in my stomach begin to loosen. "I couldn't imagine working anywhere else."

"And he must be an okay boss, I take it?" I nod apprehensively towards the closed door. This is by far the best job I've ever had, working for the best company, with the best pay. I'm half expecting something to go wrong. Knowing my luck Mr Maxwell Billionaire will be a total prick to work for.

"He's the best, and a gentleman too. Anyway, first things first, let's get you settled in."

Chapter 8

Ella

The next few hours whizz by. Judy gives me a tour of the top floor which mainly consists of meeting rooms, finance, legal and the breakout area. I get set up on my snazzy new laptop and start ploughing through my induction emails and online training. By early afternoon the nerves have gone and I'm feeling settled. I still can't quite believe I've landed this job, working for an established company like this, in a sexy, swish building such as this one. Every time my gaze drifts towards Tower Bridge and the Thames out of the window I have a "pinch-me" moment.

"Here you are," Judy stands by my desk brandishing my ID badge. "All sorted. That will let you into the building too."

I feel a tingle of excitement as I take the lanyard from her with a smile, and slip it round my neck. Now I'm a fully-fledged member of the company. "Thanks."

She sits down behind her desk and draws up the chair, tapping at her keyboard. "I think that's you all set-up with everything. Obviously, you still need to meet…" Judy trails off and peers at her laptop screen distracted. "Actually, his last call has just ended." She picks up a piece of paper off her desk and looks at me. "Would you mind taking this invoice into him to sign. It's urgent. I'd do it myself, but he's just emailed and asked me to chase something up urgently with Legal."

"Of course." I jump to my feet and take the paper from Judy, happy to be of help and actually do something.

She gives me a grateful smile. "Thanks."

I knock on the door, politely wait for a few seconds, then enter.

Every inch of the building I've seen so far is modern and sleek and the CEO's office is no exception. The light grey polished floor stretches out towards floor-to-ceiling windows that line the far side of the office and look out across the river. To the left is a low-backed modern black leather sofa, with a smoked glass coffee table in front, housing a jug of water and three upturned glasses. Behind are two panelled sliding doors that conceal another room, perhaps. A large glass desk dominates the right-hand side of the office. Beside the laptop, desk phone and couple of pens on there, sits a chessboard. The walls are dove grey and a large modern canvas depicting swirls of greys and white, hangs on the wall behind the desk.

I expect to find a fifty-something, grey haired guy behind the desk. But I don't. Across the office a man stands with his back to me. One hand's against the window and the other's holding a mobile to his ear. A ray of light peeks through a break in the grey clouds and bounces off a gold ring on his long index finger, splayed out on the glass. His height hits me first. Even from across the room he's strikingly tall; six foot three at least. The back of his grey suit jacket pulls taught across a broad, muscular back and shoulders. Expensively cut trousers hang from his slim waist and frame a firm backside. I feel a tug between my legs as my eyes roam over him.

He carries on talking in a low voice, making it impossible to hear. I chew my thumbnail. I have no idea who the fuck this guy is, but I know one thing for sure, he's not Maxwell White. Nerves I thought I'd seen the back of ping in my stomach. He clearly hasn't heard me knock and has no idea I'm here. I don't want him to think I'm earwigging. Plus, I'm standing here like a lemon.

The office door clicks shut behind me and he straightens, realising he's not alone.

"I need to go. Yeah, okay. Later," he says so I can hear.

He slides the phone into the back pocket of his trousers and turns to face me.

I'm floored.

It's *him*.

G.

The cocky, good looking, rich git from Saturday night. His captivating eyes settle on me. Time and space hang. My world tunnels to focus only on him.

This is a fucking joke, right?

He studies me for a few moments, like he expects me to say something. When I don't, he lightly rests his hands in the pockets of his trousers and slowly advances towards me like a panther stalking its prey. The air in the room grows thinner the closer he gets. I shift uncomfortably from foot to foot beneath his penetrating stare and struggle to think. The pale grey herringbone three-piece suit wraps around his ripped body and makes my heart rattle in my ribs. Power. Control. I can almost taste them in the air.

I forget how to breathe.

He's beautiful.

His lips curl into a slow, heart-stopping smile as he stops within touching distance. He doesn't look half as surprised to see me as I do him.

This can't be happening.

This *is* happening.

"Ella *Anderson*." My name sounds perfect on his lips, like he should never say another woman's name again. He stresses my last name to make a point that he knows it. "It seems the universe is trying to tell us something."

The unwelcome memory of Saturday night flashes into my mind. The lines he spun. What I admitted. How he backed away. Anger fires in my belly dampening my feelings of attraction. Humiliation burns. He made a fool of me. And I'm not going to allow him to do that ever again.

He cocks an eyebrow at my silence. "You're a lot quieter than you were on Saturday night. I can see you're struggling, so I'll help you out. I'm Gabe White, CEO of White House Developments. I own the building you're standing in and half of the city you call home."

His words confirm everything I thought about him and more. He *is* a cocky, arrogant, self-entitled prick. And he's not just rich. He's a fucking millionaire. And he's my boss.

Reality lands hard. I knew this job was too good to be true. There had to be a fly in the ointment. And here he is. The best job I've ever had is working for a guy who's the walking, talking epitome of everything I hate in a man. And then some.

I force my expression to remain neutral. I'm not letting him know how much he gets to me. "That's quite an introduction. You're not G today then? Or was the whole 'my-friends-call-me-G' thing, something you made up?"

The annoying smile leaves his lips. "Why would I make that up?"

"Because you didn't want me to know your real name?"

His brow twitches in confusion. "Why wouldn't I want you to know my real name?"

I shrug, glancing around the room. His eyes haven't left my face yet and I need a reprieve because when he looks at me I can't focus – I need to focus. "I dunno. You seem to get a kick out of playing games."

He takes a step closer to me, forcing me to look up at him.

"I don't play games. I say what I mean. And I mean what I say."

I laugh lightly, noting the flash of irritation in his eyes at the challenge. "So you keep saying, but I've yet to see that." My mouth's firing off all on its own , but I won't be made a fool of. Not again. Especially not by someone like him. And he needs to know that, boss or no boss.

His gaze hardens. I've touched a nerve. This guy doesn't like being pushed and it makes me want to do it all the more.

"My friends call me G," he says stiffly.

I thrust the invoice into the space between us showing him I've no time for any more of his lines. "Judy needs you to sign this urgently."

He takes it from me, pivots on a heel and at the very last second pulls his eyes from mine. I can't believe I'm working for this arrogant prick.

He puts the invoice down on his desk and picks up a pen. I'm given a full view of his delightful arse and solid, broad back as he bends forward slightly and signs the paper with an irritated flourish. Forbidden thoughts twine themselves around my focus splintering it in two. I'm beneath him, bent over the desk, pressed against the glass as he fucks me.

Stop it.

He's totally out of bounds. Not just because he's my boss, but because he's an arsehole.

He stops a few steps in front of me and breaks out into a winning smile which makes my pathetic heart leap in my chest.

You're not making that mistake again. Focus.

"When did you know that I was working here?"

"About three hours ago when I was asked to authorise your ID badge and saw your photo. Like I said. It's fate."

I ignore him. "I thought Maxwell White…"

"My dad. He retired five years ago and I took over."

Makes sense. I read it was a family business on the internet, however the details about Maxwell stepping down from the CEO role were certainly lacking.

He offers me the invoice.

Thank God. I want out of here. I need to get away from him and sort my head out.

I grab the paper, but he tightens his grip, forcing me to stay put. We stand in silence, locked in some weird battle of wills with the paper pulled taught between our fingers. His heated gaze burns into mine.

"I don't bullshit."

I curl my lip in disbelief. "Really?"

"I meant what I said to you on Saturday night."

There are so many reasons why his admission is inappropriate, I can't even count them all. I stop my brain from reading into what he's insinuating, because it's all bollocks. Lies. A game. The guy's got a chess board in his office. If that doesn't scream game player, what the fuck does? This girl isn't going to be taken for a ride again. The shutters came down on this heart a long time ago.

I tilt my chin upwards and meet his bullshit head on. "Which bit? The bit where you said you wanted me, or the bit where you told me not to get involved with someone like you?"

"Ella…"

My hands fly up in protest; at the horrid way my stomach flips at the sound of my name falling from his lips and what he could be about to say. I'm shutting this down. Now. I'm pretty sure this guy isn't used to hearing stuff straight but that's what he's getting.

"Here's the thing. I need this job and I'm not going to mess it up. So, can we just pretend like Saturday never happened and we didn't say…what we said. To be honest, I've forgotten about it already."

He reaches out and takes a curl of my hair, playing with it contemplatively. Just like he did on Saturday night. I hold my breath.

"That was *almost* believable. I meant what I said. You deserve better than me." He studies my reaction closely as he delivers the next line. "But it doesn't change the fact I want you, and you want me."

I suck in a lungful of air, steeling myself for the bullshit I'm about to spill. "Wanted."

His mouth quirks into another annoying smile. He's not buying it. "*Want.* You want me."

Arrogant prick.

I fold my arms. "This is wholly inappropriate, you know. I could have you for sexual harassment."

My threat does nothing to chip away at the smirk on his face. "Yeah, and that could work two ways."

"What are you talking about?"

He leans into me a fraction. I'm hit with the scent of him; sandalwood and pheromones and my stomach dances. "You haven't taken your eyes off me since you stepped foot into this office. I saw you checking out my arse when I was on the phone." His full lips tug into a wicked smile and he all but whispers. "Not to mention when I was signing the invoice."

What the fuck? How could he see?

Before I get the chance to give him a piece of my mind, his desk phone rings but he makes no move to answer it.

I glance over his shoulder at the phone.

"Ignore it," he tells me.

"You should get that. People will be wondering why you're not answering."

"People can wait, Princess."

I need to move because if I stay here a minute longer I'm not sure I trust myself, or him.

"I need to get back to my desk."

He tilts his head to the right, considering what I've said, then reluctantly hands me the invoice.

I snatch it from him. I need to move. I turn and head towards the door, trying to piece together the events of the last five minutes.

"This isn't over," he calls after me.

"It's over, all right," I declare, reaching the door. I glance over my shoulder. "I wanted you. Past tense. I know it might come as a shock to your ego but not *every* woman wants to fuck you, Gabe."

He laughs softly. "You're right, Princess, they don't. But you do."

I shake my head. Standing here arguing the toss isn't going to achieve anything. And I need to get out of here. Away from him. Clear my head.

I throw him one last withering glance, before heading out of the office without looking back.

Chapter 9

Ella

My concentration is smashed to pieces. I spend the next half an hour, clicking through my online training, not taking any of it in, as I replay the conversation and this whole fucked-up situation in my head. He's my boss. That jumped-up arse is the CEO at the best job I've ever had. Just my luck.

A tiny part of self-doubt begins to burn through the steely shutters I've pulled down and I hate it. I didn't go easy on him, but he didn't seem to mind me standing up to him. In fact, the smirk and twinkle in his eye gave me the impression he was getting a kick out of me giving him a verbal dressing down. I need to remain strong because if I make one wrong move, if I let him in, there will be no going back. I'm not going to screw this opportunity up by falling for some silver-tongued charmer. Been there. Done that. Got the scars to prove it. I swore to myself I'd never be so bloody naïve again.

I don't want him.

I *can't* want him.

"Afternoon, Jude. How are you?"

I look up from my laptop and blink in surprise. The security guy from the club the other night is standing in front of Judy's desk, dressed in black jeans and a jumper. He looks even taller and broader in daylight then he did in the club, if that's possible.

What's he doing here?

Judy gives him a wry smile. "I'm fine, thank you. What brings you here, or don't I need to ask?"

He cocks his head in the direction of Gabe's office. "He mentioned he'd got a spare half an hour, right about now. Am I okay to go on in? He's expecting me."

"Of course, if you're quick. His next meeting's at four."

"Thanks." He gives her a cheeky wink, and starts to head towards the office when he notices me. There's a flash of recognition in his eyes, and he goes to say something but seems to think better of it and stops himself. A sly grin spreads across his face and he disappears into Gabe's office.

"Who was that?" I ask, unable to help myself.

"Oh, that was Jake White. Gabe's older brother. He often pops by to talk… business."

He doesn't look like he works here. He looks more cut out for the gym. "What department does he work in then?"

"Oh, he doesn't work here. He deals with the other side of the family business." Judy busies herself, tapping away at her laptop. I don't know why, but I feel the need to probe further. "What, like the nightclub?"

She stops typing and looks at me in surprise. I realise I sound like a right nosy cow. "Sorry, I know it's a family business from the research I did for my interview. I'm just keen to learn more about things and how everyone fits in. It's nice that the business has been kept in the family, given its success."

Judy smiles fondly. My interest has clearly won her round. "Maxwell wouldn't trust anyone else to take it over. He had investors lining up to buy it as soon as they got whiff of his retirement, but he wouldn't budge. It was always going to be Gabe's. He's the only one out of the three of them that's got a head for business."

"Out of the three of who?"

"His sons."

"Maxwell's got *three* sons?"

"Yes, of course." She hesitates. "Jake's the eldest, then there's Gabe, and Spencer's the youngest."

Spencer White.

The penny drops. That's why Gabe was at the club opening, he was supporting his brother. It also explains his weird response when I asked him if he was friends with Spencer. Why didn't he tell me they were brothers?

I must look totally confused because Judy asks, "I presume you've heard of Spencer? He was in that awful reality TV show." She purses her lips in disapproval. "Of course, I never watched it, but his shenanigans were all over the papers."

"Yes, of course. Actually, I went to the opening of the club on Saturday, but I had no idea he had any brothers."

"Oh yes, they're all *very* different though. Chalk and cheese. Gabe and Spencer especially." Judy's eyes twinkle with enthusiasm, like she's talking about her own children. "Jake's eight years older than Gabe, and then there's three years in between Gabe and Spencer. Even though Jake's the eldest Gabe's always been the one with the sensible head on his shoulders. I suppose he's had to have." A look of sadness flashes in her eyes, then it's gone. She quickly carries on before I can ask any more questions, "I've known them since they were kiddies. They've all made their father proud. Even Spencer in an odd way. Anyway, listen to me rabbiting on." She gives me a tight smile, like she's remembered herself and is scared of divulging anything she shouldn't. "I'm going to head off in a bit. My husband's not been too well recently, and Gabe lets me leave a little earlier so I can get back home to him."

The CEO's got a soft side, then, even though he's an arrogant twat.

"Yes, of course."

"Gabe's last meeting's at four. It's just a project update so he shouldn't need any support with that. And Jake's still in there at the mo, so he won't bother you."

My eyes land on the closed office door. Oh, how I wish I could be a fly on the wall in there.

Chapter 10

Gabe

Today's been a write-off. I've spent all day firefighting and sorting out shit following the text from K at the weekend. I need to hit the gym and pound the fuck out of a punchbag until my knuckles bleed and muscles burn. Exercise is the second-best stress relief.

I sink back into my chair, close my eyes, and pinch the bridge of my nose, like it's somehow going to get rid of the throbbing at my temples.

The gym's not going to help get rid of this. Only one thing will.

The devil on my shoulder prods at my thoughts. I open my eyes to see her face on the screen. Hazel eyes stare back at me, instantly turning my thoughts carnal. Ella Anderson. The new girl. *Another* fucking complication, but one that's somehow made my shitty day bearable.

I scroll through her CV, which I've had HR email through to me. Asking Judy for it would raise too many questions that I can't answer, seeing as I never usually show an interest with the recruitment of my support staff. I've spent all day getting to know our newest team member despite her CV prompting more questions than it answers. She's twenty-six, lives in a shit-hole part of Hackney. She got good grades from a good college, and I would have expected her to go to university, but she didn't. For the past eight years she's racked up a lot of experience temping for some big-name companies and got a few on-the-job qualifications under her belt, but her employment history is peppered with gaps, all with the explanation of "personal issues."

I want to know more.

And I want her.

But I can't have her.

That's not a notion I'm familiar with.

The door to my office clicks open and I minimise her CV on screen. Jake strolls in, wearing a knowing grin.

I don't need to ask the cause of it.

He sits down on the chair opposite, picks up a black rook from the chessboard and lounges back in the seat, tossing the piece in his hand.

"So, as we thought. Your guy's a snake."

"Did he talk?"

"Sang like a bird. He's been playing us for fools. Taking money from us and the others, turns out they paid him more, so he sided with them. He'd sell his fucking mother if he thought it would make him fifty."

A muscle in my jaw twitches with tension. I rest my elbows on the arms of the chair, steeple my fingers and lift them to my lips in thought.

Everything always comes down to money. Money *does* make the world go round, whether you have it or not, but growing up wealthy and privileged brings its own challenges. It skews people's thoughts about you, breeds misconceptions and envy. And it makes you suspicious; of others' motivations for wanting to get to know you, be photographed with you, invite you to their charity reception, fuck you. After thirty-one years I've managed to fine tune my sponger radar and developed an instinct for those who are genuine, or not. Pity my little brother hasn't.

Jake tosses the rook in the air and catches it. "Bad news is the others are offering a pretty big cash sum."

"Then we'll double whatever they've offered."

He rolls the piece round in his fingers and gives me a thoughtful look. "You're deadly serious about winning this deal aren't you?"

"When am I not? Come on, you know the score. Whites are winners, and I'm sure as fucking hell not going to lose out for the sake of a couple of hundred grand. We stand to make millions in two to three years if we get it. You track down the owner. I want to meet him and make him an offer he can't refuse."

Jake puts the rook back down on the board and slides it forward in front of my knight.

"Precarious position," I warn.

He laughs. "You know me. Always living on the edge."

"Not as on the edge as Spencer." I don't really want to ask the next question because I know I'll get pissed off with the answer. "You heard from him?"

Jake raps his finger against his knee and shoots me a hesitant look. He's choosing his words. For all Jake's big, bad appearance he's the mediator between me and Spencer. He hasn't had to put up with as much of his shit as I have though. When Jake was away in the army, I was back home, juggling studying and keeping our little brother on the straight and narrow; covering up his misdemeanours and keeping the family name clean. As well as battling my own demons.

"Tell me. He's going to the club tonight?" I say firmly.

"I called him up on my way over here. He was still in bed with some girl. I woke him up, but yeah he's going."

"He'd better not fuck this up. I've given him a golden opportunity to do something with his life instead of partying it away and dragging the family name through the shit. I've sunk too much money into that place for him to piss about. If he fucks this up, I'm cutting him off once and for all."

"Relax G, I'll swing by the club later and make sure he's stuck to his word." His mouth tugs into a smile and he puts his feet up on the desk. "So, what's with the stunning brunette behind the desk out there?"

The throb in my head intensifies, a tell-tale sign that I'm tense as fuck. Ella *is* stunning, but to hear someone else talk about her that way, even Jake, stirs something deep within me I can't afford to dwell on.

I turn my attention back to my laptop and scroll through my emails looking for a distraction. "She works for me."

"Fucking hell G, I can see that. She's the girl from the club isn't she?"

"There were lots of girls at the club."

"You know the one I'm talking about. The one who was getting felt up and you had us throw the guy out. The one you couldn't take your eyes off."

He was in the SAS, did I really expect him to not notice?

I jut out my bottom lip and shake my head as if it means nothing. It *doesn't* mean anything. Does it? "I didn't recruit her. Judy did. It's nothing more than a coincidence."

"A very hot coincidence."

I give him a stern look. "I don't fuck my staff. So get whatever it is you're thinking out of your head. Do you really think I'm going to risk all this; everything *we've* built, not to mention our family name and reputation, for a quick shag with my PA's Assistant. I'm not Spencer."

Business and pleasure don't mix. A rule I've lived my life by, which has served me pretty well so far. And that's why I don't need Ella Anderson coming in and messing it up. Because when I'm around her, I forget who the hell I am.

And I can't.

I don't fuck my staff.

Her quick mouth and sass make my balls tight.

I don't fuck my staff.

Jake lifts an eyebrow and gives me a look I've seen before. It's a look he saves for when he's going to give me an older brother talking-to. "Sometimes, you're so focussed on the business, the family, sealing the next deal, proving to Dad you can run this thing just as well as him, if not better, you forget to be you. I know you're nothing like Spencer, but she's the first woman you seem genuinely interested in. What's her name?"

Bloody Jake and his laser-like accuracy.

I straighten my tie and glance at the clock on my laptop screen. Three fifty-five. I can't have this conversation. I've no desire to pull on the thread that will undoubtedly unravel if I start discussing this. And I don't have time. Or the inclination.

"Ella. I've got a meeting in five."

"Yeah, yeah. I can take the hint." Jake stands and pushes his hands into the front pockets of his jeans. "I'll let you know when I've set up a meeting with our guy."

Chapter 11

Ella

Gabe's office door opens and Jake strolls out, giving me a cheeky wink as I look up from my laptop. Seconds later, the man himself pokes his head around the door.

"I need you to take notes for my four o'clock," he says disappearing back into his office. He leaves the door open, I presume as a cue for me to follow him.

Rude git.

And so much for Judy saying he won't need me.

I close my laptop and clutch it against my chest like a shield as I head into his office, but the laptop does nothing to protect me from what I walk in to. His jacket hangs on the chrome coat rack beside his desk. His waistcoat and white shirt hug every inch of his tall, broad physique. I stop in my tracks, my eyes rooted to his large hands as he carefully rolls the sleeves of his crisp white shirt back to his elbows. The sight of his toned, inked arms pulls me back to Saturday night and I'm remembering; the feel of his strong hands gently holding my foot, his long fingers massaging my ankle with the lightest of touches.

"We're through here."

I snap back to reality and watch him head across the office to the sliding doors. "This is a short cut to the meeting room."

Stop gawping like a silly teenage girl. Move.

I expect him to open one of the doors and carry on ahead but he doesn't. He waits for me and when I reach him, he steps alongside me, lightly placing a hand on the base of my back and guiding me towards the door.

My body prickles in awareness. His palm feels hot and heavy on my lower back, scorching through the thin material of my blouse and he's barely touching me. I silently will him to move his hand lower.

Stop. It.

He slides the door open and removes his hand from my back. "Ladies first."

The polished grey floors and light grey walls carry on in here. The far wall is floor-to-ceiling windows like next door and a long glass table dominates the room. A man and a blonde woman are already seated and look up expectantly as we enter. I instinctively follow Gabe towards the top of the table. He draws out a seat.

"Ella." He gestures at the chair before sitting down in the empty seat beside it.

Of course, he wants me next to him.

I sit down, open up my laptop and become acutely aware of his delicious, tattooed forearms resting on the glass table on the edge of my vision. Roses of various sizes and designs cover his right arm, disappearing beneath the edge of his white shirt. Some are shaded black, others in grey. In the darkness of the club I didn't get to appreciate how impressive they are. From the indentations on the leaves to thorns on the prickly stems, it's as though someone has grabbed a pencil and drawn onto his skin.

I shift in my seat uncomfortably and stop my thoughts from running away with me. I'm here to do a job. Not ogle my boss. *Who's an arrogant prick,* I remind myself.

I catch the fresh, sandalwood scent of his aftershave as he shifts in his seat and I'm mentally transported back to the club again; when he held me in his arms against his firm, warm body.

Jesus, this is going to be a struggle.

"Before we start, I'd like to introduce Ella."

I snap back into the moment at the mention of my name.

"She's joined us today." Gabe glances in my direction then to the guy sat to my right. "This is Simon Adams, he's PR."

Simon sits up in his chair and straightens his navy tie at the mention of his name. He runs a hand through his sandy hair and flashes a charming smile as he turns his attention to me.

"Hi, Ella. Welcome aboard."

"Hi, nice to meet you."

For a split second Gabe's eyes narrow a fraction at Simon, before he shifts his focus to the platinum blonde sat to his left. Her dark eyes light up as his attention lands on her causing her crimson painted lips to broaden into a smile.

"This is Sarah Cross, Legal."

She assesses me with a smile that doesn't reach her eyes.

"Hi."

I smile politely, despite the prickly vibe I'm getting from her.

Gabe sits back in his seat and glances at Simon. "Update me on the Cedarwood Grove Project."

"The local ..."

"The residents have gone to the local rag to create a stir," Sarah butts in. "The Councillor's got involved too."

"He's got an interview with the press and is going to be interviewed on the evening news tonight." Simon interjects and gives Sarah a firm look from across the desk, letting her know he doesn't appreciate her stepping on his toes. "They've got people protesting outside the site holding placards with *"Save our neighbourhood"* emblazoned on them. You know, the usual."

The usual. Has this happened before? What type of business am I working for?

"Of course they have," Gabe mutters dryly. He catches the confused look on my face. "Ella, sorry, I should bring you up to speed with this project so you're fully briefed. We've purchased a large property on the Cedarwood Estate in a prime location for investment."

I nod. "I know the area." Cedarwood is an affluent estate, full of Edwardian houses and is a sought-after location for families.

"Plans have been approved for us to build an exclusive, gated apartment complex on the edge of the estate. The residents are objecting to it, but quite frankly, they don't stand a chance."

There's a harsh, competitive edge to his tone which I've not heard before. This guy never loses. It's his way or the highway. I just know it.

"Legally they haven't got a leg to stand on. It's a done deal. They need to suck it up," Sarah announces.

Gabe taps his fingers on the table, deep in thought. And then I see it. The letter "W" carved into the black onyx stone of his gold signet ring. W for White. W for winner. I was right. He *never* loses.

"So, we focus on damage limitation. What's the plan?"

"I'll draft a press statement in response to their interview with the local press, ready for tomorrow," says Simon. "I'm expecting the usual response, but I'd like to wait to see what their angle's going to be before I tweak it."

"We already know what their angle's going to be," Sarah scoffs. "They'll say it's ruining their little quaint neighbourhood and that it's not befitting with the rest of the estate. I don't know what the problem is, it's hardly going to devalue their properties. We're doing them a favour, if you ask me. It's the same old thing – the big bad property company coming in and ruining people's lives. So narrowminded."

My mind spins. This has more than a few uncomfortable parallels to what's potentially happening with my mum's shop. What if the landlord's selling up to a company like this one, that plan to put up some horrid new builds that will undoubtedly look like an eyesore.

"Even so, we need to manage this carefully," Gabe tells her. "What do you think, Ella?"

Sarah shoots him a *what-the-fuck-are-you-asking-her-for* look, but he's not paying her any attention. He's watching me carefully.

My cheeks colour as three pairs of eyes turn to me.

Why does he give a shit what I think?

"Do you think we're the big bad property company ruining people's lives, or do you think we're doing something positive for the community?"

"To be honest –" I glance around nervously, anticipating what reaction my answers going to get, "If I lived on that estate, I'd probably be upset too. It's a nice area, with beautiful houses, and well … I'd probably be holding a placard up too."

"Some people just don't like change," Sarah pipes up, checking her red painted fingernails.

Gabe gives me a long look. "All the more reason to manage this carefully." He turns his attention back to the others. "Thanks. Keep me informed of any changes. Simon, I want the press release by nine tomorrow morning."

"Sure thing." Simon and I stand to leave, but Sarah puts her hand on Gabe's forearm.

"Can I just grab five minutes with you? I need to speak to you about a couple of contracts," she purrs.

An unsettling feeling sparks in my stomach. A feeling I haven't felt in a long time; one I don't want to admit to. Her fingernails press into his flesh ever so lightly, like she's claiming him, and I despise it. Another thought swoops into my head making me feel even worse. Maybe she *has* already claimed him. She hasn't taken her eyes off him for the whole meeting. If she hasn't already, she definitely wants to.

I drag my eyes away from her hand on his arm and pick up my laptop, pushing the unsettling thoughts to the back of my mind.

Stop it. He can sleep with whoever he likes.

"Five minutes," Gabe tells her.

I don't look his way because I'm scared if I do he'll be able to read me like a book – then it'll be game over. I hold my laptop to my chest and follow Simon out of the room.

Don't look back.

Don't look back.

Shit.

My resolve crumbles and I glance over my shoulder. Sarah's chatting away to him, but Gabe's eyes are fixed on me.

Chapter 12

Ella

"I still can't believe your new boss is *him*," Kate squeaks in delight, for the tenth time in thirty minutes. "What a small world. Gabe White. Spencer's successful, extremely handsome older brother."

"Yeah, well, believe it. Just my fucking luck," I grumble, taking a swig of rosé and absentmindedly flicking through the TV channels. I can't concentrate. Since I've got home from work and updated my friend on my new boss situation, everything else has gone out of the window.

"What do you mean?" Kate puts her glass down on the wood floor and curls her legs beneath her on the sofa. "You're talking about it as though it's a bad thing."

"It *is* a bad thing."

She rolls her eyes and taps away at her phone. "How can it be a bad thing if you get to look at this hot piece of arse all day?" She thrusts her mobile in my face forcing me to look at press shots of Gabe dressed up in a suit, looking knicker meltingly hot as he attends some reception or other.

"It complicates things," I mumble, dragging my gaze back to the TV, even though I'm not really watching it.

Kate laughs. "I bet it does. Especially when you want to shag each other's brains out."

Bloody Kate, and her innate ability to hit the nail on the head.

I shift in my seat, uncomfortable at the thought of getting that close to him. I'd combust. I'm sure of it. The man's sex on a stick with his clothes *on*. "We don't."

"Of course you do. You admitted it on Saturday, and what about this afternoon in his office?" says Kate flatly. "Has he got a girlfriend?"

"Maybe." The memory of Sarah Cross's hand on his arm flashes into my mind. I take a long drink of wine to quell the prickle of unease in my gut. "Even if he hasn't, I'm pretty sure he's got a queue of women waiting to take up that position."

"There are a few photos of him with women, but they're all different. There aren't any that seem to have hung around. Look."

Kate thrusts her mobile in front of my face again, and despite myself I look. She's right. He's by himself in some of the photos, but in other's he's with women, and they're all different. I look at some of the names and feel a stab of unease; models, heiresses. They all share the same qualities though; tall, beautiful, blonde. The total opposite of me. Sarah Cross's face flashes into my head and the unwelcome feeling of jealousy from earlier creeps back into my thoughts.

I neck my wine, squashing it down. I can't feel this way. I've no right to. He's a cocky, privileged prick and the photos reinforce everything I think about him.

"He doesn't really want me. This whole thing's a game to him. The man's got a bloody chessboard in his office for God's sake. He's a player, who's probably got Heiress Far-la-la or whatever lining up to be with him just because of who he is. I *am not* going to fall for a pretty rich guy who's used to sweet talking women into bed. It's bullshit. Now, can we *please* stop talking about Gabe bloody White."

Kate gives me a look which tells me she doesn't agree and settles back into the sofa. She frowns. "Can you hear that?"

"What?"

"That rumbling noise."

I shrug. "It's probably the wind or something. Aren't we meant to be looking into what we can do about the shop?"

She picks up her glass of wine from off the floor. "Ah ... well, I might have a bit of news on that for you."

"Really? How?"

"Gemma from work, her sister works in the council planning office and I mentioned the whole thing about the shop. She rang her to see if she could find anything out."

I frown. "Isn't that a sackable offence; disclosing official business, or something?"

Kate pulls her hair over her shoulder and waves a hand dismissively, clearly not worried about Gemma's sister putting her job on the line. "It'll be fine. Anyway, she did a bit of digging and said there's been a lot of stuff going on with the old shops and the warehouse for ages, but it's been kept hush-hush." She pauses before carrying on and I know whatever she's about to say isn't good. "She said a property company have got their eye on the whole area."

My hearts sinks. "Property company?"

"Yeah. Darknight Properties. I remembered the name because of Batman. Sorry, El, it doesn't sound good."

My worst fears have come true.

"The council are going to sell it to some developer aren't they? I know it. They're going to tear down shops that have been there forever, and replace them with hideous monstrosities. Think of the space, it's a massive area, right by the canal too. It's a prime location." Bitterness wraps itself round my heart. "This is just so some fat cats can get even richer. They don't give a shit about the people who live here. It's all about money to them. I know. I heard it first-hand in the meeting this afternoon. They just care about themselves and lining their own pockets and to make matters worse I'm working for one of the ruthless bastards who'd do this to a community."

"But you're not, are you? White House Developments isn't doing this, it's another company."

I'm not listening. I pull my phone out of the pocket of my hoody and Google "Darknight Property," but it tells me nothing other than where the headquarters are based and a brief overview of the services the company provides.

"Why don't you ask your new boss about them?"

I look at her as though she's mad. "What? Why?"

"Because he's probably heard of them, and he might be able to fill you in on what type of company they are. If they're only a smaller company, then just maybe we've got more chance of stopping whatever it is they've got planned."

A feeling of hope springs in my chest. "Do you think?"

"Can't hurt can it?"

"But he'll want to know why I'm asking, then I'll have to tell him about the shop, and probably Mum…"

"So what?" Kate shoots me an incredulous look. "I know he's stinking rich and hot, but he *is* a human being you know. You can talk to him."

Of course I know she's right, but talking to Gabe about me and my life would be allowing him that step closer, letting him in. Keeping my guard up and thinking he's an arrogant prick is far safer.

"We're talking about him again," I warn.

"Are you sure you can't hear a rumbling noise?"

"It's probably a motorbike or something."

She looks at me thoughtfully. "You know what will stop all of this pent up lusting you've got?"

Talk about a swift conversation change. "I have not."

"You bloody have. You haven't had sex in over a year," she reminds me. "That'd be great if you were a nun, but you're not. You need some." She raises a hand in anticipation of my protest. "Think about it. Once you do I reckon all this sexual tension that's going on between you and Boss Man will disappear. Things will be far easier."

I don't want to admit it, but she might be onto something. "And don't tell me, you know just the guy."

"Look." Kate flashes her phone in my face, yet again. "What do you think?"

I peer at the photo on the screen. The guy's got short dark hair, slicked to the side and has a boyish, clean-shaven face. My eyes slide to Kate suspiciously. "This is Tom from work, isn't it?"

"Yes. What do you think?"

I need more wine.

"He looks nice."

"Oh bloody hell, that noise is getting on my nerves." Kate jumps to her feet and storms over to the window, peering through the gap in the grey curtains.

"Mmhmm. It's not a motorbike. It's a big black car. It's stopped in the middle of the road outside."

"Fascinating. Have we got any more wine?"

The roar of an engine speeding off down the road drowns out the TV.

"Well, whoever it was, has gone now."

I stifle a yawn. "They were probably just lost or something."

Kate flops back down on the sofa beside me. "So?"

"So what?"

"Are you going to let me set you up on a date with Tom?"

I start to protest but she cuts me off. "Seriously. Think about it. Just a date, a bit of casual sex, nothing heavy. I think you need to get it out of your system. You'll feel less … stressed."

I heave a sigh. Maybe going on a date *is* what I need. If I focus my brain on another guy for a while, Mr White won't affect me so much. There's no way I can manage the knicker-combusting intensity of today's encounter over and over again, that's for sure.

I take a deep breath, hoping to God I'm not going to regret this. "Okay. Do it."

"Yes!" Kate cries, fist pumping the air. "You're making the right decision. The best way to forget about one guy is to get under another. Trust me, I know, in fact I'll text Tom right now and make his night." She taps away at a text and gives me the side eye. "He's asked me a few times if you're still single, you know?"

"Oh?"

"Yeah, he's very keen."

My hesitance must show on my face because Kate gives me a firm look. "*Don't* be like that. Tom's nice."

Nice. There's that word again. The same word I used to describe him.

I tell myself to stop being horrible. I *need* a nice guy. Someone who'll look after me, not an emotionally unavailable, arrogant self-entitled prick who thinks he's God's gift to women.

Kate's mobile beeps and her eyes light up with excitement as she reads a text. "I told you he was keen. He says he'd like to take you out on a date tomorrow night. He's really looking forward to it."

I take a fortifying drink of wine. And I will too. I just need to get used to the idea first.

Chapter 13

Gabe

Golden rays of sunlight peek from behind The Shard and the high-rise office blocks across the wharf. Dawn's my favourite part of the day. This high up, I've got a bird's eye view of this spectacular city. Not that I'm in any frame of mind to admire it today. Tensions are starting to take their toll. I cannot fucking think straight.

I head straight to the bathroom, turn the shower on, spin the temperature dial to cool and step out of my sweaty gym gear. Ice cold water stings my flesh as I step beneath the shower, closing my eyes and wincing.

I'm not getting any more used to these. I open my eyes to see my erection, flat against my stomach – and they're not fucking working either. Nothing is. Three days of cold showers and intense morning workouts have failed to clear my head, like they usually do. When I close my eyes at night, wide dark eyes burn into my mind, and when I wake up they're still there.

I prop a hand against the wet tiles and fist the other around my cock, feeling it twitch with gratitude. I need to get laid, but not with just any woman. There's only one dark haired beauty that's going to fully satiate this need.

I close my eyes and conjure a mental image of her. She's on her knees, gazing up at me, closing those perfect lips around my cock, taking all of me. And I know she would. Just to make the point that she's the best head I've ever had. My pumps quicken as I remember how good she felt in my arms. Her skin gossamer smooth. That sweet, floral scent of hers. She'd taste divine. I know it. I come hard, on a long exhale, hot release spurting up my abs and chest, leaving streaks against the dark ink etched on my skin which acts as a permanent reminder of my rebellion.

I wash up, turn off the shower, wrap a black towel round my waist and head into the kitchen. My mobile lies beeping on the grey marble counter top, telling me I'm in demand.

I press a couple of buttons on the Sage coffee machine and it whirs into life, spurting boiling water into the espresso cup on the tray, then pick up my phone. Two texts; one from Laura, the other from Jake. I delete the text from Laura without reading it, and open the one from Jake.

Meeting with our guys on. This Friday @8.

He's come up with the goods again. I can always rely on Jake.

I close the text and absent-mindedly scroll through my contacts. My thumb hovers over Ella's number. I got it from her CV, just like her address.

I chuck my phone on the counter, disgusted with myself.

Who the fuck am I turning into?

Before she turned up I was in control of my thoughts and my cock. Now, I'm not sure who I am. Trailing by her house in the dark, checking out where she lives to see if it's good enough – it wasn't.

What the hell's the matter with me?

I grab the small black espresso cup and take a sip, wincing in pain as the coffee burns my lips. Right now, I'll take the distraction because anything's better than facing up to reality.

I want her.

And she wants me.

But she's out of bounds. A risk I can't take.

And that makes her all the more desirable.

I slam down the cup in frustration, spilling coffee across the shiny counter.

Fuck it.

I need a plan so I don't mess this up. Judy. *She's* my PA. I don't *have* to go to Ella.   Sorted.

Today, I vow to stay the fuck away from Ella Anderson. And everything will be okay.

Chapter 14

Ella

I'm keeping the hell away from him today. The delectable Gabe. As much as I can working for him and being in the office next door to his, anyway. My thoughts will focus on Tom and our date this evening. We're going to a bar. I'm not sure which one yet, but we're going out and we're going to chat and have a nice time, and Gabe White will be nowhere in my thoughts. I'm determined. And I'm doing pretty well up until the point I arrive at work.

I put my handbag down and hang my jacket up on the coat stand. Judy's not behind her desk. Her chair's tucked under and everything is exactly how she left it when she went home last night.

Something's off.

The second my arse touches down in my chair, Gabe's door swings open like he's got a radar. My heart skips annoyingly in my chest as I look at him. He's dressed all in black today, apart from a white shirt. Smart. Sexy. *Shit.* He pushes a hand through his hair, making it flop across his brow in that sexy way of his, and his stubble seems a touch longer. Is it possible for a guy to become more attractive overnight?

Concentrate. Tom, remember?

"Ella. Do you have a moment, please?" He turns and disappears into his office, leaving the door open for me, like he did yesterday. But this morning he's different. There's a tension in his broad shoulders as he disappears into his office. He's stressed.

I find myself ignoring his rudeness and wanting to know the cause of it. My money's on Judy.

He's sat behind his desk, with his fingers interlaced in his lap when I enter. "Judy won't be in the office today. Her husband was admitted to hospital last night."

"Oh, dear. She mentioned he'd been unwell. I hope he's okay."

"He's out, but she understandably wants to spend some time today with him."

"Of course."

He casts a long look at his laptop, choosing his words. "I know this is only your second day but I'm in back-to-back meetings for most of it. I need you to cover for Judy."

I give a no-nonsense nod. It's not the first time I've had to step-up or cover for someone else.

"Of course. I've access to your diary and got to grips with the phone system yesterday. Let's see what's booked in for today." I walk round his desk and stand beside him, peering at the electronic calendar on the screen. Back-to-back meetings up until early afternoon. He's right – today's full-on. "Do you need my support with any of these?"

He's stares at me with an unfathomable look in his eye. "All of them. I'm afraid I'm going to be taking up a lot of your time today."

So much for keeping away from him. But this I can do. Work. It is after all what he's paying me for. I'm relieved the weird sexual tension from yesterday's gone. He's being professional and I'm damn sure I'm going to be.

I smile politely. "That's fine. I'll go and grab my things ready for your nine o'clock."

***

The first meeting is an update about the controversial Cedarwood Grove Project and the press coverage the previous evening. As I walk into the boardroom, Simon from PR is already at the table, tapping away on his laptop.

"Ah, you came back after your first day?" He flashes me a smile. "We can't be that bad then?"

I take up my position where I sat yesterday and switch on my laptop, ignoring the way his eyes sweep over me with interest. I smile and turn my attention to the various drawings and photos laid on the table in front of me.

"Yes, I suppose. What are those?"

"These are the before and afters of Cedarwood. What the site looks like now and the designs of what it will look like once we've finished. The buildings earmarked for demolition are two disused care homes. They've stood empty for fifteen years and they've attracted arsonists and vandals over the years. Despite that, the residents don't want to see them go because the buildings have been there forever. Like we said yesterday, people don't like change."

The photos show exterior shots of the dilapidated buildings. A rusty skip overflowing with rubbish sits on the cracked driveway. The once white painted roughcast is grey and coming away from the brickwork in chunks. All the windows are either smashed or missing entirely; there are large holes in the roofs. Over the years, ivy has interwoven itself around the rotten window frames. Everything's in a terrible state.

Simon pushes a couple of computer-generated designs across the table to me.

The mock-ups show two blocks of apartments which have been sympathetically designed to tie in to the surrounding properties and blend in with the traditional-style houses either side of them. They're far from the monstrosities I feared.

"They look ... really good," I admit, recalling my blunt response to Gabe's question, in this very meeting room yesterday afternoon. "I get why the residents are so unhappy, but when you see these photos ..." I trail off not quite ready to admit that I was maybe a little hasty in my answer.

On cue, the sliding door opens. Gabe walks in holding an iPad and sits down in the chair beside me. My skin gooses at the closeness. *Damn. This isn't a good sign. I've got to spend pretty much all day with him.*

He gestures at the images on the desk. "What's all this?"

"I thought it might be helpful to remind ourselves what the whole project is all about," Simon tells him. He glances at me and smiles. "And I was just showing Ella."

Gabe gives me a thoughtful look. "And do you still have the same opinion as you did yesterday – or has it changed?"

Why do I get the feeling he's not just talking about the project anymore?

His disarming eyes hold mine. I try to swallow, but my mouth dries. "It's getting there."

He looks at me for a second too long, then turns to Simon. "Right. First things first. Where's this press statement?"

***

The morning disappears in a whirlwind of meetings that all blur into one. There's no reprieve. The Cedarwood Grove Project is the focus of discussion along with deciding the plan of attack in response to the contentious press interview from the Councillor, the previous evening.

My fingers barely leave the keyboard as I take down actions and arrange meetings for Gabe. While I seize the chance to dash to the toilet or grab a quick drink in the few spare minutes in between meetings, Gabe remains. For five hours he discusses strategies; answering questions and dealing with an endless torrent of shit thrown his way. The staff nod in agreement with his ideas. It's clear they've got his back, but it's more than that. He possesses an effortless charisma which means all eyes are on him. As he sits at the top of the table dishing out instructions and strategizing, I think about the first time I laid eyes on him. Power. Control. The guy's got it in spades and then some, but not in a cocky way. The Gabe who told me he wanted me less than twenty-four hours ago is nowhere to be seen. This version possesses a quiet, authoritative vibe which means there's total silence in the room as his staff hang on his every word, waiting to hear his next thought.

Once the final meeting winds down I leave him in deep discussion with a guy from finance and take the chance to escape back to my desk. I put my laptop down and turn to look out of the windows, grateful for the change of scenery. The afternoon sunshine bounces off the glass windows of The Shard and glistening waters of the Thames. Last time I looked out at the view it was morning.

A familiar niggle aches between my shoulder blades. I straighten my spine and gently roll my neck from side to side, trying to un-bunch some of the knots in my muscles from being sat down for five hours. Talk about being thrown in at the deep end.

"Hey."

I jump with a start. Gabe's on the other side of my desk, pulling his black jacket on.

"You okay?"

"Erm ... yeah, I just needed to stretch."

His brow twitches into a concerned frown. "Oh?"

"It's nothing." I wave a hand dismissively. "It's just a thing I get sometimes ... when I've been sat typing for too long."

"You should have said. I'd have made sure you were able to take regular breaks this morning."

My cheeks grow warm. He's being nice and I'm not sure how to handle it. I think I prefer him when he's being a cocky git. "I'm fine, really."

He nods satisfied with my reply. "I'm heading out to grab a bite to eat. Would you like me to get you anything?"

I'm on the backfoot.

"No, thanks." I laugh nervously, awkward at the kind gesture. He's the CEO. I don't expect this. "Shouldn't *I* be getting *your* lunch?"

"I'm not sure whether you've noticed but I don't run that kind of ship around here. I don't expect my PA to run around making me coffee and fetching me lunch. You've got far more important things to be doing."

I nod. I've felt like nothing more than a skivvy in some of the offices where I've temped in the past. Making drinks, picking up lunches, collecting and dropping off dry cleaning has all been in a day's work.

My stomach grumbles. I'm starving but I can't possibly take him up on the offer. It just doesn't seem right. "No, I'm good. Thank you."

Gabe nods slowly like he anticipated my response. "Okay, well make sure you have a break," he warns. "I'll be back in five."

He walks into the waiting lift and the doors close behind him.

For some unknown reason I stand looking at the lift, until my mobile rings snapping me out of my weird stupor. I retrieve it from my handbag.

It's Amy. My stomach sinks and I immediately feel guilty. I shouldn't react like this, but when she contacts me it's usually only for one thing. The one thing I haven't got very much of at the moment.

I take a deep breath and answer it. "What's up Ames?"

"I need your help."

As I thought. I briefly close my eyes. "How much this time?"

There's a pause. "If I don't get it, I'm going to be in trouble." The tremble in her voice unnerves me. I snap open my eyes.

"Why, what do you mean? Trouble? What's it for?"

"My degree. I need to buy some specific textbooks for legal terminology. I really need them, otherwise I won't be able to finish my course."

"Hang on, I thought you'd bought all that stuff at the start of term?"

"I did ... most of it."

"What do you mean, *most* of it?"

She sighs heavily down the phone and I know a sob story's coming. "It's hard work here, Ella. There's *loads* of studying, but the social side of things is crazy too. I want to make new friends and fit in and can't do that if I'm stuck in studying all the time."

I want to tell her that *I* wouldn't know because I never had the opportunity to go to university. But she knows all this and it means nothing to her. "You mean you spent your money for course materials on booze."

"Not all of it," she snaps defensively.

"I haven't got much money, Amy."

"Ella, *please...*"

"I'm not saying this to be horrible. I won't have much money until I get paid at the end of the month."

"*Please* Ella. I need the stupid books."

A tension headache throbs at my temples. I rub a hand across my forehead. Kate's right about her. Amy's spoilt. Because of Mum working all hours to look after us, and then her illness, I had to look after Amy from my early teens. When Mum got worse I was the one who would take time off work to look after her and go with her to chemo and hospital appointments. Amy was protected. She carried on going out with her mates, she continued to study and was able to get into university. Mum really wanted that for her. I do too. I want her to make something of her life, not waste it temping like I have.

"How much do you need and by when?" I ask, fearing the reply.

"Two fifty by next Monday."

"Two hundred and fifty pounds!" I fight to keep my voice down. "Are you joking?"

"There's loads of them," she whines. "I've got that interview tomorrow, I'll pay you back once I get the job."

"You've got to get the job first, and you need the money now." I remind her.

"I'm sorry." That tremble's back in her voice.

I exhale deeply. The throb in my temples is now a full-on headache. I've no idea how I'm going to get this money. Sometimes I could kill my sister. "I need to go. I'm at work. I'll have to see what I can do."

"Okay. I've got to go, my next lecture starts in five."

And she hangs up.

I part sit, part collapse down into the chair feeling sick. *How on earth am I going to get that much money in four days?* A whisper of an idea pops into my head and I push it down. No. I'm not doing it. Not unless I have absolutely no choice.

I check my online banking on my phone to make sure I haven't won the Lottery overnight and haven't yet got the email. Sadly not. I've a grand total of two pounds fifty left in my savings account. Only another two hundred and forty-seven pounds fifty pence to go.

What the fuck am I going to do?

I've some money left but that's for bills and food. Until I get my first wages from this job, I'm pretty much skint.

Shit.

I chuck my phone down on the desk and rest my chin on my hand as the glum reality takes hold. I've only got one option left. The thing I gave up over a year ago, and told myself I'd never do again, unless I was desperate. And now I'm desperate. And not for the first time. When Mum stopped working because of her illness, my temping job wasn't bringing in enough money to cover all the bills. Once the carers had put Mum to bed I'd go to work. I told her and Amy I'd got a second job working as a waitress in a bar in Soho.

I scroll down the contacts in my phone then type out a text. He might say no to the favour I'm asking. I'm praying he doesn't. For one night's work I'll definitely make the two fifty Amy needs. I take in a deep breath, re-read the grovelling text and press send. Within a minute he replies. I'm in.

Chapter 15

Ella

A Starbucks coffee cup appears on my desk with my name scrawled in black marker pen on the side, interrupting my self-loathing. I look up in confusion.

Gabe's standing in front of my desk with a hand on the cup. There's a brown paper bag tucked underneath his arm and he's balancing a cardboard tray with another cup in his other hand.

"Coffee?"

Yes, please!

After the day I've had I'm in urgent need of caffeine and food. I haven't eaten anything since last night. I eye the drink like it's liquid gold.

"Thank you." I reach out to take the cup, but Gabe keeps his hand firmly on the lid.

"One condition." He nods towards his office. "You take a break."

In his office. With him. Is that a good idea? It's pretty innocent ... isn't it?

He cocks an eyebrow at my hesitance. "Have you had a break yet?"

"No."

"Then you're having one now." Without waiting for a reply, he picks up the cup and walks off into his office.

He's telling me, not asking me. I glare at the open door and toy with the idea of staying here purely out of defiance but after five seconds, my empty stomach grumbles in protest. It needs coffee, and so do I.

I follow him through the door. The two cups sit on the glass coffee table, along with the brown paper bag.

He's hanging his jacket up on the coat stand. "Today's been pretty manic. You need to take a proper break, otherwise you'll burn out. Take a seat."

I *do* need a break.

Nerves fizz in my stomach as I close the door. I perch on one end of the black leather sofa as Gabe joins me on the other. He takes one of the cups and slides the other towards me.

"Thank you." I smile gratefully, closing my hands around the warm cardboard.

"I took a risk." He picks up the paper bag. "I brought you a vanilla latte. That okay?"

"That's my go-to order."

He grins and opens up the bag. "I also took a gamble –" he shoots me an uncertain look "– do you like sushi?"

I can't stop the stupid smile from spreading across my face. The words are like music to my ears. "I love it."

"Excellent." He pulls out two cardboard trays filled with delicious looking rolls and nigiri and puts one in front of me. I'm a little lost for words. "You, erm … you didn't have to buy me lunch?"

He rolls his shoulders into a dismissive shrug and settles back into the sofa, tucking into his sushi. "I was at the sushi bar. See it as a thank you for today."

"But I've just been doing my job."

"Technically, it's Judy's, now shut up and eat your lunch," he orders, a playful glint in his eye.

I give in. Not that I can wait any longer. The sushi looks delicious and I'm starved. I tuck in, savouring the flavours and trying not to ram it all in my mouth at once. We sit, eating in contented silence. It should feel awkward but it doesn't. What *is* weird, is that it doesn't feel weird in the slightest. I've been on first dates that have felt more awkward than this.

Date.

Oh God.

I shove the last sushi roll into my mouth to try and forget my plans for the evening.

Gabe puts his tray down on the table and wipes his mouth with a paper napkin. "You like it?"

I've wolfed it down. "I think my empty tray speaks for itself. It was so good. I think it's the best I've ever tried."

He picks up his coffee. "I'm glad. It's only five minutes away and open twenty-four hours. I'm not much of a cook so it's too tempting to drop in for supper some evenings."

Supper? He sees the questions in my eyes. "I live in The Madison. It's a ten-minute walk away from here."

I nod slowly, making a mental note of where he lives so I can Google it later. It will be some ultra-exclusive, modern apartment block on the docks, no doubt.

"That's really close to work. Saying that, it must be handy, not having to bother with the Tube ... it's always a mad dash in the mornings ..." I stall, realising I'm admitting I'm shit at time-keeping to the big boss. Not the best quality in an employee.

Shut up, Ella.

"It *is* convenient." He takes a sip of coffee. "Sometimes too convenient."

"How do you mean?" I ask, unsure why the hell I'm probing. He's invited me to take a break and have some lunch, which I have done. I should be getting back to work. But as we sit here chatting away easily, I'm find that I'm relaxing in his company, and the desire to be anywhere else fades away.

"Living so close means I can walk home and don't have to sit and commute, but some nights I'm here until late and some mornings I'm here at the crack of dawn."

It makes sense, but I can't help thinking his work-life balance is probably a bit out.

"Do you think you'll like it here?"

And just like that, the conversation shifts to me. "It's easily the best job I've had. The best paid, best prospects" - I look towards the afternoon sun setting across the city skyline - "the nicest view." *The hottest boss. Stop it, Ella.*

"So you think you'll stay here for a while?"

I put my empty tray down on the table and pick up my coffee. *What's with all the sudden questions?*

Gabe turns his body towards mine and rests an arm along the back of the sofa. "I noticed on your CV, that you've worked for quite a few different companies since you left college."

A stab of unease slices through me. The reasons for his questioning becomes crystal clear. It figures. As an employer he's working out whether I'm worth investing the time, money and training in, in case I decide to move on to somewhere new in a few months' time.

"You got good grades at college, how come you never thought about going to university?"

I suppose he *has* warned me he's direct.

I tuck a lock of hair behind my ear and twist the plastic lid of the cup round, avoiding his gaze. There's no way I can't tell him about Mum if I go into this. Even now, talking about it's no easier.

"I always planned on going to uni. It was a given; school, college, then uni. But, in my final year at college, Mum became ill. I stayed home to look after her and my younger sister. Amy was only thirteen at the time. All my time went into caring for Mum and making sure my little sister was okay, and I never really invested any time in getting a decent, permanent job. After Mum passed away, it took a while to sort everything out, but I decided I wanted to find something better and more permanent. Mum always believed in me. She made me promise that I'd do something with my life. This job is the first step in me *doing* something and making her proud."

I immediately feel stupid. I've no idea why I've admitted that to him. For a start, he won't get it. I'm sure he's led a charmed life. I'm betting he's never had to make sure his little brother has eaten his tea, done his homework and has a clean uniform and dinner money ready for school the next day. How can Gabe possibly empathise? We're from completely different sides of the tracks.

I take a sip of coffee and finally look at him. He's watching me carefully. The judgement I expected to see in his eyes, because I haven't been to university and got a high-flying career at the age of twenty-six, isn't there.

"I'm so sorry. That must have been really tough." He gives me a reassuring smile that warms my chest. "I'm sure you're making your mum very proud."

My throat tightens with unexpected emotion and I look down, inspecting my fingernails. *What's happening to me?* I came for a break, not to give him my life story. I'm on the edge of dangerous territory.

"Actually, I have a sort of property question for you?" I ask, pushing the conversation off me.

His lips curl into a smile that makes my heart tighten in my chest. "Anything."

Chapter 16

Ella

"Have you ever heard of Darknight Properties?"

He narrows his eyes at the question. "They're competitors. Why the interest?"

"I heard their name recently and wondered if you knew anything about them."

"*Where* did you hear their name?"

I can't tell him without going into the whole shebang about the shop. I've already told him too much about me. I'm sure he doesn't want to hear about all that sorry business as well.

"Ella?" he pushes.

"It doesn't matter."

"It does, or you wouldn't have asked. Tell me. I'm not going to let you leave this office until you do. Your choice." He lifts his eyebrows and takes a sip of coffee. The sureness in his tone tells me he means it. God, he's frustrating.

"My mum ran a florist's. When she died, one of the ladies who worked in the shop took it over. The landlord who owns it and some of the other buildings in the same row is selling up to Darknight Properties, or so I've heard. I'm worried they're going to knock everything down and build houses."

Gabe takes a long drink of coffee, considering what I've just said. "Much like we're doing with the Cedarwood Grove Project?"

I give him an uncertain look.

"At least it explains why you were so dead against it yesterday."

"I'm not *dead* against it. I admit at first I was, and yes, it made me think about mum's shop but then I saw the images of what you plan to do with the site."

His perfect lips twitch into a smile. "And you changed your

mind?"

"I came round to the idea, I suppose."

"We don't demolish buildings for the fun of it. There's always a financial reason. Often the buildings are in too poor a state of repair to be financially viable for us to sink money into. Your mum's shop. Where is it?"

"Hackney high street, by the canal."

He gives me a long look, before finally saying, "Darknight are a smaller company. That's all I really know."

So much for him knowing the gen on them.

"You say you have a younger sister?"

I guess that conversations over.

I roll my eyes and sit back in the sofa, turning to face him. I prop my head against my hand and sigh at the mere thought of Amy.

"Yeah, she's at uni, studying law. She's more trouble now than she was at home."

He laughs, but his smile doesn't quite reach his eyes. "You don't need to talk to me about pain in the arse younger siblings."

This is the first time he's made any real reference to his brother. Judy's told me snippets but I want it from the horse's mouth. "Do you and Spencer not get on?"

Gabe pushes a hand through his hair, making it flop forward across his brow. "We're very different. He enjoys the media and limelight and all the shit that lifestyle brings." His eyes settle on me. "Tell me you didn't watch that fucking awful reality TV show he was in?"

I shift uncomfortably in my seat. My reaction must say it all.

"Oh, Ella." He feigns mock disappointment and his blue eyes sparkle.

"I didn't watch it *all* the time, but it was kind of hard to miss. Spencer was the star of the show."

"Yeah, for fucking a different woman every episode, or so I've heard. Like I say, we're very different."

His eyes meet mine and he takes another sip of coffee.

His message lands loud and clear. He's telling me that he's not a womaniser like his brother, but surely he must be beating them off with a stick. Do I believe him? It's easier if I *don't* believe him, because that makes him harder to like. I don't want him to be easier to like. He needs to be the arrogant, womanising, self-entitled prick I thought he was. He needs to prove that some of my first impressions of him were right, even though they're slowly being overturned with every minute we sit chatting.

"Why do you do this?" I ask, unable to help myself.

"Do what?"

I glance around the office. "This. I'm pretty sure you could lie on a beach for the rest of your life and not bother about the stresses of work."

"You mean why do I bother working when I don't have to?"

"Yes, I suppose."

"Apart from the fact I'd go crazy lying on a beach, this is the family business. Dad's built this up. My eldest brother, Jake, always had his heart set on the army and then the SAS, and Spencer's Spencer. It fell to me to carry it on."

He feels he has a duty to his family. I look at his signet ring. "The W engraved on your ring, I suppose that stands for White?"

A smile plays at the corners of his mouth as he studies me. "We all have one. What else could it stand for?"

I shrug. "I dunno… winning."

"Why do you say that?"

"I get the impression that's something you love."

"You're either first or last, there's no second place."

"You've a chessboard in your office, it's obvious playing games is something you enjoy."

"No. Like I've said before. I don't play games," he says firmly.

He *has* said this before, but I'm still not sure I believe him. "Then why the chess board?" I quiz.

"It helps me think. When I've a problem I need to work through, it helps clear my mind and decide what I should do next."

"You've a very competitive attitude. You must place a lot of pressure on yourself to achieve."

He wrinkles his nose, like he doesn't agree. "I thrive on pressure. Always have."

"What if you don't win?"

"I *always* win."

Is he talking about in business or fucking?

Gabe White, conqueror of property deals and women.

"And let me guess when you've won, you move onto the next business transaction?"

I'm definitely talking about fucking.

He lifts his cup to his lips and is about to take a sip when the white plastic lid somehow dislodges, sending coffee spilling all down the front of his white shirt.

"Fuck!" He leaps up, slamming the cup down on the table as the coffee stains spreads across his chest.

I press my lips together to stifle a laugh and offer him a napkin. "Do you need one of these?"

He pushes a hand through his hair and looks at me, breaking into a smile.

"I'm glad you find it funny." He glances at the napkin in my hands. "No, it's okay. I've got a spare."

He unfastens his tie, throws it in my direction and flicks me a grin.

I stare at the black tie in my hands and frown in confusion as he walks across the office to the black cupboard behind his desk. "What? You mean … a spare shirt?"

"Of course," he says, as if it's perfectly normal. "Fail to prepare, prepare to fail."

He slides open the cupboard door to reveal a rail of shirts. Two of each colour, white, very pale pink, light blue, ink blue, grey and black. All hang in a perfectly neat, colour co-ordinated row.

He keeps a change of clothes in his office. This guy sure doesn't like surprises.

I expect him to pull out a shirt and go and get changed in the toilets. But he doesn't. He begins unbuttoning his shirt.

I drag my gaze to the black tie in my hands. He's stripping off. In front of me.

Fucking hell.

The idea of him standing semi-naked only a few metres away and me not peeking, is like putting a delicious chocolate cake in front of a toddler and telling them "Don't touch." I'm looking at him before I even realise. As my eyes travel over the muscles of his back I no longer care. His upper body looks even broader in the flesh. Hard, toned, perfect for sinking my nails into.

Fuck.

He throws the dirty shirt over the back of his chair and pulls a clean one from a hanger. When he turns to the side to pull it on, all the questions I've pondered about his beautiful body are answered in one delicious look. My body locks rigid as I admire him. His defined abs and the beginnings of a V confirms he looks after himself.

Both arms and his upper chest are covered in tattoos. One side is made up of the roses I've seen, the other depicts a black snake that curls all the way up his arm and finishes on his chest.

Then they're gone. Gabe puts his arms through the sleeves, fastens up the shirt and looks at me. I immediately drop my eyes to my lap a second too late and turn his tie over in my hands.

Damn it!

He's caught me eyeing him up good and proper. Just like he did at the club. But this time things are different. This time he's my boss.

I draw in a steadying breath and lift my eyes. But he's moved. He's standing in front of me, fastening the cuffs of his shirt, watching me intently.

Shit.

I awkwardly offer him his tie because I'm not sure what else to do.

He takes it, slides it round his neck and begins to tie it, all without taking his eyes off me. And I really wish he would.

"Finished?"

"Finished what?"

"Checking me out."

"I wasn't." I scoff as if it's a ridiculous suggestion.

He lifts an eyebrow. He doesn't look convinced. "Really." He doesn't sound convinced, either.

"I noticed your tattoos *actually*."

He takes a step closer, fastening the knot in his tie. "Oh yeah, and what did you notice?"

They're hot.

"They're very ..." *Come on Ella, think of something.* "Interesting."

Even I don't believe that feeble reply.

Gabe runs a hand through his hair, making it look even more tousled.

Is he doing this on purpose?

"Right, because from where I was standing it looked very much like you were checking me out." He flashes a wicked smile. "You were giving me the same look as you did on Saturday."

His eyes hold mine in that way of his that smashes my focus. Usually. Not this time. This time I'm standing my ground.

I fold my arms and meet his eyes challengingly. "I don't know what you're talking about. What look?"

"The I-wanna-fuck-you-look."

"Like you were giving me."

"I'm not denying it."

I stall at his honesty. "This is wrong ..."

"What is?"

"Talking like this."

"We're just talking."

"About the fact we want to fuck each other."

"I'm so glad we finally agree on something. Saturday happened and we're talking about it like it didn't."

"*Nothing* happened on Saturday."

"No, it didn't, but there's something here, isn't there?" He gestures between me and him. "I saw it in your eyes when we first met."

I can't deny it because then I'd be a big bloody liar. There *is* something here. And it runs deeper than me wanting to know what he'd feel like inside me. When I look in his eyes I see a glimmer of sadness lurking behind that shiny exterior. There's more to him than just being a White. And the more I'm around him the more I want to find out what it is.

"You're my boss."

"What if we were just Gabe and Ella?"

My heart skips at his words. I hate myself for letting him affect me like this. "You told me not to get involved with someone like you."

"You shouldn't."

I shouldn't ask him to elaborate. I should shut the conversation down right now and walk away. But my feet are rooted to the spot. "I don't understand. You're talking in riddles."

Gabe takes another step closer, filling the small space between us and making my stomach twist. Serious eyes hold mine. "You shouldn't get involved with someone like me. But I …"

A knock on the door interrupts him mid-flow.

Fuck it!

A part of me wants to hear what he's got to say, but the other part doesn't, because I feel like there might be no coming back from it. This interruption is a sign. It's the universe's way of telling us that we need to stay the hell away from whatever we were about to unleash.

"Thanks for lunch." I avoid his gaze and quickly head over to the door, before he has a chance to say anything we both might regret.

Sarah Cross, stands the other side of the door as I open it. Her dark eyes narrow suspiciously, swinging from Gabe to me, then back again.

"I've been calling your PA for the last half an hour to see if you were available, but there's been no reply." She throws me an accusatory look.

"Judy's off. Ella was taking a well-deserved break," Gabe tells her, without taking his eyes off me.

Sarah waltzes past me into the office, throwing a look of disdain in my direction. "Close the door on your way out."

Chapter 17

Ella

Torture. That's what the next forty-five minutes are. I replay the whole conversation over and over in my head. What did he mean? What was he about to say? He's warning me off him one minute then contradicting himself the next. My head hurts. To make matters worse, every now and then the sound of Sarah's annoying laughter filters through the door, shattering any form of concentration I've managed to scrape together. God knows what they're up to.

The moment the minute hand hits half-past on the clock on the wall, I start packing up. On cue, Gabe's office door opens and Sarah saunters out into the waiting lift, without so much as a glance in my direction.

She clearly *isn't* a fan of mine. The feeling's mutual.

I shrug on my coat and pull my hair out of my collar.

Gabe appears in the doorway to his office. "You're leaving?"

"It's four thirty and I'm going out tonight. Besides, it's been a busy day," I tell him, annoyed that I've given him too much detail. What is it about this guy that disconnects my brain from my mouth?

"I didn't realise the time."

"I guess time flies when you're having fun."

The barbed comment tumbles from my mouth before I can stop it.

A ghost of a smile plays at the corners of his mouth at my faux pas.

Shit!

I need to get the hell out of here before I say something else I regret. I've told him far too much today.

I sling my handbag over my shoulder and fix him with a firm look, determined to hold onto my last thread of dignity.

"Night, Gabe."

The beep of my phone from inside my bag gives me a welcome distraction from the massive fuck-up I've just made, as I hurry over to the lift.

I angrily stab at the call button and pull my phone out of my bag. It's a text from Kate.

You're meeting in Old Street Records at 8. Don't be late. Tom's VERY excited. x

After a bottle of wine the prospect of going on a not-so blind date with Tom sounded far more appealing than it does now, three and a half hours before we're due to meet up.

"Who's Tom?" A familiar male voice asks from the left of me.

Gabe's peering over my shoulder reading my text. His eyebrow cocked quizzically, awaiting my response.

Great. Just what I need.

The lift doors open and I head in, stuffing my phone into my handbag. Gabe follows me.

Is he doing this on purpose?

I stab at the button to the ground floor and lean against the side of the lift, making sure I'm as far away from him as I possibly can be.

"Well?"

I stare straight ahead at the closing doors. "You're leaving work early. What happened to you staying at the office until all hours?"

"I fancied an early night. Who's Tom?"

"No one."

"Doesn't seem like no one to me."

"That was a private text," I snap.

Gabe pushes his hands in his trouser pockets and smiles smugly. He's enjoying watching me squirm.

"It was from someone I'm seeing tonight, if you must know," I continue loftily. "Not that it's any of your business."

"Lucky Tom. No wonder he's so excited. He's got an evening in your company. So, what's he like?"

I fold my arms and sigh at his questioning. "I dunno. It's the first time we've met."

"Like a first date?" There's a disapproving tone to his voice. My hackles rise.

"So what? How many dates do you go on in a week?"

"None."

I roll my eyes. "Of course, not. Guys like you don't date, do they?"

"Guys like me?"

"Yes, guys like you." I fix him a look. "Guys who've got it all. They're used to having whoever they want because they've got the looks, the money, the family name ... they've a harem waiting for them. They take whatever they want from whoever they choose, then drop them once they're done because they don't really give a shit about anyone but themselves." My gob's run away with me. I've just unloaded on my boss. Big style. He could sack me in a heartbeat.

Regret prickles in my stomach. I glare at the LED display telling me we've still got thirty floors to go until we reach the ground floor.

Hurry the fuck up.

"That's quite a character assassination."

I can't look at him.

"What's caused all the hate?"

His question floors me. "What?"

"Don't get me wrong, you've not said anything that I've not heard before. Some people have misconceptions of me because of the upbringing I've had. Usually that hate comes from jealousy, but I don't get that from you." He tilts his head and looks at me thoughtfully, trying to figure me out. "So, what happened?"

I suck in a deep breath and stare at the floor. I'd prefer it if he were angry and annoyed, hell I'd even take him sacking me, but not this. He's trying to work me out, and I'm not ready for that.

"Maybe I just don't like self-entitled pricks."

He laughs, which surprises me. "You keep telling yourself that." He closes the distance between us in two easy strides. And then he's staring down at me and it gets a whole lot more difficult to breathe. "You might not like me, but you *do* want me, Princess. Very much. Just like I want you."

I shake my head. I'm not falling for it. One flash of his platinum credit card and a few cheesy lines probably works on the others. Not me. I'm not a naïve seventeen-year-old anymore. That shit doesn't work. "I don't."

"Yes, you do. Drop the ball-buster act, it doesn't suit you."

"Why, because I'm not agreeing with you?" I snap. "I'm not hanging on your every word like all the other women?"

"There's not much talking that goes on with the other women."

I want to slap him.

"I don't want you," I say looking him straight in the eyes. "And I still won't want you tonight when I'm with Tom. Or when I'm kissing him. Or when he's fucking me."

His spine stiffens. For the first time I've managed to wipe the cocky smirk off his face. I wait for his witty retort but nothing comes. The momentary elation I feel at the fact I've manage to silence him, is swiftly swiped away by regret. But I can't afford to think about it. I need to get out of here.

The lift comes to a stop and the doors slide open.

Thank god!

I force a polite smile. "Night, Gabe."

Then I hurry out of the lift without looking back.

Chapter 18

Gabe

Right, left, right, left.
Sweat drips down my forehead, stinging my eyes and blurring my vision. I force myself to keep focussed and blink through it, keeping the hits going, reigning punch after punch down onto the bag. I won't stop. I *can't*, because if I do ...

"When you said you'd finished work early, I didn't expect to find you in here."

Jake strolls towards me, dressed in a black hoody and joggers, tossing his phone in his hand. "I thought you hit the gym in the mornings. You miss it today, or something?"

I drop my hands and swipe the back of the boxing glove across my face to get rid of the sweat. "No."

He props himself against the wall and gives me the once over. "You okay?"

I pull off my gloves and throw them into my gym bag, dipping down to grab my bottle of water. "Fine. Why?"

"Coz you're hitting the gym twice in one day."

I shrug like it's nothing and take a long drink of water, so I don't have to answer.

"What's up? A deal gone tits up or something?"

I shake my head and shoot him a look. My big brother should know me better. I wouldn't allow that to happen. But then, *that* feeling I'd know how to handle.

"Nope. How's our owner?" I ask, steering the conversation back onto business.

"Good, last time I checked. Like I said in my text. All on for Friday. You think he'll come our way?"

"Yep. If we make him the right offer. And we will."

Money. It *always* comes down to money.

"So, if it's not business that's got you like this..."

"Got me like what?"

Jake smirks. "Pounding the fucking shit out of a punchbag."

I shove my bottle in my bag. "I've got a lot going on at the minute. I need a distraction." That's not a lie. I *do* need a distraction. "What time is it?"

He glances at his watch. "Just gone seven. Why?"

She'll be getting ready to go on her date.

"You fucked her yet?"

"Who?"

"You know who."

"How's Andi?" I ask, pushing the conversation back to him.

Jake blows out a long breath and rubs a hand across his buzz cut. "You know, being Andi."

That translates into being her obnoxious, difficult, spoilt self. Serves him right for getting involved with a gang leader's daughter. She hooked up with Spencer a few years back but when she realised his love for banging other women and partying would always be the most important things in his life, she set her sights on me. But I didn't take the bait. Her immature, self-obsessed ways do zero for me. When she finally took the hint she moved on to Jake and struck gold, because in a moment of weakness he thought with his dick instead of his brain.

Is that what I'm doing?

"You haven't, then. Figures, that's why you're in here trying to forget about her."

Being with another guy. Kissing him. Fucking him.

I force down the unfamiliar feeling rising in my gut. I need to be sensible. Something I'm incapable of whenever I'm around her. One look at her and all rational thoughts are wiped from my brain. This can't go anywhere. I can't risk everything. There's too much on the line.

"Like I've already said. It's never going to happen. She works for me. She's off limits."

"You know, G, life's too fucking short. What happened to Mum should tell you that."

That's not what I want to hear. I want Jake to tell me that I'm absolutely right. Not make me doubt myself. I can do that, without his help.

I pick up my gym bag and sling it over my shoulder. "So, how come you've dropped by?"

"Andi's decided to tell me she's holding a party for my fortieth next week."

I throw Jake a look. He hates fuss.

"Without asking you?"

He frowns and shakes his head, clearly pissed off. "I get the feeling it's just another excuse for her to show off to her friends, rather than for me. Anyway, thought I'd mention it."

"Of course, I'll be there."

"Dad's coming."

I guess it's a given, I know, but I haven't spoken to him in months. There's no point. Things are strained between us. They have been ever since Mum. That day we found her. *I* found her. We've not been the same since. And as the years have gone on, I've seen a side of him I never knew existed. And I despise it. The secrets we're carrying and hiding from the others have driven a wedge between us and as the years have passed, the wedge has grown into a huge fucking boulder and neither of us has any inclination to try and move it.

"That'll be nice and awkward then."

"I just … thought I'd warn you. Do you want to hang out tonight?"

I shake my head. "Not tonight. There's somewhere I need to be."

Chapter 19

Ella

The bar is rammed for mid-week. The deafening sound of chatter fills the room as I step in off the street. A guitarist sits on the stage beside the bar, singing a sad love song no one's listening to. The exposed brickwork and industrial feel to the place means it's a popular Shoreditch hang-out and it's buzzing.

I squeeze past the customers at the bar and weave round the tables, craning my neck to see if I can spot Tom. I hope to God I haven't got to wander round looking for him too long. The soles of my feet burn. My very lovely chocolate brown leather boots are already starting to rub – not a good sign. Now I remember why I don't wear them very often. Thankfully, I'm not looking for him for too long.

He shoots up from the seating area over by the windows, looking pretty similar to his photo, except he's clean shaven, and his dark brown hair's slicked back.

"Ella." He straightens his red and navy check shirt and hesitates, like he can't decide whether to go in for a kiss or just shake my hand. He hovers awkwardly for a few seconds doing a weird jig, then pecks me on the cheek. "Nice to meet you."

"Nice to meet you too."

We sit down on the light brown leather seats and I shrug off my faded denim jacket.

Silence descends between us.

I hate this. The butt-clenching awkwardness of a first date. I'm quickly remembering why I don't bother with them.

Tom gives me a tight smile which tells me he's feeling just as awkward as me. "So, tell me a bit about yourself?"

I flounder at the question. This is the first time in two years I've actually taken the plunge and done anything like this. I've dusted off my crippling, yet beautiful knee-high boots, worn my cornflower blue, floaty floral skirt and painted my nails. I'd anticipated a bit of light chit-chat and possibly a compliment.

"Oh, I er… started a new job just this week."

"Great. Where?"

And he's back; the guy I've been trying my hardest to forget about, springs to the front of my mind.

"White House Developments, Canary Wharf."

"Sounds interesting."

That's one way to describe it I suppose. "Mmhmm."

Tom launches into telling me about his job at the bank. After a few minutes of talking interest rates and mortgages my mind starts to wander. Back to this afternoon. Gabe. His muscles. His tattoos. His arrogant remarks.

"… really good pension fund."

He's talking about pension funds. On a first date. Jesus!

Tom rubs his hands together. "Anyway, I'll tell you a bit more about my role and what I do in a bit. Shall I get us some drinks?"

"Oh, yes, that would be lovely," I say, a little too eagerly. I need something to take the edge off. "A glass of rosé for me, please."

"Coming right up."

Tom disappears off towards the bar. I smooth the material of my skirt across my thighs and cross my legs, wincing in pain as my leather boots dig into my ankle. They hurt like hell but look sexy. Not that my date seems to have noticed.

I run my fingers through my hair and pull my phone out of my bag. Two text messages; the first from Kate telling me to have a good time, the second's from an unknown number sent a few seconds earlier. I open it.

Unknown: *Your hair looks fine.*

I frown. *What the hell?*

The three little flashing grey dots at the bottom of the message tell me there's more to come. Sure enough, another message pops up.

Unknown: *You look beautiful.*

Who the fuck is this and how have they got my number?

I glance around the bar uneasily. I'm clearly being watched but no one seems to be watching me. Everyone's having far too good of a time. Whoever this creep is, they're going to get a piece of my mind.

Me: *Who is this? How do you have my number?*

Unknown: *Guess.*

Me: *I'm not playing games with you. Fuck off.*

Unknown: *Do you want a clue?*

I stare at the phone aghast. Whoever it is, is pushing their luck big style.

Unknown: *You're thinking about it, aren't you?*

I'm about to tell them to fuck off, when another text pops up.

Unknown: *Hold that thought. Your date's coming back.*

Sure enough, Tom's heading my way with our drinks.

Where the hell *is* this creep? The bar's crowded. They can't be that far away.

"Everything okay?"

I smile politely and push my mystery texter to the back of my mind. I need to focus on tonight. And Tom.

"Erm ... yeah, I think so. Thanks for the drink."

He sits down beside me and takes a sip of his pint. "So, how long have you been single for?"

"A couple of years."

"Right, yeah, I hear you. I split up with my girlfriend six months ago. We'd been together since school, it was really hard."

"Oh, I'm sorry."

Tom rubs a hand across his chin. "It's all right. She said I was boring, that all I talked about was work." Hurt flashes in his eyes. "She said I wasn't enough for her anymore." He stares sadly into his pint. "I mean we lived together and everything. It's difficult when you've been with someone so long, especially when you thought they were the one."

I take a sip of wine, wondering whether Tom may not be quite over his ex. "That must have been really hard."

He takes a steadying drink of lager. "Yeah, it was. But now I'm ready to start dating again. I want to meet someone. I want the house, the marriage, the kids and all that."

Tom would be the sort of guy Mum would have loved me to be with. Polite, sensitive, good job. The fact he's so open to a relationship would be music to some women's ears – so why do I not get a warm fuzzy feeling when I look at him, or a buzz when he talks about the future. *What's the matter with me?*

"Would you excuse me. I'm just going to pop to the loo."

Tom smiles. "Yeah. Of course."

As usual the ladies' is rammed and there's a queue. By the time I've limped my way there, stood in line for an age, and limped back, the bar is busier than ever. I head through the customers back to our table. And freeze. I'm hallucinating. I *have* to be.

Gabe's sitting where I left Tom. His arms are flung across the back of the seat and one brown leather boot is casually perched on his knee, like he's got every right to be there. A tight, grey t-shirt does nothing to hide his sculptured body and a fine dusting of dark hairs peek out from beneath his v-neck top. He looks in total contrast to boardroom Gabe, but no less smoking. My heart gallops in my chest like a runaway horse at the sight of him.

He breaks into an annoying grin. "Surprise."

Get your brain in gear.

"What the hell are you doing here? And where the fuck is Tom?"

Gabe glances around the bar before returning his gaze to me. "I just happened to be in here with some friends, having a few drinks."

I narrow my eyes in disbelief. "You just happened to be in *here*?"

"Why? Don't you believe me?"

"No, I don't bloody well believe you." I slump down on the seat next to him, still in shock. "Out of all the bars in London, you turn up here?"

His smile widens at my annoyance, only pissing me off further. "What can I say, it's a small world."

I look into the crowds of customers not entirely sure why I'm bothering. I know his friends aren't here. That's a lie. He saw my text earlier. That's the explanation – I know it. He saw my text and for whatever reason decided to come along and ruin my date. Because it's all one big bloody joke to him. I can't dwell on the only other reason why he'd do this, because it makes my stomach feel as though I'm on a dodgems ride.

"Where's Tom?"

"Ah, see now that *is* unfortunate." Gabe pulls a face and steadily brushes the back of his hand across his thigh. "I'm afraid he's gone."

"I can see that," I snap. "But where? And more to the point, why?"

"The poor guy was on his own for ages. So, I popped over and we … got talking."

Horror strikes through me. "About what?"

He wrinkles his nose again, like he's choosing his words because he knows I'm not going to like whatever he's about to say. "You. Him."

"What about me and him?"

Gabe lifts his shoulders into a shrug. "I did him a favour. You weren't into him."

I don't believe this!

I want to punch his extremely handsome face. "What are you talking about? How dare you! How the hell would you know…"

"Because I watched you. Those hazel eyes of yours didn't light up when you first saw him. There was no spark there. You didn't want him to kiss you. You didn't want to fuck him." He deadpans and looks me straight in the eye. "You didn't want to know what he feels like inside you."

My chest tightens. Of course he's right. And I hate it. Just like I hate the fact that I don't know whether to slap him or kiss his gorgeous face off. An unsettling thought dawns on me as I go over his words. He *watched* me.

"It was you, wasn't it? You're the one who's been texting me tonight?"

He drags a hand across his jaw and drops his gaze.

It *was* him. I jump to my feet. "I don't fucking believe this! How did you get my number?"

"I've read your CV," he says, in an isn't-it-obvious-tone, that makes me want to punch him.

This is the final straw. I've heard enough. Red hot anger courses through my veins. I need to get the fuck away from him before I *do* hit him.

I snatch up my coat and angrily pull it on. "I don't know what the fuck you're playing at, and I'm sure as hell not spending a second longer in your company to find out."

Chapter 20

Ella

I barge out of the bar into the cool night air, taking a right towards the Tube station. My thoughts are a tangled mess and I don't even know how to begin to unravel them. I *do* know I need to get away from Gabe. He's dangerous. To my self-respect and my heart. I will not get drawn into whatever game he's playing. I swore to myself I'd never be played again, especially not by someone like him. And I won't.

"Ella, wait."

I spin round. He's already just a few paces behind me.

"Leave me alone."

"I don't think I can do that."

I'm incensed, yet somehow his words make my stomach flip. I cannot waver.

"Who the fuck do you think you are? Taking my mobile number, turning up here, sabotaging my date."

He folds his arms and gives me a firm look. "I didn't *need* to sabotage your date. It wasn't exactly love's young dream, was it? I was doing you both a favour."

"That's not the fucking point and you know it." I angrily stab my finger in the air at him. "You're my boss. This is my private time. You've no fucking right."

He grabs my wrist, stopping me from pointing and tugs me towards him. I stumble on my heels at the unexpected contact and crash into him. Warm, firm, hard as nails; he feels just like I remember. My skin burns beneath his touch. I rest a hand on his chest to steady my wobbly legs and lift my gaze to meet his. Ocean blue eyes hold mine, burning deep into my soul. I stop breathing.

We stand like that for an age and when he eventually speaks his voice is like velvet. "Be honest about who you want. It's not Tom."

He knows. He's always known. And he wants to hear me say it. He wants me to admit I want him, so he can pull back, just like he did in the club. And I'm not going to be a pawn in anyone's game.

I yank my wrist from his grip and take a step backwards putting some much needed distance between us. "Don't tell me what I want. You don't know."

I turn and begin to walk off, but he catches my hand in his, stopping me. "Where are you going?"

I shoot him an incredulous look, and snatch my hand from his. He needs to stop touching me. "Home."

"So, you're going to drag yourself to the Tube in boots that have been killing you all night."

How the fuck does he know this?

He cocks an eyebrow at my confused expression. "You practically limped to the ladies. *I* noticed. I doubt Tom did."

I narrow my eyes at the dig. "Well, I'd rather endure feet full of blisters than spend another minute in some cocky prick's company."

"One of these days that smart mouth of yours is going to get you in trouble."

My brain scrambles. I should fling back some witty retort but can't. The warning in his tone and heated look in his eyes make my insides clench.

I draw in a shaky breath. *Steady.*

He looks at me. "I'm giving you a lift home."

"What?"

"Your chariot awaits." He extends an arm to the right. It takes all I've got to drag my eyes away from his annoyingly perfect face and look at what he's showing me.

A matt black Bugatti sports car is parked on the side of the road. They cost an absolute bomb, I'm sure. But I'd expect the son of a billionaire property tycoon to drive nothing less.

"Are you joking?" I scoff. "I'm not getting in there with you."

He smiles, not in the least bit fazed by my reply. "It's getting late, it's getting cold" - his eyes slide down to my feet – "your boots are killing you."

"I've told you. I'll take the pain."

"You're a woman walking the streets of London, alone. What sort of gentleman would I be if I left you by yourself?"

I boldly meet his gaze even though the prospect of catching the Tube doesn't fill me with pleasure. "The sort who pays attention to a woman's requests? I can look after myself."

Gabe reaches into the pocket of his jeans, pulls out a fob and opens the car with a blip, all without taking his eyes off me. "I'm not taking no for an answer."

"I'm not getting in the car with you."

"Give me one good reason why not?"

I've got loads, none that I can verbalise though because then I'd be admitting what he wants to hear. The bottom line is that I don't trust myself. To be strong, if he isn't.

"It looks unprofessional." He gives me a disbelieving look and I quickly carry on. "You're the big boss. If people were to see –"

He frowns and glances around. "What people?"

I know I'm clutching at straws. "People from work, what the hell would they think?"

"I've given Judy a lift home before."

"That's not the same."

"Why isn't it?"

"I doubt you've told Judy you want her."

His lips twitch into an annoying smirk. "True. Nevertheless, I'm not leaving without you. You can complain all you like, but I'm not moving until you get in the car."

I fold my arms. "You're so bloody stubborn, do you know that."

"You'd rather be cold, in pain and extremely vulnerable than get a nice, warm, safe lift home?"

I wouldn't be safe. Not in a car with Gabe White, and his bloody charm and his to-die-for body.

Then the decisions made. The heavens conspire against me. Big, wet drops of rain begin to fall and a chilly gust of wind blows down the street. I can't afford to call a taxi to take me home. Pay days still a few weeks off yet and I don't want to go into my overdraft.

Fuck it!

I wrap my arms around myself. This is the universe's way of telling me to get on with it. Game over. He's won this round.

Gabe lifts an eyebrow and I know he's not going to stand for any more of my defiance. He reaches across and opens the passenger door. "Get in the car, please."

I know I have a choice. But a ten-minute walk on a cold rainy night to the Tube, in boots which are ripping my feet to shreds, is growing less appealing by the second. Maybe, if I just sit there and keep conversation to a nice, safe minimum, everything will be okay.

I glance inside the car. It's all shiny black with deep red leather upholstery. It even *looks* warm.

I tilt my chin upwards and give him a firm look. "Okay – but *only* because it's raining."

He flicks me a grin. "Get in, then."

I climb in and sink into the soft leather seat, suppressing a sigh of relief that I'm no longer standing in these bloody evil boots.

Gabe closes the door behind me, heads round the car and climbs in. He presses a button beside the steering wheel, making the engine start with a throaty roar. The dashboard lights up and classical music fills the car. He turns down the volume and catches the smirk on my face.

"What?"

"Classical?"

"Why? You didn't think I'd listen to classical?"

I shrug. "I dunno." I glance at his tattoos. "You just don't seem the type."

"It's relaxing. When I've got a problem to work through, it helps me think."

"Like chess."

A smile plays at the corners of his mouth at the fact I've remembered something he said. "Like chess."

I look out of the window, not entirely sure why I'm asking the next question. "So, you've got a problem?"

"A permanent one," he mutters as he pulls into the traffic.

As we head home, I fidget in my seat every few minutes because I can't get comfortable. My feet are as sore as hell and every little movement and bump in the road, causes a fresh wave of pain to slice through me. Evil boots.

"You know, you can always take them off," Gabe tells me, glancing knowingly at my feet. "Rather than sit there in pain."

I'm not going to argue.

I unzip the right boot, carefully slide it off my foot and do the same with my left. Bliss. Thank God.

"Better?"

"Much better," I agree, wiggling my toes.

"I don't get why you'd wear something that would cause you pain."

"I don't expect you to understand. It's a woman thing. I wanted to make an effort and look pretty for *my date*."

"You don't need to wear a pair of stupid boots to look pretty."

My chest tightens and I force myself to keep staring out of the window. If I'm going to make it out of the car without my knickers bursting into flames, he needs to stop saying things like that. I focus on the streetlights whizzing past the window and try to think about something else but it's difficult. The scent of leather mingles with his aftershave and turns my brain into cotton wool.

"I'm still pissed off with you," I tell him, making sure he knows his line's had no impact. "And I don't suppose I need to bother to give you my address. I'm guessing you already know it being as you know my number."

Gabe gives me a look that confirms my suspicions.

Bloody git!

"You've ruined my night," I huff.

"We've already been over this. You didn't seem too excited, from where I was sitting."

"Oh, yes, with your *friends*."

We come to a stop at some traffic lights. Gabe rests his elbow on the door. "That's right, with my *friends*."

If he was in the bar by himself, he's not admitting it.

"What did you say to Tom, anyway?" I ask worriedly, conscious I'm still in the dark about the tiny detail that made my date walk out.

"I didn't *say* anything. I told him we knew one another." Gabe catches the worried look in my eye. "For fuck's sake, Ella relax. I didn't tell him I was your boss."

That's something at least.

The lights switch to green and we start moving again. "But what *exactly* did you say to him?"

"I told him we had unfinished business and that it was probably best for him if he didn't get caught in the crossfire."

I nearly jump out of my seat. "You said fucking what? Are you insane? What the hell did you do that for!"

Gabe glances at me unperturbed. "Because it's true."

I fold my arms, seething. "No, we do not. Everything *is* finished. The day I started working for you put a big bloody full stop against whatever the hell went on, which was *nothing* in the first place."

"He didn't put up much of a fight," Gabe carries on, ignoring my tirade. "He accepted what I said and pissed off. You deserve more than that. You deserve a guy who'll fight for you."

I glare out of the window silent with rage. I can't bring myself to speak for the remainder of the journey home. The whole sorry night turns over in my mind, along with Gabe's words. I *do* deserve more than that. I deserve someone who'll give a shit. Not scamper off at the first whiff of trouble. I know Tom wasn't right for me. Now I've got to break the news of my rubbish date to my friend, the matchmaker.

Chapter 21

Ella

By the time we arrive home the weather's got worse. Rain rattles against the top of the car roof and water streams down the windscreen, making the blades struggle to clear it.

I gesture towards a gap in the line of cars parked on the side of the road. "You'll have to pull in here. There's never any room to park outside our house at night."

For once, Gabe does as he's told, pulls into the space and turns off the engine.

I hurriedly reach for my boots, desperate to get out of here. "I think it's best I go."

"You're actually going to go out in this weather. It's torrential."

"It's better than the alternative," I reply loftily, sliding my foot into the boot. But it won't go. My sore ankles are red, grazed and swollen and the boot just won't budge. I wince in discomfort and slide my foot back out. The universe is well and truly conspiring against me today. "Shit!"

"Trouble?"

I sigh and flop back into the seat defeated. "I can't get my boots back on my bloody feet. They've swollen."

Gabe shakes his head. "You'd better make sure you throw those fucking boots out when you get home." Then he jumps out of the car and I watch in stunned silence, as he darts round in front of me and flings open the passenger door.

He offers me his hand. "Come on."

"What do you mean?"

"I mean come on, I'll carry you."

He's lost it. "What? No."

"For fuck's sake, I'm getting drenched. For once, can you do as you're asked?"

His light grey t-shirt is swiftly turning black. I feel a stab of empathy and shuffle round on the seat to face him. Before I know it, his hands are beneath me and he scoops me up. I wrap my arms around his shoulders, clinging onto my boots and him as he lifts me out of the car, bumping the door closed with his hip. I hold on tight as he dashes across the pavement and up the front path to my house, taking shelter from the rain in the vestibule of the front door.

I make the mistake of looking into his eyes to find him already staring at me.

"Thank you. You need to stop doing this."

"Carrying you?"

"Rescuing me; first Saturday night and now this."

His eyes slide to my lips. "Never."

I don't want him to stop either. The realisation hits me like a train, forcing all the air from my lungs.

What am I doing? I need to be sensible.

"Maybe you should put me down."

For a few seconds he resists, then gently lowers me down. I wince as the soles of my feet hit the cold, damp tiles.

He glances at the floor. "Step onto my feet."

"What?"

"Stand on top of my feet. *Your* feet won't be cold then."

"But won't it hurt you?"

"You're as light as a feather."

I think he's mad but do as I'm told, stepping onto his feet. I wobble a bit as I get my balance and he puts his hands on my hips to steady me. He smiles. "Better?"

I nod mutely. This is wrong. I shouldn't be this close to him, but a little voice in the back of my head is telling me to go with it, because it feels so right.

He touches a lock of my hair, smoothing the ends in between his finger and thumb.

"Why do you always touch my hair?"

"Because it's wild, and untamed and beautiful. Like you."

My stomach back flips. "Don't ..."

"I want you, Ella. You know I do."

"Stop ..." I whisper, faltering at the first word. I'm struggling to breathe let alone string a sentence together.

"Do you *really* want me to stop, Princess?"

No.

"We've been through this, Gabe..." I'm determined not to let myself down and fall for any more of his lines, but he cuts me off.

"Don't. Say. My. Name. Like. That."

I want to ask why the hell not, but he lowers his lips to mine. I can't think straight. He's so close. I can feel his warm breath against my face as his breathing deepens and his eyes lock on mine.

"You're my boss."

"No. We're Gabe and Ella."

My stomach cartwheels at the possibilities his words conjure. Dangerous. Forbidden. He shouldn't be doing this. *I* shouldn't be doing this. Should I? I hate this. I'm a confident, independent woman, usually. But there's something about him that unravels me. And I'm intrigued and a tiny bit scared.

He rests his hands on my shoulders and looks deep into my eyes; like he senses my hesitance and plans on putting a stop to our dance once and for all.

"I know you don't believe me, but I don't play games..."

"Neither do I," I snap with certainty. That's the only thing I *am* certain of right this minute.

Irritation dances in his eyes. "Always with the fight."

"Oh, I'm sorry. Are you used to a more meek and mild personality in your conquests?"

"Conquests?"

"Yeah, conquests. Because that's all they are to you isn't it? The long line of models and princesses you've shagged in the past. They've just been another win."

His lips curl into a smug smile. "Sounds like someone's been Googling me."

"There're photos of you all over the internet."

"Yeah, if you search for them."

"Don't flatter yourself. If I were going to cyber stalk anyone it would be Spencer." I fix him with a fierce stare. "*He's* more my type."

I expect him to get pissed off at the out and out lie. At the very least I'm hoping that he'll get annoyed enough to leave. I need him to. If he stays he's going to do something I'll regret. I know it.

My words bounce off his Teflon coated exterior. He barely flinches and shakes his head, pinning me with his navy-blue eyes. "No. He's not."

"Anyway," I carry on, determined not to be beaten, "if anyone should be accusing anyone of stalking, *you* turned up on *my* date tonight."

"Yeah, I did. As soon as I found out you were going on a date, I couldn't stop thinking about you being with someone else."

I freeze. I had my suspicions, but to hear him admit it makes it real.

"I want to possess you, Ella. I want to know what you taste like, sound like as you come, feel like around my cock as I take you. Hard."

I suck in a sharp breath. Sparks of desire ignite deep in my belly. No one has ever spoken to me like this before. However much I've wanted them to.

He narrows his eyes knowingly. "And you want me to find out."

Oh my God.

Warm lips seal mine as he kisses me for the first time. Soft, firm and expertly hard. He tightens his grip on my waist and roughly pulls me to him, closing the distance left between us in one move, licking the length of my tongue and claiming me. My boots slip from my hands and fall to the floor with a thud. All I can think about is him. Having all of me. Fucking me. *This isn't enough.* I need more. And so does he.

He reads my mind, cupping the backs of my thighs and lifting me up against the wall with a satisfied groan. I wrap myself around him, raking my fingers through his hair and tugging him closer, moaning into his mouth, deepening the kiss. His erection stands between us, pushing against my thigh as our bodies press tight together. My stomach flips at the thought that I'm doing this to him. He wants me. And I want him. I'd let him have me right here.

"I crave you, Princess."

His simple words weave through my lust filled brain and make my centre throb with desire. He kisses me like he's running out of oxygen and I'm his air. Every inch of his taut, firm body is pressed against me, like he can't get close enough. I'm lost in him, in the kiss, in the moment of never being wanted like this ever before.

The hall light flicks on, sending light pouring through the frosted glass in the front door.

Kate.

"Stop," I gasp, pulling away. "My friend's coming." He carries on kissing me, ignoring my pleas. I close my eyes at the feel of his hot lips against my throat. It takes will power I don't even know I possess to plant my hands on his shoulders and firmly push him away. "Put me down. Now."

He looks confused, like he's not used to people telling him what to do, and for a second I'm not sure he's going to do as I've asked. After a few seconds he reluctantly lowers me down and I manage to step away from him, just as the front door swings open.

Kate pulls her white fluffy dressing gown around her tightly, her eyes widening at the sight of Gabe. "I thought I heard voices."

I scoop up my boots and try my best to act natural. If anyone's going to smell a rat it'll be Kate. "It was raining. Gabe gave me a lift."

"Right," Kate says slowly, her eyes darting between me, my boots and Gabe. "What happened to Tom?"

How the hell do I answer that? Oh, my boss turned up on our date and scared him off?

"I'll leave you to it," I hear Gabe say. I can't bring myself to look at him. Embarrassment and self-hatred coil tight within my chest. I swore I'd never let anyone like him in again.

Silly cow. What the fuck was I thinking?

Just like that, the years fall away and I feel seventeen again.

I mentally count to five and glance up to see him retreating down the path. Walking away. Just like he did the night we met at the club. Just like all men do.

Kate gives me a wry smile and I brace myself for the inevitable barrage of questions coming my way. "You my friend, have got some bloody explaining to do."

Chapter 22

Ella

I don't sleep a wink. For the first time ever I'm going to be exceptionally early for work. Ironic, given that's the one place I *really* don't want to be today.

My boss kissed me.

And I kissed him back.

I can still taste him.

This is going to be a long day.

I head downstairs needing coffee. Today's going to be as awkward as hell and I need to be mentally firing on all cylinders. As I enter the kitchen, Harry's leant against the counter with nothing but a white towel wrapped around his waist. He's on the phone and looks up when I enter.

"I need to go. I'll see you later," he mumbles, swiftly ending the call. He rubs a hand through his damp corny blond hair and gives me an awkward smile.

I grab a cup and flick the kettle on, casting a suspicious glance in his direction. "Sorry, hope I wasn't interrupting anything."

My gut's telling me something's amiss, and I can't quite put my finger on it.

"Er no, no. It was just my mum." Harry messes with his hair again and glances around the kitchen, looking shifty.

"Oh right." *Why would he look awkward about talking to his mum?*

I grab the jar of coffee out of the cupboard and twist the lid off. "Do you want one?"

Seconds pass. He doesn't reply. I look over my shoulder to check he's still there. He's still there all right. He hasn't moved a muscle. The only thing that have, are his eyes which are blatantly roaming all over my backside.

What the fuck?

I clear my throat and he looks up at me. "Have you quite finished?" I snap.

"What?

I frown. "What do you mean what, you were looking at my arse!"

He laughs with a snort, like what I've said is nonsense. "You must be imagining things. I'm a one-woman man. Unless, of course, it's wishful thinking."

What a prick!

"I don't think so."

He smirks. "Are you sure, coz I heard your date didn't go too well last night."

Bloody Kate. I turn back to making my drink. "You could say that."

"Yeah, Tom's not the most exciting of guys." Harry chuckles to himself, clearly thinking *he* must be.

The kettle comes to the boil and I fill my cup with water, giving it a stir. It's definitely going to be a strong, black coffee type of day, if my encounter with this dickhead is anything to go by.

I pick up my mug and turn round to face him. "You know, Kate's been messed around by guys in the past."

He shrugs. "Yeah, I know. What's that got to do with me?"

I fix him with a don't-mess-with-me-look. "Everything, if you two are together. I'd hate for her to be messed around."

He folds his arms and puffs out his chest like a peacock. Kate really knows how to pick them. He shakes his head dismissively. "I don't know what you're talking about. I'm not messing anyone around." He curls his lip. "I make your friend *very* happy."

I'm two seconds away from giving him a piece of my mind but bite my tongue at the sound of heels clicking down the hallway.

"There you are," Kate exclaims making a beeline for him. She throws her arms around his neck. "I wondered where you'd got to. I came out of the bathroom and you weren't in bed."

"I had to take a call." He kisses her on the cheek and gently pulls her arms from round his neck. He gives her a playful slap on the bum. "I'd better go and get ready for work, babe."

Babe. I roll my eyes.

Kate giggles watching him head out of the kitchen, with an arrogant swagger. I take a sip of hot coffee to occupy my mouth from saying something it shouldn't.

She turns to me beaming. *Oh God.* She likes him. A lot. Of course, she does. She's been stuck on him for months.

"How's everything going with you two?"

She smiles blissfully. "Wonderful."

"It's still early days though, isn't it?"

"I know, but we get on really well."

I nod and try to look a little more convinced than I feel. "Yeah, but you've not been seeing him a week yet."

Her smile fades and she flicks her hair over her shoulder. "Thanks for the vote of confidence, El. For the first time in ages I actually feel happy. I thought you'd be happy for me."

Shit! I'm making a complete hash of things.

She's right. She *is* happier than I've seen her in ages. I might not like Harry but at the moment he's putting a smile on her face. I can't shatter her loved-up bubble.

"I am happy for you. I just worry. I know how upset you were after what happened with Gav. I just don't want you rushing into things and getting hurt again."

She straightens her white work blouse and smiles. "I'm not stupid. I know this thing with Harry might not go anywhere, but for now it's going all right. I know what you mean. I'd be saying the same to you." She folds her arms and scans me up and down. "Speaking of which. You're up early?"

"Yeah, couldn't sleep."

"So? Have you thought about what you're going to do?"

I sip my coffee and run a hand through my curls, knowing full well what she's referring to. "About what?"

"About the fact you snogged the face off your boss last night."

"He kissed me first."

"And you didn't exactly fight him off by the sounds of it. I can't say I blame you though. He's smoking."

I'm fully aware of that issue.

"But he's my boss. What should I do? This is the best job I've ever had. I can't leave."

"Just keep your head down and ride it out. For a few weeks it'll be awkward, but then you'll probably both forget about it."

I'm not convinced. "Really?"

She screws up her face. "Fuck no. Honestly? I think things are going to be awkward as arse between the two of you for ages."

Great.

"Just keep out of his way."

"I work for him. I sit in the office next to his. I *can't* keep out of his way."

"Positive mental attitude. You work for his PA, who works for him, so theoretically you've slightly more of a chance of keeping out of his way. I dunno, just keep it formal and try to ignore him as best you can." Her lips twists in thought. "Although, he's pretty hard to ignore. He's so tall and big, but it's not just that, he's got this charisma hasn't he ..." She trails off, staring into space.

"Yeah, that's really helpful."

"Sorry." She shoots me an apologetic look. "To be honest I'm amazed you get any work done at all."

I'm about to demand a change of subject when the sound of a mobile ringing filters down the hall.

Kate looks at me. "That's your phone, isn't it?"

Shit!

I dash to my handbag slung over the bottom of the stairs and dig my hand inside, pulling out my phone. Margot.

"Hi, everything okay?" I ask, even though I've a horrible suspicion it isn't.

"Morning, Ella. I'm not interrupting you, am I?"

"No, not at all. I was just about to leave for work."

"Oh, good. Well, I'm glad I caught you. It's about the shop.

It's bad news, I'm afraid. We've found out the owner's selling up for apartments. The empty warehouse is being taken down too. The whole lot's going for a new housing development. That's why they want us out."

This is what I feared would happen. Mum's place gone, and with it so many of our memories of her wiped out. All in the name of profit.

"Are you okay?" Margot asks, when I don't reply.

"Yeah, it's just a shock isn't it. To think of it not being there anymore."

"The shops have been there forever. If they think we're going down without a fight, then they're mistaken." Margot scoffs. "Derek from the grocers and a couple of others are going to start a petition and design some flyers to drum up a bit of publicity about this. The local community have a right to know what's on the cards. They'll be up in arms."

"Count me in," I say, thinking back to what I've learnt in the short space of time I've been at my new job. "And it might be helpful to try someone from the council – after all, they're meant to work for us, aren't they?"

I hear a gasp of excitement down the phone as my idea lands. "What an excellent idea. I'll see what I can do. I'll be in touch."

Chapter 23

Ella

Something feels off again. But today it's not Judy. She's behind her desk, typing away on her laptop when I arrive in the office. I breathe a sigh of relief. No more one-to-one with Gabe.

"Morning, Judy. Is your husband feeling better?" I ask, hanging my coat up.

"Morning, love. Yes, thank you. He had a fall, but he's as right as rain now. Were you okay yesterday? I'm so sorry to land you in the deep end on your second day."

I sit down at my desk and switch on my laptop. "Yes, of course. Don't worry, everything was fine. The morning was back-to-back meetings, but the afternoon…" I glance at Gabe's open office door and push the memories from my lunch with him to the back of my mind, "was quieter."

"Hmm." She nods briskly, her usual sunny countenance has been replaced with a frown as she follows my gaze.

"Is everything okay?"

"Yes, yes. It's just Gabe's decided to transfer the management of one of the big projects to another team," she huffs, clearly not impressed by his decision to relieve her of some work.

"Oh, right," I say, not entirely sure how to respond. My eyes drift to his office door. "Is he in yet?"

She laughs under her breath, seemingly to herself. "No, he's not. And he's not going to be. I'm having to rearrange his schedule for the next two days."

I focus on my laptop screen and not on the unnerving feeling of disappointment in the pit of my stomach. "Oh, has there been a change of plan?"

"It would appear so." Judy heaves a sigh and flashes an apologetic smile. "Sorry to be a grump. But I'm very organised and I hate it when he throws curve balls like this my way."

"Does it happen often?"

"Almost never."

He's avoiding me because we kissed. He's probably woken up this morning regretting every single second of what happened and wondering what the fuck to do about it.

He *should* regret it, and so should I. Nothing can come of it.

***

Site visits. That's what occupies Gabe's calendar for the next two days. I don't hear from him or see him. It's like he's fallen off the face of the earth. The work still keeps on coming though and I'm glad. It helps keep my mind busy. That's what I'm here to do. Work. Nothing else, I tell myself.

Judy and I chat in the afternoons just before home time, when the office is quieter. I learn she's been married to Roger for fifteen years and has a son, daughter and a cat called Mr Tibbs. Roger took early retirement after a heart attack and triple bypass. She's the breadwinner. I tell her about Mum and her illness. In a strange way, Judy reminds me a bit of her. They're both around the same age.

By the time five o'clock on Friday rolls round, I've got a whole new pressing issue at the front of my mind which makes kissing my boss pale into insignificance.

I tidy my desk, pull on my jacket and hear the beep of my mobile from inside my handbag. I pull it out and hold my breath. It's Amy. I don't want to look. What the hell does she want this time?

GAP just called. I didn't get the job. Can you get me the money I need? x

She finishes the text with a smiley face emoji and praying hands.

My stomach turns with nerves. I can get the money, it's just what I've got to do in order to earn it.

"So, how was your first week?" Judy asks, bustling in from

the break-out area holding her clean flowery cup, ready for next week.

"Great. It seems a really nice place to work. And everyone seems really ... nice," I say meaninglessly, shoving my phone back in my bag.

Judy looks pleased at my assessment. "You've done very well. But with your experience I'd expect no less. Gabe's been very complimentary, especially given you were pretty much left to hold the fort on your own so early on. He may not have been around much the last few days but he's been keen to check in on how you're getting on."

I pull my handbag onto my shoulder and force a smile, trying hard not to read into what she's just said. "Oh, that's good to hear."

"It's refreshing."

"What is?"

Judy puts her cup down on her desk and gives me a measured look. "We've had a few girls in your role over the past five years. *Quite* a few. A couple stayed for a few years and went onto new jobs, but the others" – she hesitates as though she's trying to decide whether she should be telling me this or not – "they were dismissed."

"Dismissed?"

"Some were bright young things with lots of potential, very much like yourself. It saddened me to see them go."

"Why were they dismissed?"

"Because they let their emotions get in the way of the job."

I frown, more confused than ever. "What emotions?"

"Like I've said, I've worked here from the start. I've known the three boys since they were little and they've all inherited their father's charm in one way or another. Not only that, everyone knows the White family, which makes them even more appealing. Some of the girls became rather taken with Gabe. *Very* taken, in some cases. And we had to let them go. It was affecting their performance."

I grip the strap of my handbag tight. I feel sick. "What are you saying?" I ask, not entirely sure I want to hear this. "Gabe fired them, because they ... fell for him?"

"Without hesitation. He's far too straight down-the-line for all that nonsense. And he's got far too much at stake to be fraternising with his staff."

I fight to keep my expression neutral. If that's true, then what the fuck's been going on between us?

Uneasiness twists like a knife in my side as an unwelcome thought hits me. All the pieces slot together. What if he does that with all the women? Judy *says* he's not like that, but how does she really know? What if he reels them in, just like I fear he's doing with me. The night we met. Outside my house. What if he takes what he wants and then sacks them, so he can move onto the next one? Or, what if he tries it on and then sacks them if he *doesn't* get what he wants. It would explain everything; the way he walked away, the fact I haven't heard from him since. That's why he's not been in the office the last two days. The bastard's warming up to fire me.

Judy smiles fondly, oblivious to the inner turmoil I'm going through. "It's such a refreshing change to have someone like you working here. You've got a sensible head on your shoulders and I know you won't get drawn into any silliness like that."

Just when I thought I couldn't feel any worse, Judy proves me wrong.

***

I check the clock on my phone for the tenth time in two minutes. Six thirty. Tonight's one of those things I *cannot* be late for. I've too much riding on it. Well, Amy's stay at university and everything but my self-respect. That's got to be left at the door. The same as every other time I've done it.

I stuff my false eyelashes into my black leather satchel and pull on my short black leather jacket, catching my reflection in the bedroom mirror. Skinny ripped black jeans, white t-shirt, black and white Converse pumps and zero make-up. A far cry from what I'll look like in an hour and a half.

I grab my things and head downstairs, relieved to hear shrieks of laughter coming from Kate's bedroom. It sounds like she's preoccupied with Horny Harry. Good. I need to slip out unnoticed otherwise I'm in for the third degree. She'll flip her lid if she finds out where I'm going and I don't need the added stress.

I scoop my keys up off the hall table and I'm just about to open the front door and make my escape when I hear, "Where are you going?"

Shit.

So near, yet so far.

I freeze with my hand on the door latch and glance over my shoulder to see Kate walking downstairs, looking perplexed. I feel like a teenager caught trying to skulk out of the house at night.

"Shouldn't you be with Harry?"

"I was just coming downstairs to make us a hot chocolate." She eyes what I'm wearing suspiciously. "Where are you going?"

"I'm just popping out."

"I can see that, but where?"

There's nothing left for it. I'm going to have to fess up. All the time I'm standing here I'm not on my way. "Amy texted me a few days ago. She needs some money to buy some stuff for her degree otherwise they'll throw her off her course."

Kate rolls her eyes. "That bloody sister of yours! I've told you, Ella …"

"I know. I know she's spoilt and it's about time she stood on her own two bloody feet, but she's got no one else, Kate. If she doesn't get the money by Monday they'll throw her off her degree and I don't want that. Mum wouldn't have either."

"I know," she says softly. "But that still doesn't explain why your sneaking out the house at half six on a Friday." As the last word leaves her lips, her eyes widen in knowing. She presses a hand to her forehead. "You're not … tell me you're not going to do what I think you're going to do?"

"I've got no choice."

"You said you weren't going to do it again."

"It's just for tonight."

"That bloody sister of yours!" Kate snaps. "How much money do you need?"

"Two fifty."

"Fucking hell. You know I'd help you if I could, but I don't have that sort of spare cash."

"I know you would."

Kate blows out a long breath and angrily shakes her head. "The next time I see Amy, I swear to fucking God."

"Like I say, it's just for tonight."

"I just worry about you …"

"It's fine." I cut her off because I don't want to think about it. I'll be living it soon enough. "I've done it loads of times before. I'll be back by midnight."

Chapter 24

Ella

"All right, Ella. Long time no see." Dave, the doorman, who's usually standing guard at the stage door, greets me with a grin.

My nerves abate slightly at the sight of a familiar face. "Evening. How's your mum?"

"Good, thanks. The last hip op she had sorted her right out. Sorry to hear about yours."

I force a smile because I don't think I'll ever get used to people's well wishes. "Thanks. Is Red in tonight?"

Dave glances at his watch. "Of course, it's Friday night. She's warming them up for the main act as we speak." He smiles and nods towards backstage. "Go on in, before you catch cold."

There's something oddly comforting about the sound of laughter echoing down the corridor from the dressing room, against the backdrop of Beyoncé's 'Partition'. It's Red's signature tune and I can tell by the mounting beat that her act is reaching its climax.

I reach the manager's office and I knock on the door. Nerves flurry in my stomach. I did not expect to be doing this again. I pause for a few seconds out of courtesy, then push the door open.

Big Steve's leaning against the desk staring up at the wall of TV screens showing CCTV footage of the club. He grins. "Ella, good to see you. How've you been?"

"Fine. Thanks for letting me do this as a one off, I need ..."

"It's fine," he cuts in, sensing my awkwardness. He gives me an understanding smile. "I'm not going to turn you down if you ask to come back, even if it is just for one night."

I fiddle with the zip of my jacket, thankful he's being so nice about it all. I was so relieved the previous owner, Art Black, passed on the ownership of the club to Big Steve when he decided to call it a day. The girls couldn't ask for a nicer guy to work for.

I smile. "How's Lucy?"

He grins. "*They're* both grand."

"Both?" My eyes widen in surprise as I realise what he's getting at. "Don't tell me you're expecting?"

He folds his arms, looking as proud as punch. "Yep. Six months."

"Wow, congratulations to you both."

"Yeah, well, we planned on getting married first but ever since Art and Sophie had little Mia, Lucy's been as broody as hell." He chuckles. "And me, come to think of it. So, yeah, it's all change." He looks at me. "How about you? You doing okay since your mum?"

"Yeah, fine," I reply automatically. "Amy's doing my head in, even though she's not at home anymore."

His mobile starts to ring and he pulls it from the pocket of his black jeans, glancing at the screen. "Sorry, Ella. It's Luce. She probably wants me to pick up pizza on my way home from work. Cravings and all that. You okay for tonight?"

The mention of "tonight" causes my stomach to tighten. I force a smile. "Sure, I'd better go get ready."

There's no backing out now.

***

The dressing room is a predictable hive of activity. Girls are everywhere; tweaking their outfits, preening and beautifying themselves, all in the name of work. You look good, you attract more attention, you earn more money. And that's the reason we're all here. Not because we enjoy parading round half-naked in a room full of mostly men, but because we need the cash.

Five dressing tables with illuminated mirrors line the right-hand wall, each one occupied. The rest of the room is made up of changing booths and several clothes rails filled with outfits, hair extensions, wigs and all sorts of dressing-up paraphernalia, just as I remember.

"Sweetie!"

I turn round to see Red heading towards me. Her trademark flame coloured hair trails down her back to her bum. She's wearing a black PVC bra and hot pants, fishnets, and five-inch heels to finish off the look. She's been here forever and always looked out for me.

"Hi, Red."

"Come here." She pulls me into a bear hug, then looks me up and down. "You look good. When Big Steve said you were performing tonight I couldn't believe it. How you doing?"

"Yeah, good."

She lets go of me and puts her hands on my shoulders. "You ain't doing *that* good, otherwise you wouldn't be back here."

I wrinkle my nose. "I know, it's just ..."

"You don't have to go into it. Just as long as you're okay."

"I am." I smile. *I am.* In the main.

Her scarlet lips widen into a smile. "Come on. I've sorted your old outfit ready for you."

Thirty minutes later, I've transformed into another version of me. False eyelashes, bright red fingernails, a bit of body glitter and a tonne of make-up. As I stare at my reflection in the dressing table mirror, I look nothing like little old Ella Anderson. And I'm glad; it helps me to slip into the character I need to be for the next half an hour.

"You've still got it, lovely." Red stands behind me and rearranges my hair which has been tweaked and smoothed so the chestnut waves fall effortlessly over my chest. "Your tits always did look fab in that basque."

Fab. They're bordering on obscene. I haven't got the most generous of bosoms but the black corset forces them three inches higher than normal. I'm glad my act doesn't involve any running about, because otherwise I'd have a serious wardrobe malfunction.

I worry my red lip and ask the next question out of necessity rather than choice. I need to know. I can't afford to freeze and if anyone's going to give it to me straight it will be Red. "How busy is it out there?"

"Honestly? Rammed, even for a Friday, but you got this." She rests her hands on my shoulders and looks at me through the mirror. "You'll knock 'em dead. You always do."

I need to. I haven't got a choice.

***

The knot of nerves in my stomach tightens as I head through the backstage door and up the couple of steps onto the stage in the darkness. I've not worn stilettos this high since the last time I performed. I'm part relieved how easily I've adjusted to walking in them again. I pray to God everything else comes back to me as quickly tonight.

Right now, the only thing that's separating me from the crowd is a black velvet curtain. The loud hum of conversation and chink of glasses drown out the dance track that's playing in the background. Red was right. The place is humming.

Fuck.

"Hey, you ready to start?" A black-clad stagehand calls from the other side of the stage.

It's now or never. "Sure."

He gives a nod and disappears off behind a curtain stage-right.

There's no backing out now.

I stand behind the single black chair on centre stage and turn my back to the audience, briefly giving myself the once over. My black stockings are attached to the basque and my chest's still inside my corset. So far, so good.

The music quietens and with it the chatter of the punters.

I close my eyes, put my hands on my hips and take two deep, steadying breaths in.

You can do this. You performed almost every Saturday night for nearly two years. You'll be fine.

"Now we've got an extra special treat for you this evening." The announcer's voice booms over the mic and interrupts my focus. A couple of male whoops come from the other side of the curtain.

Fuckety-fuck.

I need to calm down and adopt my old strategy for keeping the nerves at bay. Pick out a guy in the audience and focus just on him. Zone all the other fuckers out. In five minutes it'll all be over and I'll be three hundred quid richer.

"Hold on to your hats gentlemen, because for one night only we bring you the beautiful, seductive temptress that is Amber Rue."

The opening bars of 'River' by Bishop Briggs start up, drowning out the male cheers. My eyes snap open as I feel a breeze against my back as the curtains part. The wolf-whistles coming from behind tell me I'm on show. They ain't seen nothing yet. The audience is mine and they don't even know it. For the next five minutes it's my job to make every guy in the house want to fuck me.

Chapter 25

Gabe

I take another sip of whisky, wincing as it burns my throat on the way down. This is meant to be their best stuff? Mind you, the quality of whisky on sale isn't what draws the customers here.

"How about another?" Jake spies my empty and beckons over a waitress.

"Count me in." Diego flashes a smarmy grin, the same one he's been wearing all night. The one that makes me want to punch him.

He relaxes back in the padded chair and runs a hand over his black slicked back hair, eyeing up a passing girl. Fuck knows how many drinks he's had. Too many. Ordering two at a time. This is a business meeting. I don't need him pissed, I need him coherent and giving me his fucking word. Not knocking back shots and staring at tits and arse. He's taking advantage, drawing out the deal because I said tonight's on me, and he's getting his fill. Jake told me he'd sorted it for tonight. He *did not* tell me we were coming to a strip club. But now I've met Diego I wouldn't expect anything less. He's got lecherous fucker written all over him.

"Hey, babe. You're looking mighty fine," he purrs lasciviously at the waitress who's come to take our drinks order. She gives him a funny look and turns her attention to Jake and I.

"What can I get you, gentlemen?"

"Two tequilas and a Scotch on the rocks," Jake tells her.

"None for me."

"Come on, Gabe, it's Friday," he coaxes.

"Yeah, come on, Gabe," Diego echoes with a smirk.

I swear to God this fucker's walking on thin ice.

"I said I'm good."

Jake gets the hint. "In that case just the tequilas."

Diego's eyes remained glued on the waitress's backside as she leaves.

"You should have had another drink." Jake shoots me a pointed look. He can tell I'm wound up, and this is his way of telling me to chill out.

"I've already had one and I'm driving," I say, knowing that's only part of the reason I'm taking it easy. I need to keep a clear head. This is a deal that should have wrapped up half an hour ago. I'm getting tetchy. After the week I've had, all I want to do is go home, turn my phone off and sink a few *decent* whiskies. I've got nothing against strip clubs; this one's got a good reputation, a guy I went to Oxford with used to own it, but I prefer barely dressed women in my bed back home.

I give Diego a firm look. "It's time to talk business."

He tosses his head back with a snort. "What's the rush, man. We're all having a good time here."

"I'm a busy guy. Got places to be, people to see. You know why we're here."

His dark eyes narrow. "Yeah, this is the bit where I name my price."

My fingers tighten around my empty glass. If this guy were any other fucker he'd have my hand around his neck. He's a cocky prick for someone who's been made bankrupt twice. In fact, there's not much I don't know about Diego Martinez, thanks to the background checks I've had run. This guy would sell his own mother if he thought he'd make some money. His arrogance is misplaced and it's gnawing away at my patience.

"Within reason," I warn.

"Two million."

Two million pounds to seal the deal. It's one million more than the others offered him. But it's worth it. That kind of money is a mere drop in the ocean and we're set to make it back three-fold within the first quarter.

For a split second there's a flicker of hesitance in his shifty eyes as he watches me, unsure which way I'm going to go. Jake's engrossed in the pole dancer on stage, barely listening to our conversation. There's no need for him to. He knows exactly which way I'm going.

"Two million and it's ours?" I check, because I don't trust this guy as far as I could throw him.

Diego nods. "It's yours."

"Then we have a deal." I stick my hand out and he takes it, giving it a quick shake. "I'll instruct my legal team to draw up a contract on Monday, then we can sort out payment."

"Nice doing business with you, Mr White." He sinks back into the chair, grinning from ear to ear, pound signs rolling in his eyes.

He's happy. I'm happy. Kind of. I'd rather not have to do business with a slippery little shit like him, but needs must.

"Tonight's been a … pleasure, but I need to dash, gentlemen."

"Ain't you stopping to watch the main act?" Diego points at the stage. "Whoever she is, she's drawn a crowd."

I skim my eyes across the club as the house lights go down. The place was busy when we arrived but now each one of the tables in front of the stage is filled with customers, and those that can't get a seat are standing up by the bar at the back.

"Now we've got an extra special treat for you this evening," a male voice announces over the mic, "hold on to your hats gentlemen, because for one night only, we bring you the beautiful, seductive temptress that is Amber Rue."

I guess I'm staying.

"This is going to be good." Jake shifts in his seat, getting comfy. He's making the most of tonight. If Andi knew he were here, she'd cut his balls off.

The opening beats of a song echo around the club and the black stage curtain swings open. The girl stands centre stage with her back to the audience beneath the glare of the spotlight. She looks tiny, standing alone with nothing but a solitary black chair to keep her company. Black stockings and a basque cling to her petite hour-glass figure, and deep brown hair cascades over her shoulders in waves. Just like Ella's.

And she's back. The woman I've worked damned hard to forget about over the last forty-eight hours has reclaimed her spot, right at the front of my mind.

I shunt all thoughts of her to the back of my brain where they need to stay. I overstepped the line by kissing her; letting my cock rule my brain, something I don't do. I'm not my stupid little brother who struggles to keep his dick in his trousers. I keep the family image clean. Not risk everything by fucking my PA. The easiest solution is to let her go. The only way round this is to get her out of my life once and for all, I tell myself, but the idea lands flat. She's good at her job, one of the best we've had in the role. That's the only reason the thought of never seeing her again leaves a bitter taste in my mouth. It has to be.

The stripper slowly moves round to the side of the chair, swinging her hips seductively, distracting me from my tumultuous thoughts. She plants her foot on the chair in time to the beat of the music, running her hand down her fishnet clad thigh and swooshing her hair forward so it covers her face. She's good. Sexy. Tempting. Hot as fuck. Another beat drops as the vocals kick in.

She flicks her hair back to reveal a beautiful face that looks far too familiar.

It can't be.

She walks round to the back of the chair, looking into the audience. I know that face, I've studied every beautiful angle of it. The cheekbones, the bee-stung lips.

My heartbeat screeches to a halt.

Ella-fucking-Anderson.

"Isn't that … ?" Jake begins but I hold up a hand to silence him, without tearing my eyes away from her. Who am I kidding? I couldn't, if I wanted to.

She sashays round to the front of the seat and sits down, pushing her legs apart, eyes scanning the audience like she's searching for someone. Our eyes lock. She doesn't miss a beat, steadily keeping my gaze as she runs her hands down her thighs, looking at me until the last possible moment when she dips her head and swings her hair from side to side.

My cock tightens like it's got its own radar for her. I don't know what the fuck to think. This woman's got a knack of knocking me on my arse. Half of me wants to rush up there, throw her over my shoulder and get her out of here; away from these sleazy guys who're all enjoying every minute of this. But the truth is, I'm no exception. I'm rooted to my seat. Fucking hell, I'm scared to blink in case I miss a second of her. I'm transfixed, along with every other punter in the house. And it's not hard to see why she has this spellbinding effect. Smooth porcelain skin peeks temptingly from beneath black lace. I can still smell her sweet perfume and remember the feel of her in my hands as we kissed. The way our bodies moulded together. She admitted she wants to be controlled in bed. Fucking hell, the things I'd do to her.

The wall I've spent the last two days carefully building between us crumbles with every second she carries on working the room. Logic and rational thought are chased away by pure, hot-blooded need. I'm hypnotised as she casts her seductive spell and takes control of every cock in the room, including my own.

She twists the chair round and sits down, legs open wide for her grand finale. The music starts to fade and she drops her head as her act closes.

A chorus of wolf-whistles and cheers erupt from the audience as the curtains close. I stare at the swathe of black velvet hiding her from view, bringing me hurtling back down to the earth with a bump. A million questions rush me.

And I'm not stopping until I get some answers.

Chapter 26

Ella

I'm in the chair in the dressing room with no idea how I got here. I walked off stage on autopilot. The commotion and noise from the other girls fades into the background. I'm reeling. What just happened?

Gabe-fucking-White. That's what just happened.

My secret's out in the most spectacular fashion. Of all the people to be here tonight, it had to be my boss. The guy I kissed. The man who's been avoiding me and who's most likely lining up to sack me. There's no getting out of it. He recognised me, all right. He didn't take his eyes off me, but I couldn't read his reaction. In true Gabe style, he gave little away.

"Whoop, whoop, I told you, you've still got it, girl," Red cries, bouncing up behind me. "You slayed them out there. When I was on my way back here, a guy stopped me and asked about having a private dance with you." She waggles her eyebrows at me in the mirror.

Her words push Gabe out of my mind. "No chance. This was one night. One dance. I'm done."

"He said you could name your price."

I freeze. I can earn the most through private dances, and during the entire two years I worked here, I was never made an offer like this. "He said what?"

She breaks out into a smile at my stunned reaction. "He said you could name your price, and, at the risk of sounding unprofessional, it wouldn't be a chore if you catch my drift, because he's fucking hot."

Shit! Why the fuck does life like throwing a spanner in the works?

"You came back for the money, right?" Red says, sensing my hesitance. "I say do it. One dance. Name your price. You've already done the hard bit, out there."

I know she's right. Tonight's performance will cover the money Amy needs, but a lap dance will mean I don't spend the next few weeks living in fear of maxing out my overdraft.

Sod it.

I take a deep breath, not quite believing what I'm about to say but I need to strike while the iron's hot. "Okay, I'll do it."

Red smiles. "Good. I thought you'd say that. I've shown him into booth one. He's waiting for you."

***

I touch up my make-up and spritz myself with perfume, mentally steeling myself for what I'm about to do. I've not given a private dance in a while, but like tonight proved, I've still got it. There's no room for nerves now.

The VIP area is away from the main club and has a quieter, subdued vibe. Booths line the left-hand side of the room where the dances take place. Low lighting adds to the low-key feel and deep purple curtains separate each section, allowing dancers and customers to have total privacy.

Faint chatter from the other booths can be heard above the backing track as I arrive outside booth one. I give myself a minute.

You can do this. Five more minutes. It's all about the money.

I part the curtain and slip inside.

And stop.

All the oxygen leaves my lungs.

Gabe's sitting on the black leather sofa with his arms draped over the back in that annoyingly cool, calm and collected way of his. He's dressed smartly casual; in black jeans, a white shirt, open at the collar and with the sleeves pushed back, displaying his ink. Desire wraps itself around my heart and squeezes. The last time I saw him this close up his tongue was in my mouth and we were practically dry-humping against my front door.

I crave you.

His words from that night threaten my focus. I can't allow them to. Not when the entire notion of what's about to happen is so completely wrong.

His gaze rakes up the length of my body. There's nothing cool about the fire in his eyes as they level with mine. My skin gooses. My mind's a mess. Shock and anger take over. I close my mouth that's fallen open in surprise and force my brain to form a sentence.

"Is this some sort of joke?"

He cocks his head enquiringly, lifting an eyebrow. "I was about to ask you the same thing."

"I'm not fucking dancing for you."

"I don't want you to dance for me."

I fold my arms. "Then why did you ask for a private dance?"

"Because I want you to tell me why the fuck a woman like you, is doing this."

"How dare you come here, judging me. You don't know anything about me."

"Why? Why are you working here" – he pauses as if he doesn't want to say the next word – "stripping."

"Did you see me remove my clothes? No. I'm not a fucking stripper. I'm a dancer."

Gabe shifts to the edge of the seat. "Don't split hairs. Why?"

"Are you serious? Why do you think? Money. The same reason every woman works here. To make money. Lots of it. Fast."

"Your only option is to dance half-naked for a room full of strange men?"

"I didn't see you complaining. In fact, you couldn't take your eyes off me," I point out.

Gabe drops his gaze. "Don't change the subject. You're better than this. If it's money you need, you could have come to me for help."

"I'm not a fucking charity case. I don't need your help. I don't need anyone's help. I'm fine by myself. Always have been, always will be."

He jumps to his feet, his calm countenance cracking. "Clearly you're not fine, if you have to resort to – selling your body."

I see red. "Don't you dare stand there, preaching at me when you have zero fucking clue what it's like in the real world. Money's not an issue for you. You've always had it. You're just another well-off prick, living in his ivory tower. So detached from reality it hurts."

He draws his head back as my words land. "Good to know what you think of me. Even if it is completely fucking wrong."

The curtain behind me swings open and a burly bouncer steps inside. "Everything okay in here?" he asks, eyeing Gabe suspiciously.

Of course, there's CCTV everywhere.

"Yes," I announce. "The gentleman was just leaving."

And with that, I spin on my heel and storm out.

**

Red's gone back to work by the time I get back to my dressing room. I'm relieved. She'd want a blow-by-blow account of my private dance with the "hot guy" and I'd have to lie. There's no way I could tell her the truth. That he was my boss. My boss who kissed me. Who watched me perform. Who managed to insult my dignity and pride in one fail swoop by offering me money like I'm a charity case.

Fuck him.

I scrub my make-up off, step out of my outfit and pull on my own clothes. Within ten minutes Ella Anderson's back and Amber's left the building.

I say goodbye to the girls, tell them to let Red know I'll text her later and head towards the backstage door.

"Ella!"

I stop at the sound of my name being called. All I want to do is go home, have a bath, consume half a bottle of white wine to blot out the catastrophe that this evening's turned out to be, and draft my email of resignation ready for Monday.

Pixie, one of the dancers, heads towards me holding something.

I smile. "Hey. You just caught me, I was about to leave."

"Yeah, you'll be glad I did. Mick asked me to give you this." She thrusts a wad of notes into my hand.

I frown. Payments for performances are usually paid directly into my bank account. "Who's Mick? What's this for?"

"One of the bouncers. It's for the private dance. Your guy gave it to him. I thought it was a bit odd," she continues, clearly seeing the look of confusion on my face. "I mean usually they pay directly, don't they. But Mick says the guy said there'd been a bit of a misunderstanding."

I stare down at the money in my hand. All pink notes. Christ knows how many fifties. I reckon there's easily two grand in cash. I've never seen so much money before in my life.

Fury ignites in my gut as my brain catches up. Gabe. After everything I said about not wanting his charity. I told him I didn't want his cash and he's forced it on me anyway.

I give her a tight smile. "Sure, thanks Pixie."

"Cheer up, Ella. If I'd have just landed a tip like that I'd be celebrating." She smirks. "Whoever he was, you damn sure made an impression on him."

I stuff the money into my bag. I'm about to leave another.

Chapter 27

Ella

Drops of rain splatter against the window of the Uber as I stare out into the night. The starkly modern high-rise apartment block stretches upwards in the darkness, dwarfing the buildings either side of it. I should be going home. But I can't. I'm going to end this. Tonight. I'm here to tell Gabe to stick his money and his job, and I'm going to walk out with my self-respect intact.

The inside looks just as grand as the outside. A dark grey slate floor stretches on and on, disappearing round a corner. Seating areas with trendy white bucket seats and low-backed leather sofas occupy either side of the lobby and a light grey, polished marble reception desk sits in the centre of the foyer with *The Madison* engraved on the front. An ostentatious looking arrangement of white lilies sit on one end of the desk. This is exactly the type of place I expected Gabe to live. Slick. Hip. Modern and soulless.

The concierge, a grey-haired middle-aged man, flashes a polite smile as I approach the desk.

"Good evening, madam. Welcome to The Madison, how may I help you?"

"Hi, I'm here to see Gabe White."

The concierge hesitates. I see questions in his grey eyes as he takes me in. I'm guessing the type of women who have previously rocked up asking after Gabe weren't wearing ripped jeans and trainers.

"Certainly, madam. I'll see if Mr White's available. Is he expecting you?"

He has no fucking clue what's about to arrive on his doorstep. "No."

He nods, taps away at the keyboard in front of him, and

picks up a phone. "One moment please." I hear the sound of a phone ringing out, then it stops. "Good evening, Mr White. This is the concierge. There's a young lady arrived in reception, asking to see you." He looks at me. "What's your name please?"

"Ella."

I chew my thumbnail. There's a significant possibility that Gabe's going to tell him, to tell me, to get packing.

"Ella." The concierge repeats down the phone. He gives a nod. "Certainly. Right away, sir."

He puts the receiver down and gets to his feet. "This way, please, madam."

For a moment I worry that Gabe *has* instructed him to sling me out, and I'm being escorted off the premises, but then the concierge starts to head across the lobby towards two lifts at the back of the foyer.

He gestures with his hand towards the first waiting lift. "Please, madam, this way."

Once I've stepped inside, he retrieves a card from the front pocket of his smart navy uniform, and swipes it through the card reader inside the lift. "This will take you to the desired floor." He steps back as the doors start to close. There's a twinkle in his eye and he smiles. "Have a good evening, madam."

I force a polite smile, knowing that I will one hundred per cent absolutely not have anything approaching a good evening.

The lift ride up takes forever, prolonging the agony of our inevitable showdown. I find myself running through what I'm going to do; the thought of knocking on his door, throwing his money at him and giving him what for, seems very appealing. Eventually the lift comes to a stop and the doors open.

A hallway stretches out ahead of me with doors leading off in either direction. Floor-to-ceiling windows at the very end provide a glorious, unadulterated view of the London skyline at night. The soft notes of classical music turned down low float through the apartment. I'm taken aback. I didn't expect the lift to bring me right into Gabe's apartment. *But of course, why not,* I think cynically. The super-rich are clearly far too important for menial tasks such as opening their own front doors.

I roll my eyes and head down the hall, glancing through the doors leading off either side and spy a bedroom, bathroom and office. Pieces of art hang from the light grey walls, but to my untrained eye they look like a mass of different brushstrokes in various shades of greys and purples; like something a child would paint. I've no doubt they're ludicrously expensive. As I reach the end of the hallway the apartment opens up into a huge open-plan living space. A smartly modern, integrated pale grey kitchen stretches across the right-hand side of the apartment. A circular white six-seater dining room table and chairs stand in front of a set of doors that lead outside onto a terrace. A floral arrangement of white lilies, similar to the flowers in the lobby, are displayed in a clear glass vase in the centre of the table. To the left; a large, low-backed L-shaped sofa looks out across the Thames with a frosted-glass coffee table in front. Both stand on the largest fluffy white rug I have ever seen. The same strange-looking pieces of art are hung around the white walls, showing swirls and brush marks of different colours, but are all in keeping with the dialled back, neutral vibe of the décor. Everything's immaculate and in its rightful place. It doesn't look lived in. It looks like an eye-wateringly expensive show home.

"'Clair de Lune' helps me unwind."

The sound of Gabe's voice pulls my attention to the single, charcoal grey armchair over to the left. He's sitting with his back to me, looking out across the city.

The fact he can't even be arsed to get up and face me like a man irks me.

Cocky prick.

He'd better get ready.

I storm over to where he sits, looking totally relaxed with his bare foot propped on his knee. He's changed into a white t-shirt that fits him like a glove, and grey sweatpants. He lifts a tumbler of amber liquid, which I presume is whisky, to his lips and takes a long sip, without looking at me. He's purposefully stretching out the moment between us and winding me up like a spring in the process. And I don't care how hot he looks, it's not going to distract me from how fucking mad I am.

Arsehole.

He slowly puts the glass down on a side table next to him continuing to draw things out.

I'll show him.

I pull my bag off my shoulder, dig my hand inside and pull out the wad of notes. "Firstly, I've come to return this. I specifically said I *do not* want your money."

Gabe's eyes slide from the cash to me. "It's yours."

"No, it's *yours*. I thought I made myself pretty clear when I said I don't want your bloody charity."

"It's not charity…"

"Oh, give it a rest. Of course, it is. I saw it in your eyes back at the club. Pity. Well, I don't need your pity and I don't need your fucking money either."

His brow creases in irritation. "You think I pity you?"

"The answer to everything in life isn't to throw money at it, but I'm guessing in *your* life that's been the solution to everything."

"Tonight you said that I know nothing about you, but we're more similar than you think."

I laugh. I can't help it. "Are you for real? You and I are polar opposites. You have no idea what I've been through. So, don't you sit there and tell me we're the same."

"You'd be surprised."

"Bullshit. We're from two totally different worlds. Let me guess, you've had a private education, probably went to Oxford or Cambridge or somewhere like that. Were given a job at daddy's billion-pound property firm straight out of uni. Tell me I'm wrong."

He glares at me in silence. I carry on, pleased that I'm finally getting some sort of reaction. "Have you ever had to worry about how you're going to afford to pay the next gas bill, or how you're going to buy next week's shopping so that you can feed your little sister and terminally ill mum?" I pause to make my point. He remains silent. "No, didn't think so. I managed then and I'm managing now. On my own."

I drop the pile of notes onto the coffee table. A few notes float onto the rug. Neither of us make any attempt to pick them up.

"You think you're the first person to judge me because of my family's wealth?" He angrily shakes his head. "Sorry to disappoint you, but you're not. My life hasn't been a bed of roses. Growing up with money brings its own set of problems."

"I'm damn sure it solves a few as well," I snap.

He swipes his glass from the side table and gets to his feet, downing his drink in one and slamming the tumbler back down.

"What's with all the hostility?" He takes a step towards me and I instinctively step back. He can't get close to me. Bad things happen when we get too close. He narrows his eyes like he's trying to work something out. "Like I said before, you're not jealous."

"Too fucking right I'm not."

"Then what? Why do you hate people who've had a privileged upbringing? What's happened to you?" He pauses as a thought strikes him. "*Who's* happened to you?"

I tilt my chin upwards and fix him a defiant stare. He's getting too close to the truth and I don't like it one bit.

"Spare me the deep and meaningful. I'm not interested. I came here to give you your money back and to hand in my resignation."

"I don't accept it."

"Fine, but don't expect me to turn up for work on Monday."

"You said it's the best job you've ever had."

It is. By far. The thought of what I'm giving up makes my voice weaken and I hate myself. "It's wrong. You're my boss, we can't…"

"I won't let you go."

The commitment in his voice sends a shiver down my spine. I can't afford to read into it. "What, are you disappointed I got in there first and resigned before you could sack me?"

His brow twitches into a frown. "What?"

"Judy told me about some of my predecessors. How you sacked some of them because they developed feelings for you. Does it boost your ego to know the hired help fancies you – or was it more than that? Does Judy only know half of the sticky tale? Did you reel them in, just like you were doing with me? Did you fuck them? Is that why you had to get rid of them? You'd got what you wanted out of them and then they were superfluous? Or maybe they didn't put out and it dented your ego? Is that what it's all been about with me? Gate crashing my blind date, kissing me. 'I crave you.'" I pull a face and mimic him. "Bullshit, Gabe. You've been out of the office for two days. You're lining up to firing me?"

Before I can blink his hands are on my shoulders and he pushes me backwards against the window. All the breath leaves my body as my back slams against the glass. He covers my mouth with his hand and inches his face closer until the tips of our noses touch. One hand remains on my shoulder, keeping me in place. Piercing eyes burn into me. Every nerve ending in my body tingles at the closeness and the feel of his heavy hand on my mouth, silencing me.

"You need to shut the fuck up and listen. I don't pity you. You did what you needed to do to look after your family. You've made sacrifices and put their needs above your own for years. Fucking hell, Ella, I *admire* you."

I'm floored. I want to quip that he's throwing me another line, but can't. His hand's still over my mouth. I suspect he's far from finished putting me in my place and the serious look in his eye tells me he means what he's saying.

"I didn't give you the money out of charity. I gave it to you because I wanted to make sure you never have to go back to that club again and dance. I need to know no more men are going to see you looking like you did tonight. Ever."

My heart thuds in my chest at his possessiveness. The most Ryan did was accuse me of being a slut when he found out I worked there. He never delved deeper and asked why I was doing it; tried to help me, gave enough of a shit.

"In the VIP area tonight, I went in all guns blazing and I shouldn't have …" He trails off, his beautiful eyes searching my face looking for the right words. "I shouldn't have judged you. I was still in shock at seeing you in the club. I was there on business."

I roll my eyes in disbelief and he grips my mouth tighter. "I was there on business. The *client* chose to go to Dark Desires. It was pure chance. I was about to leave and then you appear looking like a wet fucking dream." His jaw tightens. "Everything Judy told you about the other girls was right. As soon as I realised … I stopped it dead. Nothing happened. With any of them. I don't fuck my staff. So, you *are* right about one thing. Me and you, we shouldn't." Even though I know it's true, even though *I* said it, my heart plummets to my feet. "I shouldn't have turned up on your blind date. I shouldn't have kissed you. You shouldn't be here. We shouldn't be this close. I'm your boss, you're my employee, we can't kiss, we can't touch" – he shakes his head and looks like a lost little boy – "we can't fuck. Because I'm the CEO with the glowing rep and if we cross that line we're risking everything." With every word he leans into me a little closer, his body contradicting his words. "I've spent the last two days trying hard to get you out of my head. And do you know what I realised? I don't want to get you out of my head."

Fuck.

He slowly removes his hand from my mouth and steps back, looking at me. Then he moves closer again and leans against the glass, his hands on either side of my head. My gaze falls to his perfect mouth and I'm remembering what his soft lips felt like on mine.

Kiss me.

"Tell me you're not going to resign."

My eyes snap to his and I push my improper thoughts to the back of my mind.

"You're right, I shouldn't be here. You need to let me go home," I tell him, knowing full well that if I wanted to duck beneath his arms and leave, there's nothing to stop me.

"I'll let you go, once you promise not to resign."

"I don't understand. You've just stood there and pointed out all the reasons why nothing can happen between us and yet you won't let me resign. You're full of fucking contradictions."

"Because of you," he snaps. Anger burns bright in his eyes. "I was in control of everything, until *you* came along."

"Don't blame me. It's not my fault that you … you like me."

His top lip curls. "I more than like you."

My core tightens at his words. I fight it. "This! This right here is why I need to resign."

His voice rises to meet mine. "You're not resigning."

"Yes, I am! It's the only way I can get away from you."

"I don't want you to get away from me."

We're both incensed, shouting in one another's faces.

"Well, tough shit. I'm resigning"

"I don't want you to!"

"Whyever the fuck not?"

"Because I can't not see you again."

Chapter 28

Ella

The apartment falls silent. My mind's racing at a mile a minute.

He can't mean it. Because if he does ... he just absolutely can't.

Gabe's jaw twitches with tension. His brow pulls into a deep frown as he stares down at me.

"You're angry?" I'm stating the obvious but right at the moment it's the best I can do.

"Fuming."

I swipe my tongue over my bottom lip. His eyes drop to the movement, before sliding back up to meet mine.

"At me?"

"At myself. For wanting you as much as I do. Part of it might be because I shouldn't, but it doesn't change the fact that I want you. Right here. Right now. Up against this window."

I press my thighs together and draw a shaky breath in. I've managed to keep my emotions out of it so far by getting in there first and putting him in his place, but if he rolls out the big guns I fear I'll fold like a pack of cards. He breathes charisma, and he's dangerously beautiful.

"Gabe ..." I begin.

"On the dining table, over the sofa. I'll take you every way and everywhere." His eyes darken, erasing the anger and replacing it with lust. "And you'd be left with no illusion that it was anything more than just fucking. There'd be no gentle and romantic bullshit, Princess. It'd be rough and hard. I'd bury myself so deep inside you, you'd scream my name for the whole of London to hear."

My eyes close. I swallow hard at the indecent images in my mind. I want him to do everything he's just described and a whole lot more.

My eyes snap open at the sound of him chuckling. "And you want me to."

"You're wrong."

His smile dissolves. He grabs my chin and tilts it up forcing me to look him in the eyes. "You're lying. I felt it in your kiss."

"You're wrong," I insist.

"Look me in the eye and tell me you don't want to fuck me."

I want to scream in his face that I don't want him, but can't.

I expect him to flash a cocky, self-satisfied grin at my silence, but he doesn't. He brushes his thumb across my bottom lip, leaving it tingling in his wake and places his mouth so close to my ear his lips graze my ear lobe.

"You can't, can you?" His voice rolls over me, making me tingle all over.

I close my eyes, loosing myself to the closeness of him and the memory of his lips on mine. "No," falls from my lips in a barely there whisper.

"Give me tonight."

"Tonight?"

"One night. When we're just Gabe and Ella. When we forget about everything else."

I open my eyes. "Then what?"

He nuzzles his nose against my neck, making me press my palms flat against the window behind me to stop myself from bunching them in his hair, and pulling his lips to mine.

"Then we move on. Because we'll have scratched the itch."

"It doesn't sound like a good idea."

"Sounds perfect to me."

"I've never had a one-night stand," I admit, suddenly feeling nervous.

His warm breath bats against my cheek. "They're not all they're cracked up to be, but I've a feeling one night with you will be hard to beat."

"You don't know that."

"Yes, I do," he says with so much conviction, I fear my heart's going to explode.

Most of my life I've been the sensible one, done the right thing whether my heart was in it or not, but as his lips brush my throat, my grip on right and wrong vanishes. The idea that someone like him wants me sends my mind into a spin. So what if it's just for sex? We'd both be using each other. One night. With Gabe White. Then we go back to normal. It doesn't sound so difficult. Does it?

He closes the small gap between us, pressing the length of his firm body against mine and delivering the final devastating blow to my self-control.

"I want to know how you like to be touched. Show me."

"You know how to touch a woman," I tell him, fighting to keep the control in my voice.

"I want to know what *you* like. Teach me how to please you. Stay the night."

His words dance across my skin and I can't think straight. He grabs my face in his hands and kisses me like he never wants to stop. As his tongue dances with mine, all the niggling doubts I have about why what he's suggesting is a terrible idea combust into flames.

Fuck it.

Check mate.

"Okay."

A low moan sounds from the back of his throat at my agreement. He tears his lips from mine and trails a scorching line down my neck. I tilt my head to the side, exposing my throat, giving more of myself to him. He pushes my jacket from my shoulders and with it my handbag, both fall to the floor in a heap.

"Arms."

I raise them above my head.

"I quite like compliant Ella."

"Don't get used to it."

His mouth quirks into a half-smile. "We'll see."

Before I get a chance to argue, he whips my t-shirt off over my head too.

"Perfect." His voice is a breathy whisper. Hooded eyes roam over my breasts as he presses his lips to my collarbone, teasing my nipples with his fingers through the red lace of my bra.

I close my eyes at his touch and press my lips together to suppress the shudder that threatens to rise from my core.

"Red hot. Like you," he murmurs into my ear, pushing the straps down and undoing the clasp at the back. In two swift moves my bra's gone. He drinks me in with a growl, like he's never seen a pair of breasts before. "Beautiful."

My nipples pebble at his words. I want to be the most beautiful woman he's ever seen. I know I'm not, but his enamoured gaze makes me feel for a moment that I could be.

He moves lower, burying his face between my breasts and nipping the soft skin of my cleavage, before latching onto my right nipple. I cry out in pleasure, opening my eyes to see him slowly circling the areola with his tongue, like he's got all the time in the world. Like he's *enjoying* it.

"You like this?"

Fuck yes!

"Speak to me."

"Yes," I gasp. Muscles deep inside tighten with every swirl of his tongue around my sensitive, pink skin. Watching him doing this to me is the most erotic thing ever. No one's taken the time to explore my body before, or cared enough to turn me on.

He kneels on the floor in front of me, undoes my laces and takes off my Converse. Then, reaches up and unfastens my jeans, tugging them down to my ankles and helps me step out of them. My body heats beneath his sizzling gaze raking over my body. When he finally speaks his voice is hoarse with lust.

"I could stare at you forever – but we haven't got forever, we've got tonight, so I'm going to make each second count."

A weird feeling of disappointment overshadows me at his words, but when Gabe presses his lips against my belly button it's gone. He pulls my knickers off and lowers his mouth to my pubic bone.

I squeeze my eyes tightly shut, slightly unnerved. I'm completely naked in front of a guy who makes women go weak at the knees. And he's had a lot of women. All stunning. I've seen the photos.

"There aren't enough words in the entire world to describe how utterly beautiful you are."

My heart's going to explode, I'm sure of it.

His warm breath bats against my swollen clit as he murmurs his awe filled words. I flicker open my eyes, my chest heaving at the sight of him gazing up at me with admiration brimming in his eyes.

He nuzzles his face between my legs, and scores his hot tongue all the way up my inner thigh, stopping inches from my vagina. I bite the inside of my mouth to stop myself from gasping.

"I can smell how wet you are."

If he expects me to be embarrassed, I'm not. I boldly keep his gaze as he runs his hands up the back of my thighs. He flashes a wicked grin, then licks a line from my vagina to my clitoris.

My spine peels off the window, eyelids shutter closed and I stop breathing. Every nerve ending in my body is on fire as I stand there panting, waiting for him to repeat what he's just done, but he doesn't. I look down at him.

A self-satisfied smile appears on his face as he watches my reaction. "You want me to do that again?"

I nod, drawing in a steadying breath.

"Tell me you want me."

He wants me to say the one thing, I've never admitted out right. Those three words that he's said to me, but I've not reciprocated.

"Why does it matter?"

"Tell me," he demands.

He should know by now ordering me around won't get him very far. "No."

"I can see how much you want me. I can taste it."

"And how do I taste?"

"Like the nectar from the Gods, just like I imagined."

My breath catches in my throat. "You've thought about it?"

"I've thought about tasting you every single minute, of every single day since we first met. All you've got to do is say it, and I'll give you what you want. You want me, in spite of yourself. And I want to hear you say it."

"You'll be waiting a long time."

"Always with the fight. Don't worry, by the end of the night you won't have any fight left in you, Princess."

"Is that a promise?" I fly back. "Because you promised me hard and rough and so far, all I've seen is a lot of fannying around."

Chapter 29

Ella

He leaps to his feet. Before I know what's happening, his hands are on my hips, he flips me round and I'm pushed against the window. I hiss at the feel of my heated flesh against the cold glass. A biting realisation takes hold. I'm stark naked on display for the whole of London to see.

"People will see me," I say worriedly.

He pushes my hair away from my face with his hand. "It's tinted. Do you really think I'd let anyone else see you like this?" He plants a possessive kiss on the base of my neck. "You're mine, Ella."

And I want to be, but I'm not about to admit it.

"I planned to start off nice." He pulls one hand behind my back, then the other, holding both of my wrists in place with one of his hands. "I was going to fuck you with my mouth, slowly." He kicks open my legs, forcing them wider and snakes his free hand around my waist. "But now I'm going to drag you to the edge, screaming." He roughly rubs his fingers across my clit and I bite down on my lip to stop myself from proving him right. I close my eyes as he starts tortuous, slow, steady movements, dipping his fingers into my wetness and spreading it across my folds.

"Every part of you is ready for me," he mutters in my ear, biting down on my earlobe. "You like this, don't you?"

"Yes," I reply without hesitation and stick my backside out, pushing it into his erection and making him groan. He pushes a finger inside me, quickly followed by a second. I'm glad there's a window in front of me for support, because I'm pretty sure I'd be on the floor if there wasn't. His long fingers twist and explore as he trails them across the nerves to find that sweet spot. I moan into the glass, fighting the muscles clenching deep in my stomach as he starts the same circular motions as he did on my clit.

"You like that, Princess?" He rasps against my ear, and it takes all my concentration to focus on not coming. "Tell me how much you like me touching you there."

He's doing this on purpose. As if he can't tell.

"Ella," he warns when I don't reply.

I open my eyes to see pockets of steam on the window from my breathing that's all over the place. He removes his fingers and teasingly runs a finger over my clit.

"I need you to tell me how much you like me touching you."

"You know," I grumble, irritable at the fact he's stopped.

"Then tell me."

"Yes," I snap. "Yes, okay. I like it."

He thrusts his fingers back inside me, deeper than before and I'm going. Heat sweeps my body as he steadily slides his fingers in and out of me. I lean my forehead against the glass, close my eyes and cling on to my last fibre of self-control.

"I can't wait to feel you around my cock."

His dirty mouth and fingers prove too much. My thighs begin to shake and my core contracts as an orgasm tears through me, knocking the wind out of me and turning my legs to jelly. Gabe's arms are around my waist in a flash, pulling me against him and keeping me upright. We stay there for a few moments, until my breathing slows down.

"Are you okay?" He sounds concerned.

I slowly open my eyes and draw in a deep breath. "Yeah."

He plants a gentle kiss on my shoulder. "I was worried. You nearly collapsed."

"Well, it's been a while," I toss back. That could be the reason, but the fact I've never had an orgasm that intense might also be the reason. I'm almost scared to fuck him. Almost.

He unwraps his arms from around my waist and twists me back round to face him, cradling my face in his hands. A warm, cosy feeling hits my chest as worried eyes hold mine.

"Are you sure you're okay?"

I smile, touched by his concern. He said there'd be no gentle romantic bullshit and this is bordering on that. The devilish side of me wants to point this out to him, but the other side of me stops it. The part of me that quite likes this soft and gentle side to him, the one I'm guessing people rarely see; the same part of me that enjoys it when he holds my face and looks at me adoringly.

"I'm okay."

His hands leave my face and slide to rest on my shoulders. His gaze runs over my naked body. "I'm glad, because that was just the start."

That sounded like a challenge and I'm always ready for one of those. Especially where he's concerned. "Good." Just because I'm butt naked doesn't mean he's got the upper hand. "I was starting to worry that's all you've got."

I'm purposefully pushing him. And he knows it.

In the blink of an eye, he picks me up and throws me over his shoulder.

"Put me down," I demand as my head meets his back, as he carries me through the apartment.

"I warned you that smart mouth of yours would get you in trouble," he says, giving my bare arse cheek a slap.

I cry out at the sting. "Bastard."

"Yeah, but a bastard you want. Even if you won't admit it."

Git.

He throws me down onto the softest, largest bed I've ever been on. The bedroom's massive and has the same neutral vibe going on as the rest of the apartment, but I barely get two seconds to take in my surroundings, because my focus is pulled to something a whole lot more impressive.

Gabe pulls his t-shirt off over his head and flings it over his shoulder, then steps out of his sweatpants in one move. I don't know where to look first. Every single inch of his body is toned and taut. The black and grey tattoos decorate each arm from the wrist up, and cover part of his chest. A smattering of dark hairs sit across his chest and trails a line down the centre of his abs, all the way to his v that disappears beneath the waistband of his black Dolce & Gabbana boxers. I know I'm staring. The man's a god in a suit but out of it he's utterly fucking breathtaking.

I hope I'm not dribbling.

The embarrassing thought pulls me back into the moment, and I'm relieved to find I'm not the only one who's in a stupor. Gabe's standing motionless at the bottom of the bed, his impressive erection tenting the material of his underwear. He's looking at me in a way that causes my stomach to flip-flop, and then he says something that makes my heart squeeze so tight I think I'm having a heart attack.

"I'm pretty sure I could get used to you looking like that, lying in my bed."

Before I can question what he's said, I'm pulled down the bed so my feet are on the floor. He flips me over so my arse is sticking up in the air.

"Because of your smart mouth I'm not going easy on you." He smacks my backside again. "But I've a feeling you'll like it."

I will. But I'll not tell him that.

I hear the sound of material hitting the floor and turn my cheek to the sheets. Just because he's got me physically where he wants me, doesn't mean I'll be any less defiant.

"Whatever. Less talk, more action."

He leans over me and strokes my hair away from my face. "Always with the fight, Princess."

"Condom," I demand, even though I'm on the pill. Ever since the termination I've never been off it. And God knows how many women Gabe's fucked; a thought I don't want to dwell on right now.

"Always."

I hear the tearing of foil then feel the tip of his cock press against my vagina. I grip the grey bed sheets between my fingers and brace myself. I haven't even seen his cock yet, but I know he'll be big. Nothing that I've seen so far about Gabe White has been disappointing. He pushes inside me a few inches and his breathing labours. He pauses, then rears back and drives forward, filling me completely. I twist my face into the sheets to stifle my gasps as my body registers burning pain. After a few seconds the uncomfortable tightness gives way to pleasure. I was right. He's huge.

"Jesus fucking Christ," he sighs on a long exhale, stilling inside me, as we get used to the feeling of us together. He's as hard as steel, stretching me in ways I've never felt before. A tight ball of heat starts to build at my centre at the feel of him deep inside me, touching me in places that I've never been touched. My muscles throb around him as he rests his hands on my hips, cautiously sliding out of me, but I'm growing impatient. He's ignited the fire and slow and easy won't cut it.

"You said you weren't going to go easy on me."

"I don't want to hurt you."

A tiny part of my heart melts at his concern for me again, but I ignore it. I've wondered what he would feel like inside me ever since I first clapped eyes on him last week. And now I know he feels just as divine as I thought he would I want it fast and hard. And I want it now.

"Trust me, you won't. You're not *that* big."

It's a lie but I'm not going to stroke his already huge ego by admitting he's the biggest I've ever had.

"Shut the fuck up." He pushes my head down into the bed and keeps his hand there, pinning me in place. He grips my other hip with his free hand and drives forward hard, reaching deep inside me.

The way he's possessing me with his strong hands and cock is bliss, but I'm never one to be outdone. I push back, delighted in the hiss of pleasure that falls from his lips as I match his every thrust. We're both relentless; fucking the anger and repressed scorching attraction out of one another. If he keeps this up all night, I might not see morning, but it would be a wonderful way to go.

A delicious ache starts to build between my legs as Gabe alternates his thrusts, between shallow and deep, reading my body like no man's bothered to before. The sound of our heavy breathing, and the slickness of my arousal interrupts the silence of the bedroom.

"Can you hear that?" he pants. "That's you wanting me. Stop fighting it. Say you want me."

My muscles tighten around his cock and the ball of warmth at my centre builds, rising through my body. It's all I can do to open my mouth. "No."

He removes his hand from the back of my head and runs his fingers through my hair, winding it round his hand and tugging my head from the bed. "Fuck, you're so tight. Don't hold back, Princess."

Another delicious contraction ebbs through my body, swiping away all my fight with it.

I'm a hot, panting mess. Every one of my limbs is shaking and I can feel my orgasm hurtling towards me at breakneck speed. "Gabe."

"Come for me."

I don't want to, just to defy him, but my body's disobeying me this time. I don't stand a fucking chance. Every muscle in my body tightens as my second orgasm hits me hard. Wave after wave of sweet tension rolls through me. I cry out his name and see stars. He releases my hair from his grasp and my head hits the bed. Eyes closed. I'm breathing hard. My body's in shock and my brain's playing catch-up. I've always wanted a guy to touch me and fuck me and control me like Gabe. Now I've found one, I don't know what to do with him.

Chapter 30

Gabe

I gently rest my palm between the smooth, glistening porcelain skin of her shoulder blades and glide my hand down her spine, soothing her. The rise and fall of her chest slows as her breathing returns to normal and she stops shaking. With any other woman I might get a sense of sexual pride that I've made her legs buckle and left her trembling beneath me but I feel nothing of the sort. Her long dark lashes cast shadows against her pink cheeks, and as she lies there in sleepy silence, I'm struck by an overwhelming urge to know she's all right.

I skate my fingertips up her left arm to her shoulder and sense her stir. "Are you okay?"

She doesn't open her eyes, but the slight nod of her head, reassures me. I'm used to submissive women who let me fuck them how and when I want. But Ella's a wild cat. Everything with her is a fight, fucking her is a verbal and physical sparring match and every time she comes back at me, it makes me harder.

I pull out of her, then, gently roll her over onto her back. The sight of her flushed naked body makes my cock throb harder than it already is. Her rosy nipples stand erect, begging to be sucked. Cream skin and curves; and she owns every fucking one of them. She's a weapon and she knows it. She's fire, who throws curveballs at me and always takes me by surprise. Her wayward curls splay out across the sheets behind her. She's beautiful. I could spend the rest of my life looking at her and never get tired of it.

She's watching me. A gentle smile plays at the corners of her mouth. "It's rude to stare."

I prop my head on my hand. I like fighty Ella, but this playful version of her is refreshing. I'm not sure who else gets to see it – hopefully no one. I want her to save this version of herself just for me.

"Then I'm going to be the rudest guy in the world, because I'm never going to stop staring at you. You're stunning."

Her expression remains impassive but her breasts heave, telling me my compliment's caught her off guard. Has no one ever said that to her before? What kind of men has she been with? I close the thought down quickly. I don't want to know. Tonight, I'm thinking of no one but me and her.

"Sounds like a line." My fighty girl is back.

"I've told you Princess, I don't do lines."

"Yeah, and I've told you I'm not sure I believe you." Her eyes sparkle playfully. She holds my gaze for a moment then lowers her eyes to my erection. I catch the sharp rise and fall of her chest, but this time it's for a whole different reason. "You've not come."

I deserve a gold medal. Fuck knows how I've done it. Then I say something that takes *me* completely by surprise. "I want to look you in the eye as we come apart, together."

I don't do that. Not eye-to eye. It breeds intimacy, a connection, risks them getting the wrong idea. That's not what I'm about. Harsh but true. For me, it's about a quick fuck with them face down on the bed or bent over the sofa. No feelings involved.

Her eyes widen a fraction. She swipes her tongue across her bottom lip and looks at me with a mischievous glint in her eye.

"Well, are you going to get on with it, or do I have to wait all night?"

Her lips make my balls tighten and I barely suppress a smile. I cup her face and gently stroke my thumb across her cheekbone, the challenge dissolving from her gaze with my touch. I've no desire to get on with this, I'm going to savour everything about her. Etch her into my brain for eternity.

I kiss her softly, tasting her sweetness. She bunches her hands in my hair and tugs me closer, deepening the kiss. Her body tells me a thousand times over what she refuses to admit. But she will. In time.

You don't have time.

My logical brain kicks in, but I'm determined to ignore it. I shift over her, resting my hands on the bed either side of her head. She shuffles her legs wider, making room for me and I sink down between them, all without lifting my lips from hers. I line myself up and she wraps her limbs around me, pulling me closer, and I sense she's getting impatient. I'd love to draw it out, tease her, make her beg but I don't have the self-restraint to be inches away from fucking her and not.

I enter her tight, wet heat in one smooth push, growling into her mouth because I can't stop myself. She tries to arch against me but I dwarf her, pinning her to the bed as I set the pace; smooth, rhythmic thrusts, fighting through her twitching muscles, wondering how the hell I'm managing it. I'm digging deep, holding myself back and fighting every single urge to unleash thrust after thrust upon her. I need to see her come again, feel her clench around me and make those little noises she makes, but most of all I need to pleasure her.

I don't have to wait long to get my wish. She slides her hands down my back to my backside, digging her fingernails into my arse, willing me on with every thrust, silently telling me to hurry because she's close. I feel her tighten around my cock. I'm right.

"Gabe." She says my name in a breathy whisper. And I nearly go. My cock jerks inside her and she gasps.

Refocus. I look at her through hooded eyes. "Hold on for me."

She scrunches her eyes closed adorably, like I've asked her to do the impossible. "I don't think I can…"

"Wait," I pant. "Look at me." Hazel eyes brimming with fire lock with mine. "Keep looking at me."

"Gabe, I'm…"

Her entire body tenses, her hands fly to my shoulders, nails digging into my flesh as she looks at me, fighting every urge she's got to close her eyes. Even now she's determined not to be beaten, like she's got something to prove. She forces herself to keep eye contact until the very last second and she screams.

Vulnerability flashes in her eyes before they flicker closed, and I know I've seen something no other guy has. I've cracked her open, she's laid bare and split in two. The thought alone is enough to make me lose control but I don't get a chance to think about it. Shudders rack through her body, pulling me along for the ride. I lose it; pounding into her like a crazy man, growling like a wild animal until I explode, rolling my hips, again and again until I'm spent.

I crumble on top of her. Her head's tilted away from me, her eyes are closed. She looks totally content. I withdraw gently and shift off her, tying the condom off with a snap and glancing over my shoulder. She hasn't moved, her breathing's deep and steady. She's exhausted.

I slide back onto the sheets beside her, grab the sable throw from the bottom of the bed and cover us both up. She turns onto her side, away from me, and when I sidle up behind her and drape an arm over her waist, she shuffles back a little, pressing her arse into my cock. Her petite curves fit snugly against my body like she's custom made. I push the thought aside and close my eyes, nuzzling into her hair, smelling her perfume. As my fighty Princess lies in blissful contented silence in my arms I banish all thoughts from my mind. Like how I don't do cuddling after sex. Right about now, I'd usually be taking a shower while the woman let herself out. But above all, I don't think about how none of this feels weird at all.

Chapter 31

Ella

The September morning sunshine floods in through the floor-to-ceiling windows and bathes the bedroom in light. The warm rays dance across my naked skin, pulling me from sleep. I flicker open my eyes to be greeted by clear, blue skies and for a moment I can't remember where I am. I prop myself up on my elbows, mesmerised by the view. The dome of the O2 and the familiar turrets of London Bridge are visible in the distance. God knows how high up we are. The view is totally stunning. Tourists would pay an arm and a leg for this. I didn't get to appreciate it last night. *Last night.* The harsh sting of self-hatred creeps into my thoughts. It doesn't matter which way I look at it. I slept with my boss. We overstepped the line so far it's a fucking dot on the horizon.

"Morning."

I look over my shoulder. Gabe's standing in the doorway, wearing nothing but a pair of white boxers and a grin. My eyes trace down the contours of his abs and I feel a tug of desire deep inside. *Stop it. It's over.* Now for the awkward as arse part, where we make small talk then I make a sharp exit. And we somehow pretend last night never happened.

I force my gaze back to the window. "I was just admiring the view."

"So was I."

My heart squeezes in my chest. I hate that he has this affect on me. He walks over to the bed and sits beside me. I feel awkward; lying on my front, butt naked. I want to reach down and pull the throw over me but can't because he'd see everything and that possibility, in the harsh light of day, seems wrong.

"What's the matter?"

Where do I start? "Nothing."

"Ella," he warns.

"I feel as though I should put some clothes on."

He laughs softly, admiring my naked backside like he can't stop himself. "I saw a lot more than that last night."

A memory of us going at it on the bedroom floor flashes into my mind, making my stomach twist. I swallow and tell myself to get a grip. He's had loads of one-nights stands, and I'm betting all the women go gooey-eyed and clingy afterwards. Not me. He's in for a surprise.

"Yeah, well, that was last night. Now, I feel like you should turn around and let me at least get under the covers."

He looks at me thoughtfully for a moment, like he's deciding something. "No chance."

He dips his head and kisses me slowly. He shouldn't do this. One night, he said. But as his tongue tangles with mine, I've no desire to stop him. He pulls away, breathless, placing his lips a fraction from mine.

"It's a sin for you to cover up. The sight of you lying naked in my bed is more beautiful than a thousand sunrises over this city."

His adoring words fling me into a mental tailspin. I'm worried my heart's going to burst out of my chest, but in a beat my sensible head kicks in. Reality check time. We're playing with fire and I won't get burned. Not again.

"I need to go. We agreed one night. Now it's morning. That's my cue."

"Yeah, about that –" He tucks a tendril of hair behind my ear and gazes deep into my eyes. "I'm not done."

I'm on the back foot. "What do you mean? We agreed…"

"I mean, I'm not done." His tone matches the firm look in his eye. "I'm not done, with this, with you …"

I draw my head back as what he's getting at sinks in. "You have to be. This is already complicated. We shouldn't have done … what we've done. It's totally wrong."

"Is it? Because it didn't feel wrong when I was inside you last night. And you lying naked in my bed doesn't feel wrong now. Does it?"

Serious eyes look at me expectantly, waiting for me to answer. I feel awkward, but it doesn't feel wrong. None of it does, in fact it's the total opposite. Every single thing; from the way he kisses me, to the way he touches me feels so perfect I feel like crying with frustration.

He shakes his head, reading into my silence. His voice softens. "It doesn't feel weird, does it?"

I swallow hard. It's confession time. I owe him the truth. "No. But it doesn't change anything. We are who we are. If people at work found out about this, well, if *anyone* found out. Can you imagine if the press got hold of this?"

"Stop thinking."

"What?"

He pushes his hands through his hair in frustration and looks out of the window ahead, his eyes narrow in thought. "I've spent my whole life thinking about the next step. My entire fucking life has been mapped out for me since I was fifteen. When I was at school it was about getting the grades to get into Oxford. When I was at Oxford it was about acing my degree. Then, when I graduated it was about shadowing Dad in the business for two years so he could prime me up ready for when I took over. Now I'm there, every single day of my life is dictated by the next deal, the five-year business plan, projections, always about the next move. My life's like one big fucking game of chess." He rubs his hands together and shakes his head. "I just want to stop thinking. I want to be in the moment."

Sympathy tugs at my heart. The last ten years haven't exactly been the greatest for me, but I've at least lived in the moment. Mum being ill and knowing we were going to lose her made us make every day count. Towards the end we took each day as a bonus, taking enjoyment in the little things, like the warmth of the sun on your face and smell of grass after a rain shower. It made us take time, to stop and take stock of what's important. Gabe's life sounds sad. Claustrophobic. Extremely stressful. To be fifteen, knowing you're expected to follow in your dad's footsteps, is an unbelievable amount of pressure.

His privileged lifestyle is sounding more and more like a poisoned chalice.

"What are you saying?"

He shifts to lie on the bed next to me and takes my hand in his. "I'm saying one night with you isn't enough." He brushes his thumb across the back of my hand. "For once in my life I don't have all the answers, but I'm going with it. Enjoying being with you in the moment. Enjoying being just Gabe and Ella. And I'm asking you to do the same."

I look down at him gently stroking my hand. His words hit home. I've spent the majority of my adult life looking out for everyone else. Being the sensible one, keeping things ticking over and all the plates spinning in the air. But everything's different now.

Steely blues search my face, waiting for my reply. My heart constricts. He's so beautiful. And he's made everything sound so simple. *Damn it.*

He lowers his lips to mine and kisses me languidly. The scrap of resolve I had left disappears with every flick of his tongue. "And I haven't even come close to scratching that itch yet," he murmurs into my mouth.

Neither have I.

Before I know it I'm on my back on the bed and he's moving over me, taking up position between my thighs, where he spent most of the night. "Stay with me. I want you," he pants between kisses.

He wants me to say it back.

"I hate you," I gasp.

He gently bites my bottom lip and releases it with a chuckle. "You don't. You hate yourself for wanting me."

Fuck him for being so right.

"Hey, G. You up?" A male voice calls from somewhere inside the apartment.

My head jerks up in panic. "Who the fuck is that?"

Gabe drops his head and groans. "My ever-punctual older brother."

"He's here?"

"He's got a key card. Don't worry, he won't give a shit about us."

Us. The way he uses the word so freely makes my heart spin.

He kisses me lightly on the lips then reluctantly lets me go and stands. "I'm sorry. I'll make it up to you later. For now, make yourself at home. Feel free to grab a shower, there's fresh towels in the en suite."

"Aren't you the perfect host," I quip. I don't know what else to say. Cocky Gabe, I can deal with. Nice Gabe pulls the rug from under my feet.

He flicks me a grin and starts to head out of the room then stops, pausing in the doorway for a few seconds. "How about later we drop by your place." He turns to face me and hesitates. "You can collect some clothes and overnight things, if you like." He looks completely awkward, waiting for me to answer. A far cry from his usual, super together self.

He wants me to stay over. I'm nodding before I know it. "Okay."

He gives me a full-on smile and one last lingering look. "I'm going to kick my brother in the balls for making me leave you naked in my bed." With a shake of his head, he disappears.

**

The bathroom is like something out of a five-star luxury hotel. Not that I've ever been to one, but I can imagine. It's all polished white floors and walls and has a huge walk-in shower, roll top bath and jack and jill wash basins. The shower's got one of those super-powerful shower heads that make you feel as though you're being massaged from the head down and makes your scalp tingle. In the absence of my toiletries, I use the stuff in the posh-looking turquoise bottles in the rack, then bundle myself into a soft, white, fluffy towel and head into the walk-in wardrobe next door.

The room is the same size as my bedroom. An assortment of pristine shoes; smart brogues, trainers and leather boots sit neatly paired up on the floor to ceiling shelves, along with carefully folded jumpers and t-shirts. I feel like I've walked into a boutique shop – this room is every girl's dream. Wardrobes fill the rest of the room, and my curiosity gets the better of me. I slide open one of the white gloss doors and peek inside. A row of suit jackets hung by colour; black through to light grey. I've seen enough. He's a neat freak.

I step into my underwear and pull on my jeans and t-shirt that have been put on one of the spare shelves, along with my handbag, and pull my fingers through my damp hair in a bid to untangle it. My eyes land on my handbag and my thoughts flicker back to real life. Kate. I never went home last night. And I haven't let her know where I am. She'll have gone fucking nuclear.

I dig my hand inside and retrieve my mobile. I almost don't want to look at how many missed calls and texts I've got. I stab at the screen but nothing happens. It's completely dead.

Shit!

Don't tell me it's playing up. I can't afford to buy a new one right now, even with the money I earned last night.

I heave a sigh. It'll have to wait. I can't do anything while I'm here. I shove it back into my handbag and hear raised voices. My curiosity piques. I can't quite make out what's being said but Gabe doesn't sound happy at all.

Chapter 32

Gabe

"Is he having a fucking laugh?"

The crease of frustration on Jake's forehead tells me not.

I blow out a long breath and tip my head back, closing my eyes. I knew today was going too well. Something was bound to fuck up.

"I knew he was a dodgy motherfucker. I've had a bad feeling about dealing with him from the start. Diego's out for all he can get. You've seen the intel on him." I look at Jake. "Can we believe him? How do we know he's not playing us off against them, just to make more money?"

"We don't." Jake rubs a hand across his chin. "He called me this morning. I came as soon as I knew."

"Why didn't he call me? I'm the one holding the purse strings."

Jake laughs. "He's scared of you."

"Good." I clench my jaw and glance over Jake's shoulder towards the bedroom door, lowering my voice. "He should be fucking scared of me."

Jake watches me and narrows his eyes. "Is there someone else here?"

"Next steps," I press, ignoring him.

"We've three choices; give him what he wants, pull out, or I'll go and pay him a visit."

I rest my arm along the back of the sofa and prop my foot on my knee. "Although there's nothing that I'd like more than for Diego's slippery arse to be given a kicking, I don't think that's going to get us what we want." I nod. "We've another option."

"What?"

"The other company are the one's raising the stakes, so we take them out."

"You mean ... ?"

"Diego's just a middle-man. He's a pawn. Expendable. We take the others out of the equation, we remove the problem at the source."

Jake smirks. "Add another one to the portfolio – are you serious?"

My gaze flicks back to the bedroom door. "We need this deal. It's non-negotiable."

"Checkmate."

"Checkmate, indeed."

Jake folds his arms behind his head and stretches his long legs out in front of him. "So, what do you want me to tell Diego?"

"Go fuck himself, we've got bigger fish to fry. I'll sort it with Legal first thing, Monday."

Jake's eyes glint with amusement. "You mean, you're not going to fire off an email right now? What's happened to workaholic G?"

My eyes slide to the bedroom door. Right now, I've got more important things on my mind. "It can wait. You got any more bad news for me?"

Jake pulls a face, weighing up whatever other crap he's got to tell me.

"Next Saturday. You *are* coming, aren't you?"

I rub a hand through my hair and glance out of the windows to the city beyond, wishing I was out there, rather than in here right now, for this conversation. "I'm not going to *not* go, if that's what you're getting at."

He cocks an eyebrow. "Wouldn't be the first time."

"I'm going."

"Yeah, well. You know what Andi's like. She has all these good ideas but getting her tan topped up and her nails redone is more important, so Maria's taken control of the organising." Jake rolls his eyes at the mention of our step-mother's name. For her to even have that title is a joke. She's only five years older than Jake. We all thought Dad had lost his fucking mind the day he announced they were getting married. She seemed to appear out of nowhere. Met through the golf club Dad's a member of. She's a masseuse. It's hardly a love story. She's got gold-digger stamped all over her. I can't believe Dad doesn't know it, I just think he's past caring. His money's never going to run out and in the meantime he gets to shag a beautiful, much younger woman. It's just something else for me to hate him for.

"I bet she has. When and where?"

"Next Saturday. The Savoy. Starts at seven."

I shake my head. "The Savoy. Bet Dad's platinum card's taken a beating."

Jake's lips straighten into a firm line and he shifts to the edge of the sofa. "Probably, knowing Maria. She wanted some place classy, apparently. You know what it's like. What Maria wants, she gets."

Not always.

"So, what happened to you last night?"

"What do you mean?"

"After you took off?" Jake's watching me carefully. "What happened? I know it must have been a shock to see Ella there."

I look behind him to the bedroom door and he follows my gaze.

"You sure there's no one else here?" he says, turning back to me.

The sound of ceramic hitting wood and a cry of "Shit!" comes from the hall. I jerk up to see Ella clutching the weird looking ornament that once sat on the hall table. She puts a hand on the table to stop it from wobbling and cradles the ornament under her arm. She exhales deeply, a crimson flush creeping up her face as she notices us staring at her.

"Sorry. I bumped into it."

She carefully puts the vase back on the table. I couldn't give a toss if she smashed it. The thing's hideous. It came with the apartment, like everything else in here.

Jake gives me a knowing look and smirks. "So *that's* what happened last night?"

I ignore him and give her a reassuring smile. "It's fine."

Jake jumps to his feet and heads over to her, sticking out his hand. "It's nice to properly meet you."

Her eyes slide to mine briefly as she gives his hand a shake. "You too. Jake, isn't it?"

"Yeah. I'm the eldest. The brother no one knows about." He laughs and bobs his head in my direction. "Has he mentioned me much?"

She wrinkles her nose in that cute way of hers, and slides her hands in the back pocket of her jeans. "A little."

"Wow, I'm honoured."

"In between talking about work, of course," she teases.

Jake throws his head back and laughs. "Yeah, he's Mr Workaholic, all right."

Amusement dances in her eyes and she playfully pokes out the tip of her tongue at me. *Fuck, I want her.*

I stand and fight the urge to rush over there, throw her over my shoulder and carry her off to bed.

"Anyway, I need to get off." Jake's gaze slides from her to me. "I'll leave you two to enjoy the rest of your day." He pats the pockets of his black tracksuit bottoms and frowns, then heads back over to the sofa and scoops his phone up off the table. "I like her," he murmurs quietly, giving me a look. "Good to meet you," he says, heading towards the hall. "I'll see you around."

She smiles. "Yeah, you too."

Moments later I hear the lift doors slide closed. Finally, we're alone. I make a beeline for her.

"He seems nice."

I'm not really listening to her. I grab her face in my hands and kiss her deeply. It's all I want to do. It's all I ever want to do. I kiss her until my lips sting, then look down at her adoringly. She's panting. Flushed. Her eyes wide. Exactly as I like to leave her.

"What was that for?" she asks breathlessly.

"Do I need a reason? You're beautiful."

Her lips pull into a smile and she slides her arms around my neck. "You need to stop saying that, otherwise I'll get a big head."

I frown. "Has no one ever told you that before? Has no guy ever told you how beautiful you are?"

Sadness flashes in her eyes, wiping the smile from her face at the same time. "Once," she says quietly. "But he didn't mean it."

I graze my thumb across her cheekbones, a thousand questions on the tip of my tongue. The more I'm around her the more I want to learn *everything* about her; the cause of the sadness behind those hazel eyes, the reason why she's built a hard shell around herself. I know about her mum, but it's more than that – I know it.

I place a kiss on the tip of her nose. "How about we drop by yours, collect your things, then grab some lunch?"

She anxiously glances out the window, then back to me. "Out?"

"Yes. Out."

"But what if someone spots us together?"

"There are around one and a half million people living in central London. The chances of someone we know actually seeing us are minute."

"I suppose you're right."

"And we need to get moving, otherwise the cleaner will be doubly cross."

She frowns perplexed. "The cleaner. Why?"

"Because if we don't move soon, I'm going to fuck you up against that window again, and that'll be another smear they've got to clean off the glass."

She looks over at the window, breaks out into a cheeky smile, then looks up at me. "Well, in that case we'd better get a move on then, because if you try it on, I'm not sure I'll be able to stop you."

Chapter 33

Ella

The Bugatti looks out of place parked up outside my house, almost as much as Gabe. A couple of women slow down as they pass us, distracted by eyeing him up. I can't blame them. Dressed in tight blue jeans, white trainers and a snug fitting t-shirt showing off his ink, he's smoking hot.

I stop at the top of my front path and hesitate as he goes to follow me. He's a neat freak. I hope to God Kate's tidied up. "You're coming in?"

His lips quirk into a bemused smile. "Why wouldn't I?"

"Erm, well..." I glance behind him at the car. "That might be on bricks when we come out."

He shrugs, like it's no big deal. "Then we'll catch a cab."

Of course. He'd probably just buy *another* car if that happened. It's not like he's short of cash.

Nerves dance in my stomach as I head down the path with Gabe hot on my heels. I push my key in the lock and feel his firm chest press against my back. His hand squeezes my waist and he puts his mouth to my ear. "Is there any chance we'll be alone?"

God, I hope so.

I push open the front door and step inside. For a few seconds I think our luck might be in, then I hear a scuffling noise, followed by Kate's angry face popping round the living room door. "Where the bloody hell have ...oh!"

The sight of Gabe following me through the door makes her stall. Her eyes widen as she takes him in and her cheeks turn pink.

I close the front door. We all stand in awkward silence for a few seconds, waiting for someone to speak first. It's not going to be Kate. Her mouth's gaping so much she could catch flies.

"We've not had an opportunity to properly meet, I don't

think," Gabe announces, offering her his hand. "I'm Gabe White. Nice to meet you."

She snaps out of her stupor with a giggle and throws her hair over her shoulder, the way she always does when she's in the company of an attractive man. "Lovely to meet you," she gushes shaking his hand. "I'm Kate, Ella's friend and housemate."

"Kate, can I have a word."

She's lost in her own little world looking up at him dreamily. An inane grin on her face. She hasn't heard a word I've said.

"Kate!"

She looks at me with a start.

I nod upstairs. "Can I have a word?"

"Er, yeah," she replies, grinning at Gabe. "The living room's just through there. Make yourself at home."

She's acting totally weird. And using a voice I've never heard before.

"Thank you." He smiles graciously. Of course, he must be used to this; women going a bit crazy when they're around him.

I leave him to it and push my friend up the stairs and into my bedroom.

"Oh my God!" she cries as soon as we're alone.

I cringe and make sure the door's firmly shut. "Shush, he'll hear."

"Oh my god, oh my god, oh my god." She presses her hands to her cheeks. Her eyes widen like saucers. "Have you done what I think you've done? With Gabe White? You have, haven't you?"

"Shush." I insist opening my wardrobe door. I need her to calm down. He doesn't need his ego massaging by overhearing this.

"No!" Kate declares remembering herself. "Firstly, I should be pissed off with you. I was worried sick last night. You said you were coming home and you didn't. I tried calling and texting you loads."

"I know. I thought you might have." I shoot her a sheepish look. "I'm really sorry, I was going to call you this morning, but my stupid phone died."

She tries and fails to stop a smirk spreading across her face. "Well, if you were with *him* last night, I can almost forgive you. You were, weren't you?"

"It's complicated."

"Eek! You were! I knew this was going to happen after he snogged your face off on the doorstep. Tell me everything."

"I'll have to give you the abridged version. We're going out for lunch."

"Ooh ... where?"

"Mhmmm ... not sure." I stare at the contents of my wardrobe. That's a good point. I have no clue where he's taking me, so have no idea how to dress.

"Well, it's bound to be somewhere very nice. Now, forget about that for a minute and spill. I want to know all about your night of passion."

I know there's only one way to get Kate off my back so I can get sorted, and that's to tell her.

"Nothing can come of it," I add, as I finish up filling her in.

"Why not?"

I give her an incredulous look. "How long have you got? Firstly, he's my boss, secondly, we're from totally different worlds"– I turn back to my wardrobe, pull out a couple of t-shirts, and drop them on the bed,– "and he's, well, he's a White, it's ... wrong."

"They say opposites attract."

"Yeah." I scoff. "We're certainly *that*."

She twists her lips in thought and plays with the tie of her dressing gown. "If you're *so* different and if this is *so* wrong, why is he downstairs right now? Why are you packing an overnight bag to stay over at his? Why is he taking you out for lunch?"

"Bloody hell, all your questions. Why don't you shine a light in my eye and be done with it," I grumble, pulling a short white, summer dress with a ditsy print in pink and blues, out of the wardrobe. *Is this suitable attire for wherever the hell he might be taking me?*

"Well?"

She can be a pushy sod, sometimes.

I decide it will have to do. I can't stand much more of this interrogation. "We're just enjoying it while it lasts."

"Or maybe he wants you, and you want him."

I pull my t-shirt off, throw it on the bed and take my shoes off. I step into my dress. "I don't …"

"You do," Kate says firmly. "You both do. He's made it pretty clear from the start and you've been walking round totally distracted since you met him."

"It really doesn't matter, does it," I say buttoning up my dress, refusing to listen to her. "In a day or so, it'll be over."

Kate folds her arms. I know she's not going to let this drop. "You don't know that."

"Yes, I do." I pull my hair out the neck of my dress and bend down, peering into the bottom of my wardrobe to find my shoes. "We're attracted to one another. That's it. Once we're bored with each other, which is bound to happen, that'll be that."

"What if it doesn't happen like that?"

"It will," I say firmly. *It has to.* The novelty will wear off in a few days. Then we'll be back to being boss and employee. Even though I'm not exactly sure how the next step is going to work. "Aha!" I yank my white Converse from the bottom of my wardrobe and step into them.

"Well, whatever happens, he's hot." She smiles wryly. "And I'm guessing the sex was hot too?"

I engross myself in tying the laces of my trainers and not on Kate's question. I don't know where to start. He was everything I expected and more; and I know he's got more to show me.

I straighten up. "I don't ask for details of your sexual endeavours."

Kate rolls her eyes. "Okay, okay. Well, I'll take it from the smile on your face, you had hot sex and he's got a big dick."

I didn't realise I was smiling. I glance in the dressing table mirror. Yes. Plastered across my face is a massive grin.

"Anyway, where's Harry?," I ask. "I thought you two were attached at the hip."

"He's been busy."

Before she can elaborate her mobile begins to ring. She pulls it from the front pocket of her dressing gown, looks at the front screen and breaks into a smile. I don't need to ask who it is. "Speak of the devil." She fixes me with a firm look and points a finger at me. "My advice? Switch your brain off and enjoy yourself." She answers her phone with a "Hey babe," as she disappears out of the room.

I need to get a move on. Gabe's been left by himself long enough. At this rate he'll be sending up a search party. I comb my hair, apply a little mascara, blusher and lip gloss, then throw some clean underwear, t-shirts, jeans and a couple of jumpers in my small case and head downstairs.

Gabe's standing looking out of the front bay window when I enter the living room, his hands in his back pockets. His tall, broad frame make the room feel instantly smaller.

"Are you checking your car's still there?" I joke. "I know it's Hackney, but I was only pulling your leg earlier."

He turns and flashes a perfect smile, walking over to me. "I know you were. It's somewhere I've not been much. I was just looking at the local neighbourhood."

"Why? You're not sizing up properties to buy up, are you?"

His smile tightens. "I'm not *always* thinking about work." He puts his hands on my shoulders. "Not anymore, anyway. What are those?" He looks towards the stack of leaflets sat on the coffee table, with "Save Our Community" printed on the front.

"Margot must have dropped them off for me to deliver. She took over Mum's shop. Her and a few of the other shop owners have got a campaign going to try and drum up some publicity to overhaul the plans for the site. I said I'd help wherever I can."

A smile plays at the corners of his mouth. "You must have lots of ideas. You've seen first-hand how effective local support can be at throwing a spanner in the works of these sort of deals, look at the Cedarwood Grove Project. They threw MPs, the local press – the lot – at us."

"But you still won, even after they did all that," I remind him.

Gabe slides his hands down my arms. "We did." He hesitates and links his fingers through mine, looking down at our hands. "I know this is important to you. To your mum. If you believe in it, don't give up on it. We all need to do what we need to do."

I squeeze his hand. "I will. I owe it to Mum."

"Are your things in the hall?"

"They are but…"

"But what?"

I wrestle with my thoughts. I hear what Gabe and Kate have said, to be, to forget and enjoy, but I still can't resist my gut reaction to pull back. "Maybe you should drop me back here later."

He cups my face in his hands and looks deep into my eyes. "I don't want to drop you back here later. I want to take you to lunch, then take you back to mine and take you every way imaginable." He skates his thumb across my bottom lip and lowers his mouth to mine. "I'm going to spend our weekend buried deep inside you. You're going to count the ways I make you come. By the end of it, you'll be screaming you want me."

My chest squeezes, taking with it every last bit of fight in me. I stare into his eyes and realise that I'm never going to win this. I can't. He's already won. He wants me and I want him. He's everything and nothing like I thought he'd be. And the bits I don't know I want to find out about.

Gabe presses his lips to mine and tangles his fingers through my hair, pulling me close. He kisses me languidly, for eternity and I'm seeing stars when he pulls away. I feel the gallop of his heart in his chest as he presses himself against me.

"Now, the sooner you get your stuff, the sooner we get lunch and the sooner I get to tear this very pretty dress off you."

I smile. "Is that a promise?"

"It's a fucking certainty."

Chapter 34

Gabe

Sixty minutes later we're sitting outside at the top of the OXO Tower restaurant. The afternoon sun beats down on the terrace, burning through the couple of fluffy clouds floating in the otherwise crystal-clear sky. The sound of chatter and the chink of cutlery and glass fill the air. It's busy, even for a Saturday afternoon.

When Ella and Kate were having their tête-á-tête earlier, I took the chance to make a call and pull in a few favours with the maître d', wrangling one of the best tables here.

Ella sits opposite, holding her menu but paying it no attention. She's tilting her face upwards, eyes closed, basking beneath the sun's warm rays.

I feel a tug deep inside as I study her; wearing barely any make-up, dark brown curls framing her heart-shaped face. She's flawless. And I'm not sure I'm ready for it.

"What?" she asks, catching me looking at her.

"Nothing. I've been watching you since we sat down. I don't think you've even looked at your menu."

She twists a dark curl of hair around her finger. There's a glint of mischief in her eyes as she says, "It's nice, and I haven't been here before. We can't *all* dine at the finest places."

People prejudge me. Have done all my life. I've learned to not give a shit in the main, because most people's opinions mean fuck all. But even though she's teasing me, I've a burning need to put her straight. "Actually, I'm not the biggest fan of posh restaurants and fancy meals. Give me pizza, any day."

She giggles. "Really?"

"Really."

"Then why are we here?"

"Maybe I want to impress you."

"You needn't have bothered." She glances out at the river for a moment before looking at me. "I'm already impressed." She keeps her eyes on mine and licks her bottom lip.

"I'll remember that for next time."

Her eyes widen a fraction. "There'll be a next time?"

"You'd better believe it, Princess."

One night wasn't enough. I'm damn sure one day won't be either.

The waiter appears to take our drinks order. Ella says she's not fussy when it comes to wine, so I order a bottle of Pinot Grigio and jug of water.

"So tell me about Dark Desires?" I ask, once the waiter's left.

Ella sits back in the chair with a resigned look on her face. There was no way I wasn't going to ask about her working at a strip club.

"What about it?"

"How long have you worked there?"

"Technically I don't work there. I mean I did, but I stopped. Last night was a one off."

"Because you needed money."

"Yes, quickly."

"What for?"

She fiddles with the edge of the white cotton napkin on the table. "It's for my sister. She needed some cash quickly to buy some stuff for uni, otherwise she'll get into trouble. Dancing was the only way I could get the money I needed." The defensive tone from last night is back in her voice. "I don't expect you to get it..."

"Because I'm a self-entitled prick?" I cut in, unable to help myself. She's not the first person to think this, but for some unknown reason the idea of *her* thinking this about me cuts a thousand times deeper.

She gives me a rueful smile. "Maybe I was wrong to call you that."

We're interrupted by the waiter returning with our drinks. I thank him, pour a glass for Ella, a smaller glass for me and two glasses of water.

"Like I said last night, I don't judge you. I admire you for doing what you needed to do. Why did you start working there?"

She slides the glass of wine towards her on the table and curls her fingers round the stem. "Desperation. My temping job wasn't bringing in nearly enough money to cover the bills. Amy was at college. I saw an advert online. I applied and got it. God knows how." She takes a sip of wine. "I had to have a stiff drink before the audition. I pole danced at first. When I got more popular, they suggested I have my own act. It paid more, so I said yes."

Popular. A possessive part of me deep down inside, jars at the use of the word. She's using it like it's a good thing. Of course, it was for her. But all I can think of is how many men have summoned her to dance for them, stocking up their wank banks with mental images of her.

I take a long drink of water to try and extinguish the unfamiliar feeling of jealousy rising in my chest. All she was doing was looking after her family.

I reach across the table, put my hand on hers and give it a squeeze. She was the older sister. She stepped up to the plate. Did what she needed to do. Every single thing about that chimes with me and cements what I thought. We *are* similar. She just doesn't know it.

"What you did was amazing; nursed your mum, looked after your sister, survived, all the time in the shadow of your mum's illness. You're not to be judged. You're to be put on a pedestal and admired." She swallows hard and watches my fingers graze her knuckles.

"I've never met a man who's been able to see that, or who's said anything like that to me." Her voice is quiet. She bites her bottom lip, to keep the emotion at bay.

"How come you stopped working there?" I ask, moving the conversation on because I don't want her to feel uncomfortable.

"After Mum died, Kate moved in. She'd split up with her boyfriend and needed somewhere to live, so it made sense. An extra wage in the house meant I didn't need a second job."

"Did anyone know you worked there?"

"I told Amy and Mum I'd got an evening job, waitressing. They didn't know about our money problems. I hid that stuff from them. Mum had enough stress and Amy was sitting her exams." She smooths her hands across the napkin and avoids my gaze, clearly uncomfortable in the lie. "The only person who knew was Kate. She went batshit crazy when I first told her, but she understood, not like …" She stops herself and lifts the wine glass to her lips, taking a sip.

"Not like?" I prompt.

She frowns. "Hmmm?"

She's avoiding the question and it only makes me even more adamant to learn what she was about to say. "Who didn't understand about you working at Dark Desires?"

She looks out at the river. "A guy. When we met, I'd been working there for about six months. Everything was going great. After a while I worked up the courage to tell him, but he couldn't get his head around it." She shakes her head at the memory. "It wasn't pretty."

"What did he do?"

A breeze whips through her hair as she stares out at the river. Sadness clouds her eyes at the memory. "He went crazy jealous. Called me a whore and a slag. He couldn't understand that I was only working there because the money was good. He got it into his head that I chose to work there to pick men up. I told him to fuck off and haven't seen him since. Thank God."

I clench my jaw at the thought of anyone calling her those names. My insides fizz with rage. No fucking respect. The stupid fucker clearly didn't deserve her. "What a prick. Sounds as though you're best shot of him."

She smiles weakly and looks at me. "Anyway, what about you?"

"Me? No, I've never danced at a strip club."

She laughs. "No, but I'm guessing you've been there before?"

"I knew the guy who used to own it. We went to Oxford together. I've only been there a couple of times before." I give her a purposeful look. "Those places don't really appeal to me."

A smile tugs at the corners of her mouth. "I'm sure you don't need to go to that type of place to see women half naked, anyway."

"Meaning?"

"Meaning the great Gabe White must have ladies queuing around the block." Her teasing eyes hold mine and she takes a long drink of wine, suppressing a smile.

"Is that what you think?"

She laughs, but there's a challenging look in her eyes as they hold mine. "Come on, Gabe. Don't say it's *not* like that."

"It's *not* like that."

"I'm not like the others who'll just fall for whatever line you feed them." Her voice becomes taut. "I wasn't born yesterday."

She's right about one thing – she's not like the others, in the absolute best possible way.

I frown and lean forward on the table. "What *do* you think it's like? Because you already seem to have made your mind up about my sexual past."

Never one to back down from an argument, especially not with me, she mirrors my body language. I catch the steely glint of determination in her eyes. "I'm not going to pander to your ego and say all the reasons why women would want to date you. It's obvious *lots* do, and judging by the photos on the internet you've made the most of it."

"Are you jealous?" I shoot back, unable to help myself.

Her cheeks flush instantly. She'd be a shit poker player with that tell. She claws it back in a heartbeat, giving me a look that says what I've suggested is absurd. "Of course not."

"You sure about that?"

"Positive," she snaps. "By the looks of things the others were far more your –" she pauses and watches a boat pass by on the river as she chooses her words "– class, anyway."

"What the fuck does that mean?"

"It means Princess whoever-of-fuck-knows-where and the catalogue of models you've screwed are all part of the same super-rich scene as you." She gives me a scathing look. "You're positively roughing it, fucking me."

My eyes narrow into slits. "Are you serious?"

The defiant sparkle remains in her eyes. "I'm not stupid. I'm just a bit of rough for you, and soon the novelty will wear off."

"Are you ready to order?" The waiter asks returning to the table, but I barely hear him.

I don't know whether she's baiting me on purpose, or whether she really believes this is true. Either way, I'm setting the record straight.

"There's been a change of plan. We're not staying," I announce.

Her eyes widen in surprise.

Yes, Princess. You're going to see what happens when you push me.

I pull out my wallet, take out a couple of notes and throw them on the table, getting to my feet.

The waiter collects them. "Of course. Thank you, sir."

Ella reluctantly stands, draining her glass of wine. "But I thought we were here for lunch."

"Change of plan. We're going home."

"What do you mean?"

I fix her a firm look. "I mean, we're going home."

She opens her mouth to protest but I don't want to hear it. Whatever she's going to say is bound to piss me off even more. And I've a feeling we're about to have a show-down.

Chapter 35

Ella

I can barely keep up. Even in trainers I still only manage to keep two paces behind him. He storms out of the restaurant and onto the sun-drenched street, heading towards the car. His shoulders are stiff with tension. It's clear he's annoyed.

"Gabe. Wait," I gasp, but he's not listening. He's charging ahead like a man on a mission.

If he thinks I'm going to carry on chasing after him, he can think again. I've only ever chased after one guy, and swore I'd never do that again. I come to a halt in the middle of the street.

"You know what, if you haven't even got the decency to tell me what the fuck's going on, you'd better go home alone."

He stops in his tracks and slowly turns to face me. His face like thunder. I'm on the backfoot. His calm and collected exterior has well and truly cracked. I've never seen him look so angry. He stalks towards me. "Don't ever talk about yourself like that again."

"Like what?"

"All that stuff you said about class back there. About you being my bit of rough. It's total bullshit."

"Is it?"

He grabs my chin and forces me to look at him. "Don't push me."

"Why, what are you going to do about it?"

Angry blue eyes burn into mine. "Take you home and show you how wrong you are."

My chest heaves at his words. I press my thighs together. I'm standing out in the street in broad daylight getting turned on. "How?"

"I'm going to take you over my knee and smack that perfect arse of yours, so it's as pink as your flushed tits after I've fucked you."

My chest squeezes. I feel like I'm running out of oxygen. From somewhere I find my voice. "Are you going to get on with it then? Or are we going to stand out here all day?"

"That smart fucking mouth of yours." He grabs my hand and pulls me across the road, muttering expletives under his breath as he unlocks the car.

We don't speak on the journey home. Classical music pours from the speakers and I stare out of the window. He says he listens to this when he has a problem. Today, I'm it. Tough shit. I spoke the truth and I stand by it, whether he wants to hear it or not. Maybe this is how our bubble's going to burst. It's going to at some point. One last argument and one final fuck to put a full stop to it. Because it should stop. *We* should stop.

Gabe parks the car in the underground car park of the apartment block. We climb out of the car, slamming the doors behind us. He grabs my hand, impatiently tugging me towards the lift.

The lift doors close as we enter. I decide to take the bull by the horns. I'm growing tired of his mood. If he's bringing me back here to fuck me then finish this, I'm not letting that happen. I'm determined to get in there first. "Listen ..."

I don't get chance to get any more words out. He's on me, pinning me against the wall, with his body and mouth. His hands grab my waist pulling me to him, forcing his arousal into my hip as he kisses me hard. He catches my bottom lip between his teeth, then let's go with a growl, warning me to shut up. He's fucked off *and* turned on.

I yank my fingers through his hair, twisting and tugging, eliciting another moan from him. He slips his hands beneath my buttocks and lifts me up so that I'm balanced on the handrail of the lift, then he shifts between my legs and pins me in place. Our tongues tangle between hot, angry kisses as he spreads my legs wider and ducks his hand beneath my dress, finding my knickers. His fingers curl around the lace and he rips them off in one move, like they're paper and stuffs them in his pocket.

"You won't be needing these for the rest of the weekend."

"Eight quid they cost me," I tell him, "I'll invoice you, shall I? I can't afford to throw away eight quid knickers."

"Shut up," he says, and then his lips are back on mine, silencing me.

His lips remain on mine, silencing my gasp. Fireworks go off in my head. I'm knickerless and his words imply that he wants me for more than one more night. But I don't get a chance to dwell on it. The lift starts to slow.

Fuck.

I tear my lips from his and put my hand on his chest, pushing him away. "We're stopping."

Hooded eyes look at me, and for a second I'm not sure he's even heard me. Just in time, he registers what I've said and lowers me down to the floor.

The doors slide open and a grey-haired man wearing trainers, tailored brown shorts and a white polo shirt steps inside. "White! How's business?"

Gabe recovers in a blink of an eye and flashes the guy a perfect smile. "Great. How's retirement?"

I blush at our close call. We're making a habit of nearly getting caught out.

I discreetly straighten my dress and smooth a hand over my hair. My lips sting. God knows what I must look like.

"Fantastic. Just going up to the pool," the man says.

This place has a pool. Of course it does.

Gabe and the man launch into a discussion about the stock exchange. Before long the lift stops, the man gets out and a couple enter, forcing us to shuffle back to make room. No sooner have the doors closed, Gabe pushes a hand up my dress and squeezes my arse, hard. I bite the inside of my cheek to supress a squeal and control my ragged breathing. The sting of my soft flesh between his fingers registers sharp pain then pleasure. Muscles deep inside clench. Is this his way of telling me he's still angry, or what's in store for me when we get back to his?

As soon as the lift reaches the apartment, he grabs my hand and yanks me inside, leading me into the bedroom.

The look of anger from earlier has been replaced with a burning need. There's only one thing on his mind right now. "Take your dress off."

"What? Are you fucking serious? You haven't said two words to me since we left the restaurant, and now you're telling me what to do."

A deep crease etches into his brow. "Stop with your fucking mouth. For once do as you're told." He reaches forward and tears my dress open.

My mouth gapes in shock. I'm furious and aroused at the same time. But I'll not show him. I'll let him see the anger but not the desire. Just like I won't ever admit that I want him.

I glare at him. "I love this dress. You fucking dick."

"I'll buy you a new one. No, you know what, I'll buy you ten." He walks right up to me and looks me in the eye. "I'm not a patient man." He pushes my jacket and dress off my shoulders. I hear them land in a heap on the floor. "And you test my patience with that mouth of yours."

I boldly meet his gaze. "That's too bad. Tough fucking shit. Oh yeah, throw money at the problem. This is what I mean, you arsehole. Because it's just money to you, isn't it? There's nothing that can't be fixed. But you're wrong. You can't buy ten more. That dress is two years old, what, are you on eBay AS WE FUCKING SPEAK looking for another one? Don't get arsey about being called a rich bastard wanker if you're going to act like a rich bastard wanker. I'm not going to bow and scrape and bend for your every whim."

Renewed anger flashes in his eyes. He grabs my shoulders and pushes me backwards. I cry out in surprise as I lose my balance and fall back onto the bed. I don't get a chance to moan. He flips me over onto my front and pulls me down the bed. I feel the mattress shift as he sits on the end and pulls me over his lap.

"What the fuck are you doing!" I cry, struggling, but his

hands push down on my waist, keeping me in place.

He slaps my arse cheek, making me yelp.

"What are you doing!"

"Exactly what I said I would."

He dishes out another smack, this time harder than the first.

I gasp as the stinging sensation gives way and is replaced by a pleasurable ache between my thighs.

Fuck.

I close my eyes. I've always wanted a guy to do this to me. It's one of those dark little kinks I've carried around inside me for years, like the fact I like to be controlled in bed. I'd never plucked up the courage to share what I like with anyone until I met Ryan, and he didn't get it. None of them did. Until now. Gabe knows what I like. He sees into my darkness, without me having to say a word.

I brace myself for another slap but it doesn't come. He gently smooths a hand across the warm flesh of my backside, soothing it instead.

"Don't ever talk yourself down. Do you hear me?"

"I wasn't. I was telling the truth."

Smack!

My head jerks up at the impact. "Shit!"

"Tell me, you're important."

"Are you fucking crazy?"

I earn myself another sharp slap, but I'm getting used to them by now.

"I'm starting to think that maybe I am. Now say it."

Smack!

This pleasure pain thing is melting my brain. After each slap he smooths his hand across my stinging arse cheek.

"Say it!" he demands.

"Fucking hell, okay. I'm important."

Once again, he gently caresses his hand over my arse, carefully kneading my stinging flesh. I close my eyes and squeeze my thighs together to try and supress the dull ache between my legs.

"Don't ever say stuff like that about yourself again, and don't tell me how I feel about you." His voice matches his gentle touch. "I've had people telling me how I should feel about stuff most of my life, don't you be one of those people too."

I snap open my eyes. A million thoughts ping round my head. *Who is he talking about? How does he feel about me?*

He plants a soft kiss on the base of my spine, wiping all thoughts from my brain and making me shiver. Goosebumps prickle across my skin as he glides his palm over the curve of my backside and slides his fingers between my legs. My eyes close and I instinctively push back, seeking his touch.

A low moan falls from his lips as he pushes the tip of his finger inside me and I wriggle my arse back further, needing him to deepen the penetration.

"Not like this." He removes his hand between my legs, refusing to give me what I want. Now he's got me where he wants me, this will be on his terms.

He unclips my bra and tugs it from beneath me.

"You're so, so perfect." There's a softness to his tone, but it's more than that. There's awe and admiration too that makes me feel ten feet tall.

He slides his arms beneath me, gently lifts me up and lies me on the bed face down. I turn over to see him tearing his clothes off. He steps out of his jeans and stands totally naked at the end of the bed.

He's called me perfect. I say so is he. He's over six foot of dangerously lean, toned, tattooed gorgeousness and that's not even the deadliest weapon in his arsenal. He's got this disarming quality I'm not even sure he's aware of. The way his hair falls across his forehead. How his striking gaze starts my heart beating a little faster with just a look. And when he touches me I'm a goner. He's deadly.

I drink in the sight of him as he heads over to the bedside table and pulls out a condom. The roped muscles of his back flex as he tears the wrapper open and rolls it onto his length, then walks over to me.

I don't know where to look first as he stands over me. Beautiful and erect. He reaches out a hand and caresses my cheek before sinking to his knees in front of me and kissing me. I go with it, sliding my arms around his neck and lower myself off the bed to straddle him.

I rest my hands on his shoulders, wriggle into position and I sink onto his cock as our gazes lock. He tips his head back and closes his eyes, drawing in a lungful of air. My aching muscles throb around him as I adjust to the feel of him. The sight of his face, contorted with pleasure, is almost enough to make me come. His eyes open and he looks at me as I start to rotate my hips.

"Ella." He breathes my name and puts his hands on my hips. His heavy gaze roams over my breasts. "You beauty," he whispers, making me feel like a million dollars.

I bask beneath his words and I speed up my pace, rolling my hips, feeling the delicious tension build at my centre. I catch his bottom lip between my teeth and release it.

"I'm coming."

"I know you are, Princess," he pants, gripping my hips tighter. "Wait for me."

"I can't."

"Wait for me."

I cling onto his shoulders as a fresh wave of pleasure starts at my centre and rises through my body, taking hold of me. And he feels it too.

"Wait for me!"

"I can't."

Even when we're fucking it's a battle of wills. And this has been building all afternoon. I dig my fingernails into his shoulders and feel liquid as I pierce his flesh. His lips land on the valley between my breasts. "Fucking hell," he chokes out.

His cock tightens inside me, nudging me over the edge. My spine snaps straight, forcing my head back. I feel him let go. His fingers dig into my hip bones so hard it hurts as he pushes me down on to his length and his hips buck and roll.

My eyes snap close and I cry out, falling into an abyss of pleasure as tremor after tremor rack through my body, wiping my brain and leaving me weak. I collapse against him, curling my arms around his shoulders and feeling the rise and fall of his chest as his breathing slows. He nuzzles his nose into my neck and plants a tender kiss on the curve of my shoulder. We hold each other for ages in contented silence. He leans forward and puts his hands on the bed behind me.

"Hold tight," he tells me. I do as he's asked, clinging onto his shoulders. He pushes himself up to standing and puts his hands under my bum to stop me from falling.

"Do you want to put me down?" I ask, because it would be much easier.

"No."

That's fine by me. I don't really want him to put me down either.

He steps forward and carefully lowers me onto the sheets. With a kiss, he slides out of me and lies down beside me.

I immediately miss the feel of his body on mine and tell myself not to be stupid. Then, he scoops an arm around me and crushes me to his chest like he's read my mind. Or does he feel the same? The thought makes my stomach twist with longing.

I follow the edges of the black and grey rose tattoos on his arm with a fingertip, distracting me from my thoughts. This is the first time I've been this close and had chance to admire them properly. The shadowing of each rose is so skillfully done, it's like a pencil drawing. I stroke the edge of a petal that's tattooed above his nipple.

"Your tattoos are beautiful. What made you have them done, they're extraordinary?"

He looks at my finger gliding along his chest, thoughtfully. "Rebellion, I suppose."

"From what?"

"My life." He looks at the ceiling and heaves a sigh. "Dad. He despises them. He thinks they're common."

I know he hasn't got the best relationship with Spencer, but

I presumed his relationship with his dad was good. He trained him up and entrusted him to carry on the business. "You don't get on?"

"Used to when I was little. But show me a little boy who doesn't think his dad's a rockstar. It's not until you get older, you start to see people for who they really are."

Maxwell White built the business from scratch. He's revered and looked up to. He's a well-known property developer with a rags-to-riches tale, yet this suggests there's another side.

"What happened?"

He looks at me for a long time, like he's deciding whether to tell me something or not. "Life. What about your dad?"

I get why he's guarded. He doesn't come from a regular family, they're high profile. I go with the swift change in conversation.

"He wasn't around. Amy was about one when he left. Mum was crushed. We were fine, she saw that we never went without, but she had to be both a mum and a dad to us. For the first few years after he left, I remember wishing every birthday and Christmas he'd come back. After a while I realised he wasn't going to. When I got older, Mum admitted he was the love of her life, but we were better off without him."

Gabe curls his fingers around my wrist and strokes his thumb across my pulse. "He left her to raise two little kids by herself? Your mum sounds like an amazing woman."

I smile weakly. "She was the best."

He shifts, sitting up in bed and cups my cheek with his hand. "Listen, given lunch was cut short, how about we order some food? I'm starving."

I smile. "It was your own fault for storming out."

"I think you'll find that it was yours." He lowers his head and kisses me lightly on the lips. "And this mouth of yours."

"You could try and control yourself," I counter.

"Around you? It's impossible." My heart squeezes. He kisses me then pulls away, looking serious. "Don't believe everything you read or see on the internet. I'm not a playboy like Spencer.

And don't ever think that just because someone's richer, or because they're a different class, makes them better than you."

"I don't think they're better," I clarify. "I just think they probably have more in common with you."

"Why, because our fathers go to the same golf club?" He cocks an eyebrow telling me he doesn't agree. "I'm the judge of who I've more in common with, and it isn't any of them."

As he kisses me deeply and his body covers mine. I know I want it to be me.

Chapter 36

Gabe

The burnished orange sunset fills the early evening sky and casts the towering office and apartment blocks in shadow. The rays of the disappearing sun fill the apartment with a dream-like ethereal glow. I glance over my shoulder at my laptop, sitting closed on the corner of the grey marble counter where it's been since I came home from work yesterday. In five years, I can count on one hand the non-working days when I've not checked or sent emails. My mind and hands have been full of something else this weekend. And I don't have one single regret.

"Women are trouble. The more money you've got, the more they want to fuck you. They're good for one thing and one thing only. Take my advice kid, don't get yourself tied down to one."

Dad's words echo in my mind. The same way they have done for years, influencing my life and views on relationships. That's exactly what he wanted. If I'm wed to the business, with no other distractions, it can only mean more success. And it suited me, too. There's never been a woman in my life long enough for me to form any sort of emotional connection to them, because I didn't want to. Until now.

The thought hits me like a punch to the chest.

It's just fucking, I tell myself.

But as I watch the sun disappear behind the silhouette of St Paul's Cathedral, I'm left with the stark realisation that maybe it's not. I've never asked a woman to stay over before. I've never wanted to. It's happened by default a couple of times, followed by an awkward exchange the next morning while she waits for her cab.

I rub a hand across the stubble of my jaw and stare out at the river, glittering in the fading light. Things seem so easy with Ella, when in reality they're so complicated I can't even begin to unravel it.

"Hey."

I turn to see her wandering towards me, wearing nothing but my white t-shirt. Her hair tumbles across her shoulders and her legs seem to go on forever. My cock lurches in my sweatpants, the way it always does when I clap eyes on her.

"That t-shirt looks a lot better on you than it does on me."

She comes closer. "Oh, I don't know about that."

I smile at her playfulness and slide my hands around her waist. I really can't decide if I like her best like this or being feisty. "Wait. Did you almost pay me a compliment?"

She puts her hands on my shoulders and stands on tiptoes so her face is nearly level with mine. "Almost, but not quite. Now, what are we eating?"

My mouth's on hers before I know it. She presses herself against me and moans softly as my tongue slides in her mouth. "How about you?" I pant, between hot heavy kisses that elicit a louder moan from her.

"Yes," she breathes against my lips, making my cock harden.

This. Her. Everything when we're together feels so easy.

A buzzing noise sounds from across the kitchen, making her jump.

"What was that?"

"The concierge. Actual dinner's here." I place a light kiss on her lips and smile. "You can be second course," I tell her, watching her cheeks blush.

I reluctantly disentangle myself and head over to the phone on the wall.

A few minutes later I emerge from the lift holding a box. Her eyes widen in surprise as she looks at the box, then me. "Pizza?"

"Of course." I sit down beside her on the sofa, put the box on the coffee table and open the lid. "I said it was my favourite. I played it safe with Margherita. That okay?"

"Perfect," she says eyeing the contents.

We each take a slice and settle back into the cushions.

"I'm famished," she admits, taking a mouthful and hooking

her legs over mine.

I watch her tuck into her slice with gusto. Some of the women I've dated wouldn't have allowed pizza in the same room as them. Not Ella. She's refreshing.

She takes another slice and settles back into her seat.

"So, do you still think I'm a self-entitled prick?"

Her eyes swing to mine. "I said last night, maybe I was wrong to call you that."

"So you *don't* think I'm a self-entitled prick?"

She takes a bite of crust and shrugs. "You're not as bad as I thought you'd be."

"Careful. That sounded *dangerously* like a compliment," I tease.

A smile curls at the corner of her lips. "Maybe it was. I dunno, sometimes people like you ..."

"How do you mean, people like me?"

She pops the last bit of crust in her mouth and chews thoughtfully. "I mean, people who've had a privileged upbringing, that have been born into money."

Ever since we've met she's had a stick up her arse about my wealth and I'm determined to find out why. I take a slice out the box and hand it to her, then reach for another. "Okay. Go on."

"Thanks. Well, sometimes *those* people just aren't very nice. They think they're entitled to treat people like shit and act in a certain way, like they're somehow allowed to be horrible, just because they're loaded."

I'm getting somewhere. "And how many of *those* types of people have you met before?"

Her chewing slows. She lowers her eyes to the pizza box and puts the slice back inside, like her appetite's vanished. "One."

The sadness in her eyes says it all. Something happened to her and I'm determined to find out what. I mentally shuffle through the bits of information I've learnt about her. "Ryan?"

She shakes her head, and straightens.

"Then who?"

"It was a long time ago," she says firmly, avoiding my gaze.

I put my pizza back in the box, wipe my hands with a napkin and take her hands in mine.

"Shit eats away at us if we don't talk about it. Take it from me."

"I know," she whispers, shifting closer to me and touching her forehead to mine. The wall she's built around her heart is slowly crumbling, I can feel it. She's opening up to me. I don't know what the hell has happened to her, but I want to make it all better.

The sound of my mobile shatters the silence. She tugs her hands from mine, looking out of the window, her guard snapping back into place. I pull out my phone. It's Jake. *Cheers, bro.*

"What's up?" I snap.

"You need to come down to the club," he shouts over the blaring music in the background. "It's Spencer."

"What's he done now?"

"Got into a fight."

I dash a hand through my hair in irritation. "He's meant to be running the fucking place."

"I know, I know. Listen, G, I've broken it up, but you might want to come down to sort shit out."

Like I always do. Clear up after his mess. "Is he hurt?"

"Yeah, a bit. Nothing serious."

"Okay, I'm leaving now."

I cancel the call. I can always rely on Spencer to screw things up.

"Is everything okay?" Ella asks.

Fuck knows what she must be thinking overhearing snippets of that conversation.

"Spencer's been in a fight at the club. I need to go down there." I push my phone back into my pocket and stand up. "I'm sorry. I'll try not to be long."

"I'm coming with you," she declares, getting to her feet.

If the rational, sensible part of my brain were in charge I should want her to stay here. That way she and the family side of things are kept totally separate. As they should be. But my brain isn't running the show anymore and neither is my cock. Something deeper is at play here. I want her by my side. Always. Fuck the consequences.

She catches my hands in hers and links her fingers through mine. "Besides, you can't leave me here by myself, I'll get lost in this place."

She gives me a teasing smile that seals the deal.

"Okay," I agree. "But remember, I'm nothing like my little brother."

Chapter 37

Ella

It's dark by the time we arrive at Whites. Gabe pulls the Bugatti into one of the spaces marked *Reserved* in the small car park round the back of the building.

He cuts the engine and shoots me a hesitant look. He seems uncharacteristically on edge. "Are you sure you want to come in?"

"No, I want to stay out here in the cold." I roll my eyes. "Of course I'm coming in."

Concern flashes in his eyes and he puts a protective hand on top of mine. "You're cold?"

A warm fuzzy feeling hits my chest at the fact he's worried about me, again. Of course, Mum cared about me in a motherly way and Kate's always got my back but I've never had a guy in my life that's ever given a shit enough about me to worry. And I've been just fine, blazing my own trail and looking after myself. Until now.

"I'll be okay once I'm inside."

He peers up at the entrance, looking unconvinced. An uncomfortable thought hits me. Maybe he doesn't really want me here. This part of his personal life is still a bit of a mystery. 'Work' Gabe I'm familiar with, but this place is a link to his family and the side of his life he guards. Maybe he's not ready to let me in just yet. Maybe he'll never be ready.

"What's the matter?"

He's watching me. I need to know.

"Do you … do you wish I'd stayed back at yours? Because if that's the case, if you don't want me to come in, I'll stay in the car. Your brothers are in there. I know I've met Jake but that was kind of by accident, and they're your family, and this is … well, we're not …" I'm rambling like an idiot.

A smile plays on his lips at my awkwardness. "No, I want you to come in. It's just Spencer's a prick at the best of times. If he's been fighting, that means he's drunk. I don't want him to upset you."

I feel a tingle of relief. He's worried his little brother's going to upset me. "I worked in a strip club for two years. I think I can handle putting Spencer in his place if he oversteps the line."

He laughs. "Actually, now you put it like that, I'm quite looking forward to this." Something he said a while ago clicks into place. "Is this what you meant when you said you and I are more similar than I know? We both have to keep bailing out our younger siblings?"

He looks at me thoughtfully. "Amongst other things."

Before I can prod further, he squeezes my hand and says, "Come on, let's go and see what the damage is."

***

The bouncer standing guard at the back door of the club bobs his head in acknowledgement as we enter. The thumping beat of dance music can be heard in the distance as we head down a long white corridor, with doors leading off either side.

The sound of raised male voices filter towards us and grow louder as we come to a stop at a door marked *Cloakroom.*

Gabe pushes open the door. Around the edge of the room are lockers. On the far end is a small kitchenette, sink and fridge. In the centre is a round, four-seater table. Jake leans against one of the lockers, arms folded. He's glaring at Spencer who's hunched forward on one of the chairs, holding his nose with his hands. His mousey brown hair has fallen over his face and it's obvious he's totally out of it.

Jake's frown dissolves as he sees me. He straightens in surprise. "Ella."

"What the fuck's happened?" Gabe asks, ignoring the questioning look in his older brother's eyes.

"Dipshit here thought it would be a good idea to hit on someone's wife. Funnily enough, her husband didn't take too kindly to it and gave him a kicking. He's in the office, calming down." He looks at Gabe. "Thought you might want to tidy up a few loose ends."

Gabe narrows his eyes in anger and turns his attention to his younger brother. "For fuck's sake, Spencer. You're the manager. This is your job, have some fucking accountability for once in your life. I didn't buy this place for you so you could get pissed every night and hit on women. This is a business. *Your* business."

Spencer slowly lifts his head, squinting at us both with one eye closed, like he's only just realised we're standing there. His hands are covered in blood and he's clutching a sodden tissue to his bleeding nose. A red line trickles down his forearm and splatters onto the white linoleum by his foot.

"Never fear, the cavalry's here," Spencer slurs. He frowns in confusion as he homes in on me. "Now, what do we have here?"

"Shit. Sorry, G. I forgot." Jake puffs his cheeks, blowing out a long breath, looking awkward.

Spencer chuckles. "Oh dear, he's had to excuse himself."

What the fuck are they talking about?

I look to Gabe for reassurance, but he's gone. Jake looks sheepish and nods in the direction of the corridor outside.

What's going on?

I head out the room to find Gabe leant forward against the wall. His fingers are splayed out across the white breezeblocks and his head is dropped forward as he takes deep, steadying breaths in and out. His eyes are closed tight, his face pale. Beads of sweat collect on his brow. I don't know this Gabe. Panic grips me.

"Oh my God, what's the matter? Are you okay?"

"Go back inside."

I don't want to do anything of the sort. "Is there anything I can do?"

"I said, go away." His voice is tight and full of warning.

He's scaring me. I know he doesn't want me here but I can't leave him in this state. "Please, let me help."

"Just do as you're fucking told and go back inside!" He grinds out through clenched teeth.

The fact he's pushing me away when he clearly needs help, hurts more than the pain of seeing him like this.

I fight to keep the emotion out of my voice. "If that's what you want."

I slope back into the cloakroom trying to work out what the hell's going on. Spencer has sat up, tilting his head back and holding the blood-stained tissue to his nose to try and stop the bleeding.

Jake catches the troubled look on my face and gives me a reassuring smile. "Give him five. He'll be okay."

I look around the room feeling like a spare part. I'm not sure what the hell's going on with Gabe, but it seems like I'm the only one in the dark. Is it the blood? For now, I need to make myself useful.

I head over to the kitchenette, grab a couple of hand towels from the dispenser and run them under the cold tap.

I sit down beside Spencer and offer them to him. "Here. You should try to clean up. You're making a mess of the floor."

Jake snorts with laughter. Spencer casts me a curious sideways glance. He straightens his head and takes the wet paper towels from me without so much as a thank you.

"So, where did he find you?

I can hardly say work, can I? Jake knows our secret, but I'm pretty sure Spencer can't be trusted with that information.

"He hasn't found me from anywhere," I reply stiffly. "And I'm not a fucking object, so don't speak to me like I am."

Spencer's mouth pulls into a bemused smile as he wipes his nose clean of blood and takes me in. Apart from sharing the same colour eyes, he and Gabe look nothing alike. He's wearing a creased black t-shirt and tight fitting faded black jeans with black lace-up boots. He's got poor-little-rich-boy stamped all over him. I catch sight of the W ring on his right hand. If it wasn't for the family branding, I wouldn't have believed they were related.

"You're a bit different to his usual type. Me, on the other hand, I like them when they've got a bit of fight."

"From what I hear about you, you're not picky." He laughs and leans into me, waggling his eyebrows. "Yeah, but you've heard of me."

There's something about him; he exudes arrogance and the cocky smirk he permanently wears reminds me of Logan.

"Half of the country followed your bedroom antics on the TV, but it's hardly something to be proud of. You treated some of those girls like shit."

His eyes narrow at my challenge. He's definitely not used to being pulled up. "I made that fucking show. And trust me, darling, I'm not the only brother who treats women like shit."

Alarm bells ring in my head at the veiled jibe. It's clear he's talking about Gabe, but is he telling the truth or just trying to yank my chain because I'm getting to him?

My mobile rings in my pocket interrupting our verbal sparring match. I pull it out. It's Amy. Her timing is impeccable, as always. I've no doubt she's calling to check I've got the money she needs. She'll have to wait. I cancel the call and put my phone on the table.

Spencer looks at the photo on my phone of me and Amy, taken on her birthday last year. "Who's the blonde?"

"My sister."

"She's hot."

"She's too good for you."

He flashes a lascivious smile. "Is she as feisty as you, because if she is, I'm sure we'd get on like a house on fire."

"You'll never meet her to find out and even if you did, you're not her type," I lie. Spencer is *exactly* her type. She was obsessed with watching *Young, Rich & Reckless* just to catch a glimpse of him.

"I'm *everyone's* type, babe."

Cocky prick.

I'm about to launch at him for calling me babe, but don't get the chance as Gabe enters the room. He's back to his usual collected self.

"I've sorted things with the guy," he tells Jake. "There'll be no comeback."

How's he sorted it? And what type of comeback?

He throws Spencer a look of disgust. "Go home and sleep it off. And for fuck's sake, lay off the drink in future. I'm done with bailing your arse out. This is your final chance."

Spencer silently glares at Gabe's instructions, like he's heard it all before.

Gabe takes my hand and turns to me. "Come on, let's get out of here. I've had enough of this place."

***

Gabe doesn't say much on the walk back to the car. A lot's happened in the last thirty minutes and I'm still trying to work it all out.

We get into the car and Gabe turns on the ignition. I know he's not going to elaborate if I don't push it and I'm definitely going to push it.

"Are you okay after what happened back there?"

"Bailing Spencer out is sadly par for the course. I'm used to it."

That's not what I'm talking about, but go with it. "Yeah, I got that impression. What did you say to the woman's husband?"

"I sorted it."

"Yeah, you said, but how?"

"Spencer's high profile because of the TV show. People are tempted to go to the press. They'd lap it up."

"What are you saying?"

"I'm saying, everyone's got a price."

My eyes widen. The penny drops. "You paid him off?"

Gabe drags a hand across his jaw and glances out of the window. "Like I said, everyone has their price."

"Isn't that bribery?"

"No, it's an agreement."

"And how do you know he won't go to the press?"

"Trust me. He won't."

There's a glint of malice in his eyes, the same look I saw that night at the club when he grabbed Sam round the throat. I was right. He does have a dangerous side. "And how many times have you done this?"

He rolls his shoulders into a shrug. "Fuck knows. I've lost count."

"But he'll never learn. Why do you keep doing it?"

"What he does reflects on the family, which reflects on the business. I'm not going to let everything everyone's worked so hard for, get undone by my stupid prick of a brother. Why do you keep helping your sister out?"

"Because I'm the only one she's got left."

He smiles. "Younger siblings are a pain in the arse." He pulls his seatbelt round him like it's the end of the conversation. He's done talking, but I'm not.

"Why did you rush out of the room back there? I was worried about you. What happened?"

He clicks his seatbelt in place and stares straight ahead. For a moment I'm not sure he's going to say anything. "I was fine."

"You didn't look it."

"After a few minutes, I'm always fine."

"What happened?" I press.

He hesitates. It's clear whatever he's about to say he doesn't share often. "I don't like the sight of blood. It's no big deal. Everyone dislikes something, don't they?"

My brain mentally rewinds. I was right. He'd been fine until Spencer began dripping blood all over the floor. "You looked like you were about to pass out. How long have you been phobic?"

He shakes his head at the word. "I'm not ... I developed it as a kid. Like I said, it's no big deal."

I've a burning need to know *why*. It's true most people don't like something. I'm not keen on heights but I don't nearly pass out every time I walk over a bridge. Gabe's reaction seemed pretty severe.

He drags a hand across his jaw, still avoiding my gaze. I'm peeling back the layers of him, and he's clearly not comfortable with it. And I don't want to push him.

"You're right, younger siblings are a pain in the arse," I tell him, changing the subject.

He looks over at me and smiles. "Come on, let's go home. I want to forget about tonight, and I know just the thing to distract me."

Chapter 38

Ella

I wake the next morning to sunlight filtering through the windows and a note on the bedside table.

I'm going to hit the gym. Won't be long. Order up some breakfast for us. Menu's on the kitchen counter. xxx

My heart traitorously skips at the sight of the "x" for a moment, before niggling doubt beats it down. It means nothing, just like the use of the word "us" means nothing, just like this weekend means *nothing*.

I sit on the edge of the bed, gazing out across the city. It's too easy to get carried away; the sex, the fancy apartment, the flash car and Gabe himself, but the bubble's going to burst soon and I need to face facts. There's a physical attraction between us. The connection we have is purely sexual. We've scratched the itch. A lot. It'll be time to move on soon. Just like he has with God knows how many other women who've been in my position before.

I take a shower and pull on my light blue skinny jeans with the rips in the knees and a sleeveless black t-shirt. I put on a little blusher and mascara and run my fingers through my hair and head to the kitchen.

The menu's on the counter as promised. I climb onto one of the padded grey velvet stools and flick through it. My stomach growls at the delicious food on offer; everything from smoothies to a full English breakfast.

A phone rings from somewhere in the apartment, making me jump. It's not my mobile, unless it's Gabe's. Curious to know where the sounds coming from, I slide off the stool and wander round the apartment following the ring. Then it stops, a loud beep sounds, an answerphone kicks in and Gabe's voice says,

"Hey, I'm not available right now. Leave a message after the beep."

My gaze lands on the black answerphone on the console table in the hall. There's another long beep.

"Hiya. It's me." A woman's voice fills the apartment. She gives a coy little laugh which makes me uneasy. "I was wondering whether you fancied hooking up tonight, because well, I've been feeling lonely, I miss you G, G ..." My stomach drops to my Converse. "I was lying in bed, touching myself, thinking about you, wishing you were with me. You've got my number. Call me."

Silence fills the apartment.

Jealousy stabs through my heart like a knife. My mind launches into fifth gear.

Who the fuck was that?

One of his string of women, or worse?

I press a hand to my forehead and briefly close my eyes as a horrid thought hits me.

His girlfriend? Fiancée?

I *presumed* he was single, but it stands to reason he's not. He's one of the top twenty most eligible bachelors in the country. There's bound to be someone. He's not going to be upfront about it, is he? Not when there's sex on the cards. He's just a guy after all. They all think with their dicks.

I stalk into the walk-in wardrobe and yank my overnight bag from the top shelf, scooping my clothes and belongings off the shelves and cramming them into my bag. Anger spurs me on, squashing all the emotions I have no right to feel; disappointment, sadness, jealousy. I zip up the bag and sling it over my shoulder. He *almost* got me. *Fucking bastard!*

The odds aren't in my favour today. I hear the lift doors open and steel myself as I emerge into the hall.

Gabe's navy t-shirt and shorts are damp with sweat and his hairs sticking up all over the place. He's a hot mess. *Fuck.*

He breaks into an easy smile. "Morning Princess, hope you've ordered..." his eyes drop to my bag and he trails off, his smile dissolving. "What's going on?"

I steel myself and glance at the blinking red light on the answerphone. "Your girlfriend rang," I say, nodding at the phone. "Apparently she's touching herself so maybe you should get over there before she goes off the boil."

His eyes slide to the phone. "What do you mean? Who called?"

You mean, there's more than one woman? Of course. Silly me. Why should he just have one woman when he's probably got a line of them throwing themselves at him!

Unwelcome emotion bubbles in my chest, and I bite the inside of my cheek to stop it from taking over. I'm not getting into this with him. I'll sound like a crazy, jealous bitch and I'm not giving him the satisfaction. I need to get the hell out of here.

I fix him a firm look. "I think that it's best that I go."

The frown line on his forehead deepens. "But I don't want you to."

"Tough shit, I'm going."

His eyes darken. He glances behind me to the bedroom and tilts his head, giving me a thoughtful look. "Shall I take you back there and remind you why you should stay?"

I'm determined to stand strong.

"This is over."

"And you're deciding that, are you?"

"I just did. Let's be realistic. We fucked, we shouldn't have done. We're on borrowed time. It needs to end. Now."

"That's quite a speech, how long did you practise that?"

"I'm serious."

"So, am I. If you think I'm going to let you walk out of here, you're wrong. Instead, I'm going to drag you into the bedroom and fuck some sense into you."

His words have my heart in a vice-like grip. Surely he should be pleased. I'm ending it. I'm giving him an easy way out. He'll have free rein to move on to the next woman, which is highly likely to be Miss-answer-phone-message. *Why is he making this so fucking difficult?*

"No."

"If there's one thing I've learnt over the past two days, it's that we're permanently ready to fuck each other. Even now, even though we're arguing, I'm hard." His heated gaze rakes over my body. "And I know if I pushed my hand down your knickers right now, you'd be wet for me, Princess."

He delivers the last line with so much conviction I shiver. I try not to smile as I press my thighs together.

He's right. I know it. He knows it. I do want him, all the time. I've never felt this level of attraction before. I should be doing a happy dance at the fact he's admitted he feels the same, and I would under any other circumstance, but not now. Not when I know he's a potential cheat.

It's clear he's not going down without a fight. I need to dig deep and do what I need to do, to end this.

"Don't be so fucking naïve. You're Spencer's brother, from a famous family and worth fuck knows how much. You're a *White* for God's sake. What woman wouldn't like to say they've fucked you."

My words wipe the smile off his face. He draws his head back slightly. I can see the cogs turning in his head. "What are you saying? That you only slept with me because of who I am?"

He wears a hurt look that I've never seen before. My heart aches. I step round him and make a dash to the lift, unable to look at him any longer. I need to remain firm.

"What can I say, you got me," I toss out, stepping inside and turning to face him.

"I don't believe you." The firmness of his voice matches the look in his eye.

"Believe it, because it's true," I snap, keeping my hard-faced bitch act going and desperately jabbing at the lift button.

Relief sears through me as the doors start to close.

"Face it Gabe, for once in your life, *you've* been played."

***

'Walking on Sunshine' by Katrina and The Waves blares down the hall from the kitchen when I get home. Even Kate's out of tune singing and the smell of freshly baked cookies wafting down the hall can't lift a smile.

I've spent the Uber ride home convincing myself I've done the right thing. So, why do I feel like a Queen Bitch?

Kate appears in the kitchen doorway holding a mixing bowl. White flour is streaked across her cheeks and blue top.

"I thought I heard the door go. What are you doing back?"

I dump my bag on the floor and puff out my cheeks, blowing out a long breath. Where the fuck do I start?

She gives me a long look and pulls a face, sensing somethings up. "Hang on." She disappears into the kitchen and seconds later reappears holding a plate of chocolate chip cookies.

"Your face tells me you need one of these."

Ten minutes later we're slumped on the sofa with an empty plate between us, and I feel sicker now than I did when I arrived.

"I still can't believe you dumped him." Kate wipes the crumbs from her mouth with the back of her hand and looks at me like I've gone mad. "Bet there's not many women who could say they've done that."

I throw the remaining half of my cookie down on the plate. "I haven't dumped him. That would mean it *was* something more than sex, and it wasn't. One of us needed to end it."

"Yeah, well I'd say it's pretty much over after you told him you only shagged him because of his money."

"I'm not exactly proud of what I said, but I needed to get out of there and that was the only thing I could think of that would make him hate me. Anyway, now he's free to hook up with Miss-booty-call or his girlfriend, or whoever the fuck she is."

"Do you really think he's a cheat?"

I shrug and heave a weary sigh. "I don't know. I don't know what to think anymore. I'm *tired* of thinking."

"Well, so what if the other woman called? He's hot, loaded and a White. He'll have banged loads of women. You sound a bit jealous to me."

"I'm not jealous," I snap.

Kate gives me a doubtful look. "Honestly?"

I slam my head back into the leather sofa and squeeze my eyes closed, hating what I'm about to admit. "I'm jealous," I groan.

"I knew it!"

"When did this get so fucked up? I shouldn't feel this way. There are so many reasons why this is totally wrong. He's my boss. We're from completely different worlds …"

"Why does that matter?"

I pick at the frayed knees of my jeans. "It's just my track record with men like him … isn't great."

Kate raises her eyebrows. "You're not seriously comparing Gabe to that fucking bastard, Logan. Fucking hell, he's not even in the same league."

"Isn't he? I don't really know anything about him, he's a bit closed off when it comes to his personal life, and I get that but …" I try to find the right words that won't make me sound like a needy sap.

"You want more."

That's exactly it. "But I can't have more."

"You want to know more about him. You're looking for a sign from him, that he doesn't see you as just another woman he's fucked."

"It doesn't matter anyway, now, does it. The whole thing's a moot point. I won't see him again. There's no way I'll have a job after this, and that's for the best."

"You think he'll fire you?"

"Of course I'm fucking fired. It doesn't matter anyway. I'm resigning. I can't possibly turn up at work tomorrow after this."

"Has he tried to call you?"

"Dunno. My phone's in my bag in the hall."

"Don't you think you should maybe check?"

Not yet. I need a bit more time to process everything that's happened in the last couple of hours.

"Later." I nod at the pile of flyers on the coffee table which Margot dropped off for me. "I need to pull my finger out and get posting those. Anyway, a walk will help me take my mind off this shit for a while."

Kate looks out the window behind me and frowns. "Are you seriously going out delivering in this weather?"

"What?" I twist round and follow her gaze. Heavy black clouds fill the sky and rain splatters against the glass.

"I'll take an umbrella. I need to do my bit and help Margot and the others." I eye the plate with the half-eaten cookie. "Anyway, how come you're baking again?"

Kate pats the back of her messy bun and scrunches up her nose. "No reason. Just fancied it, I haven't done any for a while."

A while. The last time Kate started a baking frenzy was when she split up from Gavin. It occupied her mind, and gave her hands something to do, to stop herself from texting him. It worked wonders, but wasn't so good for our waistlines. Needless to say, the smell of freshly baked goods and the sight of a mixing bowl have me feeling equal amounts of pleasure and concern for my friend's emotional welfare.

"How are things with you and Harry?"

"All right."

"Only all right?"

"He's been busy, doing a lot of overtime this weekend, so I haven't really seen him, but we're going out tonight."

There's an uncertainty in her voice which makes me worry.

"Are you sure everything's okay?"

"Yeah."

I'm not convinced. She's thrown herself headfirst into this. "It's just, you don't seem okay."

She absent-mindedly brushes flour off her t-shirt with the

back of her hand. "I think maybe, because I've liked him for so long, I built it up in my head that it was going to be fantastic…"

"And it's not. Are we talking about the sex here or everything?"

"Everything, more or less."

"I thought the sex was good with Horny Harry?"

She shrugs. "It's all right, just a bit wham-bam. I dunno, maybe I expect too much."

"Of course you don't. You deserve someone who'll tick every box, and after all the shit you went through with Gav, you doubly deserve it. If Harry's not matching up, then, well … you know what to do."

She pulls a face which tells me she knows I'm right. "Yeah well, I'll see how tonight goes. Anyway, I think it's about time you took your own advice."

I look at her, confused.

"You deserve someone fantastic too. If they don't measure up, like Ryan, then by all means move on, but if they do, don't be scared to take a risk and let them in."

I sit forward on the seat and push my hands through my hair, uncomfortable at the x-ray vision she's got when it comes to my love life. "It's just I was worried that if I took a risk, he'd break my heart."

Kate sidles up beside me and puts her hand on mine. "He stalked you when you went on a date with someone else, then carried you to the front door and snogged your face off, even though he shouldn't have done any of it. Not to mention the fact you've spent nearly all weekend with him. Think about it from his perspective, he's got loads at stake here. You can walk away if it goes tits up, he can't, he's the boss, yet he's still done it all…doesn't that tell you something?"

I pick up the pile of leaflets from off the coffee table and thumb through them. "Yeah, it tells me when he gets someone in his sights, he'll do whatever it takes to seal the deal."

I can feel Kate's eyes on me. I don't dare look at her because I know she doesn't buy it. And I'm not sure I do either. But I'm tired of thinking about Gabe White. Hitting the streets, pushing flyers through letterboxes in the pissing rain seems incredibly appealing compared to sitting here all afternoon driving myself mad, thinking.

"Listen, El, I think he ..."

I'm tired of talking about it. I leap to my feet and swipe the pile of flyers off the table.

"I'd better head out, these won't jump through letterboxes by themselves."

Chapter 39

Ella

I've misjudged. Misjudged how wet it is. How I really should have spent another five minutes looking for an umbrella before I left the house, and how pushing flyers through grotty letterboxes does nothing to distract me from the horrid, unsettling feeling I get in my stomach every time I re-run the day's events through my head.

By the time I'm nearing the end of my flyer-pushing round, I've convinced myself this has all worked out for the best. So what if I've got to leave the best job I've ever had. I'll just get another one, where the boss isn't the sexiest thing to walk the earth and I won't develop feelings for him.

Feelings. I've let myself down. I've allowed my stupid fucking heart to rule my head, something I said I'd never do again, because the last time I did I ended up in the shit.

I've no idea how long I'm out pounding the pavements. I walk until the last flyer is posted and I'm soaked to the bone. My faded denim jacket is sodden, my hair's hanging like rats' tails and my Converse squelch.

It's dark as I head down the front path. The light peeking from behind the living room curtains tells me Kate's not yet left for her date. I brace myself for the telling off I'm about to get for wandering the streets for God knows how long, in the rain.

I step inside to find her all dolled-up standing at the hall mirror, applying a coat of pink lipgloss. Her eyes widen at the sight of me.

"Jesus, you're fucking soaking. I should have a go at you, but there's no time for that." She looks worried. "Thank god you're back."

I close the front door and push my soaking wet pumps off my feet. "Why, what's up?"

"Didn't you see the car?"

"What car? It's dark outside, and" – I pluck at my soaking wet t-shirt with my fingers – "pissing it down, if you didn't know."

"Gabe's car."

My stomach somersaults at the mention of his name. "What do you mean?"

"He's been here five minutes," she whispers, nodding towards the closed living room door. "I tried calling you, but your phone's still bloody switched off."

I peel off my soaking wet jacket and hang it on the radiator to dry. There's only one reason why he's come to see me. "He's probably come to hand me my P45 in person."

Kate pushes her lipgloss into her bag and gives me a funny look. "He asked if you were in. When I told him you weren't, he said he'd wait for you." She steps into her black heels at the bottom of the stairs.

A car horn beeps outside.

"That'll be Harry. I'm staying at his place tonight." She gives me a meaningful look which I ignore and opens the front door, glancing over her shoulder at me. "If you're still looking for a sign, I think this is it." Then she's gone.

My stomach feels like it's rolling down a hill. I look at my bedraggled reflection in the mirror. My hair's sticking to my head, my t-shirt and jeans are glued to me like a second skin, but by some miracle at least my mascara hasn't run.

I put my hand on the living room door handle and take a deep breath, steeling myself. This isn't going to be easy. There's no doubt Gabe's come to give me a piece of his mind. I push open the living room door and step inside. The Tiffany-style lamp on the side table by the sofa, and a fire blazing in the fireplace, bathe the room in a warm glow. I'm on the back foot as I stare at the flames flickering in the hearth. It's the first time the fire's been lit since Mum died.

Gabe kneels on the hearthrug, prodding the coal basket with the poker. I close the door and go to stand beside him, staring into the dancing flames. The warmth from the fire fills the room and I'm grateful after trudging about in the rain all afternoon.

"Kate said she didn't think you'd be much longer," he says without looking at me. "I was going to give you another five minutes before I came looking for you."

"You didn't need to bother." I know I sound like an ungrateful bitch, but I'm struggling to process the fact he's come looking for me. Those aren't the actions of someone who's pissed off.

"Walking the streets on your own at night isn't safe. Kate tried to call you but your phone was off."

"I left it here."

He heaves an impatient sigh. "Fucking great, so if anything *had* happened, you wouldn't have been able to call anyone."

"Nothing *has* happened to me though, has it? Anyway, there's no point me taking my phone with me, the battery's knackered."

He glances at me, the irritation clear in his eyes. "You're soaked. I knew you would be, that's why I lit the fire." He hangs the poker back in the holder on the hearth and stands up.

There he is again; looking after me, caring about me, worrying about me. His protectiveness tugs at my heart strings. "We had an open fire in our living room back home," he carries on, his voice softening. "When we were little, Dad used to get me and Jake to find kindling from the garden, then we'd help him light the fire. Open fires always make a room feel warm and cosy. I kind of miss it."

"Kate and I never bother. We just bung the heating on. The last time it was lit, Mum was alive. But I kind of miss it too," I admit, wrapping my arms around my chest and staring into the flames.

"What was earlier about? You almost had me."

The swift change in conversation pulls me back to the here and now. I carry on staring into the fire, unable to look at him. "I don't know what you mean. I said what I said because it's true."

"Cut the bullshit." He turns to me, a determined glint in his eye. "You expect me to believe you only slept with me because of who I am?"

"Why not? I'm sure I wouldn't be the first."

"No, you wouldn't, but one thing I've got really good at over the years is working out who's fake and who's genuine. Who sees me as a meal ticket or a step up the ladder. You're not like that. Why pretend to be?"

I need to push this. I need to make him believe me. He needs to hate me and walk out of here in disgust, because it's the only defence I've got left.

I look him dead in the eye. "You don't know me. I *am* one of those women."

"No, you're not. Trust me, I know a gold digger when I see one and that's not you. You're selfless and big hearted and loyal and those women aren't fit to walk in your fucking shadow. You're lying. I can see it in your eyes, just like I saw the sadness in them when I first met you."

His words weave through the cracks in the defence I've built around my heart like ivy. The fortress I built eight years ago to prevent anyone else getting close. If I don't let them in, they can't hurt me. And I've never wanted to let anyone in, until now.

When I don't reply, Gabe puts his hands on my shoulders and gently pulls me round to face him.

"You heard Laura's voicemail message, didn't you?" he asks.

My defences might be crumbling but I'm still not making this easy for him. I fix him with a firm look. "I'm not jealous. At no point did we ever say we're exclusive…"

"Oh, we're exclusive all right." His eyes search my face. He frowns. "What did you think? She and I were together? That I was cheating on her?"

"Can you blame me after the message she left? Anyway, who you fuck has nothing to do with me."

He tightens his grip on my shoulders. "I haven't seen her

since the night I met you. I couldn't stop thinking about you, so I hooked up with her to try and fuck you out of my head."

His words land hard. Even though he's telling me the reason he was with her was because of me, I can't stop the bitterness in my voice. "I'm so pleased for you, did it work?"

"No, it fucking didn't, did it. I've not been able to stop thinking about you, since we met, how many times do I have to say it?"

He needs to stop saying stuff like this. "Can you get on with the real reason why you're here? Just sack me, then fuck off."

"You think I'm here to sack you?"

"If not, why are you here? I made my feelings perfectly clear earlier."

He rushes me. One second I'm standing in front of the fire, the next I'm against the living room wall. His hands are on my shoulders, pinning me in place.

"I'm here for you."

His lips hover dangerously close to mine. My breath catches in my throat.

"Stop. This isn't right."

"Tell me why?"

"You're my bo..."

He presses two fingers against my lips and silences me. "Don't say it's because I'm your boss. That's workable. There's more to it, isn't there? Be honest."

"Like you have, you mean?"

"I've been honest."

"We barely know each other."

He stares deeply into my eyes and strokes his fingertips across the tops of my bare shoulders, unravelling me with every touch. "You always do this. Deflect. Jump to the defensive. Tell me why this isn't right? You and I *should* be complicated. So tell me why it's not."

My heart swells as I take in his words.

He ghosts his fingertips across my cheekbones and along my jawline. "Kissing you, fucking you, just being in the moment with you is a dream, and I don't want to be anywhere else."

He glides a hand down my neck and across my collarbone to my chest, pressing his palm against my heart. "Open up. Let me in."

I stare into his eyes and for the first time I feel hope. That this is more than an affair. That this could work out. "If you hurt me, I'll cut your dick off."

Sincere eyes tug at the final threads of my resolve. "I won't let anyone hurt you ever again, Princess, including me."

He presses a kiss to my forehead and I close my eyes as his lips slide to my right cheek. They skim lower, planting a teasingly light kiss millimetres away from my mouth, igniting flames of desire deep within me and leaving me wanting more. His lips trail a line of fire down my throat. He plants an open mouthed kiss on the curve of my neck and unfastens my jeans, peppering my flesh with soft kisses and pushing a hand down the front of my knickers.

My teeth catch on my bottom lip at the sound of him groaning in approval at what he finds.

"You're waiting to be fucked," he breathes against my ear, massaging my clit with his fingers, evoking a tug of desire between my legs as he carries on the tortuous motion.

"Shut up and kiss me."

He laughs at my impatience and removes his hand from my underwear, then tugs my knickers and jeans down my legs. "Better?"

"Hardly. I'm half naked while you're fully clothed."

He flashes me a wicked grin and rests his hand either side of my head on the wall, leaning into me. "Why don't you do something about it?"

I smile at the challenge, lock my gaze with his and slide down the wall, unfastening his jeans and pulling them down his legs, kneeling in front of him. I skate my hands up the backs of his muscular thighs, over the firm peach of his backside and to his boxer shorts where I pause, tucking my fingers beneath the waistband. His eyes haven't left mine the whole time and his breathing is coming in short bursts. He's just as turned on as me, and the thick outline of his erection in his boxers tells me I'm right. I curl my fingers around the top of his boxers and tug them down his legs, freeing him.

His gaze shimmers with desire. "Take your top off."

I do as I'm told, pulling my damp t-shirt off over my head and letting it fall at his feet.

"And the rest."

I reach behind my back, unhook my bra and discard it on the floor.

His eyes brim with fire. "My beauty," he rasps, voice thick with lust at the sight of me kneeling before him, totally naked.

The way he says I'm his, fans the flames of desire inside me. I can't imagine being anyone else's.

I raise myself up on my knees and push the bottom of his jumper up, exposing his abs. I keep my eyes on his as I lick a line down the shallow valley in the centre of his muscles all the way to his belly button, savouring the taste of him; soap and manly musk. I'm hungry for more.

I dig my nails into his arse cheeks and run my tongue over my lips before steadily taking him in my mouth, all the way down to the root.

I close my eyes, fighting my gag reflex. He's the biggest I've ever had and I want this to be good.

'Oh, fuck.' He moans in ecstasy, weaving his fingers through my hair and spurring me on.

I slide him out of my mouth, almost to the tip and give myself a couple of seconds to prepare, before I take him all the way again, feeling him twitch and throb on my tongue.

"This is so fucking good … but I want to be deep inside you when I come."

He wants me to stop but I ignore him. I want to carry on, I want to pleasure him until he can't take any more. I take a tighter grip of his backside and slide him back down my throat, hearing the mangled hiss of pleasure and protest fall from his lips. The salty taste of precum lands on my tongue. He's close.

He bunches his fingers in my hair, forcing my head back. I release him.

"Not like this," he says.

I hold his gaze determinedly and wipe my mouth with the back of my hand. "Are you going to fucking kiss me then, or what?"

A muscle in his jaw twitches at my defiance. My backchat turns him on. The sooner his resolve snaps the sooner he'll fuck me.

He tugs me upwards by my hair, making me wince and get to my feet. Dark, hooded eyes glint with lust as he winds my hair around his hand, tilting my head back, forcing me to look at him. "You sure you want to goad me, Princess?"

I want everything he's got to throw at me. I'll never back down. "Shut up and fuck me."

His lips curl into a smirk. "Very well, have it your way."

He pulls me a few steps to my right by my hair, then pushes me backwards onto the sofa.

Within seconds he discards his jumper and stands naked in front of me. The glow from the fire bounces off his muscles and casts him in shadow. My lungs stop working as I take him in. He's a God. I'm physically aching for him to make the next move. And I know I'd wait forever.

"Like what you see, Princess?"

"I said shut up and kiss me, White."

He grabs my knees and yanks my thighs open. I open my mouth ready to impart a witty retort but nothing happens, because he glides his hands up my inner thighs and my mind blanks. He gently parts my folds with his thumbs and licks a scorching line with his hot tongue from my vagina to my clit. I press my lips together to stifle the cry threatening to escape. I glance down to see him watching me with a wicked grin. "You asked me to kiss you. You didn't say where."

Smart arse.

"Now, do you want me to hurry the fuck up, or do you want me to do this some more?" he asks in an annoyingly measured voice. He's playing with me.

More. Always more. "Don't stop," I plead.

"Good, because I could taste you like this, all day."

I practically sigh as he delivers another long, leisurely lick and I moan with pleasure. I dig my fingernails into the leather as my insides tense. He puts his hands on the tops of my thighs holding me steady as he carries on the mind-blowing assault with his tongue. Each languid lick is followed by him encircling the throbbing bud with his tongue, again and again until I'm squirming beneath him.

He squeezes his fingers into my trembling thighs. "Stop fighting it."

I suck in another breath, clinging onto my self-control feeling the tension ratchet inside me. I force myself to focus, blanking out the feel of his mouth and stubble grazing my inner thigh.

"Are you going to fuck me or what?" I gasp, growing impatient.

He chuckles, humming against my clit sending a shockwave of pleasure through to my centre. "All in good time, Princess. I'm going to fuck you with my mouth first."

"But I want you inside me," I pant.

He sinks two fingers inside me without warning and every, single muscle in my body tenses. My head snaps back, my eyes close and it takes every ounce of self-control I have not to come.

"Gabe!"

'Is that better, Princess?" he asks pressing his tongue against my clit and snaking his fingers higher inside me. I bite down on my bottom lip to stop myself from screaming.

"Do you have any idea how beautiful you are? Look at yourself."

I open my eyes and lower my gaze. I'm dancing on the brink of orgasm, and his voice is thick with lust. He's watching me intently as he takes one uneven breath after another. My nipples have pebbled and my breasts heave as I fight to keep some semblance of control.

"You're a fucking work of art. A thing of beauty bestowed upon us mortals, and you're mine. Every single part of you."

His declaration knocks me sideways. Thoughts and feelings compete for brain space. I tense my trembling thighs to stop myself from falling over the edge. Heat prickles up my body. I'm not going to be able to hold this off much longer.

"You're so close it fucking hurts. If I touch your clit, you're going to go."

I look at him through narrowed eyes. Fucking Gabe is just as much a verbal sparring match as everything else.

"Fuck me already," I demand.

He flicks me a devilish grin. "You know all the right things to say to make me crumble, Princess. First, you're coming on my tongue." He lowers his head between my legs. I know what he's about to do and can't stop him.

"Gabe," I begin, but I don't get to finish. His firm, tongue licks my clit one final time and I lose it. A high-pitched squeal falls from my lips as I arch back into the sofa, my eyelids close. Fireworks go off behind my eyes and I come apart in his hands. As the tension slowly ebbs from my muscles, I sink down into the cushions, sleepy, satiated and completed relaxed.

I hear the tear of a wrapper. Hands grip my thighs and open them wide. I feel the wet tip of his cock at my entrance as he lines himself up, before pushing inside me in one thrust.

I moan at the feel of him where I want him to be. He swears under his breath. I open my eyes to see him above me, his eyes locked on mine as he moves over me, into me, deeper and harder every time. After two orgasms it doesn't take long before I'm right back up there again.

"Mine," he rasps on every thrust, over and over reinforcing it.

"I want to be." The words are out of my mouth, before I have chance to register what I've said.

A guttural groan erupts from his chest and his cock tightens making me clench around him and moan. He drops his head forward and stills. The tendons in his shoulders and neck bulge and flex as he fights off his own undoing. He gives himself a few seconds then slowly raises his head and looks at me.

"That mouth of yours. It's going to be the end of me."

Good.

He keeps his eyes locked on me and drives forward, reaching deep and it's too much. I fall apart beneath him, riding the crest of my climax and he's right up there with me. His hips stutter as he pounds his way through, calling my name as he comes, before collapsing over me.

I close my eyes and wrap my arms around his broad shoulders, listening to his breathing slow. The gallop of his heart thuds against mine as he lies on top of me. As we lie there, wrapped up in each other, a warm, fuzzy feeling of contentment descends as I think back to his words from earlier. He was right. This. Us. It feels right. When we're together everything fits. I swallow down the unexpected ball of emotion in my throat.

He shifts off me and props his head on his hand. As he gazes at me adoringly, I'm sure my heart's going to burst out of my chest.

"I've never had this before."

I smile. "What? Sex? I don't believe you."

He laughs, stroking his fingertips across my brow with the gentlest of touches. For a second he hesitates before carrying on. "No, I've had that. I've dated my fair share of women. I've treated some of them like shit too. I never cheated on any of them" - he looks at me to make his point - "but it was just sex."

"Why are you telling me this?"

"Because I want to be honest with you and I want to make you see that things are different with you. None of the others lasted more than a couple of weeks."

"The same thing could happen to us."

"It won't."

My chest tightens at his words. "You've never had a serious relationship?"

He glides his fingers down my arm. "No. I'd take them out for dinner, we'd have sex, and I'd let things peter out. Sometimes, I'd call them and arrange to meet up just for sex."

"I'd have told you to fuck off."

"Yeah, well maybe they should have done. It would have served me right. The past few years I've been focussed on the business. I didn't want anything that would distract me. And I never met a woman who would." There's something in his voice which makes me think there's a "but" coming and my stomach fizzes with nerves. But he doesn't and I feel stupid. Instead, he asks, "What about you? Have you ever been serious with anyone?"

I swallow hard and shake my head. "Not really."

He ghosts his fingertip across the tip of my nose, trailing it down to my bottom lip. "What about the guy who told you, you were beautiful?"

"We were only seventeen."

"So, were you in love?"

"I thought he loved me but it wasn't real."

"You said he didn't mean it when he said you were beautiful."

I focus on the shadows dancing across the wall from the fire. "He only said it to get me to sleep with him."

He cups my cheek in his hand and tilts my face round so I'm looking at him. "Well, obviously he was a dick. I've never wanted any woman the way I want you."

My heart sings as he kisses me. I tangle my fingers through his hair and give myself to him. I've been waiting for him to say those words from the first day we met.

Chapter 40

Gabe

Today's a good day. It's a fucking fantastic day. The best I've felt in a long time. Rays of sunshine peek from behind the high-rise office blocks of the wharf as I take my usual morning route to work.

Everything seems lighter and brighter. It could be like this every morning, but I wouldn't know, due to having my phone glued to my ear for the duration of my walk here.

I head into the building and the waiting lift.

My phone. *Shit!*

I pull it out of the back pocket of my grey trousers as the lift starts heading upwards. I haven't looked at it since Friday. It's been on silent all weekend, sitting beside my untouched laptop.

Guilt creeps into my thoughts at the fact I've neglected my duties, but the scent of Ella's sweet lingering perfume inside the elevator swipes it away. I head out of the lift, scrolling through the unread emails on my phone, not paying attention to any of them. I left her sleeping soundly when I crept out of her bed at some ungodly hour this morning.

"Good morning, ladies," I say, heading into the office.

She's at her desk and doesn't look up.

"Morning," Judy calls, peering over the rim of her glasses. "You're still alive then? I was beginning to think something had happened to you over the weekend."

I grin, knowing full well where she's headed with this. "How so?"

"You know how so, young man. Firstly, you're not here before I arrive and secondly for the first time in forever, I haven't come in to a pile of emails that you've sent over the weekend."

I shrug, toss my phone in the air and catch it. "There are more important things than work."

I can feel Ella looking at me from over her laptop screen and desperately want to see her face, but I can't risk it. Judy's a shrewd cookie who doesn't miss a beat. She slides her glasses off her nose and puts them on the table as if she can't quite believe what I've said. "*I* know that. I just never thought I'd see the day *you* realised it."

"Yeah, well you know what they say Jude… all work and no play…" I flash her a cheeky smile and reach the door to my office.

She chuckles. "Well, it's about time you saw the light."

Her phone begins to ring and she answers it. I take the opportunity to steal a glance at Ella, who's typing away on her laptop with a slight frown on her face, like she's struggling to concentrate.

I know the feeling, Princess.

"Morning, Ella."

She stops typing and looks up at me. There's a polite smile on her face, but the twinkle in her eye tells me of the mischief that lies beneath.

"Morning, Gabe."

Her blush pink blouse sets off her creamy skin. The top couple of buttons are undone, begging me to unfasten them further and kiss the soft skin of her neck.

I flick her a grin and force myself into my office before things become blatant. I've already been staring at her longer than I should have.

I shrug my jacket off, hang it on the coat stand beside my desk and settle into my chair, tapping the space bar of my laptop to wake my machine up. One hundred unopened emails sit in my inbox waiting for me, and that's after Judy's sifted through stuff I don't need to have eyes on. A reminder pings on the screen, telling me I've a meeting with Legal at ten o'clock. I should start prepping for that, but I've opened up a blank email and started typing before I even realise what I'm doing.

Me: *You look beautiful. x*

Her: *Thank you. Why didn't you wake me to say goodbye this morning? x*

Me: *I didn't like to wake you, and it's not goodbye, this is only the beginning. x*

Her: *Charmer. x*

Me: *It's going to be more difficult than I'd imagined keeping my mind on task and you the other side of that door today. x*

Her: *You need to try harder. Some of us have got work to do. x*

Me: *Cheeky – carry on like that you'll be earning yourself a spanking.*

I can't help but smile as her email pops up. *Good. X*

***

I thought the day started too well. Back-to-back meetings and a fuck-up at the Birmingham office means every single second of the day is taken up with conference calls and meetings. The one saving grace is a text from Jake telling me he's sorted shit with Diego. That slippery motherfucker is out of the picture. I'm dealing with the organ grinder from now on, not the fucking monkey.

By the time four o'clock rolls round I'm beat. I've not seen Ella and I've barely left my desk all day. I'm pissed off and worn out and my day's far from over. When I finally get a chance to venture out of my office, Judy's packed up her things and is zipping up her leopard print waterproof jacket.

"Weather's looking gloomy. That means the Tube will be even busier," she mutters.

And the motorway, I think to myself.

"I've rearranged your diary for the next couple of days. See you Friday?"

I rub a hand through my hair and smile wearily at the very thought. Friday seems a long way off at the moment. "Yes, thanks Jude."

She slings her handbag onto her shoulder and nods. "Okay.

Ella's still here if you need anything."

On cue, she appears looking briefly in my direction, before heading over to her desk.

The black material of her skirt hugs her curvaceous figure and her black heels make her hips swing in an oh, so sexy way. The woman's fire. One look at her and I forget all my troubles.

"Right, I'm off. I've got the kids coming round for tea tonight."

Ella smiles. "Of course. Have a good night. See you tomorrow, Judy."

Judy heads off into the lift, and I watch the doors close behind her. Silent seconds tick by then Ella looks at me and gives me a smile. "Are you okay?"

I am now. "I'll live."

"You look tired."

I'm tired of this place. But I'll never tire of looking at her face. I tug at the knot of my navy tie, loosening it. "Can I have a word?"

I head back into my office and hear her footsteps behind me. "Close the door."

It's barely closed before I pounce on her. A day's worth of stress; of her on one side of the door and me the other, of the fact I haven't even seen her, bubbles to the surface now we're alone. My body flattens against hers, pressing her into the door, trapping her. I sweep her hair away from her neck, revealing the nape and plant a line of kisses across her soft skin. Everything about her is intoxicating, from her sweet, warm flesh, to the floral heady scent of her perfume, to the way her body relaxes against mine with every kiss.

"I've wanted to get my hands on you since I saw you this morning," I admit, nipping her ear lobe.

"You had your hands on me this morning," she tells me, the smile evident in her voice.

"I want more."

I always do where she's concerned. I spin her round to face me, crushing my lips to hers. She sighs against my mouth, her body moulding to mine, the way it always does. She rakes her fingers through my hair, pulling me closer and deepening the kiss. But I still want more.

My hands are on her waist and I walk her backwards to the sofa, steadily lowering her down so she doesn't fall. I know where I want to be, where I need to be and my brains on autopilot. I ruck up her skirt to her waist and she opens her legs wider for me to settle in between.

There's no thought to how risky and entirely inappropriate this is. A visceral urge to claim her rises up inside me, gripping me by the balls the way it always does when she's around. It's the same thought I've had from the word go.

"Fucking hell, I want you," I murmur against her mouth, caressing her breast through the cotton of her shirt. I glide my hand lower and tug her leg behind my back, pressing my cock against her. She gasps and makes my already rock-hard dick tighten. All that stands between me fucking her brains out is three pieces of clothing. I've never been so tempted in all my life.

"Do you have any idea how much willpower it's taking me not to fuck you right now?"

"Then do it," she pants.

My cock jerks at her sassy mouth. I've never met a woman that makes my self-control as thin as ice. But I've never met a woman like Ella.

"I've got a meeting in twenty minutes."

"That's a passion killer." She laughs.

I press my forehead to hers, and look deep into her eyes. There's nothing I want to do more than ignore my duties for the rest of the day and spend it in bed with her. But I can't. The sense of responsibility I've always worn with pride hangs around my neck like a dead weight. Reality creeps back, sobering me.

"Tell me about it." I prop myself up on my elbows. "I've got to go away for a few days."

"I heard Judy mention it."

"Something's fucked up at the –"

"Birmingham branch," she interjects and gives me a small smile. "Yeah, I heard."

I place a chaste kiss on her lips, then get up and help her to her feet.

"I'm sorry."

She rearranges her clothing and smooths a hand over her hair. "Why are you apologising? It's not your fault. It's business and we're at work. Of course your job's important to you."

Her simple words hit home. I'm not sure it is anymore. I planned to spend every evening buried inside her. Not a hundred and fifty miles away in a hotel room.

"Is everything all right? You seem a bit... troubled."

I take her hands in mine. "Sure. There's just a lot going on at the moment." I kiss her forehead. "You need to get out of here and give me time to calm down before my meeting with Greg and Barry from Finance." I glance down at the bulge in my trousers.

She giggles. "You were the one who asked me to come in here, remember?"

"Any chance for time on my own with you."

Her smile dissolves as a thought strikes her. "When will you be back?"

"Friday."

A renewed smile is on her lips, but it looks forced. Disappointment shines in her eyes. But this is Ella. She's not going to admit it.

"Okay. Well, I hope everything works out." She glances around the room, looking awkward. "I'll, um ... see you when you get back." She hesitates, before turning and heading towards the door.

That goodbye just won't do.

I dash after her, grab her hand and spin her round to face me, bringing her colliding into my chest. My mouth on hers silences the squeal of surprise on her lips as I guide her back against the door.

"I thought you needed time to calm down," she gasps in between kisses.

"Fuck it. It's only Greg and Barry."

On cue, the rumble of male voices approaching can be heard the other side of the door.

"Gabe, we need to stop."

I reluctantly tear my lips from hers and run my thumb across her bottom lip. I don't think I can, where she's concerned. And I don't think I want to. The sound of Greg and Barry on the other side of the door pulls me back to reality. I step away from her and push a hand through my hair, trying to get some sort of control over my libido. "We'll pick this up on Friday."

She smiles and this time it's not forced. It's a full-on smile that makes my chest tighten, which I try not to dwell on. "I look forward to it."

So, do I Princess.

Chapter 41

Ella

"Ella, Ella. For fuck's sake. You're going to be late! Wake up!"

I open my eyes with a start. Kate's standing in my bedroom doorway, dressed for work in her smart navy skirt and blazer.

Not again.

I push my hair out of my eyes and give myself a few seconds for the fog of sleep to clear. "Shit. What time is it?"

Kate taps her wristwatch. "Nearly eight. You're going to be late for work."

Eight o' fucking-clock.

"Why the hell hasn't my bloody alarm gone off?" I shoot up in bed and angrily swipe my phone off the bedside table, frantically stabbing the screen with my finger. Nothing happens. "The fucking battery must have died, again. Shit!"

"I'll call you an Uber, otherwise you're never going to get there."

I chuck my phone on the bed in disgust. "That's twenty quid I can't afford." I've got a bit of money left over from my work at the club, but that's for groceries and stuff until I get paid.

Kate gives me a sympathetic smile. "Don't worry. It's on me."

Bless her.

"What club? And what's on you, apart from me?" Harry appears in the doorway and gives Kate a kiss on the cheek, sliding his arm around her waist.

She blushes and pulls him off her with a giggle. "Never you mind, naughty."

Things are clearly looking up between them. I passed out as soon as my head touched the pillow last night, so had no idea Horny Harry stayed over.

His blue eyes wash over me. He smirks. "Still in bed?"

I pull my duvet around me and fight the urge to roll my eyes. "Looks like that, doesn't it."

"Come on, we need to leave Ella to get ready for work," Kate tells him, picking up on the icy vibe I'm casting her boyfriend's way.

Harry holds his hands up in the air defeated. "Okay, okay woman, I'm going."

"Thanks for sorting the cab for me," I say to her after he's gone.

Kate smiles. "No worries. Now get your arse out of bed."

***

Fifteen minutes later I'm in the back of the Uber heading towards the city and can finally breathe a sigh of relief. I pull my phone from my bag and switch it on, hoping the ten-minute charge I've just given it holds out until I get into the office and charge it up properly. *Bloody thing.*

It lights up, erupting with a string of beeps as a barrage of text messages and missed calls appear on the screen. One text is Amy thanking me for the money, but the rest are from Gabe. Thirteen missed calls, two voicemail messages and five texts all from him; asking how I am and worried that he can't get hold of me.

My phone rings making me jump. It's him.

"Erm, morning. Are you all right?"

I hear a long exhale of relief down the phone. "I am now. I've been trying to get hold of you all fucking night."

"I'm sorry. I didn't know. My phone's still playing up and it didn't hold its charge properly, so it switched itself off."

"I was one call away from coming home."

I can't ignore the skippety-skip of my heart at his admission. "You'd do that?"

"Of course. There's no way I'd be able to concentrate without knowing you're okay."

I catch my reflection in the cab window to see I'm grinning

like a fool. "Well, if it makes you feel any better, I'm now running late for work."

The tension in his voice subsides. "Where are you now?"

"In the back of an Uber. You?"

"I'm in the back of the car on the way to my first meeting of the day."

"First?"

"I've got five."

I cringe. "Busy day."

He sighs wearily. "Extremely. Days like this, I wonder why I do it."

"You know why? It's your family business. Anyway, you said you could never just lie on a beach."

"Well, that depends on who's laying on the beach with me. I think I could be tempted."

The thought of Gabe on a sun-drenched beach in just his trunks flashes into my mind. Tempting doesn't cover it.

"Listen, I'm nearly there. I'll speak to you later."

A pang of sadness hits my chest. I force my voice to keep even. "Okay, hope your meetings go okay."

"Me too. I'll speak to you later."

He ends the call. The twinge in my chest grows. I've got three whole days until I see him next. At the moment that feels like eternity.

***

When I walk back through the front door that night after work, I'm greeted by a huge bouquet of flowers on the hall table. There are at least forty white roses wrapped up in black tissue paper tied up in a cream silk ribbon. Their fragrant perfume fills the hall. Harry's clearly after something or he's in Kate's bad books. They're beautiful and must have cost an absolute fortune.

"Ella!" Kate calls from upstairs.

I shrug my black jacket off my shoulders and hang it on the hook behind the front door. "Yeah, I'm back. Your flowers are lovely. Harry's gone all out."

Kate thunders down the stairs, pulling a cream sweater over her head. "They aren't for me."

"What?"

She jumps off the last step of the stairs onto the laminate floor like an excited kid at Christmas. "They're for you."

My gaze swings to the bouquet. "For me?"

"Yep, they arrived about ten minutes ago, along with that parcel." She nods to a rectangular box wrapped in brown paper on the table next to the bouquet.

"I don't understand." I frown in confusion and look from the box to the flowers. "Who the hell's buying me stuff?"

Kate hovers over my left shoulder, practically humming with excitement. "Yeah, yeah, open the bloody envelope and find out."

I pluck the small white envelope from amongst the roses, slide the white card out, and read the handwritten message in black ink on the reverse.

'For not being there, G x'

My heart skips a beat.

"Well?" Kate demands.

She's about to burst with impatience. I can feel it.

"They're from Gabe."

She lets out a squeal of excitement. "I fucking knew it! Who else would they be from? This is so exciting. Now open the bloody box."

I stare at the package. "What the hell could that be?"

"Think later." Kate picks up the box and shoves it into my hands. "I'm meeting Harry in half an hour so need to dash, but I'm dying to know what's in here."

I put the card on the table and take the parcel from her. "I'm surprised you haven't opened it yourself."

"Don't tempt me. If you don't get a wriggle on, I bloody well might."

The box isn't addressed to me. It hasn't even got a postmark on. "How do you know this is for me?" I ask warily.

"Because it came with your flowers. The delivery guy said they're both for you. Now hurry up!"

I tear off the paper to find a brand-new boxed iPhone. A yellow Post-it note is stuck on the front with a handwritten message.

'Switch it on straight away, Gx.'

"Oh my God," Kate gasps. "He's bought you a grands worth of phone! It's like he knew yours is playing up."

I stare in stunned silence at the very expensive, top-of-the-range gift, trying to work out how I feel.

"He does," I mutter. "I spoke to him earlier."

Another excited squeak erupts from my friend.

I shake my head. "This is too much."

"No, it's not. It's a gift. And you *do* need a new phone."

"That's not the point."

"Yes, it is. It's a present. Now I say, do as you're told and switch it on."

I *do* need a new phone and it *is* a gift, I suppose. I admire the shiny new box. There's no way I could afford to buy one right now, especially not one this expensive. I slide the phone out and switch it on.

A text message immediately pings through. No surprises, it's from Gabe.

This is all set up and ready to use. I want to be able to contact you whenever I want. I'll call you later, x

"Well," Kate says sneaking a peek at the text over my shoulder. "This is *definitely* a sign. Flowers *and* a gift. It's all starting to sound quite serious if you ask me."

Serious. A tornado of excitement and nerves swirl in my stomach as I try to fathom how I feel.

A knock on the door makes me jump out of my skin and interrupts my thoughts. I put the phone down on the hall table.

"Ooh, I wonder who that can be. Let's hope they come bearing more gifts," Kate teases.

I shoot her a dubious look and open the door. "Let's hope not."

Two is enough for one day.

It's Margot, looking red faced and flustered. Her glasses are nearly falling off the end of her nose and her green and blue plaid scarf is slung haphazardly around her neck. She's out of breath.

"Are you okay?" I ask, worriedly.

"Yes, yes," she pants, putting a hand on her chest and gathering herself. "I'm glad you're back from work. I could do with your help."

"My help?"

"We've managed to garner quite a lot of press attention about the shops. There are some reporters from the local news down there right now. I told one of them about your mum's shop, and they asked if they could speak to you about it."

I baulk at the very idea. "Me?"

"Yes, on camera."

"On camera!"

"But we'll need to get a move on."

"I don't know," I say uncertainly. Dancing in front of a room full of strangers while wearing lingerie I can do. It's not me, it's Amber Rue. This *is* me. "I mean, I'm not sure I'll be any good."

"Go on!" Kate urges. "It'll be great."

"*You'll* be great," Margot encourages. "And your mum would have loved all the fuss being kicked up."

Mum. That's what this is all about. Her legacy being maintained and not destroyed just for profit. Posting out a few flyers isn't enough. I need to do whatever it takes. "Okay. I'll do it," I blurt before I can change my mind.

Margot's face lights up. "Marvellous. We need to get down there. They're all set up outside the shops."

"Okay, give me five minutes."

"Wonderful, I'll head back and let them know you're on your

way," Margot calls over her shoulder, hurrying down the front path.

Kate steps into her trainers at the bottom of the stairs.

"Are you coming too? I thought you said were seeing Harry?"

She laughs and gives me an absurd look. "And miss your fifteen minutes of fame? You must be joking."

Chapter 42

Ella

It's getting dark by the time we arrive at the shops. A couple of press vans from local TV networks are parked up in the high street and a cluster of reporters are standing talking to the shop owners. Passers-by have started to congregate. It's a hive of activity and I'm having second thoughts. I haven't been down here since before Mum died and I never dreamed I'd be returning under these circumstances.

Kate must sense my unease. She gives my arm a reassuring squeeze. "You'll be absolutely fine."

I'm not sure about that.

Margot waves from where she's standing over by The Enchanted Florist with a reporter.

I take a deep breath and we shuffle our way through the crowds towards them.

"Hi, I'm Tessa Carmichael from the *Daily Reporter*," announces a thirty-something woman with a sleek black chin-length bob, wearing a pristine cream mac. "Ella, isn't it? Can we get you to stand a little more over to the right, please?"

I shift over and look uneasily at the camera pointed in my face.

Her bright pink lips widen into a tight smile as she shoves a microphone at me. "We need to get a move on as we're running out of time. I'm going to ask you a few questions about your mum's shop, okay?"

"Erm… okay."

She gives a nod to the cameraman behind her and presses a finger to her earpiece. Kate and Margot are standing to the side, giving me a thumbs up.

"Okay, we're on in three, two, one…"

Shit!

Tessa turns to camera and flashes a smile. "This is Tessa Carmichael, live from Hackney High Street, where local shop owners are currently engaged in a dispute with the council over the sale of the leases to a developer."

Every nerve in my body jars. No one said anything about this being *live*.

"This evening I'm talking to one of the business owners, Ella Anderson." She pushes the microphone a little further in my face. "Can you tell us a little more about your shop?"

"Erm," – I cast a hesitant glance at the camera – "It's not *my* shop. It was my mum's shop. She owned it for fifteen years."

"And your mum died, isn't that right? That must have been really difficult for you."

I pause, taken aback by the question. I'm not talking about something so emotive with a complete stranger, not to mention God knows how many people who are watching. I feel sick at the thought.

"Last year her friend took over the running of the shop, after she died."

"How does it feel to know your mum's shop is going to be pulled down to make way for a regeneration of the local area?"

I open my mouth to respond, but the words aren't forthcoming. I feared this was going to happen, but knowing it for certain is something different. I look to Margot and Kate for reassurance, but they look just as in shock as I do. "Erm, I wasn't aware of that."

"I've seen plans for fifty brand-new starter homes and apartments in place of the shops here and the warehouse further down the street."

"I suppose ... I suppose that makes sense."

Tessa looks perplexed. "It makes sense? You're saying you agree with the tearing down of the shops?"

I see red. "Of course not. Some of these businesses have been here since before you and I were born. They're part of the local community. To tear them down would be a travesty."

"So, you're totally against the regeneration of an area that's struggling?"

"No, I'm not. Stop putting words in my mouth," I snap. "I get the area needs some help, but surely there must be something better than destroying perfectly viable shops. That's not going to help the local community. It's just a money-making scheme."

Tessa gives a self-satisfied smile and turns back to the camera. "There we have it. It's just a "money-making scheme." What do you think viewers? Back to Bob, in the studio."

The light on the cameras goes off and Tessa turns to me. "Thanks Ella. Your honest view is refreshing. You did well." Then, she spins on her heel and disappears off through the crowds, followed by the cameraman. Probably in search of another poor soul who's got no idea what they've let themselves in for.

"Well done," says Margot, patting me on the back. "Your mum would have been proud."

"That was bloody awful. I didn't realise it was going to be live."

Margot pushes her glasses further up her nose. "No, she didn't mention that to me either."

"Well, it's done now. I've made a complete tit of myself."

"No, you didn't. You told her straight, "don't put words in my mouth,"" Kate mimics.

I cringe. "I wish I hadn't said the last bit."

"About it being a money-making scheme? Well, it is, isn't it?"

"Did you hear what she said was going to happen? They *are* planning on tearing the lot down to put up houses."

Margot and Kate exchange glances and give me a weak smile. No one knows what to say. No one wants to admit the very real possibility that it's going to happen. All we can do is hope that we've done enough to put a spoke in the wheel of the fat cat's get-rich-quick scheme.

Kate puts her arm around me. "Come on. I think we've all enough excitement for one day, don't you?"

Margot smiles at me. "Thank you, Ella. Hopefully we've

made the Council stop and listen. I've heard on the grapevine that the plans are being taken back to some Committee or other to be reviewed."

Hope sparks in my gut at the good news. "Really? So this might all have paid off."

Margot gives me a triumphant smile. "Let's hope so, dear."

***

An hour later I'm freshly showered, bundled into my pink fluffy dressing gown and sitting on the sofa, sipping a glass of red. Kate's at Harry's, leaving me alone with my thoughts. Dangerous. I've replayed the nights events cringing at the memory, hoping the vino will take the edge off. The flickering flames of the fire pull me in. I didn't realise how much I missed it until Gabe lit it the other night.

My phone springs into life on the coffee table. My heart leaps at the sight of his name, the way it always does.

I answer it with a smile. "Hey. Did you get my text earlier?"

"Of course. You don't need to thank me, Princess."

His rich, deep voice washes over me causing my skin to pucker. I want him here, with me. Not god knows how many miles away in Birmingham.

"I still say you didn't need to buy me flowers or the phone, but thank you."

"And like *I* still say, I wanted to. Anyway, how's my TV star doing?"

I shift forward on the sofa and put my glass of wine on the table in alarm. "You know?"

"I saw."

"How?"

He laughs. "I do have a TV in my hotel room and it's a property deal. It's my business to know what's happening with the other players in the game."

I anxiously chew my thumbnail at the fact he's seen me make a prat of myself on TV. "I know. I wasn't expecting to be there. It all happened a bit quick. I came home from work, then the next thing I know, I'm live on the six o'clock news."

"I think the reporter was out of line with what she said about your mum."

"So do I. There wasn't really any need to bring up the fact she's dead."

"I saw your face when she asked you that. Are you all right?"

"Yeah, it's just I haven't been to the shop since she died and going down there brought it back a bit."

"I'm not surprised."

I sigh heavily. "Yeah. I'll be okay tomorrow. Anyway, how's your day been?"

The sound of a knock at the front door echoes down the hall.

"Shit. Sorry, there's someone at the door."

"It's okay. I'll hang on."

I stand and head into the hall.

"My day's been shit," he says.

I open the door and freeze. Gabe's standing on the doorstep with his mobile to his ear, wearing a light grey jumper, black jeans and a grin.

My heart cartwheels in my chest at the sight of him.

"Until now." His eyes remain glued on mine as he slowly slides his phone into his back pocket and steps through the door.

I shift aside to let him through in a daze. "But I thought … you're in Birmingham."

Gabe closes the front door, takes my phone from my hand and puts it on the hall table, all without taking his eyes off me. I'm too scared to look away in case him being here is all a lovely dream.

He cups my face with his hands and grazes his thumbs across my cheeks. "When I watched the news I could tell you were upset."

"You came back because of that?"

His eyes search mine. "Of course," he says, as if it's the most natural thing in the world. "I needed to know that you're okay."

My hearts banging against my ribs so loud I'm sure I'm having a heart attack. "But how did you get back so quickly?"

"Helicopter."

My eyes widen. "You hired a helicopter to fly back just to see me."

"It was the fastest way to get to you."

His words warm my heart and his touch ignites a fire deep inside my soul. I've never known anyone like Gabe before, and it's got nothing to do with his money. Hope bubbles in my chest, taking me by surprise.

Warm lips are on mine before I know it. Fingers tangle through my hair, pulling me against the length of his firm body.

It's only been a day since I last tasted him, but it feels like a decade. God I've missed him.

"How long can you stay?" I murmur against his lips, not wanting to break the kiss.

"All night. Hang on tight." He bends down and scoops me up into his arms, crushing me against his chest. I squeal in surprise, clinging to his broad shoulders as he carries me upstairs, with his mouth glued to mine.

"It's the one on the right," I mutter as we reach the landing because he's got no idea where to go.

He kicks my bedroom door closed and lowers me onto my bed, tearing open my dressing gown. I'm waiting for him to pounce, but he doesn't. He stands at the edge of the bed, reaches a hand behind his back and pulls his jumper off over his head then steps out of his jeans. Blue eyes gaze at me adoringly, like he can't quite believe I'm real. My stomach flips with longing. Moonlight streams in from the window behind me, bathing the room in light and illuminating him as his stands in my bedroom, gloriously erect. He's the most beautiful man I've ever seen. That's the only thing I *was* right about when I first met him. He's nothing like I thought he would be. He's arrogant but caring, strong yet soft. He can read my body and unravel me with a touch, like no other man ever has. He wants me to let him in, and the more time I spend with him the more I want to. The thought thrills and scares me in equal measure.

He tilts his head as his hooded eyes rake the length of my body, focussing on my breasts. "I want to watch you come."

I bite down on my bottom lip at the thought of pleasuring myself in front of him. The ache between my legs grows stronger. This is another fantasy of mine, but every other guy I've ever been with has just focussed on racing to the finishing line. Gabe savours every course.

But I need to touch him.

I slide to the end of the bed and look at his cock. The tip's wet, he's already close. This won't take long. I lift my gaze to his and lick my lips, watching the sharp rise and fall of his chest. I reach out a hand to touch him but he grabs my wrist, stopping me.

He lifts an eyebrow. "What are you doing?"

"Touching you."

"I said I want to watch you come. Now lie the fuck back and spread your legs."

The throb between my thighs intensifies at his command. From somewhere the imp inside me kicks in.

"Make me."

Irritation flashes in his heated gaze. "Don't push me, Princess."

I fix him a firm look, telling him I'm not backing down. "I said, make me."

His dick jerks. This sexual power play turns us both on and there's no denying it. He plants a hand on my shoulder and pushes me back onto the bed, then kneels on the floor in front of me. He impatiently yanks my legs open, lowers himself between my legs and props each one over his shoulder. He flicks me a wicked grin and presses his mouth against my inner thigh, trailing a line of gentle kisses upwards.

My breathing hitches at the anticipation of what's to come as he says in a steady voice against my flesh. "I'm going to spell out your name, with my tongue."

He comes to a stop, his mouth hovering inches above my clitoris. The feel of his warm breath, and the idea of what he's about to do makes me squirm against the sheets. I close my eyes. He's teasing me. And he's taken back control.

Ella's only four letters. *I can do this.* He wants me to come but I'm determined to defy him.

My back peels from the mattress and I twist the sheets in my hands as he licks the length of my folds and slowly encircles my clit, with a long leisurely suck dragging every little last bit of fight out of me.

"P."

Fuck!

He repeats the glorious motion, pressing his tongue against my clit, causing the tension in my centre to spiral and eliciting another moan of pleasure.

"R."

He's going to fucking kill me. I'm going to die being given the best oral sex of my life.

Who knew the word "Princess" was so long. I didn't, but by the time he reaches the second "s" I'm done for. Every single muscle in my body is clenching to stave off my orgasm, and just when I need him to carry on, he stops.

I blink open my eyes to see him staring up at me.

"Finish it," he demands.

The meaning of his words hits me. He's got what he wanted. He's dragged me to the edge and now he's left me with little choice. I slide my hand down my body and start slow, deliberate strokes over my clit with my fingers, keeping my eyes on him. His eyes are glued to my hand, his breathing labours, telling me how much this is turning him on. But I'm raising the stakes. If he wants to watch me, I'll give him a show he won't forget.

I shuffle my legs further apart and slide a finger inside me, followed by another. Muscles deep inside me clench around my fingers. It doesn't feel as good as his mouth or cock, but it'll do.

I see him shift and kneel on the bed between my legs, all the while watching me. He fists his cock in his hand and starts slow strokes, drawing deep breaths in. "You know, I'm going to fuck you harder than that, Princess."

I speed up the thrusts of my fingers, meeting his darkened gaze. The idea of us both pleasuring ourselves to turn each other on, scrambles my brain and makes me throb. "The rougher the better."

His strokes speed up. A muscle in his jaw clenches telling me he's fighting his climax. "You have no idea how fucking beautiful, you look. I'm going to come all over your perfect tits and then I'm going to make you scream."

Fuck!

His words wash over me as my orgasm builds, the slickness of my arousal coats my fingers. I can't take much more. "I'm close."

He pumps his cock with his fist, and his shoulders tense as he fights to keep control. "Come for me, Princess."

My spine stiffens, my head snaps back and my eyes shutter close. It's like my body has been waiting for those words of permission. Muscles deep inside me tighten and my thrusting fingers speed up as I come on a gasp. I hear a groan and blink open my eyes. Gabe's shimmering gaze takes my breath.

Streaks of his release cover my breasts and the dip of my stomach, glinting in the half light. There's something primal about it. Like he's claimed me. And I love it.

He picks up his jeans off the floor, pulls a condom out of the pocket, tears it open and rolls it onto his still hard length. He crawls up the bed and shifts over me, settling between my legs.

"I love this. Me all over you," he tells me, rubbing his fingers through his arousal and smearing it across my breasts. Then he picks up my hand, pushes my damp fingers into his mouth and sucks. "And I love tasting you."

I can't wait any longer. I need him to finish what he's started. "Fuck me."

A smile plays on his lips. "I thought you'd never ask."

He strokes his fingers through my hair and presses his lips

to mine, muttering three words against my mouth that make my heart sing. "I've missed you."

He enters me with one smooth push and scoops an arm beneath me, crushing me to his chest. Untapped emotions well inside me, but I don't get chance to dwell on them as heat courses through my body.

"I've missed you too," I tell him, but barely get the words out as he thrusts inside me with a moan, filling me deeper, driving me up the bed.

I wrap myself around him, clinging to his frame as he fucks me relentlessly, driving the air out of my lungs making my limbs tremble.

"So much," he rasps against my cheek and I'm desperate to say it back, but he delivers another punishing thrust and I lose the ability to speak. Waves of pleasure hit me sending me spiralling over the edge and he's with me, pounding through his climax until he's spent.

I catch my breath, and try to bask in the post-coital haze that's descended over me, but can't. A niggling thought in the back of my head stops me from totally relaxing. I squeeze my eyes shut tight as a realisation hits hard.

I'm falling for him. Plain and simple. I'm falling for someone I don't want to fall for. That I'm scared of falling for.

A hot, heavy kiss lands on my chest, followed by the scratch of stubble as he rests his cheek on the valley between my breasts. "I've been thinking about doing that all day."

I open my eyes. "Fucking me?" I ask, hoping that's not his answer.

He tilts his head up and looks at me. "All of it" – he shifts his weight to the side and props his head on his hand – "Fucking you, kissing you, tasting you, being with you. I've had a semi most of the day, thanks to you." A smile tugs at the corners of his mouth. "You distract me even when you're miles away. I'm glad I came home."

His penetrating gaze holds mine and tugs at my heart. "Me too."

"I wouldn't have been able to relax without knowing you were okay."

"You could have called to check, you know, you didn't need to come back."

"I did. I needed to hold you, and tell you everything's going to be okay."

My smile fades. "But it probably won't, will it? All this stuff they're doing with the shop. It's probably not going to make much difference even now they're going to review it again."

"I don't know. The Council have the final decision."

"I know. It's just hard to think the shop might not be there any more. It feels like it's the last thing. Towards the end, she made me promise to redecorate the house after she'd gone. She said she didn't want me moping about and making the place some sort of shrine, she wanted me to get on with my life. So, month by month, Kate and I redecorated the whole house. It doesn't look like the same place now."

"She'll never be gone." Gabe puts a hand on his heart "She'll be in here, always."

"I know, I guess I just feel really guilty. I haven't been to the shop since she died and soon it might not be there anymore."

"Don't feel guilty. She wouldn't have wanted you to feel like that." He tucks a stray strand of hair behind my ear. "I wish there was something I could do."

"Don't be silly. Anyway, you've done enough with the flowers and phone, *they* were too much. No one's ever bought me anything like that before."

His brow creases into a frown. "That doesn't mean it's right. Let me spoil you."

That's what I'm afraid of. He's spoiling me from wanting any other man.

"Actually, there's something I want to ask you." He plays with my hair between his fingers and gives me a long look, thinking carefully about what he's about to say. "It's Jake's fortieth on Saturday. He's having a party, and I wondered whether you'd like to come with me?"

I freeze. Jake seems nice (although Spencer definitely isn't) but what about the rest of his super-rich family, like his parents? He wants me to *meet* them. I bat away the rising feeling of nerves in my chest. "Erm, so, all your family will be there?"

A troubled look flashes in his eyes for a moment, then it's gone. "Yeah, well you've met most of them. Just not Dad and my …" He pauses. "I'd like you to come."

"I'd like that, of course, but isn't it risky?"

"How do you mean?"

"People are bound to ask how we met, isn't it going to be awkward?"

"Don't worry. Jake's got my back and Spencer doesn't know. When that question crops up I'll answer it. Leave it to me, stop worrying." He looks at me thoughtfully, grazing his fingertip along my cheekbone. "I must be mad, introducing you to my family, they're … unique, but the thought of going without you …"

He trails off and shakes his head at the inconceivable thought. My heart squeezes in my chest because I get it. Every hour we're apart I miss him more. It wasn't meant to be like this, but I have a feeling I'm on the losing team in this power play we're in. I'm in danger of losing more than the game. My heart's at stake.

I curl my hand around his neck and pull him towards me, kissing him on the lips. "Then you, Mr White, have got yourself a date."

Chapter 43

Gabe

I rest my head against the black leather head rest and glance out of the window at the motorway whizzing by. Traffic's good. I'm glad. I just want to get home. I managed to squash the final meeting of the day and claw back some time to head home early.

I shift in the seat and loosen my tie, glancing at my mobile in my hand. Ella. I want to see the look of surprise on her face when I get back earlier than planned.

The light inside the car momentarily fades as we pass underneath a bridge and I catch my expression in the window.

I'm grinning like the village idiot. The same way I always do whenever I think about her. She's fire and ice. Sassy and bold. She possesses the ability to wind me up and turn me on in the same breath. My brain short circuits. I start thinking things I never thought I would and acting way out of character; like hiring a helicopter to fly home to see her, like inviting her to a party with my family. Like letting her in.

I feel a pang in my chest as I realise I haven't heard her voice in more than twelve hours. My mobile vibrates in my hand and I hope it's her. But it's Jake.

"Hey, what's up?"

"I'm just calling to see how things were progressing with the new deal."

"We're on track. Everything's agreed. I made an offer they couldn't turn down. They signed off on it a few days ago."

"Excellent." Jake hesitates, which means whatever he's about to say will likely piss me off. "So, you still coming on Saturday?"

I clench my jaw. I'm not sure what's pissing me off the most. The idea of actually going, and having to exchange awkward as fuck pleasantries for the evening, or the fact my big brother keeps checking that I *am* going. "Of course."

"Cool. Maria wanted me to double check. I said I would, in case you'd changed your mind."

"I've said I'm going."

"Chill, G. Don't shoot the fucking messenger. Would you rather me be the one calling you or Maria?"

I heave a sigh. I don't need to reply.

"Exactly. I'll let her know. I'll catch you later, okay."

"Okay."

I push my head back into the seat and close my eyes as he ends the call. My mind instantly fast forwards to the party. The strained silences with Dad, my step-mother, Lady Macbeth on his shoulder. That fucked-up dynamic.

Why the hell have I invited Ella?

She doesn't know what she's walking in to.

I'll have to tell her before Saturday.

I snap open my eyes at the sound of my mobile ringing again.

Maria's name flashes on the screen.

What the fuck does she want?

I stare at the phone, contemplating not answering it, but I know if I don't she'll bring it up at the party and use it as ammunition to start an argument between me and dad.

"Hi."

"Hey, there." Her smooth voice purrs down the phone, instantly fucking me off.

"What do you want?"

"Oh, come on, Gabe. That's no way to talk to your step-mum, is it?"

She's goading me. She knows how I feel about her, how we all feel about her.

"I'm busy."

"Well, you know what they say. All work and no play."

"I said, what do you want, Maria," I snap, already tiring of her bullshit.

"Okay, okay, calm down. I'm calling to check that you're still coming to the party on Saturday."

"You needn't have bothered. Jake's literally just called to check, and yes I am. I thought he told you he was checking that out with me himself?"

"I just wanted to be sure." She falters at the fact I've called her out. "I'm passing the final numbers onto the caterers now, so need to know."

"Will that be all?"

"Your dad's looking forward to seeing you."

Now I know she's lying. "I very much doubt that."

"*I'm* looking forward to seeing you."

I clench my jaw. Here she goes with her loaded shit. "I need to go."

"I never see you anymore," she sighs wistfully down the phone.

"You never saw me, Maria. You know Dad and I have never been close."

"I miss you."

And there it is. The real fucked up reason for her wanting to check I'm going to this party, and for calling me up.

She's trying to draw me into an argument. She's trying to get me to talk. But I won't be drawn in.

"I need to go. Oh, by the way, being as you're calling to confirm final numbers for the party, you'll need to add one more. I'm bringing a friend."

A short, sharp laugh echoes down the phone. "Yeah, female I'm guessing."

'Yes."

"Oh yeah, and who's the hanger-on this week?" The bitterness in her voice is clear. I'm getting to her.

Hanger-on? She's got a fucking cheek. "We've been seeing each other for a while, actually."

Silence.

I smile to myself. Pleased in the knowledge she's got the message loud and clear. "So, we'll see you on Saturday."

Chapter 44

Ella

The afternoon sunshine beats down on the tree-lined square outside White House Developments. It's Friday. The morning has passed by in a flurry of emails and telephone calls, meaning I've only just had chance to grab lunch.

As I head back towards the office my phone rings. My heart sinks as I look at the screen. Amy. The last time she called she wanted money, and I've none left to give her. Another stint at Dark Desires is out of the question.

"Hi Ames, what's up?" I ask, heading through reception.

"Are you okay to talk?"

There's only ever one thing she wants to talk about. "I'm just coming back into work actually, is everything all right?" I tell her, heading into the lift.

"Um, yeah. I just want to talk to you about something, but it can wait if now's not a good time."

I frown. This isn't like my little sister. Amy wants and expects everything yesterday. I'm immediately suspicious. "Everything's all right isn't it?"

"Yeah, yeah, fine."

The lift comes to a stop at my floor. I'm not convinced, but I don't have time to go into it now. "Well, give me a call tonight, if you like."

"It's Friday," she says as though what I've suggested is ridiculous. This is more like the Amy I know. "I'm out," she sighs impatiently, clearly unimpressed that she's able to have everything her way. "It doesn't matter."

She ends the call.

Charming.

I head out of the lift and over to the office. Judy's standing behind her desk chatting to a familiar, tall figure, standing with his back to me. An expensive pin stripe navy suit hangs from the broad lines of his shoulders. Gabe.

My heart speeds up at the sight of him. He's back early.

He notices me and finishes his conversation with Judy. His blue eyes sparkle as he nods towards the Starbucks cup in my hand and smiles. "Let me guess, vanilla latte."

"Um yes," I say, acutely aware of Judy's curious gaze darting between the two of us.

The last time we saw one another after being apart he fucked me senseless.

Silence stretches on between us. Things are getting weird. I need to snap out of it and speak before Judy starts to suspect something's up.

I put the cardboard cup on the desk and my handbag on the floor. "I didn't think you'd be back in the office until Monday."

He pushes his hands into the front pockets of his trousers and tilts his head, giving me a thoughtful look. "There was something really important I needed to get back for."

Heat rises through my body. I quickly turn and shrug my jacket off, hanging it on the coat stand, before Judy can catch a look at my face.

She clears her throat. "I'm just off to the kitchen to make myself a cup of tea, does anybody want anything?"

"Not for me, thanks," Gabe tells her.

"Nor me," I say, collecting myself and turning back round to face them.

Judy gives us a smile, before heading off in the direction of the kitchen.

He smiles. "Hey."

"Hey. What was the thing you needed to get back for?"

His smile widens. "She's standing in front of me."

I worriedly glance over my shoulder to check we're alone.

He chuckles at my nervousness. "Relax."

"We need to be careful," I warn. "Judy will work out there's something going on."

His smile fades. "Maybe I'm tired of being careful. Maybe I don't care if Judy does guess."

If me and him were found out, he'd risk everything. A potential scandal in the press, damage to the reputation of the family and business, not to mention losing the hard-earned respect of his employees.

I don't get to challenge him on is ludicrous comment. We're interrupted by a cry of "Gabe!"

I don't need to look. I'd recognise that annoying voice anywhere.

Sarah struts into the office and walks right up to him. She rests her hands on her hips and flashes a flirtatious smile. "So glad you're back. Can you spare five minutes for little old me. I need to run something past you."

He's only been back five minutes. Has she got a fucking radar or something?

The familiar prickle of unease takes over me, the way it always does when she's around. I force it from my mind, sit down behind my desk and turn my attention to my emails.

"Not really. I've had a long week, and was hoping to head off early." Gabe's rebuke makes me smile.

"It's about the Nightingale Development."

What the fuck's the Nightingale Development?

No one speaks. Seconds pass by. Gabe looks troubled. "Okay, come through."

Clearly pleased to have got what she wants, Sarah throws a smug smile over her shoulder at me as she follows Gabe into his office.

Five minutes later, the door opens and Sarah comes out, heading towards the lift. Gabe follows her out.

"I'm needed on site," he tells Judy.

I shift uncomfortably in my seat. Sarah stands waiting for the lift, straightening her red blouse. I shouldn't feel like this, but I don't trust her. It's obvious she's got her eye on Gabe.

Judy casts a suspicious glance in Sarah's direction. "Okay, will you be returning to the office today?"

"I doubt it."

I catch the pointed look he throws my way as he speaks and

quickly look at my laptop screen. God, this clandestine stuff's exhausting.

He gives us a tight smile. "Night, both. Have a good weekend."

A stab of jealousy slices through me as I watch Sarah's eyes light up as Gabe approaches her and they step into the lift. I watch the doors close. The memory of the photos of Gabe from the internet with those women, all tall and blonde, burns a hole in my brain.

I'm relieved when my mobile beeps, interrupting my thoughts. I pick it up.

Be ready for 7. Pack a bag. You're staying at mine tonight. We've some catching up to do. I miss you. x

I re-read the text over and over. The words make my stomach dance with happiness and swipe all thoughts of flirty Sarah from my mind.

"What are you smiling at?" Judy peers over the top of her glasses at me giving me an inquisitive look.

I feel my cheeks heat up. I put my phone down on the desk and turn back to my screen. "Erm, nothing."

I'm so shit at acting cool but I need to get better at it. Especially if I'm going to meet the prestigious White family this weekend.

***

Like clockwork at four, Judy switches her laptop off and packs up her desk.

"What a day." She heaves a sigh, throwing her handbag over her shoulder. "I bet you're glad it's Friday."

"Why's that?" I ask a little too quickly. I seriously need to chill the fuck out.

She gives me a funny look and laughs. "Because you'll have a break from this place, of course." Her eyes narrow curiously.

"Have you got anything special planned for the weekend?"

I wrinkle my nose and keep my eyes on the screen. "No, nothing exciting." *Liar, liar, pants on fire.* "What about you?" I ask, shifting the focus off me.

Judy breaks into a broad smile. "Ooh yes. It's our fifteenth wedding anniversary, so the kids are taking us out for a meal tonight."

"Sounds lovely. Where are they taking you, somewhere nice?"

Her eyes sparkle with pride. It's clear her family are everything to her. "The Ivy."

"Very nice. I've never been."

For a moment the excitement in her eyes is replaced by sadness. "I have, but that was a long time ago. Oh, here's my son now, come to collect me," she chuckles, snapping out of it and looking towards the lift.

I watch him head our way and take him in. Tall and looks around my age. Tan chinos and a light blue shirt give him a smart, preppy vibe. But as he gets closer, an uneasy feeling creeps over me. The cocky walk. The sandy blond hair that was once collar length is now short and swept to the side. Flint-like grey eyes; the same ones that were as cold as ice and full of contempt the last time he looked at me.

My mouth dries. I can't think straight.

It can't be.

He stops at Judy's desk and flashes her a charming smile, then notices me. His gaze narrows curiously, like he recognises me and he's trying to piece things together.

I've rehearsed this moment over and over. Every word I want to say is tattooed on my brain, but it wasn't supposed to happen like this. Eight years strip away. I'm seventeen again. Curled up in a ball on the bed, thinking I'm about to die because of the amount of pain I'm in.

"Ella, I'd love you to meet my son," Judy tells me, completely oblivious to the fact my worlds opening up in front of me.

I watch as his eyes widen in surprise at my name.

"This is Logan."

My stomach drops to the floor. Logan-fucking-Marshall. The bastard who took my virginity for a bet. The guy who lied about loving me just to get me to fuck him and then left me to abort our baby, alone.

Nausea swirls in my stomach. I briefly close my eyes and press a hand to my brow.

Judy gives me a worried look. "Are you all right, Ella? You've gone a bit pale."

I force a smile. "Yes, thanks. Just tired, I think. It's been a long day."

"Ella," Logan mutters in disbelief. "Ella Anderson."

Judy's eyes swing between us, sensing somethings up. "Do you two know one another?"

Kind, caring Judy doesn't have one iota about what her darling son is capable of.

"We went to the same college," Logan tells her.

Judy's eyes widen as the penny drops. "Of course you did. Silly me. I remember from Ella's CV. Oh, isn't it a small world."

Isn't it just.

She looks at me expectantly, waiting for me to say something. This could be my moment. My opportunity to reveal what a bastard her son really is, but as she looks at me, with a great big smile on her face, I bottle it. Judy's been nothing but kind and caring to me since I started. It's not her fault Logan's a bastard.

"Yes, it is," I reply stiffly.

Logan takes a deep breath, clearly relieved I haven't spilled the beans on his dirty little secret. He turns to his mum and gives her a winning smile.

"Come on, mum. The car's outside and I'm parked on a double yellow."

Judy laughs. "Of course, dear. We don't want that lovely Ferrari of yours getting a ticket, do we? I'll see you Monday. Have a lovely weekend, Ella."

I'm on auto-pilot. I feel like I'm having an out-of-body experience, floating above it all while watching this situation unfold. "Of course. You too, Judy. Have a lovely evening."

They head towards the lift and I watch them until the lift doors close, making sure he's gone.

I slump down in my chair, put my head in my hands and close my eyes. Emotions I thought I'd dealt with rush to the surface. For the last eight years I've built a brick wall round my past. Closing it off, so I don't have to deal with it. And that bastard's just put a bomb under it. I thought I'd dealt with it. But I haven't. And Gabe doesn't have a clue.

Chapter 45

Ella

"Oh my God!" Kate squeaks with excitement from my bedroom doorway, making me jump.

I can't remember how long I've been staring at my reflection in the bedroom mirror, scrutinising the dress she's lent me for tonight.

"I told you that dress would look fab on you."

I pull a face. "Yeah, it's lovely but I'm not so sure."

"Are you joking!" She walks over to me, tilting her head to the side and examining my reflection in the mirror. "If Gabe doesn't need hosing down after he's taken one look at you, then he's not the one."

The One.

I look at her as though she's mad. "He's not … it's not like that between us."

Kate gives me a look that says she doesn't believe me, but I've more pressing matters than arguing the toss over my relationship status. I'm really not sure about this dress.

I twist round, smoothing the black velvet across my stomach and checking how much side boob I'm revealing. There's no way I can wear a bra in this thing. The halter neck floor length gown has a deep v at the front and is backless.

"I'm worried it's too revealing. I'm meeting his parents for the first time. I want to create the right impression."

"You look sexy, sophisticated and classy and you're going to The Savoy. You'll fit right in." Kate heaves a wistful sigh. "All that money floating about, and Spencer White. Are you sure I can't come?"

She's still got a thing for Gabe's younger brother, even after I've told her he's a dick in real life. Even so, right now I'd take Kate's fawning over Spencer if it meant some moral support at the party.

I anxiously chew my bottom lip and turn this way and that, in the mirror.

"Will you stop? You look stunning." She casts me a sideways glance. "Are you all right? You've seemed a bit off all day."

I sweep my hair over my shoulder with a hand and avoid her gaze. If anyone will suss me out it's Kate.

"Yeah. I'm fine."

"Are you sure? Everything's okay with you and Gabe, isn't it?"

"Yeah, fine."

"Well, something's up. What is it?"

The thought of meeting Gabe's family and friends shouldn't get me into such of a tizz, but the whole Logan-thing yesterday has knocked me off my stride.

"Nothing."

"Something's the matter. You've been preoccupied all day. Is this all because you're meeting Gabe's parents –"

"No. Well … a bit. Not really."

Kate puts her hands on her hips and gives me a look which tells me she's not going to budge. "Then, what is it?"

"Okay, okay." I take a deep breath knowing she won't drop it until I cave. "I saw Logan."

Her expression switches from confusion to surprise to anger, in a matter of seconds. "Logan Marshall? Fucking hell. When? How?"

"Yesterday, at work. It turns out he's Judy's son. He came to pick her up and take her out for an anniversary meal."

"Oh, what a gentleman," Kate snaps. "What happened? What did he say? Did he recognise you?"

"Not at first. Then Judy introduced me and it clicked. He told her we knew one another from college."

"And what did you do?"

"What could I do?"

"Tell him his bloody name with knobs on."

"Trust me, I wanted to. I know exactly what I want to say to him, but I just couldn't. Judy was there, I like her. She's been lovely to me."

Kate rolls her eyes. "She deserves to know what a nasty little fucker her son is."

I want to put this whole thing back in the past where it belongs. A showdown with Logan isn't the way to heal wounds.

"It's been eight years. Do you really think he's going to step foot inside the building again now he knows I work there? I'm never going to see him again, today was a one off. I've got to work with Judy every day. Like I said, she's a really nice lady. I think … I just want to move on. I've worked hard to put all that shit behind me. Telling Judy will rake everything up."

Kate gives me a sympathetic smile. "I get that, but I still think he should be on his fucking knees apologising for what he did and how he treated you."

I laugh sharply. "I doubt that. He was the same Logan, just an older version. Same arrogant swagger, expensive clothes, flash car."

"Have you told Gabe about what happened?'

Nerves swirl in my stomach at the thought. "Not yet."

"Are you going to?"

"I want to be honest with him."

She blows out a long breath, taking in what I've just told her. "Gabe will understand, I'm sure."

I can't think about that conversation right now. "I'm still not sure about this dress," I tell her, changing the subject. "Do you think I've got time to try any others on?"

"No."

"Are you sure? What time is it?"

"Nearly seven."

Shit! I really haven't got time. "He'll be here any minute."

Kate gives me a smug smile. "That settles it then. You're going in this dress, and you're going to be the belle of the ball."

It looks like I am.

I head downstairs and stop at the hall mirror to check my

make-up. I've worn a little more than normal tonight; smoky eyes and a red lip. The occasion calls for it.

"What do we have here?"

Harry's leant against the doorframe to the living room. His beady blue eyes sweep up the length of my body and rest on my breasts.

Dickhead.

I'm about to tell him what I think of him, but don't get chance.

"Ella's going out to The Savoy, with Gabe," Kate says coming downstairs.

Harry straightens and averts his eyes from my tits to his girlfriend. He gives her a sheepish grin and rubs a hand through his hair. "Oh, hello, babe. Oh right. The Savoy, yeah nice."

Kate puts her arms around his waist. "Why don't we go out tonight?"

He pulls a face. "Nah, not tonight, babe. I don't fancy it."

"You never fancy it."

I look back at the mirror and tweak my hair. I'm not getting caught in the middle of a domestic with these two. They haven't been going out five minutes and they already sound like an old married couple.

A knock sounds at the front door. Through the frosted glass I see a tall, broad shadow. My heart skips. And I haven't even seen him yet.

"Come on," Kate waves her hands at Harry and ushers him back into the living room. "Let's leave Ella to her night. Have a fab time." She waggles her eyebrows at me suggestively, before disappearing into the living room.

Nerves prickle in my stomach, the way they always do when I see him.

I open the door. My breath catches in my throat.

He fills the doorway. A painfully expensive light grey three-piece suit fits him like a glove and makes his sea blue eyes pop. He doesn't move an inch. The only part of him that does are his eyes, raking up my body. Without saying a word, he steps inside and presses his lips to mine, kissing me languidly. He curls a hand around the back of my neck, pulling me closer, deepening our scorching kiss which speaks a thousand words.

He pulls his lips from mine a fraction, and gazes deep into my eyes. "You're trying to kill me," he breathes against my lips.

"I'm not."

His hooded gaze washes over me and leaves me with no doubt about the meaning behind his words. "I think you're trying to give me a fucking heart attack, dressed like this."

"Actually, I was worried it was bit much and I'm overdressed."

"You *are* overdressed." Gabe watches my fading smile. "You're wearing too many clothes." He briefly glances over my shoulder to the stairs. "How about we forget about the party and I take you to bed."

I slide my arms around his neck. What an offer. "Sounds good, Mr White, but it's your brother's birthday. I think we should go."

"And I think I should fuck your brains out."

I want nothing more, but even though the thought of going to this party and meeting his family fills me with nerves, I really want to go.

"Later."

"I'm not sure that I can hold out that long."

"You need to try."

Gabe glides his hands down my bare shoulders and links his fingers through mine. He gives me a look which makes my insides dance. "For you Princess, I'll try anything."

Chapter 46

Ella

We pull up behind another car outside the front of The Savoy. An older couple climb out of the shiny black Jaguar ahead, and the man, dressed in a black tux, hands his keys to the valet. The woman is wearing a gold satin gown, with diamond jewellery draped around her neck. They're the picture of elegance and make me feel a little better about wearing my fancy dress.

Nerves tingle as I stare up the hotel. I know I shouldn't feel intimidated about being here, but I can't help it. There's no denying I'm out of my comfort zone.

A grey-haired doorman wearing a black top hat and double breasted jacket stands at the top of the stone steps that lead up to the wooden revolving doors of the entrance. I watch as he welcomes the older couple before they head into the entrance with a smile.

"There's something you should know."

Gabe's brows are pulled into a frown. He has a distracted look in his eye and is staring through the windscreen.

Nerves that had started to abate return with a vengeance. "What?"

He raps his fingers against the steering wheel. "My parents aren't together."

Other than the little I know from meeting his brothers and the research I did about the business before my interview, I know nothing about his family. He's never broached the subject. Until now.

"Oh, I'm sorry. Are they separated?"

A muscle ticks in his jaw. He carries on looking ahead and pulls the car forward as the Jag up in front moves. "No, Mum died when I was fifteen."

It was hard enough for me to deal with losing my mum as an adult, but I can't begin to imagine what it must have been like for Gabe having to handle that as a child. "I'm so sorry –"

"Dad remarried." He cuts me off, clearly in no mood for sympathy. He looks at me, like he's toying with the idea of saying more. We're interrupted by a knock on the driver's window. It's the valet.

The moment's gone. Gabe forces a smile. "Time to go."

We climb out of the car. Gabe hands his keys to the valet and walks around to me, resting a protective hand on the base of my spine and guiding me up the steps of the hotel.

The doorman greets us with a polite smile. "Good evening, sir, madam."

We head through the revolving wooden doors and into the vast foyer. A shiny black and white checked floor stretches on and on across the cavernous entrance hall. Antique chairs and coffee tables are dotted about the lobby and sit on huge expensive thick pile rugs. A large, dark wood reception desk on the far wall faces the revolving doors of the entrance. Fancy lights hang from the high ceilings with ornately carved cornicing. It's classy, elegant and has a touch of the theatrical about it. I can't stop myself from staring. It's truly splendid.

Gabe takes my hand in his and guides us through an archway off to the left and up another set of stairs. At the top is a long corridor with a set of large wooden double doors that lead into another room. The sound of chatter and the soft notes of a piano filter through the open door. The party.

Gabe comes to a stop just outside the door and turns to me. "Are you okay?"

"I'm fine. I mean" – I look towards the party – "I'm a bit nervous about properly meeting your family for the first time, but I'm okay."

He hesitates. "Listen, why don't we forget it and go home."

"But we're here."

He stares past me into the room. "I'm just not really sure I'm in the mood for the shit."

What shit?

Something's up. He's been acting odd since we got here.

An unsettling feeling takes up residence in the pit of my stomach. Maybe now I'm here, he's having second thoughts about introducing me. He's second-guessing himself about the fact he's invited me in the first place.

"Here he is!" A male voice cries from behind me.

I turn round to see Jake heading out of the party with a tall, slim blonde on his arm. "Good to see you."

Gabe's usual cool, calm façade snaps back into place and with it a ready smile. "Happy Birthday, big bro."

"Thank you and nice to see you again, Ella. You're looking lovely," Jake tells me.

"Thanks, Jake, and Happy Birthday."

"Thank you."

Gabe laces his fingers through mine and Jake notices. He looks from me to his brother and grins.

"Take your time, Jake," the blonde on his arm pipes up, with a roll of her eyes.

He shoots her a pointed look. "Of course, how could I forget. Ella, this is Andi, my girlfriend. Andi, this is Ella…" For a moment he hesitates, like he's not quite sure how to introduce me. For a second I'm worried he's going to say "Gabe's girlfriend," but he doesn't. Gabe's clearly getting jittery about introducing me to his parents, so fuck knows what he'd do if Jake called me that. "Gabe's friend," he says, eventually.

Andi tilts her head and looks at me thoughtfully, weighing me up. Her cornflower blue, off-the-shoulder floor-length dress complements her long, honey blonde hair. Large gold hoop earrings are in her ears. Her make-up is perfect. I'm guessing she's a model.

"Good evening, Andi," Gabe says.

Her pink, glossed lips pull into a smile. "So, how did you two meet?"

The dreaded question. Gabe squeezes my hand, reassuring me.

Jake raises his eyebrows and takes a sip of whatever short he's drinking from the glass tumbler in his hand.

"Through work," Gabe replies smoothly.

She arches an eyebrow. "I suppose it's not going to be any other way with you, is it, Gabe?"

She's bought the lie at least.

"Are we re-joining the party, or what?" Jake cuts in, before any more questions are thrown our way. "Come on, before Dad finishes off all the good whisky."

We follow Jake and Andi into yet another spectacular room. Every inch of the place is rammed with guests dressed in their finery, eating and drinking. Waiters wearing smart black and white uniforms weave through the clusters of people, holding round silver trays filled with flutes of champagne and hors d'oeuvres. Everything about the place and everyone in it, screams money. We lose sight of Jake and Andi as we move into the room.

"We might as well get this over and done with first," Gabe mutters in my ear.

I don't know what he's referring to, but let him lead the way across the room.

We come to a stop at an older gentleman, wearing a salmon pink shirt and navy trousers. His tan skinned makes his white, slicked back hair seem even brighter. A gold Rolex glistens on his wrist as he takes a long drink of whisky. He's in deep conversation with another older man and doesn't notice us at first. A younger woman stands beside him. Her plunging, thigh-length gold sequin dress clings to her curves and shows off her ample cleavage. Loose dark brown curls rest on her breasts. She's chewing her bottom lip and her dark eyes are glazed in boredom; she looks like she'd rather be anywhere else then here. I'm struggling to place her. Gabe hasn't got an older sister and she can't be any older than mid-forties.

The man with the pink shirt's gaze drifts to us, and he stops talking. His shoulders stiffen. "Gabe."

"Dad."

This is Maxwell White?

Gabe shares his dad's height but other than that they're

nothing alike.

A weird, strained silence descends. The guy Maxwell was talking to makes his excuses and leaves. A tumbleweed could roll across the room and not look out of place, right now. It's awkward as fuck.

The attractive brunette at Maxwell's side takes a sip out of the champagne flute and beams at Gabe.

"Hi Gabe, thanks for coming. Your dad and I are so happy to see you."

"Maria," he replies with a stiff bob of his head.

"Dad remarried."

His words from moments earlier hit me.

This is his step-mother. She must be thirty years Maxwell's junior, at least.

Maxwell takes a swig of whisky from his tumbler and turns his scrutinising gaze on me. "And who is this?"

Gabe's grip on my hand tightens. "This is Ella. Ella, this is my dad, Maxwell, and my step-mum, Maria."

"Nice to meet you, Ella."

"You too."

I look to Maria to say "hello," but I'm met with a stony smile as she scans me up and down suspiciously. I'm not getting the friendliest vibes off her.

Maxwell clears his throat. "I hear you're on the brink of closing a big deal?"

Gabe shakes his head. "Let's not talk shop. How was Monaco?"

"Oh you know what he's like, G," Maria giggles, swinging her hair over her shoulder. "Your dad never switches off."

Maxwell drains the remainder of his whisky. "Old habits die hard."

Gabe glances at me, clearly hating every second of this. "I'm sure Ella doesn't want to stand and listen to me waffle on about boring old work."

"Don't mind me," I jump in. Things are awkward as hell between Gabe and his dad, and if talking about the business eases the butt-clenchingly tense atmosphere between them, then so be it. "I need the ladies', anyway."

"They're back outside, down the corridor," Maria tells me, wearing a smile that doesn't reach her eyes,

"Great, thanks."

Gabe squeezes my hand and looks at me. "Five minutes."

He doesn't intend on making his chat very long then.

I'm just thankful for the reprieve.

***

The ladies' toilets are just as fancy as the rest of the hotel. Three white basins sit beneath three gilt framed mirrors. A large crystal chandelier illuminates the room.

I put my black clutch down on the white marble counter and retrieve my lipstick. The door to the corridor opens then closes. It's Andi.

She gives me a tight smile and stands at the basin next to me.

Great.

She pulls her mobile from her snakeskin clutch. "So, how long have you and Gabe been dating?" she asks, tapping out a text with her long French manicured nails.

I finish reapplying lipstick and glance at her worriedly. I hope she's not here to grill me, but have a horrid suspicion that's exactly what she's planning on doing. I'm shit at lying. I'm definitely going to mess this up.

"Just a few weeks."

"I see he's abandoned you already?"

"He's talking to his dad and Maria."

Andi's smile disappears at the mention of Maria. She slides her phone back into her bag and inspects her reflection in the mirror.

"How long have you and Jake been dating?" I ask, keen to steer the conversation off me and Gabe.

She fluffs up her roots with her fingers and scrunches up her nose. "Six months. I don't blame you for making yourself scarce from that awkward as arse conversation between Gabe and his dad. They *really* don't get on."

"Yeah, I gathered."

"You met Maria then?"

The question is simple enough, but I can't help but feel it's loaded.

I put my lipstick back into my bag. "Yes."

Andi casts me a sidewards glance. "You need to watch her."

"How do you mean?"

"I mean you need to watch her ... with Gabe."

I think back to the way Maria's eyes lit up when she saw him. Her comment about being happy to see him. Her clear dislike for me. I'm not sure I want to hear the answer to the next question, but have to ask.

"How do you mean, with Gabe?"

Andi flicks her long blonde hair over her shoulder and turns to face me, folding her arms. "Everyone knows she's only fucking Max to get to Gabe."

I freeze. *What the fuck do I say to that?*

"It's true. Shit went down a few summers ago," Andi carries on. Although part of me wants to tell her to shut up, the other part of me needs to hear this. "A couple of weeks before she and Max were due to get married, she pretty much laid it out on a platter for Gabe. Oh, don't worry, he didn't grab a spoon, sweetie, but she's definitely one to watch."

My mouth dries. I feel sick. He warned me his family were fucked up, but this is another level. Is this why he's barely mentioned his parents to me? Why he got cold feet as soon as we arrived?

"You said that you and Jake have only been dating six months, so how do you know ... that happened?"

"Jake told me."

I frown. My mind a mess. Andi wasn't exactly welcoming when I first met her. I can't help feeling suspicious. "Why have you told me?"

"Because Maria's a gold-digging bitch and I can't stand her. None of the family can. And she likes to cause trouble." Her green eyes narrow thoughtfully. "I've not told you this to cause trouble. I've told you so that you know what she's like, especially where Gabe's concerned. You need to watch your back."

My stomach twists with nausea. "Thanks, I guess."

Andi brushes her hair over her shoulders and gives me a warm smile. "For what it's worth, I'm pleased for you both. It's about time Gabe settled down. I don't think anyone thought he would. He's been married to the job for too long. I don't think he's ever introduced a woman to his family before. I'm not going to lie. There was a time when I had a bit of a thing for him. But then, I think most women who know him have at some point."

Andi's honesty reassures me a little. At least she's been up front about things.

"Jake seems really lovely," I say.

She smiles weakly and twists a long blonde strand of hair around her finger. "Yeah. He's the best."

She couldn't sound less convinced if she tried. She heaves a sigh and rolls her eyes. "Anyway, I'd better get back. He'll be wondering where I've got to. See you around."

I give it a few minutes and head back into the party. I scan the room and notice Gabe's still talking to Maxwell. Jealousy twists like a knife in my gut at the sight of Maria stuck in between the two men, looking enraptured as Gabe talks.

I still need time to process this head fuck. A drink wouldn't go amiss either.

Through the guests I catch sight of a table over to the left side of the room, covered in a pristine white table cloth and glasses of champagne.

Thank God.

I make a beeline to the table, pick up one of the glasses and take a mouthful of champagne welcoming the fizz.

"Hey, Ella."

Jake's standing to my right with an older lady.

"Hi. Gabe's just talking to your dad and Maria. I thought I'd leave them to it."

Jake nods his head knowingly. The woman glances down at her glass, like she gets it too. It seems everyone knows they don't get on.

"I just saw Andi in the ladies. She was heading back out here," I tell him.

Jake's brow creases into a suspicious frown, as he scans the room. "Oh. I haven't seen her for a while."

I can't help but feel as though I've put my foot in it, and I'm not sure why. "Oh, well maybe she bumped into someone."

"Maybe." He doesn't sound convinced. "Anyway, let me introduce you to this lovely lady."

The woman beside him laughs softly and pats the back of her grey bob, as though she's uncomfortable with the compliment. She's dressed in a black dress with a peter pan collar and shiny black patent sensible heels. There's a grandmother vibe about her.

"This is Nessa. She's practically part of our family," Jake tells me. "Nessa, this is Ella, she's with Gabe."

"How lovely to meet you," Nessa says in a calm, well-spoken voice.

I smile. "You too."

"Nessa was our housekeeper, nanny, second mum, pretty much everything to us growing up."

Her blue eyes sparkle. "And it was my pleasure. I was so surprised when I got an invite to this evening."

"Too right," Jake says. "Like I say, you're part of the family."

He's interrupted by the sound of his mobile. He pulls it from his back pocket, and answers it with a frown. "What's up?"

I hear a female voice down the other end of the phone.

"What do you mean, you've got to go?" The frown deepens and he places a hand over his phone, remembering himself. "Sorry ladies, please excuse me."

We watch him disappear off through the crowds.

"So, you're friends with Gabe. That's nice," Nessa says warmly.

"Yes, we met through work."

"Gabe's always been very business minded. That's why Maxwell wanted him to take over the company. He's always been the sensible one of the three, and the most sensitive, but he's had to carry a lot on his shoulders over the years."

"It must have been so hard for Gabe, well, for all of you, when his mum died."

Nessa looks taken aback. "He told you?"

"Well, erm ... yes. Only recently though."

"It's not something he talks about. At all." She smiles fondly. "But I'm glad that he felt he could talk to you about it. It was so hard for him."

"I lost my mum recently and that was hard enough, but he was so young."

"Oh, I'm so sorry my dear. It doesn't get any easier, however old we get, does it?" Nessa's eyes shine with tears and she swallows down emotion, taking a moment. "But Gabe was *so* young. Jake had just joined the army so he wasn't around. Spencer was only thirteen so was shielded from lots of things. He wasn't told *everything* that happened. Maxwell decided it was best that he didn't know."

I'm intrigued. "Why? What did happen?"

"You don't know?"

"Know what?"

Nessa gives me a worried look. "How it happened?"

"No. Gabe just said she died when he was fifteen."

She fiddles with the collar of her dress and looks awkward. "Oh, well, erm ..."

"Ness!"

Gabe appears at our side and puts an arm around her shoulders drawing her into a hug. "I had no idea you were here. It's so good to see you."

Nessa laughs and gives him a peck on the cheek. "Hello, young man."

"Not so much of the young anymore," he says, letting go of her.

"Don't be silly. You're just a young whippersnapper."

He laces his fingers through mine and suddenly looks serious. "I'm sorry. I didn't mean to leave you, but that took longer than I thought."

"You don't have to apologise, I've been talking to Andi, Jake and Nessa."

I catch her watching us both with a twinkle in her eye. "Yes, I've been chatting to your lovely Ella."

Gabe squeezes my hand and gives me an unfathomable look. "Yes, she is, isn't she."

My stomach flips. I can't decide whether he thinks that I'm lovely or that I'm his. But I'm sure of one thing; I want to be both.

We spend the next hour talking to Nessa who regales me with some embarrassing stories of Gabe when he was younger, much to my delight. They push the conversation I had with Andi earlier, and the unwelcome thoughts about Maria, to the back of my mind. The love she had for Gabe and his brothers growing up is apparent, and it warms my heart to know that even though he was only young when he lost his mum, he had someone like Nessa in his life to help him with his grief.

***

The cool night air wraps around me as we leave the hotel. We climb into the car that's waiting for us out front.

Gabe seems pensive and stares at the road, lost in his own thoughts. I welcome the silence, as I try to unravel the information overload I've been subjected to this evening. Andi, Maria *and* Nessa's curious words about his mum's death tangle in my head like knots.

"So, I'm not sure I should ask, but what did you think?" Gabe asks eventually.

I stare out of the window unsure how to respond. "How did *you* find it?"

He shrugs. "To be honest, it wasn't quite as bad as I expected."

It was a million times worse than I expected.

"You and your dad, *really* don't get on, do you?"

"No."

"Is that why you had second thoughts about coming?"

He glances at me worriedly. "Of course. What other reason would there be?"

It's time for some truths and answers. "I wondered whether you'd had second thoughts about introducing me to your folks."

Gabe shoots me an alarmed look. "Absolutely not. You're amazing, Ella."

"I was just being stupid I guess."

"Yeah, you were."

I watch the streetlights whizz past as I build up to asking the next question. "How old is Maria?"

"Forty-five."

"That's quite a big age gap between her and your dad."

"You're telling me."

"She's very beautiful."

A muscle twitches in Gabe's jaw. "Beauty doesn't mean anything when you're poison inside."

"Why do you say that?"

"She can be incredibly manipulative. She's only after his money. Plain and simple."

"You think that's why she's with him?"

"Why else would she be with him?"

"To get to you."

He pulls up outside the barrier to the underground car park of The Madison and fixes me with a firm look. "Where did you hear that?"

I really want him to deny it, but he's not. He could have laughed it off or told me I was being silly, but he hasn't. He's more interested in how I've found out. His lack of response silently validates what I've been told. It's true.

I turn and stare out of the window. I really wanted him to introduce me to his parents and let me in. Now he has, I'm not sure I want an insight into his fucked-up family.

He heaves a sigh, pissed off at my silence, buzzes down the window and punches a code in to the metal keypad on the wall. The screech of rubber against tarmac echoes around the car park as he angrily plants his foot on the accelerator, making the engine roar into life.

"Who told you?" he demands, turning the car into his reserved parking space and slamming on the brakes. "You need to start talking."

My patience snaps. "I think *you're* the one who needs to start talking."

His jaw clenches with tension. "Andi. It was Andi, wasn't it? She's the only one who *would* tell you."

"It doesn't matter who told me. It's true, isn't it? Maria threw herself at you just before she married your dad." His eyes glitter with anger and he shakes his head. His silence only serves to piss me off even more. "Did you fuck her?"

"Do you really need to ask that question?"

"I don't know. This is a pretty messed up situation," I snap. "Look at it from my point of view. At the start of this evening I didn't even know you *had* a step-mum, let alone one that wants to fuck you."

"It's not like that."

"Then what *is* it like?"

His eyes search my face. I know he's making his mind up; to finally let me in. Or not. He gives an exasperated growl and climbs out of the car, slamming the door behind him. Despite the anger coursing through my veins my stupid heart drops to my shoes. That's a no, then. Even after tonight, the wall around his heart is still there. He can't do it. He can't let me in.

I climb out of the car and watch him stalking towards the lift. This isn't enough. I don't want to be like all the other women before me. All the flings that have never really known the real him. I want more of him than he's able to give. I can't keep going along with this casual arrangement any longer. For my sanity or my heart. I always knew it was going to end, I just never figured it was going to be like this.

Emotion wedges like a brick in my throat. I force my voice to remain even and take a deep breath at what I'm about to say.

"It's over."

Gabe stops in his tracks. He slowly turns to face me. "What?"

"You and me. Whatever the hell this thing is between us. It's over."

He narrows his eyes like he can't quite believe what he's hearing and he starts towards me. "Nothing's over, Princess."

I shake my head and take a couple of steps back. He's steaming towards me and showing no signs of stopping. "Yes, it is Gabe. It's for the best."

Within a flash he's in front of me, wrapping his arms around my waist and throwing me over his shoulder into a fireman's lift.

"What the fuck are you doing? Are you crazy!" I cry, hitting my fists against his back, as he carries me across the car park. I hope to God no one's watching.

"I think I might just fucking well be."

The doors close behind us as we step into the lift and we begin moving upwards.

"Are you going to put me down."

"Not yet."

"Why the hell are you doing this?"

"Because you're talking bollocks and I need you to listen to me."

"I'm being sensible."

"I've been sensible all my life, it's overrated."

"Is this how you get all your women to listen to you?"

"No. I've never told any of them anything worth listening to before."

The lift comes to a stop and the doors slide open. I recognise the polished floor of Gabe's hallway, and watch the lights flicker on as he carries me through the apartment.

"Have you quite bloody finished?" I snap, tiring of this malarkey.

He gently lowers me down on the kitchen counter and smooths down my hair, tucking a loose tendril behind my ear and staring deep into my eyes. My head's a mess. The look he gives me turns my insides to mush. The anger from earlier leaves me.

"Now sit down and shut up, and for once, do as you're told."

And for once, I'm inclined to do just that.

Chapter 47

Gabe

I pull two tumblers out of the kitchen cupboard followed by a bottle of Johnnie Walker Blue Label and pour two fingers into each glass.

Ella's playing with her hair and staring out towards the window deep in thought. Giving her a glimpse into my fucked-up family and taking her to the party tonight was always a risk. But the time's come to put her straight about a few things.

I take a sip of whisky and welcome the burn as it hits the back of my throat. It offers a distraction. Stops my mind overthinking about what I'm about to do.

I head over to her and offer her a glass.

She takes it from me with a small smile. "Thanks. I'm not a fan of whisky but I think I'm going to need it." She meets my gaze, lifts the glass to her lips and takes a small sip.

"What do you think?"

"It's smooth." Her eyes hold mine. "And you should start talking."

I put my glass down on the counter, shrug off my jacket and throw it over the back of the kitchen stool. I unbutton my cuffs and push back the sleeves of my shirt, like I'm preparing for a fight. Maybe I am. A subconscious one, with my past.

I pick up my tumbler and take another sip, steeling myself. "What Andi told you about Maria is true. A couple of weeks before she and dad got married they had a party at their house. I drove and didn't plan on staying long, because of how awkward things are between me and Dad. Anyway, Jake and Spencer started a game of poker. It got late and I didn't realise how much I'd had to drink. I was over the limit so stayed in one of their guest bedrooms. In the middle of the night, I woke up. Maria was in bed beside me. Naked."

Ella's eyes widen. "What happened?"

I grit my teeth at the memory of her fingernails running down my chest beneath the sheets. "I leapt out of bed and kicked her out."

She drops her eyes to her glass. "Does your dad know what happened?"

"Doubt it. Maria's not going to tell him, is she? And I'm certainly not. It's just not worth the hassle. She's got him so wrapped around her little finger, he probably wouldn't believe me anyway."

"That's fucked up."

I blow out a long breath and rub a hand through my hair. "Welcome to my family."

She takes a sip of whisky and winces as it goes down. "I spoke to Nessa a little bit. She seemed really nice."

"Nessa's the best."

Ella presses her lips together and lifts her eyes to mine, like she's thinking very carefully about whatever she's about to say. "She mentioned your mum."

Now it's my turn to take a slug of whisky. "Oh?"

"She said something about Spencer not knowing everything about what happened to her."

She pauses. "What did happen?"

I drain my glass, put it down and lean against the shiny grey countertop. I'm thirty-one. I'm a CEO for fuck's sake, yet I can't say this. The words stick in my throat like knives.

Ella puts a hand on my wrist, sensing my struggle.

"It's okay," she says softly. "I know it's hard. If you don't want to talk about it, that's okay. I'll be here, whenever you feel ready."

Her hazel eyes brim with sympathy and understanding. No one's looked at me like this before. No one gets it. No one's seen into my soul. She's the balm to soothe all my worries.

I glance down at her fingers gently stroking my wrist easing my anxieties away, and from somewhere I find the words. "She killed herself."

Her fingers still.

"My mum killed herself. She slit her wrists. We'd just come home for the school holidays, and I found her. That's –" I pause as words fail me. Admitting I've got a weakness isn't something I'm used to, or proud of. "That's where my phobia of blood comes from. When I found her, there was a lot..."

"Gabe." My name falls from her mouth in shocked whisper. "Oh my God. I can't imagine." Tears spring in her eyes. She shakes her head like she can't find the right words.

"Spencer was only thirteen. To this day he still doesn't know what happened. Dad told him she went to sleep and never woke up."

"Why? Why did she do it?"

Ella asks the questions that burrowed away in my brain ever since.

"Dad said she'd been taking anti-depressants for a few months. He said she'd done it because he'd found out she'd been having affairs for years behind his back and that she couldn't live with the guilt and what it would do to the family image. That's the bit I struggled with the most, second to her taking her own life. It just didn't fit with how she was. Dad told me I just didn't want to believe she'd do something like that."

"What are you saying?"

I've pondered these thoughts too many times over the years and I know it doesn't do to dwell on them. It makes you go fucking crazy.

"I don't know. I don't really know what to think."

Ella curls her hand around my wrist and strokes her thumb across my pulse point. "Maybe you were right? We have got more in common than I thought."

I shift in between her legs and she shuffles her thighs further apart, as much as her dress will allow. I take her hands in mine.

"You get me," I tell her. "You see me. Like no one else can." I cup her cheek with my hand. "And I get you. Don't I?"

She nods her head slowly, fresh tears welling in her eyes. I want to kiss them all away. I want to make everything better, like she does for me.

"What was your mum's name?" she asks,

"Rose."

Her eyes widen and drop to the rose tattoo. "That's the meaning behind your tattoo?"

"One arm represents my mum, the other Dad. Both make me who I am."

She gently traces her fingertips over my inked skin. "The roses are beautiful."

"Mum was beautiful."

"Thank you for telling me."

I cup her face in my hands and stare deeply into her eyes. "I've been carrying this around all these years, and no amount of sitting on a therapist's couch solved how I felt about it. But you're my cure, Ella. I knew it as soon as I first saw you. I saw the sadness in your eyes and felt it, like it was my own."

"I felt it too," she whispers.

I claim her mouth with mine and kiss her deeply, like my life depends on it. Maybe it does. The next moment we're tearing each others clothes off. My finger finds the side zip of her dress and slides it all the way down, allowing the black velvet to fall away, leaving her nearly naked on the counter in front of me.

She leans back on her hands and tilts her neck, exposing more of her soft skin to my mouth, moaning as I place kisses all the way across her collarbone, darting my tongue against her flesh.

"I crave you, Princess. With every fibre of my being, I crave you."

"I want you to." She sighs in contentment, arching against me.

I open my eyes and drink in her beauty. Eyes closed, head dropped back, her perfect breasts heaving as she waits for my touch. My Princess. My Ella. My salvation.

I slide my fingers beneath the edges of her flimsy lace knickers and tear them from her hips with an impatient tug, then grab her waist and pull her to the edge of the counter, lining myself up with her.

She gasps, but there's a twinkle in her eye which tells me she likes it.

I wrap my hand around the back of her neck and pull her lips inches from mine.

"You like when I'm rough, don't you?"

"Yes."

I gently bite down on her bottom lip, then let go, keeping my gaze locked on her as I brush my fingers across her clit.

"You're wet."

"And if I felt your dick, you'd be hard."

I barely suppress a smile. I want her. "You get turned on when we argue."

"You get turned on by my mouth."

"All the fucking time."

Without warning, I slide two fingers inside her all the way to knuckle and watch her eyes shutter closed. I press my lips to hers to stifle her gasp of delight.

"My dirty little Princess."

I increase my grip on her neck, eliciting another moan and massage her clit with my thumb, keeping my fingers buried deep inside her. She quivers around my hand and the fact I'm driving her wild makes me even harder.

"You need to hurry up," she demands.

"Or what?" I tease, dragging my fingers across the sensitive spot inside her.

"Gabe," she gasps, barely able to speak. She's getting more aroused by the fucking second. I've got no intention of letting her come like this. But she doesn't know that.

"Tell me what you want,"

She tilts her head and gives me a look that makes my balls tighten. "You. I want you."

My cock lurches. The power this woman holds over my self-control and my dick is unrivalled. She weaves her spell and I'm gone. If I'm not inside her within two minutes I'm going to explode like some teenager.

I slide my fingers out of her, and she sits up, catching my wrist and lifting my fingers to her lips. She slides my fingers into her mouth, sucking her arousal, all the while keeping her eyes on mine. My cock strains against the material of my boxers so much it hurts. She knows exactly what she's doing.

Like she's read my mind, she unfastens my trousers and frees me. My relief's short lived as she curls her hand around my dick, and I tense as she glides her thumb over the tip, dampening it with pre-cum and licking it.

Fuck this woman and all that she does to me.

"Fuck me, Gabe."

She doesn't need to ask twice.

"The protection's in the bedroom."

She looks at me thoughtfully, then reaches up and pushes my waistcoat off my shoulders, and with it, my shirt, smoothing her hands across my chest.

"I'm on the pill."

I look at her for assurance, reading into her words. "Are you sure?"

"I'm pretty sure I'm clean. I've only ever had sex without protection once and that was a very long time ago." Her eyes drop to the floor momentarily and when they return to mine, they're filled with sorrow. And I want to kiss it all away.

"I'm the same. Apart from maybe a few times back in uni. I've always been careful." I kiss her deeply, then pull my lips from hers. "I want nothing more. I want to feel your heart and soul, inside me."

Her breathing deepens, as she arches into me, pushing herself against my cock, giving herself to me and battering down the final piece of my resolve.

I drive forward, filling her deeply. Her fingernails dig into my shoulders and she nuzzles her face into my neck as I fuck her. Every thrust unravels her further. Each moan she gives as I hit the spot makes my cock strain. She's fire. Everything I need and want wrapped in curls, curves and sass.

"You're mine, Princess." I growl into her mouth, making her

whimper and tighten around my cock. "You're mine, Ella Anderson."

She claws her fingers through my hair, tugging me closer to her and biting my bottom lip. "Then you're mine, Gabe White."

I never wanted to be anyone's but I want to be hers. I want to be her everything.

Her muscles contract around my cock and I groan.

"I'm close," she tells me.

I know when she goes I don't stand a chance of holding on.

She tenses around me, scoring her fingernails down my back as she comes apart on a scream. But I barely feel it. I tip over the edge in ecstasy with her, moaning her name, worshipping her mouth with my own and spilling inside her, driving into her until I'm spent.

She clings to me with trembling arms as we stand entwined. Listening to the sound of her breathing slow, feeling the beat of her heart as her chest presses against mine. I tangle my fingers through her soft curls and breathe in the heady scent of her, mingled with sweat. An unfamiliar feeling of contentment fills me. This is right. This is where I belong.

I pick her up and carry her into the bedroom, relishing the feel of her relaxing into my arms. I lay her down on the sheets, climb in beside her and pull the fur throw over us both.

Her wide dark eyes glint in the darkness as she lies watching me.

"I think ..." she pauses, as if she's unsure whether to carry on. "I think I'm falling for you."

Her words hit me in the chest, entangling round my heart and squeezing tight. My fighty Princess is nowhere to be seen. This is my pure, stripped back beauty with the biggest heart I've ever known.

I stroke the back of my knuckles against her cheekbone and gaze deep into her eyes, saying words I'm not afraid to admit anymore. "I've already fallen, Princess."

Tears brim in her eyes and I bundle her into an embrace,

pulling her to my chest. I press my lips to the top of her head and breathe her in.

I'd lost the game the moment I clapped eyes on her.

Checkmate.

Chapter 48

Ella

As soon as I arrive back home the next night I know something's amiss.

A familiar looking bright pink leopard pink suitcase sits in the hall at the bottom of the stairs. It's not Kate's, but I recognise it.

The door to the living room opens and Kate appears with a face like thunder. "Thank fuck you're back."

"Why? What's up?"

The living room door opens wider and Amy appears. Her wavy corn blonde hair is tied into loose pig tails and she's wearing a very tight, vibrant purple v neck t-shirt.

Kate nods her head at my sister. "This."

Amy cuts her eyes at my friend and gives me a sheepish look. "Erm … hi, El. Surprise!" She laughs nervously, and nibbles a pink fingernail.

"What's going on?" I ask, panicked, my mind immediately lurching to the worst-case scenario. "Are you all right? Are you ill?"

"Don't be silly. I'm fine. It's just that I've decided to drop out of uni." She tosses the phrase into the air like it's nothing. She never did have a care in the world.

"You've decided to drop out of uni," I repeat slowly, letting the words digest and the full force of what that actually means hit me. "Why?"

She wrinkles her nose. "It just wasn't for me. The degree was boring. I think I want to earn some money instead."

"Too right. If you're moving back here you need to earn your keep," Kate chimes in.

I press a hand to my head and briefly close my eyes, trying to work out the reason for my little sister's sudden change of heart. "Hang on Ames. I thought this was what you wanted to do? You can't just drop out like that."

"I can and have. I told my lecturers yesterday. They support my decision. I *thought* it was what I wanted to do, but it's just really hard and boring. It's not for me. You know you've always been the one with the brains."

If this is her attempt at getting round me, it's not going to wash. "This is a massive fucking decision. Didn't you think to talk to me about it first?"

"I did. I tried calling you the other day to talk about it, but you were too busy at work." There's a resentful tone to her voice which annoys me.

"Yes, that's right, Amy. Your sister was at work, earning money, paying her way and yours," Kate jumps in.

She's got a point. "So what are you going to do now?" I ask.

Amy shrugs. "Get a job."

"You need to, if you're staying here."

She rolls her eyes. "I will."

"I mean it Amy. Everyone pays their way in this house. You're no exception."

She huffs and inspects her fingernails. "All right, fucking hell. I get the message. I'll start job hunting first thing tomorrow. Tonight, I'm going out."

My head hurts. She's only just got here. "Out? With who?"

"Milly from college. Remember?"

Not a chance. Amy had so many friends and boyfriends at college I could barely keep up. "Not at all. And how does Milly know you're back?"

Amy gives me a look as though I've lost the plot. "I text her to let her know."

"Before you text me?"

Amy juts out her bottom lip and pouts. "Don't get mad, El. I know you wanted me to go to uni, but it really wasn't for me. I'm sorry. You do want me to be happy, don't you?"

Fuck it!

"Of course I do and so would Mum." I rub a hand across my

face, as the news fully sinks in. My little sister is back. *Oh God.* "Firstly, you need to unpack your stuff. You can't leave that here," I tell her, pointing at her suitcase.

"Okay." She looks at Kate. "I'll need my old room back."

"You what?" Kate asks her.

"I'm back now, I can't have the box room."

"Tough shit. You moved out."

"But now I'm back. For good."

Kate and Amy living underneath the same roof again is going to be a bloody nightmare.

"Kate's right, Amy. It's her room now. It's only fair. You'll take the spare bedroom."

"For fuck's sake," she moans, grabbing her suitcase and starting up the stairs. "Some people never fucking change." She glares at Kate, bouncing her case off every step.

"You okay?" Kate asks me, once Amy's disappeared out of ear shot.

"It's a shock."

"I bet. She could have tried a little bit harder to tell you."

"It's obvious why she didn't. She knew I'd try and talk her round and she's obviously made up her mind to quit."

"You need to make sure she gets a job," Kate says firmly.

"Oh, I will. I can't afford to keep her. She needs to bring some money in." I drag my fingers through my hair. "I thought things were going too well."

***

I'm glad to get out of the house the next morning. My little sister living back at home is exactly as I remember it. Noisy chaos against the backdrop of loud pop music blaring from her bedroom from the second she wakes up. Kate leaves the house even earlier than usual. I know she's keeping her distance because otherwise she'll blow a fuse.

Work is busy. Judy's at a spa day with her daughter, so it's left to me to man the fort. Gabe appears just before lunchtime, making a beeline for his office surrounded by guys from Finance.

It's early afternoon by the time they filter out and I receive a call from Gabe asking me to go into his office.

He's sitting behind his desk, scrutinising the chess board when I enter. "Close the door behind you," he tells me without looking up.

I do as I'm told and when I turn back he's heading towards me.

"Are you okay?"

He grabs my face in his hands and kisses me languidly, pulling me close.

"I am now," he breathes against my lips. "You look stressed."

"Amy's doing my head in. You look stressed too."

"Fucking work. I've got half an hour. I need to *de*stress." His hands slip beneath the hem of my skirt and ruck it up to my waist.

"Gabe!" I'm standing in the middle of his office with my arse out. "What if someone comes in?"

"I don't give a shit. I'm sick of playing the game by other people's rules. I want you, now. And the only way I'm going to stop is if you tell me no."

I have no idea what he's got planned, but right now I don't care. "Never."

He flicks me a wicked grin, puts his hands on my shoulder and pushes me back until I feel the door behind me. "Good, because I'm going to fuck you up against this door."

Shit!

He unfastens his trousers and pulls his boxers down, allowing his erection to spring between us.

I smile. "Someone's ready."

"I missed being inside you last night." He kisses me once on the lips. "And this morning." He slides a hand between my legs and pulls my knickers to the side, dipping his fingers beneath the material. He hums in approval against my lips at what he finds. "Looks like I'm not the only one who's ready."

For him, I'll always be. I hook my leg around his waist and he pushes the tip of his finger inside me, coating my clit with my arousal. I bite down on my bottom lip to stop the groan escaping from my lips.

He adjusts his position, lines up, then slams into me. I bury my head into his neck to stop myself from crying out at the feel of us together. If anyone is on the other side of the door, they'll guess what we're up to, but Gabe doesn't seem to care and neither do I.

He withdraws and drives into me again, and it takes everything I have not to cry out.

"Two more," he pants.

I nod. *Thank God.*

He thrusts into me harder, forcing me up the door with his cock, making me moan into his ear.

"That sound is enough to make me come." He pounds into me and I come hard, biting down on my shoulder to stop myself from calling his name. A stream of hot breath hits my cheek, as he lets go. For a few moments, we stand panting, breathless and in a daze.

"I've got you a door card cut."

"What?" I tilt my face upwards and look at him.

He rests his forehead against mine and smiles. "A card for my apartment. I've got you one cut, so you can come and go as you please."

My mouth drops open, as I flail for something to say. "Are … are you sure?"

"Positive. Last night I missed you. I miss you. All the time. Whenever you're not with me, I hate it. I want you to stay over at mine more. I want you to treat it as our place."

My heart rattles against my ribs and I'm sure it's about to explode with happiness. He's said everything I feel, and was too scared to admit. "I don't know what to say. I do too. I feel the same."

"I want us to be an official couple."

"But what about here?" I ask worriedly. "What will people say?"

"I don't care. I'll think of a way to handle it. All I know is that you're mine, and I want everyone to know it."

I idly push my fingers through his hair and kiss him. "I do too. I want us to be in the open. Like a proper couple."

The sound of my phone ringing from the other side of the door disrupts the moment. I plummet back to reality.

"I really should get back to my desk, before people start noticing."

He reluctantly lowers me down and fastens his trousers. Then, he helps clean me up and rearranges my crumpled disheveled clothes.

"Here," he says, retrieving a black key card from the back pocket of his trousers. This is yours, Princess."

I can't stop the stupid smile from spreading across my face. "Oh my god. Thank you."

"And tonight you're staying at mine. That little sister and best friend of yours can cope without you. I can't." He places a gentle kiss on my lips. "Ever."

***

I can't concentrate properly for the rest of the afternoon. My head's stuck on Cloud Nine.

Gabe's still holed up in the meeting room with Simon from PR at four o'clock. I grab a break and glass of water from the kitchen and head back to my desk to find a brown A4 file on top of my pile of papers. I've only been gone for two minutes. I'm sure it wasn't there before, unless Gabe popped out and left me some work to do.

I sit down, pick up the file and look at the front cover but there's no note attached or Post-it note, telling me what he wants me to do with it. I'm about to close the file, when something catches my eye.

Nightingale Project is typed up on the first page. That was the project Sarah came to talk to Gabe about the other day and he acted a bit weird about. I turn over the page. Inside is a set of blueprints for Hackney High Street. I frown. We're not involved with any projects involving Hackney High Street. There must be some confusion, but as I flick through the file, an unwelcome feeling creeps over me. The buildings are familiar. The addresses, the establishment names, I know them all. The butchers, the grocers ... Mum's shop. A set of prints of the existing shops, overlayed with computer generated designs shows rows of smart, modern looking terraces, an apartment block and recreational area. This is the development to take over the high street. These are plans showing what's going to be built in place of the shop. But how? White House Developments aren't leading the project, are they?

My fingers go into overtime, flicking through the pages, frantically seeking answers as to how and why this is happening. All the time I thought a rival company were behind the tearing down of Mum's shop but I was wrong. I come to the final page. My eyes land on the approving officer's signature. Gabe White.

I snap the file closed and chuck it onto the desk, like it's a grenade set to detonate.

My stomach rolls with nausea. Bits of the unwelcome puzzle start to piece together. Gabe's cagey response when I asked him what he knew about Darknight Property. The project that he farmed out to another team to support, which upset Judy. All the meetings with Sarah from Legal. And the guy who just fucked me up against his office door is at the heart of it all.

Gabe knew all along.

He lied to me.

He doesn't care about me.

If he did, he wouldn't do this.

He's just used me for sex.

And there I was thinking I meant something to him.
Silly cow!

I bite the inside of my cheek to stop the torrent of emotion from taking over.

I've been taken advantage of by a cocky well-off prick before. I swore I'd never allow it again. And I won't.

He may have won the battle, but he hasn't won the war.

Gabe White better watch out.

To be continued …

Find out how Gabe and Ella's story concludes in;

Out of Love

Pre-order your copy **HERE** from Amazon

Gabe

The precious White family empire is nearly on it's knees. Maintaining the family's sparkling rep has underpinned every decision I've ever made. Until now. She's tipped my world upside. Made me question everything I've ever believed in. Shown me a different way of life. I'm in love with Ella Anderson and everything she stands for.

I want more. I want her. Forever.

But the rules of the game have changed. This time it's all or nothing. And I'm faced with a choice; family or love.

Ella

Every guy I've ever cared about has deceived me. This time round it cut a whole deeper. I hate Gabe White and everything he stands for. But he's captured my heart. Found the chink in my armour. But I won't be beaten. He may have won the first round but he won't win the next. Gabe might be used to winning, but I'm one 'game' he's not going to conquer.

ALSO BY SALLYANNE JOHNSON

THE BLACK SERIES

Dark Desires #1
Dark Heart #2
Dark Soul #3

THE WHITE SERIES

Out of Bounds #1
Out of Love #2

About Sallyanne

Writer of sexy, edgy romance

Sallyanne was born and raised in the West Midlands, UK, where she still lives. She has loved reading and writing for as long as she can remember. A few years ago Sallyanne decided to put fingers to keyboard and unleash her imagination upon the world.

She loves reading and writing contemporary romance with an erotic twist, with strong, feisty women and blisteringly hot heroes with an edge. When Sallyanne's not busy with her day job, she's dreaming up new stories and pant scorching alpha males. Let's face it, there can never be too many… can there?

AUTHOR'S NOTE

Thank you for taking the time to read my book! I hope you had as much fun reading it as I did writing it. I would love to hear from you, and you can connect with me on any of the following sites:

f
o
g
BB
a

If you enjoyed the book, please tell your friends and the world by leaving a review on Amazon. Reviews are key for self-published authors like me. We really, really appreciate it.

Thanks again for reading.

Best wishes,

Sallyanne

Printed in Great Britain
by Amazon